Mist and Moonbeams

Stories from the Great Lakes Edge

Paul Michael Peters

Contents

Ebook: 978-1-7330883-9-8

Paperback: 979-8-9902614-0-2

Hardback: 979-8-9902614-1-9

For Susan and Bob

FOREWORD

Some 430 million years ago, give or take, during the Silurian Period, the basin that would later hold the Great Lakes formed. This was the beginning of what would become one of my favorite places, Tahquamenon Falls, rooted in dolomite. Over centuries, hard rock layered above, setting the stage. Then the Ice Age came, reshaping lands under ice, crafting the scene as glaciers retreated; pleasant peninsulas emerged, landscapes carved. In this light, life's changes seem less stark.

I've lived beside each Great Lake: born in Detroit, moved to Marquette, Chicago, and Toronto, aiming to settle on the Sunrise Coast. This region, vast and wild, teems with life and paths well-trodden by nature and man. Birds trace the sky in their biannual voyage; industry pulses along the Rust Belt. Here, the soil is rich, the people robust—friendly, smart, hard-working. Perhaps I'm partial, but to me, this is no exaggeration, dear reader.

The Great Lakes are rich with history. That is as true a statement as I will ever write. How could I ignore telling some stories located here?

In the early review, questions emerged about the chapters' sequence. Not by volume, nor alphabetically ordered, as seen. "Huron, Ontario, Michigan, Erie, Superior," spell H.O.M.E.S., a mnemonic for the Great Lakes. Each "HOMES" letter stands for a lake. This, to me, is clearer than ROYGBIV.

One grasps home's essence in these kitchens. Plaques, decals, pillows declare, "Home is where the heart is," "Home sweet home," "There's no place like home." In cabins, among fishing and hunting gear, "Home is not a place, it's a feeling." T.S. Eliot said, "Home is where one starts." Each story seeks that place, that someone.

Cozy up by the fire, in your reading nook, and escape your troubles. I've cut the parts you'd skip, kept only the good. Our first story begins at home.

You Can't Start a Fire With Moonlight

LAKE HURON

One

With a cautious toe, Michelle dipped into the water's edge while balancing on the rocky shore. "It's cold," she declared, withdrawing swiftly.

"Scared?" Christopher asked, standing chest-deep.

"Of you? Hardly." She gazed at the Super Blue Moon reflected in Lake Huron, a shimmering golden beam across the waters. "It looks cold."

"You baby, get in here," he taunted. "The Great Lakes are always cold. It warms up once you're in; you'll get used to it."

"I've heard that line before." Arms folding over her bare breasts, pink panties tight on the hips, she proceeded with care, each step calibrated to find a sturdy rock beneath her. "Normally, I have my water shoes on." In a sultry attempt, she'd meant to tantalize him, but when her foot slipped, her arms shot out, spoiling any illusion of poise. Recovering, she saw a glint of delight dance across his face. "Well, now you've seen everything," she remarked as she waded out to shoulder depth. Keeping her head above water—she didn't want to wet her hair—she considered the time it would take to dry it and style it, time better spent elsewhere.

"Nervous?"

"A little. I've never done anything like this before." His touch enveloped her; the cold was washed away, supplanted by a warmth radiating from inside.

"Michelle, I've been mad about you for so long."

Her cheeks flushed from his words. Their subtle dance had lasted all summer, and she'd often found herself thinking of him when alone. He had entered her thoughts, her private spaces.

"I've been thinking of you too, Christopher."

"I like that."

"What?"

"When you call me Christopher. Most people call me Chris, but not you. Hardly ever. With you, it's always Christopher."

“The boss's son gets his full name.” She whispered his name again, leaning closer with each utterance until their lips met in a pure, passionate kiss that ignited something she hadn't felt in ages. A sense of hope, of finding something—right, relaxing, wonderful—bloomed within her.

His hands, large and firm, took her. As they moved down her side to her hips, she gasped between kisses. She turned in the water, her back against his chest, and his kisses migrated—from lips to neck to ear, to all the neglected spots desperate for attention. She helped him remove her panties, something she had refused to do on the beach, being self-conscious from the years, and he threw them onto the shore.

"Nice throw," she said between breathy sighs.

Under the moon's golden eye, they surrendered to pleasure, their reflections dancing on the Lake Huron waters. Finally, as the moon ascended, they embraced, awash in wonder.

"We should go back. I'm getting cold," she said, "and there might be questions."

Carefully, they gathered their scattered clothing and began the walk back to the beach house. Fingers intertwined, they touched like teenagers engrossed in a summer fling. The house lights served as a beacon, the distant chatter growing louder with each step.

In the final stretch, where the magic still hovered, she captured a mental photograph—a keepsake. With a final squeeze, they let go, each heading their separate ways: Michelle to the house's front, Christopher to the back where conversations crescendoed.

Slipping back unnoticed, Michelle towel-dried her hair and changed into dry clothing in the bedroom closet. On her way to the kitchen, she deposited her laundry in the hallway chute. In the kitchen, she picked up a tray of food from inside the refrigerator before heading out to the fire pit where her husband and the other guests congregated.

She placed the full tray on the table, putting the last two hotdogs from the near empty tray on top before removing the empty one. She planned to take it back to the kitchen when her husband's booming voice stopped her dead in her tracks.

"Michelle."

She stood, waiting for whatever came next. Screams of anger and infidelity? Accusations and insults? A fight?

Sweetly, he asked, "Honey, what was the name of that place we visited with the kids two summers ago?"

"The one in Gatlinburg?"

"No, the one by Dollywood."

"You're thinking of Helen's, and it's nowhere near Dollywood; it's on the other side of the state. We went from Memphis to Huntsville—from rockabilly to rockets, remember?"

"Helen's! That's it. Baby, you're the greatest. I have the best wife ever."

Smiling, she absorbed his adoration. He was a good man. In the shadows beyond him sat Christopher—a man who had been good to her.

Once the guests had departed, their belongings and children in tow, Michelle and her husband Mike turned to the ritual of cleaning up. Over the past fifteen years, they had honed their roles to a seamless choreography. Mike busied himself with the grill, extinguishing the fire, stowing the chairs, sequestering the full garbage bags from curious wildlife, and filling another with the detritus of the night. Michelle, meanwhile, held dominion over the kitchen—loading the dishwasher, plating the leftovers, and scrubbing high-traffic areas from top to bottom.

Friends—no, good friends—had made it a tradition to visit each summer, drawn to Rogers City in the northeast part of Michigan. It's what a local might refer to as the "pointer finger" of the Michigan Mitten, a working town anchored by the world's largest limestone quarry and processing plant, where Mike drove a two-story dump truck and Michelle worked accounting in the office. Each August, it hosted a Salmon Tournament; come September, it marked the commencement of the Fall Festival—a promenade through landscapes tinged with autumnal splendor. This year, the event coincided with the appearance of a rare blue supermoon, the first since 2009 and the next not until 2037.

Mike leaned in to kiss Michelle's cheek as she stood at the sink, laboring over a chili pot. "You see that moon? Big moon. Gold moon, wasn't it?"

"Yes, it was," she said.

"So big, so golden. When was the last time we saw a moon like that?"

"On our thirteenth anniversary."

"Yeah, what was that... 2010?"

"2009. Boyd turns thirteen this year."

"Right, right. Great moon."

Michelle set down the pan, her prune-like fingers doing a final rinse and wiping down the counter. She loved Mike, a good father and provider, yet she wished he'd remember the little things—the dates that held sentimental value, moments that mattered. He always was close, but just slightly off.

"So, what do you think?" he asked.

Her mind had drifted; his words were but ambient noise she had grown too accustomed to, muffled by her deeper cogitations. "Sure, sounds good," she said, distracted.

She gave her favorite sponge its last rinse under the faucet. That's when she noticed the tan line on her left hand, bright and a conspicuous white. Normally, her wedding ring shielded that patch of skin from the sun. Now it was missing. A jolt of real fear struck her as she retraced her steps in her mind. Had it slipped down the drain? Was it in the closet?

Mike startled her with another kiss. "I was heading to bed. You good?"

"Good, good, all good," she assured him, a touch too much.

His eyes studied her for a moment. "Ten o'clock service tomorrow?"

"Yes, ten o'clock," she confirmed.

"Night-night," he said, heading down the hall, subtly hinting at marital expectations for a Saturday night, humming his "sexy tune" with his "sexy dance" which he had started the second year of marriage, but had lost its charm by the fourth year and third son.

Michelle went downstairs, frantically rummaging through pockets and laundry piles, but found no ring. Upstairs again, she secured the doors, dimmed the lights, and checked in on the boys. From the hall, she could hear the onset of Mike's snoring. Another night she had outwaited him.

With the dim, almost clandestine glow of her cellphone, Michelle scrutinized every inch of the closet floor, a frenetic desperation mounting in her chest as her search yielded nothing. She turned to the bathroom next, meticulously dissecting each corner and drawer like a detective hunting for that one overlooked clue. Still, emptiness. Her heart thumped a frantic rhythm in her chest as she went through the motions of her nightly ritual—applying lotion, cleansing, moisturizing—her actions robotic, as if on autopilot. Finally, she settled into bed, but rest was a distant hope; her mind was in turmoil, tangled in a tapestry of conflicting emotions. Her eyes were wide open.

Closing her eyes in an effort to get a few hours rest, she found her thoughts magnetically pulled to Christopher, the way he had touched her, the careful, deliberate manner with which he had given her attention—the sort of attention Mike had not given her in years. She saw herself in Christopher's arms again, as he lifted her off the ground, spinning her like a forgotten melody from her youth. For a moment, she had felt a euphoric freedom, a break from the stifling sameness of her life.

Then, suddenly, like the soft toll of a distant bell, she heard it in the theater of her mind—*TINK*. A sound that cut through her reverie, plunging her into a new reality. Her arm had swung over Christopher's neck, steadying her dizzying spin, and in that fraction of a second, the ring had flown off, breaking free as if it, too, yearned for liberation.

Eyes wide open. A wave of panic washed over her. The ring

would be there, on the beach, half-buried in the sand like a treasure waiting to betray her. It would be an intimate secret, one not even the dawn could keep. She felt a mounting urgency; she had to find it, had to retrieve it before the world woke up, before that tiny band of gold unraveled the life she had so meticulously built.

Two

As dawn bled its first light over the horizon, Michelle found herself on the rocky shoreline of Lake Huron. The rising sun skimmed over the water, casting an ethereal glow but lending no comfort to her troubled mind. Here she was, her eyes scanning the pebbled expanse for that one elusive glint—a gold band set with a diamond that had once belonged to Mike's grandmother. A family heirloom that signified not just their union, but a lineage of commitment and fidelity she had so heedlessly betrayed.

Her thoughts were a torturous labyrinth. She had succumbed to an impulse, an ancient tug of the flesh that spoke not of love but of immediacy, and now here she was, the weight of generations bearing down upon her. On hands and knees, she combed through the scattered rocks and pebbles, overturning each one with a frenzied urgency as if expecting the ring to cry out to her.

But time, that inexorable force, moved on. The sun climbed higher, and what was once a secluded nocturnal stage began to populate. Joggers appeared on the scene, their breath misting in the morning air, their pounding footsteps a metronome to her increasing despair. Swimmers waded into the frigid water, and fishermen cast their hopeful lines from the shore.

A gnawing realization gripped her: She would have to go back. Her family would soon be waking up. Absent her morning guidance, the children might resort to television, even though it was forbidden on Sundays, or engage in a forbidden skirmish in their video games. Mike would seize the chance for another hour of sleep, blissfully ignorant of the storm gathering in the heart of his household.

Dragging herself away felt like physical agony. Her path retraced the steps she had taken with Christopher the previous night, each footfall a heavy echo of betrayal. Her neck ached from bending, having scanned the ground so assiduously, and her spirit was ravaged by a night devoid of rest and a mind mired in guilt.

As she made her way back, ideas darted through her thoughts like frenzied fish in a shallow pond. She would need to return, armed with something more efficient than her bare hands. A metal detector, perhaps, calibrated to react to gold. Or a small spade to sift through the sand, a mechanism to jostle the rocks, to expedite this harrowing quest. What had she done? What could she do now?

Yet even amid this spiraling turmoil, the haunting beauty of the morning was not lost on her. It was as if nature itself was laying bare the dichotomy of her life—the radiant sun opposed by her darkening soul, the tranquil lake contrasting her roiling emotions. It was both a reflection and a distortion, a world moving forward while she was stuck in a moment that threatened to undo everything. And so she moved, as she had to, her footsteps weighted by the ring that was not there, the choices she could not unmake, and the secret that now clamored so loudly within her.

The scent of fresh coffee intermingled with the warm aroma of pancakes, pork sausage, and eggs, filling the house with a welcoming embrace. Mike, hair tousled and eyes still squinting against the morning light, wandered into the kitchen and stretched. "What bribery is this?" he mused, his voice gravelly with sleep.

"Huh?"

"You only cook like this when something's about to expire or you're feeling guilty."

She offered him a smile, so practiced and so effortless. "Expiration dates," she said.

Mike leaned in and mimicked a kissing sound, careful not to come too close. Morning affection had its limits, and the border was always defined by unbrushed teeth. Their oldest son, Boyd, ambled into the kitchen next, mimicking his father's stretch before taking his seat at the breakfast nook. Floyd, the middle child, went about setting the table with a practiced efficiency, while Lloyd, the youngest, joined the others in anticipation of the morning feast.

Today, she moved with a balletic grace, each gesture and step a calculated part of the familiar dance. The pancakes landed effortlessly on the plate; the syrup poured in a glistening stream. Her family watched, lulled by the practiced movements, so seemingly effortless yet teeming with a barely concealed tension. To the outside world, it was a mundane Sunday morning scene, but beneath the veneer of domestic tranquility, Michelle felt the weight of her secret pulling at her. Every perfect pancake, every well-placed fork was another brick in a façade she was desperate to maintain.

Mike and the boys may have enjoyed the spectacle of her previous culinary mishaps, laughing off the minor disasters as part of the charm of a Michelle-cooked breakfast. Today, however, the absence of such moments wasn't lost on them, though they couldn't quite put their finger on the shift in atmosphere. For Michelle, each executed task was a tiny triumph over the chaos lurking in her soul, the entropy of a life on the edge of unraveling.

She deftly flipped silver-dollar-sized pancakes, a skill honed over years of Sunday mornings, and carefully transferred them onto waiting plates. With a cautionary, "Hot! Don't touch, let your dad help," she placed a jar of warmed syrup on a trivet. Butter—soft from sitting at room temperature—and small glasses of orange juice took their places on the table, along with scrambled eggs and steaming cups of coffee for her and Mike.

Leaning against the sink counter, Michelle sipped her coffee and watched her family dig in—a daily triumph in fulfilling the very domestic dream she had vowed to achieve. A mother's vow, made against the backdrop of her own wanting childhood.

As the tempo of eating slowed, Michelle issued the day's next set of commands. "Time to clean up, everyone. We're dressing in our Sunday best for church."

The house soon echoed with the sound of water rushing from multiple faucets. Mike retreated to their bathroom, and the boys rotated in and out of the shower. Seizing a stolen moment, Michelle slipped down to the basement. There, she quickly assembled a makeshift tool, a sort of sifter cobbled together from an extendable dusting stick and an unused donut flipper basket—both products of the "As Seen on TV" display at the box store. This, she hoped, would be her secret weapon in her quest to reclaim the lost ring.

A glance at the clock startled her back into the moment. Rushing back upstairs, she threw on an older, seldom-worn dress and hastened through a truncated beauty routine. When she finally emerged, it was her family who awaited her in the living room—a reversal that was rare but not unwelcome.

"Okay, okay, I'm ready," she announced, stepping into the choreographed dance of their daily lives.

Mike opened the door, letting the boys burst forth in their usual sprint to the truck. Following behind, he locked the door, sealing the small, comfortable world they had built. There was an order to these things, a reliable sequence of events that provided a comforting framework around their lives. Some might have found it dull; for Michelle, however, amid the complexities and secrets she harbored, it was this very routine that held everything precariously in place. The good life they had built was both her sanctuary and her stage, and today, more than ever, she played her role with a desperate perfection.

Three

Amber was an avid reader and her best friend was a common raven she had named Chet. Their friendship blossomed the summer she was quarantined in her room with mumps, a period she had found rather delightful as it provided her with a span of uninterrupted time devoid of excuses to tackle her wealth of unread books. However, Amber's mother, concerned about her daughter's pasty complexion, insisted that she spend some time outdoors.

It was during one of these outdoor sojourns, a book in her lap and a plate of chicken nuggets by her side, that she first encountered Chet. He alighted on the white metal garden table, his size almost double that of a crow. Unlike crows, which moved in murders, Chet was alone, a wanderer separated from an unkindness. He had a limp and regarded her with a cautious eye.

"Would you like a nugget?" Amber inquired.

Chet's head twitched and rotated to get a better angle on her. He advanced but did not pilfer from her plate. It was only when she extended a smaller nugget toward him that he accepted it. Chet then took flight and Amber dismissed the encounter, assuming the hungry bird had resumed its ordinary avian activities.

She was astonished when, hours later, there was a tapping at her second-story bedroom window. Setting her book aside, she opened the window and screen. Chet perched on the windowsill, bearing something in his beak. He deposited the item on the sill and waited for her to pick it up. It was a metal charm shaped like a heart. Amber quickly pieced together the sequence of events: Chet received a nugget, spotted something shiny on the shore of Lake Huron while flying, and brought it to her. Evidently, the charm had broken off from a piece of jewelry.

As Chet observed, Amber repaired the clasp and threaded a string through the ring that once connected it to the jewelry. She tied the string around her neck, where the charm would remain for the next five years.

From that day forward, Amber and Chet were not just friends, but good friends. Amber ensured Chet was fed daily. With her bedroom window open, he would drop off various treasures and tidbits he discovered throughout the day. Often, Amber would sit in her bedroom chair, Chet keeping her company on the windowsill. In the summer, she would sit in the backyard, engrossed in a novel filled with adventure, wonder, romance, and knowledge, while Chet observed from a perch her father had constructed.

On this particular Sunday morning, as Amber read a new novel in the crisp August air, the high school senior pondered the implications of attending a university far from Chet. Would the dorms permit a caged raven? Could she even suffer to cage Chet, taking him away from the freedom he so cherished? How much time did they have left together, given that wild ravens typically lived 10 to 15 years?

Before she could resume her reading, she heard a distinct *TINK*. It was the sound of Chet dropping a new treasure on the metal table. "A diamond ring?" she queried, amused. "Are you proposing? Where did you find this?"

Chet cocked his head and fluttered from the table to his perch.

Amber rose and went to her room. Chet promptly followed, touching down on the windowsill. She opened her dresser's top drawer, revealing numerous plastic cups organized in shoeboxes, each filled with trinkets and treasures Chet had brought her over the years. The heart pendant around her neck was merely the beginning. Almost every day, Chet brought her something new that sparkled and shimmered in the sunlight. One box contained colorful rocks and beads, each cup labeled with the week they were received. Another box held keys, rusty nails, solitary earrings, small bones, and pieces of wire. Yet the gold ring with a diamond would be placed in a separate box, reserved for special keepsakes.

"Thank you, Chet. I do."

Four

Sun-kissed to the point of sunburn, her skin a telltale shade of crimson, Michelle felt the marrow-deep fatigue of an afternoon surrendered to the unforgiving sun. There was a raw purity in her exhaustion, as if the sun had distilled her down to her most essential self. She had spent hours under its gaze, sifting through sand and pebbles with her makeshift tool. Her pursuit, however, had yielded nothing but frustration and an acute sense of her own limitations.

After the emotionally draining morning and the taxing outdoor expedition, Michelle relished the brief respite of a shaded park bench, its slatted wood surprisingly cool against her overheated skin. The sun at her back, lowering in the sky, cast elongated shadows across the beachside, and the daylight assumed the golden quality of late afternoon.

Floyd and Lloyd, a few yards away, were engrossed in their

scouting activities. The image was charming, a snapshot of innocent endeavor. It filled Michelle with a mix of melancholy and pride—these moments of fleeting youth that she could safeguard only in her memory.

Earlier that day, the slow cooker at home had been entrusted with a pot roast, accompanied by potatoes and carrots —an offering to the domestic gods. The dish would be ready by the time they returned, a gastronomic reward for a Sunday rigorously spent in church, followed by leisure activities and chores. The aroma of the slow-cooked meal filled her mind, and she found it comforting. That simple kitchen appliance, dependable and steadfast, seemed to encapsulate all her aspirations of home and family. Her duties and cares simmered slowly through the hours, merging into something nourishing and complete.

Still, the serenity was tainted. As she sat watching her boys, the absent ring gnawed at her consciousness like an invisible stain. It was not merely an object; it was the trusted symbol of generations, a hallmark of promises and unspoken understandings. Its absence marked her betrayal. She couldn't shake the feeling that something foundational had been altered.

She sighed, feeling the weight of the day settle into her bones. A part of her longed to go back to the beach, to continue the Sisyphean task of sifting through the sand, chasing a glint of redemption. But for now, she stayed in her seat, a guardian watching over her young, nursing her secrets in the quietude of her soul.

From her bench, Michelle listened to the lesson with interest. She was always amazed at how much her sons and the other scouts learned during their outings.

Roy waved his arms to gather everyone's attention. "Alright, scouts, gather around! Today we're going to learn something essential for any outdoorsman: how to start a fire! But we're not just going to use matches or lighters. Oh no, we're going to use"—he held up a magnifying glass dramatically—"science!"

Walt chuckled beside him. "That's right! Pay close attention; this could be really helpful one day, especially if you ever find yourself without matches in the great outdoors."

The scouts looked at each other, intrigued. One of them, a kid with a cap turned backward, raised his hand. "A magnifying glass? Really?"

Roy beamed. "Yep! You'd be surprised how powerful the sun's energy can be. Now, can anyone tell me what this magnifying glass does?"

Another scout piped up. "It makes things look bigger?"

Walt nodded. "True. It makes things seem bigger. Its inventor was a philosopher named Roger Bacon in the thirteenth century, and he used them to help older people read. But for our purpose, we are going to talk about its other property. If you want to eat bacon, you need to cook it, right?"

"You need fire," three of the boys said nearly in unison.

"A magnifying glass also concentrates light into a single point," Walt continued. "And concentrated light can generate heat—enough heat to start a fire."

A freckle-faced scout with reddish hair raised his hand.

"What about moonlight? Can we start a fire with moonlight? Like the bright moon the other night?"

Walt answered, "Ah, moonlight. It's beautiful and poetic, but not quite up to the task of starting fires. Any guesses as to why?"

Another scout answered, "Because it's not as bright?"

Walt smiled. "Exactly! Moonlight is actually reflected sunlight. The moon doesn't produce light; it reflects the sun's light back to Earth. But that reflection is far weaker than direct sunlight."

Roy added, "To get technical, the intensity of moonlight is about 500,000 times weaker than the sun's light. Even with a magnifying glass, there's just not enough energy in moonlight to start a fire."

One of the younger scouts made a thoughtful face. "So, it's like trying to fill a bucket with a dropper?"

Roy clapped. "That's an excellent analogy! There's simply not enough *oomph* in moonlight to get things burning."

Walt continued to show the boys how to set up cuts of wood and identify which wood is good for campfires. He covered ideas on kindling like dried grass, leaves, and the lint in your pocket. Each of the boys took turns with a plastic magnifier, finding the right distance, and starting a smolder, growing it to a flame.

Walt checked his watch. "Well, it looks like it's almost time, boys. Next time we meet, we're going to talk about finding your way in the woods—the fancy word for this is orienteering. We're going to learn a new word: declination. Anyone who looks it up and brings me the written definition gets extra points."

The troop dispersed, chattering with excitement and newfound knowledge, all while making sure to properly extinguish the small fire they'd ignited.

As the evening unfolded, Michelle felt the tug of domestic routine drawing her back into the role she played so well—wife, mother, homemaker. Yet the sunburn on her skin was a physical manifestation of the day's earlier chaos, a reminder that not all was as serene as it seemed.

While Mike and the boys tucked into the pot roast she had prepared, Michelle excused herself to take a cool shower. The water was a balm to her sunburned skin, soothing her as aspirin coursed through her system. She slathered on a thick layer of aloe vera, hoping to mitigate the worst of the damage.

Later, in bed, she listened as Mike outlined the week ahead. His early starts and late nights meant she'd be solo on morning drop-offs and dinner duties. This wasn't new; work had always been demanding for Mike.

Then he brought up Chris—her Christopher.

"I know he's the owner's son and all, and you've got this thing about not kissing up to people. Last night, you kind of ignored him. I don't think I saw you say more than hello to the poor guy."

Michelle tensed. "I didn't mean to ignore him. I was kind of busy hosting everyone," she said, keeping her voice neutral.

"I know, I know," Mike replied. "But he's back in the area again, and you know how social dynamics work. It would look good for both of us if you were friendlier to him. Besides, the guy could use a friend."

Michelle nodded, her mind whirling. Why hadn't she been more attentive to Christopher? Could it have made a difference, smoothed over some invisible wrinkle in their life that she wasn't aware of? She couldn't shake the feeling that everything was interconnected in ways she couldn't grasp, like threads in a tapestry that she could feel but not see.

"Alright," she said finally. "I'll make an effort."

Mike leaned over to kiss her forehead, causing her to wince. "Thank you. You're the best."

He switched off the bedside lamp, casting the room into darkness. As she lay there, Michelle wished she could switch off her thoughts the same way. Instead, her mind drifted back to the day's events—the sunburn, the lost ring, the scout meeting, the subtle pressures of family life, and now, the expectation to be nice to her secret lover for the sake of workplace politics. Michelle let out a silent chuckle as she remembered her friend's candid remark: "Moms get stuff done." It had been a rallying cry of sorts, said with a mix of exasperation and admiration during a casual conversation about the juggling act that was motherhood.

All these things seemed to coalesce into a jigsaw puzzle, forming a complex mosaic of her life. Each piece, no matter how trivial, held a place and purpose, influencing the entire picture in ways she was only just beginning to understand. Yet, unlike a jigsaw puzzle, the pieces were ever-changing, and some, like her ring, were irreplaceably lost, leaving gaps that would always be felt.

Tomorrow was another day, filled with its own challenges and joys. As she closed her eyes, Michelle vowed to face it with the same resilience that had carried her so far. For now, that would have to be enough.

It was the first day of the new school year. Michelle relished the simplicity of the morning ritual with her boys—the sound of cereal pouring, the subsequent crunching, the brief interactions that often said more than long conversations ever could. Boyd was growing up, finding his own way, and while a part of her missed the days when he was younger and less independent, another part of her swelled with pride at the young man he was becoming.

As Boyd made his way out the door, Michelle was swept up in the familiar swirl of parental emotions—pride intertwined with a hint of melancholy. She embraced Floyd and Lloyd firmly, watching as they set off with their vibrant backpacks bouncing, all three venturing to the singular small town school building where every grade level was united under one roof, encapsulating their distinct worlds.

Driving to the quarry's office, Michelle couldn't help but keep an eye on the clock. Today wasn't just any day; it was a day colored by the gnawing absence of her missing ring, a symbol whose emotional value far outstripped its material worth. The missing piece had turned her into a temporary clock-watcher, its hands ticking down to the narrow window she would have to comb the beach during lunch.

Limestone dust floated in the air as she arrived at the quarry, a reminder of the hard, gritty work that took place here. She exchanged pleasantries with the front desk receptionist and nodded at Christopher as she headed to her small, organized cubicle. The look on his face in passing was one of surprise. The sunburn was deep, the color bright; no amount of foundation would cover it. Her focus for the morning was ostensibly on balance sheets, payroll, and pending orders, but in reality, her mind kept drifting back to the beach, to the stretch of sand that held the missing chapter of her family's story.

Lunchtime couldn't come fast enough. As the clock finally signaled her brief respite, Michelle wasted no time. She was out the door and in her car, driving back to the beach with a sense of urgency she usually reserved for emergencies. The sandwich she had packed sat on the passenger seat, but eating was the last thing on her mind.

Reaching the beach, she quickly got to work, scanning the ground with the makeshift sifting tool she had used the day before. Her eyes worked in tandem with her hands, mechanically but desperately scanning the pebbles and grains of sand for that glint of gold. Forty-five minutes normally was enough time to eat a leisurely lunch, but today it felt like seconds.

Finally, the clock warned her that time was up. Empty-handed and filled with a renewed sense of frustration, she drove back to the office, her untouched sandwich still beside her. As she sat back at her desk, Michelle felt like she was splintering into pieces, each shard burdened with its own set of duties and secrets.

But even as she grappled with her own internal strife, she knew that she had a job to finish, sons to care for, and a home to maintain. With a sigh, she refocused on her work. The numbers on the spreadsheets made sense, at least. They fit into neat boxes, unlike the messy labyrinth of her thoughts and emotions.

As she fell back into the rhythm of her responsibilities, Michelle found a strange comfort in the mundane tasks that filled her day. They grounded her when she felt like she was coming apart. And so, she carried on, because that's what moms do—they carry on, even when their worlds are tilted, holding onto the hope that everything will eventually right itself.

"So, how was your first day back at school?" Michelle asked.

She smiled at her sons, taking in the nuances of their simple responses. "Fine" had as many shades as a painter's palette when it came to kids, especially her boys. Floyd was always the most eager to share, his words tumbling out like a river in flood. His enthusiasm for Mrs. Hart's history class was palpable, even if his description was sprinkled with the vague terms "stuff" and "things."

Lloyd's more pragmatic approach didn't go unnoticed. He was already thinking ahead, focused on upcoming projects and the academic demands of the term. Their different personalities made each conversation a unique dance, a delicate balance between probing and listening.

But Boyd... Boyd was a different story altogether. The relationship between a mother and her firstborn is a complex patchwork quilt, stitched from the threads of many shared experiences, lessons, and growing pains. Michelle felt that bond acutely as she looked at him.

When he mentioned a girl named Amber, she caught the subtle shift in his voice, the underlying note that signaled the entrance of something—or someone—new and significant. Her son was changing, evolving, and while part of her heart swelled with pride, another part felt the bittersweet pang of the inevitable march of time.

It was a strange and pivotal moment, hearing her oldest son talk about a girl who wasn't a relative for the first time. A host of emotions flitted across her face: surprise, curiosity, but mostly a kind of melancholy joy. She knew this day would come, of course. But understanding something in the abstract is different from living it.

"Amber, huh?" she finally said, her voice tinged with a curiosity she couldn't entirely suppress. "Is she in one of your classes?"

Boyd shrugged, as teenagers often do when they're guarding a treasure of personal importance. "Nah, she's older. Just saw her around. Her locker is on the corner of the hall around from mine."

Michelle nodded, respecting the boundary he had subtly laid down. "Well, school is a time for meeting lots of new people."

"Yeah," Boyd replied, his one-word answer as layered as a

Russian novel. It spoke of things unsaid, feelings unfathomed, and a future yet to unfold.

As the family dinner continued, Michelle felt like she was seeing her boys through a new lens, one that sharpened the contours of their emerging identities. Each "fine" from their lips seemed like a veneer, beneath which churned seas of emotion, curiosity, and the restless stirrings of growth.

And she, their mother, was tasked with the privilege and challenge of guiding them through it all—even as she navigated her own complex web of emotions and responsibilities. Because no matter what, life went on.

Five

"Hey," Boyd ventured, encountering Amber by her locker.

"Hey back at ya," she replied, her eyes flicking up briefly from the interior of her locker, a small sanctuary adorned with drawings and photographs of Chet.

"You, ah, fond of birds?" Boyd inquired, stumbling a bit over his words.

She studied him for a moment, then shrugged. "Not all birds. You?"

"My father and I have gone hunting a few times. You learn a bit about birds that way," he said, cautiously optimistic.

Amber's expression clouded, a sense of resignation settling in. She recognized in Boyd the prototype of another young man who simply wouldn't understand her. "That's nice," she said evenly. "My affinity for birds is rather different."

"Oh?" Boyd looked genuinely curious, his eyebrows arching upward.

"Yes, this is Chet." Amber pointed at a photograph. "He's a raven who's been bringing me gifts daily for over five years since we first crossed paths." Her fingers delicately touched the charm hanging around her neck. "This was his first treasure to me."

Boyd paused, contemplating his options. His first instinct was to meet this peculiarity with sarcasm, perhaps a quip about her being a "crazy bird girl" to feel better about himself. But a deeper impulse prevailed, one nurtured by years of his mother's probing questions that had taught him to inquire rather than judge. "That's really unique. Tell me more?"

A smile blossomed on Amber's face. Perhaps she had been too hasty in her assumptions. "I'd be delighted to," she said, her eyes meeting his in a quiet acknowledgement that they had just crossed an invisible threshold, from the mundane to the nuanced, in their understanding of one another. For a moment, she looked at him differently—no longer just another boy who might tease her for her interests, but someone who was willing to see her as she was.

"It's actually really cool," Amber began, the initial timidity in her voice giving way to a sense of excitement. "Chet and I first crossed paths several years ago. He was isolated and hungry, separated from his unkindness—you know, that's what a flock of ravens is called. In exchange for the food I gave him, he brought me this charm." She lightly touched the pendant around her neck, as if it were a cherished keepsake. "It was as if, from that first encounter, he understood some silent pact between us, a mutual respect that goes beyond what you'd expect between a bird and a human."

Boyd was hooked. "That's amazing. What kind of gifts does he bring you?"

"All sorts of things—earrings, tinfoil, pieces of wire and string. Sometimes stuff like buttons or small coins. Ravens are incredibly smart, you know. They can solve puzzles, recognize human faces, even plan for the future to some extent."

Boyd found himself smiling, impressed by Amber's passion and captivated by the unexpected story she had just shared. "I had no idea. I've seen ravens before, but I never thought about them that way."

Amber grinned, grateful for the space to share her world. "That's the thing; we often overlook the extraordinary in what we consider ordinary. Each time Chet brings me a gift, it's like he's telling me a story—a narrative of the world from his viewpoint. It's quite humbling and endlessly fascinating."

"Wow," Boyd uttered, genuinely intrigued. "That's so cool."

Amber closed her locker, her eyes meeting Boyd's.

Boyd nodded, sensing a newfound rapport. "Well, if you're ever up for sharing more stories about Chet, I'm all ears."

Amber's smile widened. "I'd like that."

As they parted ways, Boyd couldn't help but think he had done well.

Six

Another lunch hour marred by the glaring sun; another degree of sunburn attained. Michelle sat at her desk, ostensibly reviewing spreadsheets and invoices, but her thoughts were eclipsed by the absence of her ring. When would Mike notice? What would he say? And Christopher—he hadn't uttered a word to her since Saturday. What sort of upbringing leads a person to behave like that?

On the drive home, Michelle pulled into Sam's on Second, a pawn shop she'd never visited before. She was unsure how her small-town community would perceive her making a stop there, so she parked in the secluded alley at the back. Upon entering, the electronic bell heralded her arrival. A head popped up from behind the counter; it was Sam, the proprietor. The shop was devoid of other customers, and the plexiglass barriers around the counter seemed like an overreaction in a post-COVID world.

"These barriers aren't for COVID, ma'am," Sam explained, having been asked a thousand times before. "They're here to prevent people from jumping over the counter—a sort of grab-and-go deterrent."

"Do you have metal detectors? Ones that can detect gold? I've heard not all of them can do that."

"We do have a couple of options," Sam said, stepping out from his enclosed space. "I'm Sam, by the way."

"Michelle," she offered.

"Nice to meet you, Michelle. What brings you to the world of treasure hunting?"

She hesitated. "Not exactly treasure hunting. I thought, with so many things lost on the beach, and with all the tourists leaving things behind..."

"Smart idea to come here," Sam cut in. "Folks who buy these things new are fools. Spend a ton and then give up when they don't find anything." He directed her toward three metal detectors on a shelf. "Personally, I'd go for this Chinese model. It's $150, compared to the $1,200 Australian kit."

Michelle opted for the less expensive Chinese model. "That's what I was thinking."

She noted that there was a sign over the counter that simply said "Jewelry."

"Do you sell or buy rings here?"

Sam's eyes darted to her. "It's my number one item. Are you

also looking for jewelry, perhaps? Wedding rings? Bought a few in the last four days."

Michelle's heart leapt. How did he know? Hers might have been an old, familiar story: a wife loses her wedding ring and has to find it. "Could I see them?"

Sam unveiled a tray lined with black velvet, showcasing five wedding rings—none of which were hers. "Not what you're looking for?"

"No, thank you," she replied, trying to mask her disappointment.

"So, just the metal detector today?"

"Yes, please," she said, noticing a sign that read, "ALL TRANSACTIONS ARE CASH ONLY" in all caps. "I'll be back in ten minutes. Could you hold it for me?"

Michelle took exactly ten minutes to walk two blocks to the credit union, where she withdrew $140 from her personal savings, adding it to the $10 she already had in her purse. When she returned, Sam had prepared her purchase for her, packing it in a bag that included the original box, instructions, headphones, a small shovel, a carry case, a battery, and a wand.

Feeling the transaction was fair, Michelle stowed her new purchase in her car. Once home, she plugged the metal detector's battery into an outlet in the garage, next to the treadmill that only saw use during the colder months. With each passing second, as the battery charged, Michelle couldn't help but feel that she was recharging her hopes as well.

After dinner, Michelle excused herself by announcing her intention to take a walk on the beach. She could no longer endure the agony of another day scorched by the sun, nor the breathless escapades of rushing back and forth to the beach during her lunch break.

Armed with her newly acquired metal detector and the makeshift sifting tool she had fashioned herself, Michelle ventured out. The beach had never felt so paradoxical—familiar, yet fraught with a new urgency. She meticulously navigated the detector back and forth, tracing rows on the sand that ranged from the shoreline, where water idly lapped, to the tall, sentinel-like grass that framed the beach. Every beep of the device was a thrill, every dig a fount of possibility, yet she found nothing of value. Especially not her ring.

By the time she returned home, fatigue had settled in, heavier than the disappointment that trailed her. Mike was already in the land of sleep, snoring softly, a man untouched by her present anxieties. As she slid into the cool sheets of their queen-sized bed, Michelle felt an uncanny sense of both closeness and distance. Here they were, lying inches apart, and yet her mind was miles away—somewhere on the beach, tirelessly searching.

She loved Mike. The epitome of a good man. Why would she allow herself to get into this position?

For Michelle, the notion of calling in sick for a "mental health day" was tantalizing but ultimately unacceptable. In her internal universe, a stringent moral compass seemed to turn its needle decisively away from such indulgences. She had never been one to indulge herself in such liberties—not when the kids fell ill, or when Mike was incapacitated by a kidney stone, or even when seasonal viruses made their rounds through her household. No, Michelle would not break now, not even under the weight of her mounting anxiety and looming questions.

She got out of bed, her body aching, still radiating the residual warmth of a fading sunburn—perhaps a touch of sun poisoning, she stubbornly refused to admit, even to herself. But it didn't matter. The minutiae of the day awaited her—those duties and routines that formed the foundation of her family's lives.

Cereal clinked into the boys' bowls, signaling the beginning of the morning, just like it had all week. After, she would shepherd them out the door, her heart a tangle of maternal pride and concern, always hoping they would find something valuable in their day, something beyond textbooks and lockers. Then, the familiar drive across town to work, the ritual of preparing payroll, the critical phone call to the credit union to ensure deposits were locked in. It was Labor Day weekend—she could almost smell the extra day like a season waiting just around the corner.

With a mixture of resignation and resolve, Michelle readied herself for the day ahead, determined to execute each task with the meticulous care it demanded. It was as if she were following a script, each act leading inexorably to the next, leaving no room for the nagging "what-ifs" and "if-onlys" that had been her unwelcome companions of late.

Michelle felt anchored by her rituals, even as a part of her floated adrift, continually searching. Yet she knew, as she stepped out into the burgeoning light of day, that no amount of routine could completely silence the questions that were beginning to insist upon answers—questions that circled around a missing ring but extended to domains far more complicated and less tangible. And so she moved forward, simultaneously grounded and untethered, setting in motion the events of another ordinary day.

The monitor on her desk hadn't changed in five minutes. She sat there, staring at it, while in her mind, she was across town, walking the beach. She felt hot, toasted from the sun. Her giant stainless steel mug with a protruding plastic straw had visited the water cooler twice already that morning—a new record for hydration.

"Hey..." Christopher peered over the cubicle wall, his puppy-dog eyes pleading for attention. "Hey."

She looked up the third time he said it. "Good morning."

Chris slunk into the chair Michelle kept by her desk for when others needed to talk through financials with her.

"What happened to you? You look... extra crispy."

"Yeah, I know." She tucked her hair behind her right ear.

"I was thinking," Christopher began to whisper, "I was thinking of maybe getting out of here for a few minutes. You up for playing hooky? My boat's at the marina. I could apply another layer of sunscreen, and we could be hitting the waves without anyone knowing."

Those eyes almost had her. His hands that had made her

feel so good. His strong arms, good looks, and playboy attitude just didn't move her like they used to. She had done her penance. Marching up and down the beach under the hot sun, neglecting the beautiful world she had built and the lives she was charged to care for was enough self-abasement to last a lifetime.

"Chris..." The sound of his name turned his eyes wide. "I love my husband, Mike. I love my three boys. I have a great life." She thought for a moment. "You and I had a night. A fiery night that burned me. I don't think—"

"No, no, that's cool." Chris sounded like one of her sons when their feelings were hurt. Time to take the toy and go home. "It's cool. I just thought, well." Standing up and stepping out of the cubicle, he added, "Catch you later."

It was fast and easy to fall out of Chris's world. Just as easy as falling into a lake. The hours he had spent talking Michelle up were wasted, all those moments fleeting.

Seven

As they ambled together, shoulder almost touching shoulder, there was a palpable air of ease between them. His arm, swinging naturally, had grazed her hand. This new sensation of touch, skin on skin, was breathtaking. So amazing, he made sure it accidently happened at least two more times. Boyd felt as if he had stepped into a world suspended in time, a landscape distilled to the simple beauty of this particular moment. There was no calculus of the future here—no tallying of years and stages, no musings about the feasibility of a younger boy dating an older girl. The simple act of walking together filled the space around them, a universe contracting into the span of a few feet.

"Remind me again—what exactly are we doing?" Boyd's voice carried a note of genuine curiosity, his eyes focused on the road ahead.

"We're going to sell a few of the treasures Chet has gifted me over the years. I'm saving up for school," Amber explained, her tone mingling anticipation with a tinge of regret.

For Boyd, the concept of a pawn shop was as foreign as French—something from movies or television. Savings, on the other hand, was a term that evoked the glass jar tucked away in the recesses of his closet, filled with crumpled bills and spare change. "You know, I really like that I'm always learning something new from you, Amber," he said, a note of gratitude coloring his words.

Amber looked at him, a smile softly curving her lips. "That's really sweet of you to say," she replied, visibly touched.

They both internally recognized this as a moment, but not out loud to each other.

As the two entered Sam's, Amber was greeted warmly while Boyd was subjected to the stink-eye. "Who's your friend? How old is he?"

"That's Boyd. He's sixteen," Amber lied.

"Ok." Sam's expression remained unimpressed. "What've you brought me this time? Or, should I ask, what did Chet bring?"

Amber delved into her backpack to retrieve the items.

"She tell you why his name is Chet?" Sam directed the question at Boyd.

He shook his head, still a tad bewildered by Amber's lie about his age.

"It's her mom's favorite musician, Chet Baker. Her mom loves jazz. Only one around here who buys used jazz records."

"Here they are." Amber placed a purple cloth bag with "Crown Royal" emblazoned on it onto the counter.

Sam added, "Her mom gave her the bag too." As Amber laid out the items on the black velvet board, Sam inserted an eyepiece and began to examine the contents. "Let's see what we have here."

"Okay, this one"—he pointed with a metal rod—"real diamond earrings. I can give you 50 bucks for those." He jotted down the amount and description on a scratch pad. "These are glass, and not matching. Similar, but not matching. So 5 bucks on that. Some dude with a single sailor's piercing might buy a single stud or two."

Boyd was elated. Just a few found objects and Amber already had $55. For Boyd, making money entailed pushing a mechanical mower across numerous neighborhood lawns every summer. Chores paid too, but nothing close to what Chet was bringing in for Amber, or even what he earned mowing lawns.

"This necklace," Sam continued. "That's gold, I'll give you 25 bucks on that." He recorded it like the others. "You got anything else for me?"

Amber reached into the bottom of the purple bag and pulled out a gold wedding ring with a diamond.

"Woo-doggie! Chet deserves a real treat for this one," Sam exclaimed. "Let's see."

"That's a really nice ring, Amber. Are you sure you want to sell that?"

"Of course she does," Sam interjected. "For school and stuff. Right?"

Amber nodded, although Boyd sensed a flicker of hesitation in her eyes. To him, it was the most beautiful ring he'd ever seen. There was something familiar about it. It surely held significant value, both financially and sentimentally.

"Amber, you and I go a ways back. I don't want to take advantage of you. The best I can offer is $1,500. But, think on it, there's a jeweler in Gaylord who might give you more."

"How am I going to get to Gaylord?" Amber asked, a hint of frustration in her voice.

"Well, you're not going to school for a while, you've got time to figure it out," Sam replied, nonchalant.

"But I could be earning interest on the cash starting today and getting more in the long run."

"True, true."

Amber weighed her options, the gears in her mind turning. Selling the ring to Sam meant immediate cash, but there was a chance she could get a better price elsewhere. Then again, the trip to Gaylord would take time and effort, and there was no guarantee the jeweler would offer more. And then there was the ring itself. Could she really part with such a beautiful and, presumably, sentimental piece? Amber felt a pang of guilt, aware that the ring once symbolized someone's love and commitment. She looked at Boyd, then back at Sam, and took a deep breath.

A sense of wonder caught Boyd's attention as Amber made a decision. He meandered through the labyrinthine store, his eyes feasting on the treasure trove of miscellany that Sam had amassed over the years. Everything from the archaic to the modern, from utilitarian to the purely decorative, was laid out for his perusal. For a boy who earned his money cutting grass, this was a universe unto itself—a museum of lost and found objects, each with its own untold story of riches.

"Sam? What's this for?" Boyd pointed at a curious object, his fascination momentarily pulling him away from his pondering over Amber's dilemma.

"Magnet fishing. It's a magnet on a fifty-foot rope," Sam explained, not bothering to look up from his counter. "You toss the magnet into the water and pull up metal and stuff. Some of it's valuable—stuff I'd buy. The rest is junk."

A mental cog clicked into place for Boyd. *A giant magnet and rope for fifty bucks,* he mused. The gears of his imagination started turning at breakneck speed. *I have fifty dollars. I could make that money back and more.*

Visions of long summer days spent by the river or, even better, on the marina flickered before his eyes. Images of sunken treasures waiting to be discovered, old coins hidden beneath layers of mud, and metallic objects forgotten by boaters or fishermen. Everyone drops watches, rings, phones, and wallets. It wasn't just the prospect of finding valuable items; it was the thrill of the search, the allure of the unknown. In that moment, the stack of fifty one-dollar bills wrapped in a white rubber band, tucked away in his closet felt like an invitation to a world of endless possibilities, a golden ticket to an adventure yet unwritten.

EIGHT

"Michelle, your timing is perfect. Not half an hour ago, another ring came in. You want a look?"

Michelle strained to quell the tone of desperation in her voice. "Yes, please."

As Sam sauntered toward the jewelry section, he spoke again. "How's your metal detector? Have you field-tested it yet?"

"It's less than what I had hoped, to be honest."

"What are your thoughts on magnet fishing? I happen to have a kit. You can get all kinds of treasures with it."

"But not gold. Gold is not magnetic."

"True, true. Still, lots of things are. Things I purchase every day." Sam retrieved a black velvet tray and presented the ring to Michelle. "Bear in mind, I've not had the time to clean it."

"How much?" Michelle interjected, abruptly cutting Sam

off. At once, she knew: that was the ring. Her ring. Her own ring. Someone had found it and brought it here to Sam. This was why her search on the beach had proven fruitless. It may have been discovered yesterday or even this very morning; the timing was immaterial. What mattered was that it had been found. She could slip it back onto her finger. She was able to avoid any questions, any additional lies, any arguments. She could stop the worry and get back to her life. She could finally move beyond this moment without great penalty or persecution. She was wrong, she had done wrong, and she had learned her lesson. There was no need for punishment or penalty. She would be free of this mistake, then do better.

"Well, it's valued at $3,200. But I would sell it to you for an even $3,000."

Michelle's face was a mask hiding all emotion. Inside, in her private place, roared a tempest unmatched by Mother Nature. Three thousand? Something she had never considered. Her initial astonishment swiftly curdled into ire. This was sheer highway robbery. How could Sam perpetrate such an outrage? It was *her* ring. Hers. Upon reflection, she realized the score: No police report had been filed; it was found, not stolen. She had neither offered a reward nor disclosed the loss to anyone. This was the cost—the cost of silence, the price of anonymity. The continuity of her marriage was worth more than $3,000.

"Cash only?" Michelle inquired, her demeanor impeccably calm.

"Yes, ma'am. Cash only, paid on the spot, as it were."

Michelle's mind sprang into action, contemplating the

amount and where it could be gotten. A fleeting thought skated across her consciousness, as ephemeral as it was insidious: The payroll did have a cache of cash reserved for just such large sums. She dismissed it instantly, revolted by the very suggestion, loathing herself for even permitting it entry into her thoughts. It would have to come from her savings. Yet doing so would deplete nearly the entirety of her financial buffer, leaving her without recourse should any emergency arise. Her aging car would need to soldier on for another half-decade; winter tires would have to be deferred until the ensuing year. This was virtually all she had. Yet what was at stake here was the very bedrock of her life: her marriage, her relationship with Mike, the equilibrium they had established for their boys. All of her everything, jeopardized for nothing.

"Two thousand-eight hundred," she countered with a straight face. "In cash. You hold it for me. I run to the bank before it closes for the weekend. Is that clock accurate?"

"Yes ma'am, that clock is right."

"Twenty-eight, then."

"I hope you'll not forget my kindness on our next encounter."

"Twenty-eight. Say it."

Sam was taken aback by her directness. "Twenty-eight."

"Hold it. I'll be right back."

Michelle raced toward the credit union. She couldn't recall the last time she had run like this, though it might have been when one of the boys, still a toddler, had made a beeline toward the lake—or possibly the road—mistaking a chase for a game.

The door was still open when she got there. Mary-Ann, the teller she'd worked with professionally for many years, was behind the counter.

"Michelle!" The smile was in her voice. "Didn't think I'd see you again today. Cutting it close for the long weekend, aren't you?"

"Mary-Ann, just made it. I need your help with a withdrawal. Please."

Walking back to Second Street, her purse was laden with the full weight of her emptied savings, including the receipt that signaled the account's closure—insufficient funds to keep it open. Mary-Ann had been discreet and professional, asking no questions, providing no judgments. Yet Michelle knew that in a small town like Rogers City, there were always invisible threads of curiosity weaving between its residents. Though they didn't move in her immediate social circles, Sam and Mary-Ann were now the keepers of a secret fragment of her life. They weren't members of her church, they were not in orbit around her world, but they existed in this confined universe that sat along the shores of Lake Huron.

Michelle couldn't be certain if Sam was a good man. She only knew that he was a businessman. Like many men she'd known, there was often an unspoken yearning for something more. Like with Christopher, this lingering "What if?" sat just on the periphery of conversation, ready to intrude if invited. Carrying this newfound burden—the knowledge of the ring—forward wouldn't be without its difficulties. There was always the latent fear that it could be held over her head. But at least the ring would be back on her finger.

"Sam, $2,800. Cash," Michelle stated, standing at the jewelry counter.

For a moment, Sam met her gaze in silence. He held a number of cards in his hand, each representing a different path. He could have reverted to the initial price, which she'd barely managed to scrape together. He could have inflated the price even further, opting not to sell it to her at all. He might even have tapped into darker inclinations, extracting more than mere currency.

Yet, he chose none of these paths. "Let me get my book and write this up," he finally said.

A heavy sigh of relief escaped Michelle's lips as he walked away. She felt like a taut wire, ready to snap. This had been a week burdened with too many moments held in precarious balance, and she couldn't wait for it to be over.

Nine

"Hi, Mom," Boyd said, his voice infused with cheer. "How was your day?"

"Good. It closed the week on a rather high note," Michelle replied, her back turned to her son as she busied herself with the evening's dinner preparations. "I beat you home. Did you do anything fun?"

"Hanging with Amber."

"The girl with the bird?"

"Yeah," he said with embarrassment.

"I'm glad you're getting to spend time with her."

"Me too... Mom, you know that money I've been saving, from mowing lawns?"

"Yes."

"Could I use some of it to start a new business?"

"It's your money, darling. Use it however you wish. Though I would advise saving it for something truly meaningful."

"This would be an investment in a new venture. I'm thinking of taking up magnet fishing over at the marina, retrieving valuable items."

The colander, filled with spaghetti noodles, slipped from Michelle's grip and clattered into the sink with a clang. "A magnet fishing business? Where on Earth did you get such an idea?"

Michelle turned to face her son, recognizing instantly the source of this seed that was planted.

Seated in the breakfast nook with his schoolbook, Boyd looked up at his mother and began to say, "Me and Amber—" But then his eyes landed on her hand. On the ring. He understood why it had looked so familiar, why he had thought it was the most beautiful ring he had ever seen.

She watched as his expression shifted, fading from the tender narrative of teenage romance with Amber to a slow, dawning realization that his mother had lost her wedding ring.

A fleeting thought passed through his mind: *Isn't it cool Chet found Mom's ring?* Yet, another question intruded: *Why would Mom remove her ring? Where would she take off her ring?*

Boyd was caught in a trance, staring at his mother's hands. Those were the hands that had cradled him, nurtured him as a child; the hands that turned the pages of the bedtime stories she read to him; the hands that had high-fived him in triumph and patted his back in consolation. The ring had been there. Always. He never realized how important the ring was until now.

"Mom?" Boyd finally uttered, unsure of what else to say or think.

"Boyd—"

The back door opened and in walked Mike, punctual as usual when not working extra shifts. He seemed to carry a shroud of quarry dust as he entered. Planting a kiss on Michelle's cheek, he said, "Boyd, good Boyd, doing his homework." Just as casually, he glanced at Michelle's hand and remarked, "Ah, good, you found it." His right eye gave a knowing wink. The corner of his mouth curled ever so slightly. "I thought you were going to kill yourself looking for that thing." Then he continued through to the bathroom to freshen up for the night.

Boyd shot his mother a knowing glance. He might not have had all the particulars, might not have been mature enough to know more than the innocent sensation of his hand brushing against Amber's, but he knew enough. With a clap of his book closing, he excused himself to his room.

For a moment, Michelle remained frozen, like a statue in her kitchen. Above the din of her two younger boys playing in the yard, above the simmering murmur of the sauce on the stove, she covered her mouth with both hands as tears began to fall. She allowed herself only that brief moment, blotting her tears away with the blue-striped kitchen towel. Then she collected herself. Because moms got shit done.

Lying parallel to Mike on their queen-sized bed, Michelle lay awake in the darkness after the click of the light switch signaled bedtime. "Mike, did you know? Did you know the whole week?"

He took a deep, contemplative breath before responding. "I knew. I knew long enough."

"I'm sorry, Mike. I am so, so sorry."

"I know."

"How did you find out?"

"Michelle, I know you better than you know yourself. You talk in your sleep. You tell me everything."

"Why didn't you say anything? Why didn't we fight about this? Why didn't you get mad? Are you ever going to forgive me?"

Turning to face her, Mike found her in the darkness of the room, just the thickness of bedding separating them. He breached the distance and kissed her sweetly. "I forgive you. I do."

"Why? Why would you?"

"Michelle, I meant it when I said it. For richer or poorer, in sickness and in health, till death do us part. I do."

A Hummingbird in Winter

LAKE ONTARIO

One

"Sorry. I am so sorry." Those are her first words.

I find myself falling. That uncontrollable fear of hitting the ground. The expectation of that acid burn on my knees from abraded skin. I am a child again, on the playground, being bullied, about to taste my own blood. In an instant, I can imagine the pain, the taste of pennies, the brown liquid, the bruised lip. What if I lost all my teeth? Hit the curb just right and land on the street; what would I do then? Would I gather up the teeth? Putting them in milk is what I remember. Then, get to a dentist.

In the year 2132, gravity still wins.

Here it comes, the concrete rubbing my palms raw. It's about to happen. The shooting electricity up my leg, back to my brain. Which swear word will it produce?

"Shit!"

Tongue swipe across the incisors, top, bottom, and they all feel there. My elbows took the brunt of the shock. Oh, my knees. Here comes the pain. Adrenaline heightens the senses. I can smell the cold of Adelaide Street. It is not pleasant.

I take a deep breath. "It's so fucking cold!"

I roll up. With my weight off my hands, I can feel my palms tingle. There's a burning in my knees. I steady myself and get up on my toes, trusting the ball and heel to balance. Looking down, I can see the holes in my suit pants, the abraded skin now meshed into the fabric. I can feel a warm stream racing down each of my legs. The right drip wins, reaching my socks first.

"Oh dear, I am so, so sorry," I hear her say again.

On another assessment, I notice my bag is still on the ground. I bend and pick it up by the handle, not the strap. It seems intact. I sling the strap over my neck and shoulder. It's securely in place. Reality is starting to catch up. Time is returning to its usual pace. Hands and knees are burning and bloody, elbows are sore, and a throb starts in my back where I was first hit. I turn, and time slows again when our eyes meet. I can sense the flutter of my eyelids as my brain tries to catch up. She is the most beautiful woman in the world. Her eyes are magnetic, pulling me in.

"I am so sorry," she repeats. "What can I do? How can I help?"

I gulp. She's talking to me. She caused this.

Her hand waves in front of my face. "Hello?"

"Shit."

"Oh, look at you." Her voice is laced with concern. "You're

a mess. How can I help? I am so, so sorry." She reaches for my arm, and in what would normally be a moment I'd relish, I recoil and wince in pain.

"Shit!"

"Oh, this is bad. I don't know what to do."

Her captivating allure begins to wane. Time snaps back to normal, and I recall where I am, where I was going, and the current time. I glance at my wrist, noting the time, then gingerly activate my BIOPDA to connect with a number. After two rings, I say, "Gord, I've had a bit of an accident here on my way to meet you. A real mishap with some minor injuries, but everyone's fine. Is there any chance we could reschedule?"

He responds, "Yes, of course. No serious injuries, I hope?"

"Nothing too severe."

"Alright. I have an hour free this afternoon, or we can find a slot tomorrow. I'll send over some times my team is available while you're in the city."

"Thank you very much. I apologize for this inconvenience and appreciate your patience," I reply with gratitude.

He wishes me well and reassures me that the situation will be acceptable for his team, and that I should keep him updated on the details and my condition. Feeling a tad light-headed, I thank him and end the call. Now, I can sense my lips grappling for the right words.

Then, there's an unexpected kindness. A gentle touch above my elbow. She's grasping my arm, inquiring, "Where can we go to take care of this?"

I glance up and around to orient myself. "That's my hotel."

"The Hilton?"

I nod.

"Oh, and you're a guest here, and I did this to you... I am so sorry. You should not hold ill will to the great city of Toronto or its people for this."

"It's okay. I'm okay."

"Let's get you fixed up," she suggests.

Her touch is nurturing, guiding me as we walk side by side. She isn't pulling or rushing me. Each step feels deliberate, cautious. There's an unfamiliar sway to my movements now. Even though the hotel is just half a block away, the journey feels much longer.

"The entrance is just around the corner," I point out.

Switching to my other side, she supports my left arm, positioning me to walk alongside the building with her closer to the foot traffic. Considerate in her actions, she shields me from the risk of bumping into passersby. After a few more yards—or meters, I should say—we reach the steps of the side entrance.

Noticing the absence of a railing, she assures, "It's okay; lean on me."

We ascend the steps one at a time. Once at the top, the revolving door ushers in a mix of icy and warm air. Once inside, the warmth heightens the sting on my injured skin. My knees and palms, with their dancing nerves, experience a fresh wave of pain. I can't suppress an audible gasp.

"Oh no," she murmurs.

"I'm okay," I fib.

"Which floor are you on?"

"Thirty-two."

She guides me to the elevator bank, presses the button, and ushers me in when the doors part. As we stand there, she repeatedly tries to press the button to my floor, to no avail.

"Why won't this work?" she asks after several attempts.

"Stupid me. You need the key card."

Without hesitation, before I can act, she delves into my left pocket. The unexpected intimacy of her hand exploring the space sends another adrenaline surge coursing through me. Retrieving my wallet and the key card, she examines it, turning it over with an expression of curious fascination.

"Wave it in front of that pad," I guide.

Her eyes meet mine with a hint of amusement before she makes a somewhat graceless attempt, waving the card over the entirety of the elevator control panel.

"See that little protruding black part with the yellow light? That's it," I clarify, pointing it out.

She aligns the card properly, making the light turn green, then pushes 32. With a swift motion, she stuffs both the key card and my wallet back into my pocket, causing my suspenders to stretch taut.

"We'll need the key card again," I note. "To get into the room."

"Yeah," she responds, nodding with an intensity that feels deeper than the casual gesture most people use. Her hand delves back into my pocket, maneuvering about before emerging with the card.

Choosing to savor the silence, I remain quiet. The illuminated floor numbers catch my attention as we ascend. A sense of déjà vu washes over me. She seems familiar—someone from movies or a show, perhaps? I ponder the dates of Toronto's film festival. Could she be someone famous?

When the elevator doors slide open, she guides me out with a gentle, patient touch. The ever-present urgency in my inner monologue chants its usual mantra: *Must get to the client. Must complete business.* The distinctly American pace of business, often glaringly apparent to those in other countries when I visit, feels absent around her. Nothing feels hurried in her presence.

Upon reaching my room, she deftly swipes the card, the reader flashing green on her first attempt. As we enter, the remnants of my hurried morning are evident: an unmade bed, the lingering humidity from my shower, and a slight mist forming on the window that frames the CN Tower.

"Take off your pants," she instructs.

Caught off guard, I stammer, "Pardon?"

"Those pants are ruined. We need to clean your wounds. Your jacket too," she adds.

Mouth agape, I'm sure I resemble a floundering fish. My mind scrambles to voice objections, to uphold some sense of modesty in the face of this unexpected intimacy.

"I don't even know your name."

She peels off her winter coat, revealing an evening dress that looks as though it belongs on a Hollywood red carpet. Its form-fitting design accentuates her physique.

"Cynthia" is what I hear. "Problem?" she queries.

"Nope. No problem." I comply, step into the bathroom to remove just my pants, taking a seat on the closed toilet lid.

She reaches over to turn on the sink tap, letting the water warm. While it runs, she searches the counter for a washcloth. Finding one, she dampens it with the warm water, wringing out the excess before turning back to me.

Gently, she begins dabbing at the scraped areas on my knees. The warmth of the cloth contrasts sharply with the stinging of my wounds. I flinch slightly at the contact.

"I'm sorry," she murmurs. "I'll try to be gentle."

I nod in response, trying to distract myself by watching her face. The concentration in her eyes, the way her brow furrows slightly when she encounters a particularly bad scrape—it all makes her look even more endearing.

"You're not from here, are you?" she asks without looking up.

"No," I reply. "I'm from the States, just here on business."

She hums in acknowledgment, continuing her care. "You have an accent."

"Most Canadians say that." I chuckle. "To me, you all have the accent."

She laughs softly. "Fair enough."

After a few more minutes, she finishes cleaning my wounds and straightens up, her eyes meeting mine.

"Thank you, Cynthia," I say, genuinely grateful.

Opening my toiletry bag on the counter, she finds the small first aid kit I always carry. Cynthia starts to sort through the contents. She pulls out a small bottle of antiseptic, a few sterile gauze pads, and some medical tape. Kneeling back down, she once again focuses on my wounded knees.

She peeks into the bag and comments, "You've assembled quite the collection," her tone laced with a touch of amusement. Her gaze briefly catches on the foil-wrapped prophylactic packs, then quickly shifts away, a subtle dance of curiosity and decorum.

I can feel the heat rising to my cheeks. "Prepared for everything, I suppose."

She chuckles softly. "Indeed." Her tone changes. "Hold still," she instructs softly as she pours a small amount of antiseptic onto a gauze pad.

The cold sting of the liquid hits immediately, and I clench my teeth to stop from hissing out in pain. I can feel her eyes on me, concern evident. "I know it stings, but this will prevent any infection."

I nod in understanding, trying to distract myself from the burning sensation. "You're really good at this," I remark, genuinely impressed.

She smirks a little. "Two younger siblings. I got a lot of practice."

There's something comforting in the way she talks about her past, a sort of openness that encourages trust. I can't help but feel a strong connection to her, despite only knowing her for a short while.

As she continues, layering a gauze pad over each knee and securing it with medical tape, I allow my thoughts to wander. How did I end up in this strange, yet deeply intimate situation?

From a business trip to being cared for by a beautiful stranger in my hotel bathroom, the day had taken a turn I hadn't anticipated.

"All done," Cynthia finally announces, breaking me from my reverie. She looks up, pride evident in her eyes. "Not my best work, but it'll do."

I chuckle. "I'd say it's pretty great. Thank you, really."

She smiles warmly, extending a hand to help me up. "It's the least I could do."

We both stand there for a moment, an unspoken bond forming between us. The world outside seems to fade away as we're enveloped in this shared moment, the beginning of an unexpected journey.

"Normally, I'd be unnerved by someone touching all my things," I confess, the words pouring out in a rush of nervous honesty. "I travel often for work. The blue rubber gloves in security lines might protect the wearers, but they also spread germs across the items on those conveyor belts. I love my fellow man, but let's face it, people can be gross. I can't risk getting sick. Who knows what those gloves have touched? And a mask can only do so much. When I first entered this room, I wiped down the remote and door knobs with cleaning pads. Who knows what's happened in these hotel rooms before?"

She smiles and nods, listening intently.

"Sometimes, I find evidence of a 'glitter party' in these rooms. Glitter clings everywhere, and it's persistent; it can linger for months. I doubt a scout troop was here doing arts and crafts. I sometimes think a professional dancer might have been entertaining someone on that very couch."

When I see her puzzled expression, I hasten to explain, "Many prostitutes wear glitter. It's notorious for being hard to remove." Realizing my insensitivity, I quickly add, "Human trafficking is a serious issue. It's nothing to joke about. I shouldn't have."

Yet, looking into her eyes, I see an honesty and sincerity that's hard to define. My inner teenager's voice might chant, *She's so hot*, but it's not just about that. There's a childlike innocence mixed with her mature poise. I chastise myself for only focusing on her physical beauty. This woman, who has so selflessly led me back to my room and cared for my injuries without a hint of hesitation or disgust at the sight of blood, is unique. She's genuinely here in the moment, extending kindness to a complete stranger. It's both rare and truly wonderful. I've heard stories of Canadians being friendly to stop at accidents to help, but this is different.

I take a deep breath, steadying my thoughts, and make an effort to be empathetic. "What happened?"

She tilts her head. "What happened?"

"Why were you in such a rush when you bumped into me?"

She looks down. "Show me your hands."

I extend both hands to her, palms up.

"You don't have bandages suitable for these wounds. They need cleaning."

Cynthia selects a fresh hand towel from the rack. She lets the hot tap run until it steams. Submerging the towel, she wrings it until it achieves the ideal balance of warmth and dampness. With delicate taps, she cleans my palms. I try to keep them steady as she works. Intermittently, Cynthia blows on them, hastening the drying process. Retrieving the same tube of gel, she dispenses a generous amount onto each palm. There's a meditative quality to her movements as she gently massages the gel into my skin.

Once she's finished, our eyes meet, and I'm ensnared by her gaze. She seems flawless. With a gentle smile, she says, "Let's get you dressed."

Two

"I believe you'll look dashing in this suit. The cut and color suit you far better than the one you had on."

I'm warmed by her compliment, the first in what feels like ages.

"You have a discerning eye. That's one of my tailored suits."

Cynthia strides over to the desk. As she picks up the navy tailored pants and prepares them for me, I lean on her for support. She masterfully gets me into them, guiding my arms into the suspender loops, and then adeptly fastens everything in place. The sensation of her hands carefully adjusting my shirt beneath the waistband is unexpected yet comforting.

When she reaches for the matching jacket, I interject, "I'm really not that incapacitated. Your assistance means a lot, but I'm perfectly capable of dressing myself."

She graces me with a radiant smile as she responds, "The

best way to find yourself is to lose yourself in the service of others."

I'm genuinely taken aback. "That's quite profound."

"Mahatma Gandhi said it." Holding out my jacket invitingly, she instructs, "Turn around."

I comply, allowing her to deftly help me don the jacket. There's a gentle pat and brush on my shoulders, likely to ensure a clean appearance. "There," she comments with a firm tug at the jacket's coattails, "this emphasizes your shoulders. People respect a strong, masculine presence." She signals for me to face her, and as I turn, her approving eyes meet mine, "Now, there's a handsome man."

I look at my wrist for the BIOPDA. A few taps later, an email from my client proposing an alternative meeting time for the afternoon pops up in front of me. Perfect. With the screen up, I automatically enter a mode of laser focus, allowing all other distractions to fall away. Within moments, I'm composing an email, thanking my client for his flexibility and explaining my earlier accident. I assure him I've received medical attention and confirm our rescheduled meeting time.

Being in this work zone compels me to address all my unread emails. As I systematically open, assess, and respond, time slips away from me.

Forty-five minutes fly by. I adjust the screen from my wrist on the BIOPDA and realize I'd completely lost track of Cynthia's presence. There she sits, poised on the edge of the bed, observing me with a calm demeanor.

"Cynthia, I'm so sorry."

"It's alright."

"I just dove into one email, then another..."

"I noticed," she says gently.

"It's an addiction to work really, I am so sorry. I truly apologize."

"Don't worry about it. I wanted to ensure my unexpected entrance into your day wouldn't hamper your work."

"You've been so kind, from guiding me here to tending to my wounds. I can't thank you enough."

She smiles warmly. "You're welcome." Her serenity feels genuine as she inquires, "So, what's on your agenda for the rest of the day?"

"Well," I begin, stalling as I try to grasp the situation. On the one hand, she's a stranger who ran into me, and from behind, no less. Should I be divulging personal details to her? An innate caution tugs at me. Yet, she's seen me in a vulnerable state, in my underwear, and there's an undeniable intimacy established. Moreover, there's something about her, an allure I can't pinpoint, that I find utterly enchanting. "I plan on grabbing something to eat before heading to my rescheduled meeting."

"And after that?"

I hesitate. "Some friends invited me out for dinner. I was planning to join them."

"That sounds lovely." Rising gracefully, she smooths out her dress. "I'll accompany you for lunch, ensure you reach your meeting without a hitch, and see you off to your dinner."

"Oh, well—"

"It's the least I can do after causing you such trouble," she interjects.

"You're insisting on this?"

"Absolutely," she responds, her gaze sweeping over me. "A great man once said, 'Service to others is the rent you pay for your room here on Earth.'"

"Who was this great man?"

"Muhammad Ali."

"And you're insisting on spending the entire day with me?"

"I am. It's non-negotiable."

She slips into her black winter coat with practiced ease, shrugging it onto her arms before I can assist.

"It's such a beautiful coat. Looks really warm."

"It is, indeed." She lifts her shoulder, hugging the coat closer, her eyes drifting upwards in reflection.

"You seem familiar. Are you a model? Or perhaps I've seen you in shows, or movies?"

Her cheeks tint a soft pink as she replies, "You're too kind. Yes, I'm a model—a one-of-a-kind model."

I chuckle at her playful self-description.

"It's refreshing to meet someone like you. Modest? No, that's not it... genuine. That's the word."

"Thank you." She nestles her cheek against the coat's high collar, designed for warmth. "Now, let's get you something to eat."

I swiftly slip on my shoes and follow her toward the door.

"Aren't you wearing a coat?"

"I didn't bring a winter coat. They're bulky on flights." I

keep to myself that being near Cynthia has kindled a warmth inside me that I haven't felt in a while, a sensation that's hard to put into words and even harder to voice aloud.

"No, that won't work. You need a coat."

"I'll manage for a few blocks."

"There's a place nearby. We can take a look."

As we step into the corridor, I hear the door close securely behind us. Glancing at my watch, I say, "Alright, but only a quick look."

She nods. "A quick look it is."

Three

"We've come full circle," I comment.

"How so?"

I gesture across the street, explaining, "145 Adelaide—that's where you helped me up. Or, should I say, knocked me down?"

She chuckles lightly, conceding, "Yes, I guess we've returned to the scene."

145 Adelaide is an anomaly in its surroundings. A quaint six-story structure juxtaposed against the skyline of towering modern edifices. The grandeur of its first two floors is accentuated by high ceilings graced with chandeliers, and an ornate metal arch embellishing its entrance. The windows of its third to fifth stories grant panoramic views of the bustling street. Yet, it's the sixth floor that draws the most attention. The Parisian-like green copper roof culminates in an expansive window. This

window, crowned with an arch mirroring the ground floor's aesthetic, spans almost the entire width of the building. It exudes an antiquity reminiscent of the early 21st century but retains a modern touch of elegance.

"Let's go," she urges.

My stride, initially hesitant due to the pain, becomes more assured. The aspirin from the hotel lobby is evidently working its magic.

"Where exactly is this shop?" I ask.

"Just two blocks ahead."

"Why don't we cross the street here? We could grab a bite on the other side. How does that sound?"

She nods in agreement. "Sounds good."

As we reach the intersection, the beeps signaling it's safe to cross fill the air. Hand in hand, we step off the curb and make our way across Adelaide.

"That sound is called an Accessibility Pedestrian Signal or APS," she explains. "It's an audible beacon to help those who are visually impaired."

It's almost embarrassing, the snail's pace I keep. "Really? I didn't know that."

"Yes. In fact, in 2035, Ontario passed an ordinance requiring major cities like Toronto to activate these during high traffic times, bypassing a button that one needed to press previously."

I make it to the curb, feeling the elastic of the bandage stretch as I bend my knee to step up. As one beep for the visually impaired ends, another begins, signaling our turn to cross York.

"After 8 PM, the APS beacon switches back to requiring the manual press of a button."

As we cross York, the sensation from the bandage reminds me of my gratitude for Cynthia. I might have been a mess without her.

"Is government your area of expertise? Do you work for the City?"

"No, I just find these things interesting."

With her arm locked in mine, I feel her give a slight squeeze of encouragement. When I look her way, she smiles, sharing that same sentiment.

"You'd be great at trivia night at the bar, I bet."

"I would." That smile appears again.

Finally, we arrive at the nearest Tim Hortons. And like every Tim Hortons in Toronto, there's a line.

"What will you order?" she asks.

"I'm going for a medium double-double."

"Double-double?"

"This is when the barista adds two creams and two sugars. I'm also going to get a whole grain carrot orange muffin. What would you like? My treat."

"I'll have the same."

"Very well."

After a quick check on my wrist, I realize we have time to sit after placing our order. We choose a seat near the window. I sip my coffee, peel away the wrapper from the muffin, and pull the moist chunks apart.

"The trick, you see, is to eat enough before the presentation to have energy, but not so much that you burp or your stomach makes odd noises."

She asks, "Is this meeting crucial?"

"It's the pre-meeting to the most important meeting I've had in a long time. So, yes, it's pivotal. This needs to go well, so next week, when I come back, the client will say yes immediately. I don't want them to harbor any doubt that this is not only the right choice but the best one."

"That sounds like a solid strategy. Leave them without a doubt."

I sip my coffee and remark, "You know, it's comforting to have someone to converse with before a meeting. I'm usually on my own."

"Being alone is the worst."

The coffee is still piping hot, so I pause before taking another sip and observe, "I find it hard to believe that you often find yourself alone."

"It's true. I am frequently alone. I constantly seek activities to keep occupied. If I can distract my mind, it's a relief."

I nod and empathize, "I believe that's why I work so much. It occupies my mind, distracting me from the emptiness. Most of my social life consists of watching others. It's easy to get drawn in and feel that others have happier, more fulfilling lives."

Her gaze grows distant. "When I observe others, it feels as

if they possess knowledge I lack. There must be some answer they have that eludes me. I sometimes wonder if they're withholding a secret from me. At times, I feel trapped. I just don't understand how people can seem so content, so genuinely happy."

"Trapped—what an apt description. I often feel that way too."

She inquires, "What do you do for a living?"

An unintended tension creeps into my shoulders as I reply with a shrug, "I'm just a sales guy."

"And whom are we visiting today?"

"The largest bank in Canada."

"And why do you believe you present the best option for them?"

I sigh. "I wish the answer were straightforward. It's my responsibility to simplify it for them. I believe it boils down to three things. Firstly, the technology is something they're already acquainted with. Secondly, it aligns seamlessly with their compliance policies. Their past successful collaborations with us is another reason I've secured this meeting."

She prompts, "And the third reason?"

"They'll likely want the third reason to revolve around pricing. Every client hopes for a cost-effective solution. Undoubtedly, the cost and pricing are significant considerations when finalizing a deal. However, I wish to sidestep lengthy negotiations. I desire a swift conclusion."

"So how do you expedite the process?" she ponders.

"Value. I need to show value. I must convince them that

what they're getting is worth the investment or presents such an attractive proposition that they can't decline."

"How do you demonstrate value?"

"Are you sure you want to hear this? It's somewhat mundane. You don't have to be polite just for my sake."

She grins. "I'm genuinely curious about this concept of value. As I mentioned earlier, many things intrigue me."

So I explain, holding a $8.49 muffin, that its value lies not just in its cost but in its quality—a product from a superior brand worth the extra steps. Efficiency comes next; buying saves me time and hassle compared to baking, given my tight schedule and lack of equipment. Lastly, I highlight effectiveness; I chose a nutritious whole grain carrot orange muffin over less healthy options, making it the best choice for fueling my day. Through quality, efficiency, and effectiveness, the muffin exemplifies true value beyond its price.

She nods appreciatively. "That's enlightening."

"Not interested in your muffin?"

She neatly folds the brown paper around the muffin and tucks it into her coat pocket. "I'll save it for later. Now, let's find you a coat."

Four

"You're right. That *is* a handsome jacket," I comment, diverting my gaze from the store window display. However, she remains locked in a look at the two figures in the display.

"Aren't they a lovely couple?" she murmurs.

"Yes, very."

Her eyes are fixated on the pair of mannequins donning stylish winter outfits. The female mannequin sports a jacket identical to Cynthia's, while the male one showcases the jacket she wants for me.

"You have a similar build to him, just a bit shorter," she notes.

I'm not sure how to feel about being compared to a plastic model, especially with the subtle reminder that I'm just under six feet tall.

"She and I have the same measurements. That's why this coat is perfect for me."

Looking closely, I can see the resemblance. Both boast graceful necklines, prominent shoulders, and, I realize with a start, similar chest proportions. I blanch at the thought, quickly push away any lingering observations about Cynthia's chest, especially after all she's done for me.

"You need this coat. We'd be a matching pair."

"That sounds—"

Interrupting my sentence, she takes my hand with authority and directs me toward the store's entrance.

The familiar store chime rings as the door opens. Out of courtesy, I stretch out my arm, holding the door ajar for her. A welcoming aroma of fresh linen and fabrics fills the air.

Her excitement palpable, she hurries over to the display jacket.

"Can I assist you?" inquires a lean woman dressed in black. Her striking purple mohawk and multiple facial piercings make her stand out amidst the shop's muted tones of white walls and deep reddish-brown wood floors.

Cynthia responds confidently, "We'd like this jacket. His chest measures 100 centimeters, so this size"—she points—"should be the one we need." Gently unhooking the jacket from its perch, she passes it to the clerk.

The clerk replies with a tone dripping in retail sarcasm, "Okay. Anything else?"

"That black scarf. And the gloves," Cynthia adds.

"I can't wear gloves," I interject, raising my hands to display the reddened palms.

"Oh, right. Just the scarf then."

The clerk carries the items to the counter, arranging them so the security tags are all within the deactivation field's range. The soft hum of the system starts, then stops with a distinct click. She retrieves a register tablet from her pocket and presents it to me. "That's $325 for the jacket and $185 for the scarf. Plus, there's $82 VAT on each, bringing your total to $674. Thumbprint, please."

I can't hide my surprise. "I always forget how steep the taxes are here."

The clerk's expression suggests a mix of impatience and disinterest, as if she could be spending her time better elsewhere. I take the tablet, press my thumb on the screen, and, just like that, I'm the proud owner of a new winter coat.

Before the clerk can retrieve the tablet or offer to bag the coat, Cynthia swiftly takes it from the counter, almost dancing with the coat as if it's a partner, and moves toward me.

"Arm, please," she instructs, her tone affectionate.

I obey, extending my arm. The coat slides on effortlessly. I turn slightly, and soon the coat envelops me. The fresh scent of new wool fills my nostrils. The inner lining, a shimmering silver silk, contrasts beautifully with the black exterior. The coat feels like a comforting embrace—warm but not stifling, snug without being restrictive.

Cynthia begins to wrap the scarf around my neck. Its softness is unparalleled.

She steps back, admiring her handiwork. “This is Grade A Cashmere from the goats of Kashmir. The wool is 14 to 15.5 microns in diameter, ensuring it feels incredibly smooth against your skin.”

My gaze shifts to the cashier, whose demeanor lacks Cynthia's enthusiasm. “It's a fine scarf,” she remarks, almost mechanically.

“You look very handsome,” Cynthia compliments.

The register chimes softly as the clerk reclaims the tablet. “Thank you for shopping with us today, Mr. Crease. Is there anything else I can assist you with?”

“Mr. Crease?” Cynthia inquires with raised brows.

“Yes, Crease is my last name.”

“Like a fold? A pressing? A ridge?”

“Exactly. Spelled the same.”

She tilts her head slightly, her curiosity piqued. “And your first name?”

“Dashiell.”

“Dashiell Crease?” she repeats, rolling the name on her tongue.

“That's right.”

She smiles warmly. “What a distinguished name. It suits a man like you. I wish I'd asked when we first met.” She murmurs, almost to herself, “Dashiell Crease.”

The clerk addresses me, “Is there anything else today, Mr. Crease?”

“No, thank you, we're set.” I glance at Cynthia, who seems

momentarily lost in thought after learning my name. "We have a schedule, Cynthia."

Hearing her name snaps her back to the present. She meets my gaze, nods, and gracefully guides me to and through the door, leading us back onto Adelaide Street.

FIVE

"Gord, thank you for accommodating this change in time." I extend my hand for a shake. "I must look a sight."

"Dash, are you okay? Good heavens."

"I've got a little hitch in my giddy-up, as they say back home."

Gord laughs, then his gaze shifts to the woman at my side. "And who might this be?"

"Gord, this is Cynthia. She's helping me get around today."

Gord seems taken aback for a moment, then extends his hand to her. "At your service."

I've worked with Gord long enough to recognize that lingering look. The same man who, during an outing for "drinks" last year, commented on an exotic dancer, saying, "It doesn't matter where you get your appetite, as long as you go home for supper." He holds Cynthia's hand just a moment longer than is socially acceptable. Cynthia handles it gracefully with a giggle and that captivating smile, not uttering a word of protest. She understands the importance of today.

"Let's get you up to the boardroom."

"Boardroom?"

"Yeah, Florence will be there. I mentioned that, right?"

"No, you didn't."

"Ah, don't worry about it. Just another day, right?" Gord turns to the lobby security clerk. "They're with me. I'm escorting them in." He nods to the guard.

As we move forward, I find strength in Cynthia's support—not just physically, but also in her steadying presence, giving me confidence that I can get through the day.

"Who is Florence?" she whispers.

"She's Gord's boss's boss's boss. The decision-maker. The one with the budget."

"I thought that meeting was next week."

"Me too."

As Gord holds the gate open, accessed through his key card, he watches Cynthia assist me, a smile playing on his lips. He exudes a nervous energy I've only seen him display around certain women. This becomes even more evident in the elevator as Gord begins his charm offensive.

"Do you follow hockey, Cynthia?"

She shakes her head.

"Because I played for the Laval Rocket for a season." There's a smirk on his face and his chest puffs out slightly.

"Really?" she replies, her tone hinting at mild impress.

Gord's hands find their way to his belt buckle beneath the suit jacket and hitch it higher on his waist. In the quiet of the lift, she turns her attention to the numbers ticking over as we pass each floor. I can sense Gord's confidence waning as he reflects on his revelation and Cynthia's subdued reaction. I can almost hear his inner monologue: *This used to be a sure thing. Women usually follow up, ask why I left, or who I know, or if I still get season tickets to the Leafs.* As reality sinks in, he shifts uncomfortably.

Gord breaks the silence, "You ready for this, Dash?"

"Always ready," I reply, concealing my nerves. I'm sure he neglected to mention Florence's attendance at the meeting because he too forgot. Or perhaps he only just found out himself. It might be a move to save face; a classic Gord maneuver.

"Nice jacket," Gord remarks. "Perfect for this polar vortex. I can't recall the last time it was this cold."

"It's a handsome jacket, isn't it?" Cynthia chimes in.

Gord offers a brief smile as the elevator door opens. Holding it, Cynthia guides me out into the executive lobby of this top floor.

The receptionist beams from behind her curved desk. "Mr. Crease?"

"Yes."

She gestures to my left. "Your meeting is in the boardroom right down here. Would you like some coffee? Water?"

"Water would be great. Thank you."

We proceed without hesitation. As we approach, I notice through the glass that the room is occupied. Stern expressions adorn the faces of those seated in their high-backed leather chairs. Gord might be five years my senior, but this group has a decade on him.

"You've outdone yourself, Gord. I asked to meet the decision-makers, and this certainly looks like them."

At the head of the table sits an elegant woman. The gray streak in her hair contrasts dramatically with the surrounding jet-black. Noting her commanding presence and the emerald green professional sheath dress, I venture, "At the head of the table... Florence?"

"That's her," he confirms.

"What a view." Lake Ontario looks menacingly cold from this vantage point. Ice encroaches near the shore, and the wind at this elevation must be fierce. I can almost sense the force of it pressing against the glass.

My professional smile is a fusion of warmth and seriousness —more jovial than jolly. I don it as we traverse the glass corridor leading to the boardroom.

From the corner of my eye, I catch Florence glancing up. Upon spotting us, her gaze shifts, tracking our progress intently. By the time we reach the door, every head around the boardroom table has lifted, all eyes fixed on our approach. All except for one man at the front, engrossed in his presentation as he gestures toward numbers, charts, and graphs on a massive monitor.

Drawing nearer, it becomes evident that Florence, along

with the others, isn't fixated on "us," per se, but solely on Cynthia. At that moment, I feel almost invisible. A twinge of anxiety bubbles up, manifesting as an almost audible gulp in my throat. I find myself pondering, *Is Cynthia's allure an asset in this setting, or an unforeseen distraction?*

Six

There is a tang of perspiration in the air. It's not the result of hard work, like at the gym. Instead, it hints at fear. I've been in this situation before: locked away in a room for days, pressured by a looming deadline, subsisting on lousy food, gas building up in the belly, and the only sunlight seen is filtered through UV-protected glazing. It's not an ideal environment for humans. It is, however, the boiler room for business that stokes the engine of prosperity. With the first whiff, something professional inside me clicks on. The pain disappears. I am fully present in the moment.

The speaker finishes.

I extend my hand to shake Florence's. "Hello, I am Dashiell Crease."

"Florence Morin."

"Thank you for allowing me time in your busy day." My tone is professional, firm, confident.

"Let me take your jacket," the receptionist says from behind me, holding out a bottle of water.

We trade—I hand her the jacket and take the bottle of water in exchange. Behind Florence, I notice chairs where Gord and Cynthia have taken seats.

I touch my BIOPDA and press the button to connect to the giant monitor, which then displays my slides.

There are ethereal moments in life, my father described to me. Jack Nicklaus and Tiger Woods both spoke of Zen moments in golf where they played effortlessly. Prince's performance of "While My Guitar Gently Weeps" at the Rock and Roll Hall of Fame. Abigail Davis landing Vision on Mars with just fumes left in her auxiliary tank, then taking her first steps to plant the American flag. This is my moment.

The introduction is captivating. Setting up the case, perfect. The first question, which interrupts at the ten-minute mark, occurs as if they didn't know I had planted that seed in the fourth slide to prompt me. And the look from Florence Morin, the Division President of this financial institution—which is more than just a polite smile—bolsters my confidence.

"In eight months, at a conservative rate of 2% adoption in the organization, the system pays for itself," I conclude.

Unlike in the movies, when you make a compelling argument in real life, there are no slow claps that build to applause. More often than not, there's a series of squeaks from chairs as people pivot to look at the most senior person, gauging the correct reaction from their superior's demeanor. These high-back leather chairs, well-greased, don't squeak, but the rustle of movement gives a similar impression. Each person looks up from their monitor to Vice President Morin.

With her Quebec accent slightly more pronounced than it was during our introduction, she says, "I like it. Let's get this to procurement. Fifteen-minute break, everyone."

My sigh of relief is palpable. These last six months culminated in this moment. With it behind me, the switch flips again. I feel the pain, the burn, and the wobble in my balance return.

As Florence turns to speak with Cynthia, the other eleven at the table rise and move to take their break. I steady myself by gripping the back of the nearest empty chair.

I once read a study discussing the optimal times in the day to pursue for the most favorable outcomes. The study, focusing on criminals appearing before a judge, revealed that verdicts often depended on the judge's blood sugar level. Early morning, when well-rested and satiated, the chances of a favorable ruling are high. These chances decrease as lunchtime approaches, then improve post-lunch, but drop again toward day's end. This post-lunch window seemed ideal for Florence Morin.

As I observe her interact with Cynthia, Gord steps aside. He joins other men outside the glass barrier, ogling my guide. I can read Gord's lips: "Yeah, can you believe she's with him, eh? What a lucky guy." Glancing back at Cynthia, I notice Florence jotting something down. It appears to be a business card, which she hands to Cynthia. The two exchange smiles and nods.

Florence smiles at me and says, “Nice work. I look forward to working with you,” before leaving.

Now, it's just Cynthia and me alone in the boardroom. Tentatively, I ask, “Did Florence give you her number?”

“She did. It’s her private line. She mentioned getting drinks sometime.”

“Is that normal for you?”

“Normal?”

“Do people often give you their number? Do they pay more attention to you?”

“I don’t know if it’s more than usual, but yes, they do.”

During our attempt to exit, we pass a clowder of Canadians, all seemingly searching for a reason to chat with Cynthia, and finally reach the receptionist's desk. The receptionist hands me my coat. With a bit of assistance, I slip it on, and we head toward the elevator.

As the elevator doors close, I ask, “Do you still want to have dinner with my friends tonight? I feel like I owe you a big thank you. Florence seemed to respond well to you, and that certainly helped.”

Her hand gently squeezes my arm in reassurance. She smiles. “I insist.”

I pull up my BIOPDA and quickly send a message to my friends: “Bringing +1 for dinner.”

Seven

The Edwards live on Walker Street, just steps away from the Summerhill station, ideally situated in Toronto on tree-lined streets, offering a small-town feeling nestled within the big city. Rodman and Judith Edwards are DINKs, meaning Double Income, No Kids. Only this high-income group can afford to live in Summerhill. They enjoy the green spaces and city life, residing in a series of two-story brownstones.

"This neighborhood is wonderful," Cynthia says. "All of these homes were once part of the estate of Charles Thompson, the Canadian transportation baron."

"You sure know your history."

I can feel the warmth of her arm tucked under mine. She must do cross-training. Her strength has impressed me throughout the day. I've encountered a few slick spots that threw me off balance, yet she's remained steadfast.

In the winter darkness, the expensive and historic incandescent lights from the Edwards' home shine through the front window, reminding me of a lighthouse on the shores of Lake Michigan.

My breath forms a plume of frozen vapor as I say, "This is it. We're here."

Cynthia stops and asks, "How close are you to them?"

"How do you mean?"

"Are they your best friends? Or just acquaintances?"

I pat her gloved hand holding my arm and assure her, "You'll be fine. Just be yourself."

Ascending the three steps to the porch, I press the doorbell, hearing the chime echo inside. Judith's shadow fills the opaque entrance. The clicks of the unlatching mechanism build anticipation until the door swings open, revealing her friendly smile and warm greeting. "Come inside, quickly, warm up!"

"Judith?" Rodman's voice calls from another room. "Is that them?"

"Let me take your coats so you can warm up inside."

There's a mat with shoes next to the door, where I remove and leave my pair. With her coat now off and in Judith's arms, Cynthia follows suit.

"You must be Cynthia." Judith looks her in the eye, then fully embraces her. "Thank you for saving our Dashiell." With her arms around Cynthia, cheeks pressed and nose above her shoulder, she remarks, "Oh, you smell good."

Cynthia blushes. "Thank you."

Judith turns and calls, "Rodman, they're here."

Footsteps on the wooden floor grow closer. Rodman, tall and lanky, comes around the corner, ducking under the door-frame and down the hallway to greet us. "Dashiell." He nods. "And? Cynthia?" Rodman leans down, adopting the European tradition of greeting with a kiss: first cheek, second, then back. "You do smell good."

Judith interjects, "I know! I already said that she smells good. Doesn't she, Dash?"

"I didn't, I mean... yes."

Cynthia, caught between our reactions, smiles from all the attention. "This is a beautiful entry. I'm sure the rest of the house is just as wonderful."

Judith signals, "That's our cue, boys. We're crowding her. Let's go inside. Come on, Rodman. Let's move, Dash."

I wait as the two lead Cynthia out of the entryway and down the hall, then follow them to the back of the house. As we walk, Judith recounts the story of the house and its restoration from a dilapidated state just six years ago. Every good couple has stories: the archive of what has made them "them" over time. A volume about how they first met, an instruction manual on the house, cookbooks of successful and failed meals, biographies of guests they've hosted, and travelogs of vacations (with pictures upon request). Every couple has these cherished tales. Watching Cynthia bask in the glow of newfound friendship and the warm light, I wonder if today might become one of ours. The day we met.

"Look at this girl, so thin. We should feed her something. Are you hungry? Hm? Let's sit down and we can dig in."

"Can I help with anything?" Cynthia asks.

"No, honey, that's sweet of you. Please, sit. Rodman will tell you his story about the boat." In a less intimate voice, she calls out, "Rodman, pour the red wine for our guests and tell them that story about the boat."

Turning to the kitchen, I catch Judith giving Cynthia a second look. She notices that I've seen her and mouths the words, "Smells so good."

"So, there I was," Rodman begins, taking the crystal decanter from the bar and carefully pouring over each of the glasses. Every story from Rodman starts this way: "So, there I was..." Then he fills in with the story hook: "facing down a grizzly," "nose to nose with the CEO," "shaking hands with the King of England." He is an excellent storyteller. His height makes him stand out in a crowd. Unlike many of his vertically enhanced peers, he can be a little shy. His stature grants him access and attention to social scenes us average Joes don't experience.

In confidence, during a Raptors game once (the league where the actual cloned raptors are in a pit, not that basketball thing), he confided that he doesn't always want to be "the tall guy." He said, "Hey, tall guy on a boat. Hey, tall guy in a small car. Hey, tall guy in an elevator. It's always, 'Hey tall guy in a...' followed by, 'how's the weather up there?' People think they're original with that line. It's not even funny." Nonetheless, he admitted he enjoys the adventure and the unique perspective.

As dinner progresses, Rodman, with the ease of a born raconteur, launches into another tale. "So, there I was," he starts, the room instantly quieting in anticipation, "suspended over the Grand Canyon, hanging by nothing but a fraying rope."

Cynthia, her eyes alight with humor, waits for just the right moment before interjecting, "Let me guess, you were out there chasing butterflies again?"

The group chuckles, but Rodman, with a dramatic pause, nods gravely. "Not just any butterflies, mind you. These were the rare, elusive blue morphos, the kind that can outrun a hawk. But there I was, a man on a mission, defying gravity for the sake of beauty."

Cynthia nods, feigning seriousness. "A noble cause. And here I thought you were just trying to get a good selfie angle."

Rodman laughs, tipping his wine glass in her direction. "Cynthia, you've caught me. But I'll have you know, the selfie was magnificent. National Geographic is still calling."

Their playful repartee adds a layer of light-heartedness to the evening, showcasing not just Rodman's knack for spinning yarns but also Cynthia's ability to engage with wit and charm. Their exchange, filled with laughter and mock grandiosity, delights everyone, highlighting the dynamic interplay of storytelling and clever banter that defines the night.

As we say our goodbyes and Judith helps me put on my shoes, she whispers in my ear, “Rodman and I talked. If you start dating her, we're totally into sharing.”

Confused by her remark, I furrow my brow, the implications whirling in my mind. With Cynthia supporting me down the steps and to the taxi, the comment lingers.

"Where to?" the taxi driver asks.

I look at Cynthia. "We should drop you off first."

"The Hilton Toronto, on Richmond," she replies.

"Are you sure?"

"My place is just across the street from there."

Her skin seems flawless, or her makeup covers any signs of the traumatic adolescence.

I am lost in her smile. We sit in the back seat of the taxi looking at one another in some awkward teenage stare. A flutter of energy in my tummy and I think back to my first kiss, Janet Dragger, in the backyard of her parents' house. Nestled in the long green grass of a hot summer hidden in the shade of an appliance box from her parents' recent purchase. It was unknown mechanics of the flesh programmed into my DNA. Awkward and fumbling at first, it turned quickly into a rush of excitement. Lips, sweet. Taste of sugar. Wet and hot young bodies pressing mouths, then tongues. Hands touching, fingers exploring, the senses on fire. New, yes. More, yes.

Looking into Cynthia's eyes takes me back to that original rush of unknown possibilities, where life is still a dream and the future has yet to unfold.

The lights from Yonge and Dundas, Toronto's Times Square, fill her eyes with sparkles and reflections as the universe unfolds before us. The car stops short at the signal, jostling us with the momentum of pedestrians crossing. We're jerked forward and back, and I find my hand now on hers, our fingers touching. Finding courage in the moment, I lean forward and meet her halfway in a kiss.

The chill from the back passenger door opening sweeps across the black leather seat, still warm from where our hands touched. I lean on the large metal backseat door after pulling the handle, finding my footing on the cement drop-off at the hotel. I don't blame the doorman for helping her out of the car first. Being drawn to her comes naturally. I struggle to stand, feeling the skin pull at the new scabs on my knees. The tension from the bandages strains the back of my knee. What is the name of that spot? The arm has an armpit; is this the leg pit? Once fully erect, the pain subsides, and I take a few smaller steps toward the rotating door.

Cynthia is trying to evade the attendant who's being overly attentive. She fakes left, then spins right to avoid any contact and shepherding. Breaking free, she steps next to me, sliding her arm under mine. I feel lifted, both physically and in spirit.

I flash a smile at the doorman, partly to flaunt that she's with me, but also, I suppose, out of politeness.

A sudden rise in temperature envelops us as we enter the lobby. Using my free hand, I start to undo the top few buttons of my new coat to let the warmth in. I slow my pace until I come to a stop, away from the gaze of the front desk.

She asks, "Are you in pain?"

"No. Well, not more than earlier."

"Are we stopping?"

"I want to thank you for your help today."

"You're welcome."

"I mean it. Thank you. You went way above and beyond the normal call of duty. You walked me all over town, flirted with the right person to advance my career, and charmed my friends thoroughly. You're truly impressive."

A glint appears in her eyes, accompanied by a hint of a humble smile. "You're welcome. Now, let's get you to bed."

My eyes widen. "You don't need to—"

"Don't need to what?"

I'm overwhelmed with possibilities as I glance down at my feet. Hers are right there in front of mine. I let my eyes travel upwards, following her legs, to the hem of her skirt, to that patch of skin not covered by the jacket she's so fond of. Continuing up to her neck, chin, face—our eyes finally lock. Within the iris, there are golden flecks of imperfection that I hadn't noticed before. Her right eye is a deeper shade than the left.

"You don't have to," I manage, swallowing audibly. "You don't need to come up."

"But I want to." Her response is natural, filled with an unexpected warmth and cheer.

"I didn't want to assume anything."

She smiles again. "I'm going to keep an eye on you."

Her arm returns to its comfortable position, supporting mine, and we head toward the elevator. There's no urgency; it's just two people walking to the elevator.

As we approach, she pauses. Her hand smoothly slips into

my pocket once more, a gesture less covert than the one that morning. Her fingers retrieve the keycard, and with a few more steps, we reach the elevator door. It opens, and she swipes the card past the pad with practiced ease, pressing the button for floor 32. We're on our way up.

Eight

There's a *clack* as the door closes behind us. The beautifully polished entry of the hotel room floor, the masculine stained woods and black trim, go unseen without the click of the light switch. Through the expansive window along the exterior wall, the alternating lights of the CN Tower provide just enough illumination for us. I take her hand in the darkness, turning her to me, and kiss her. There's no rush, no hurry to reach a destination, just the pure enjoyment of pressing lips together. Slow, soft, playful, and fun, we kiss in the doorway.

"I'm much braver in the dark," I say. I can feel the smile on her face as her lips retract away. In my mind, I envision her smile, as if I had stared at the sun too long and its image is now imprinted there for eternity.

Flickering light from the tower outside the window illuminates the room just enough. Her hands start to work down the front of her jacket. The tips of her fingers slide each large button through its hole until her jacket is open, then off. She retrieves a hanger from inside the closet and places her jacket there. Her hand extends in expectation to me.

A tad clueless, I look down and remove my coat, handing it to her. It's soon resting on a hanger in the closet beside hers.

She steps past me, moving further into the room. She pivots on her toes and draws her finger in my direction, beckoning me to approach. I step to her, close enough for what comes next. Her hand finds its way under my suit jacket, up to my shoulder, and she helps me out of it. In a flash, it's hung on the back of the desk chair. Her hand returns to my shoulder, freeing me from the hold of my suspenders, allowing gravity to take its course. She promptly gathers the trousers by the hem, then hangs them in the closet using the special hangers equipped with clips.

Instead of coming back to me, as I had anticipated, she heads to the bed. Gripping the corner of the tucked-in bedding, she pulls it swiftly, revealing the sheets below and folding the comforter back on itself.

"Come here," she beckons, her voice barely above a whisper.

I obey.

"Now," she murmurs, focusing on each button of my shirt, starting from the top and working her way down, "I want you to know, I'm not in the habit of doing this."

"Habit?"

"I don't typically go up to a man's room and kiss him in the dark."

"Oh, *that* habit."

"What happened this morning was unexpected." She looks up into my eyes. "Sometimes these unexpected events become wonderful opportunities."

Being this close is electrifying. Every sense of mine seems heightened. There's sheer excitement in merely being near her, taking her in.

"I fear you're about to add a big 'but' to that sentence."

"There is no 'but.'"

With the final button undone, my shirt drops to the floor. She turns, her back now facing me.

"Little help?"

I feel a tad foolish when I realize what she's asking. I locate the small hook at the top of the back of her dress. Beneath it is a delicate zipper, which I pull down. As the two halves part, they reveal more of her smooth, silky skin. Once fully unzipped, I help her shed the dress. Swiftly, she picks it up from the floor. Within moments, I hear the familiar rattle of a metal hanger on the closet pole.

I turn to see her in the entryway. The lights catch her just right, highlighting her in her bra and panties. Then comes the click. When my eyes adjust to the darkness again, her white undergarments capture the changing lights from the city, bathing the room in hues of red, blue, and gold.

She steps forward and slips past me to the center of the bed.

"Don't forget to set your alarm," she says, pulling the cover over herself for warmth.

In the darkness, I find my BIOPDA on my wrist, and the familiar lump that is the button. With a touch, it unlocks, and after three presses, the alarm is set.

Slowly, I make my way to the bed and lie next to her. She pulls at the sheet and cover, draping them over me. The weight settles in a comforting embrace. Her hand finds its way across my chest, her head rests on my shoulder, and her leg is draped over mine. I'm acutely aware of every inch of her skin touching mine, and I am fully aroused.

Her lips, now close to my ear, need to use very little effort for me to hear. "There's something so intimate about talking in the dark. Two people, this close, with so little between them, protected by the night. Just our words, with nothing else in the way, nothing between us."

I close my eyes and can still envision her smile, imagining her lips with each word spoken. "There was something different about you, I could tell, when I first saw you," she says. "What is it? I can sense something's different."

Summoning courage in the darkness, I reply, "I've never been told that before. I've never found myself feeling this close to someone. I mean, I've been with others... But..."

"It's okay," she reassures. "Don't be afraid to say it."

Taking a deep breath, I say, "We shouldn't have sex."

"I agree."

"I mean, not tonight." I feel like an idiot, too honest and too comfortable. It feels too presumptuous.

"Yes, that's what I meant too," she replies.

"I really enjoy being with you. It feels like there's something profound between us, and I would hate to spoil that. Today was so..."

She emits a delightful laugh, one I can feel as our torsos touch. "Yes."

"You are so beautiful. I've watched people fall for you today, and I just feel fortunate to be here with you, like this."

Her weight shifts, and I feel her fingers on my cheek drawing me closer as she begins to kiss me. Between kisses, she murmurs, "You are special. I see that in you, and I am the lucky one."

I instantly regret the "no sex" statement made only moments ago. She feels so good, smells so enticing, and my arousal seems insurmountable. My hand reaches out to her, cupping her breast. I hear soft moans of pleasure and encouragement as my hands explore. The goosebumps on her skin are palpable as we touch.

NINE

The sun in winter refuses to rise for another hour. There's an orange-pink glow on the horizon, gently nudging awake the world. Thanks to Cynthia's assistance yesterday, my meetings and the subsequent steps for business are deferred until next week. My flight isn't until 5:30 PM, so there's no need to scramble for an earlier departure. We can spend the day together.

Waking up beside her, I feel rejuvenated, alive for the first time in years. Even during this bleakest season, a glow of eternal summer radiates within me, stemming from the moments we've shared. With her arm draped over me, I can feel the tiny hairs on her skin rise as I whisper, "Good morning."

"Did you sleep well?"

"I did. I feel great."

"Yes, you do." She nuzzles into me. "What's the plan?"

"My flight isn't until 5:30, so—"

She's upright and straddled on me in an instant. "You're leaving?"

"Hey," I say, pinned under her, trying to soothe her. "We have the whole day together. I'll be back next week. I'm not running away. You knew I was here for business. After our collaboration yesterday, it's obvious I'll be returning."

Her shoulders drop and her posture slackens. I can see her processing this news. Although it was never verbalized, I assumed she knew. The clues seemed clear to me—staying at a hotel, visiting from the US. She seems disheartened as she collapses back beside me.

I roll toward her. "It's just a temporary parting. You'll be okay."

She buries her face in the pillow, taking a moment to accept this revelation.

"We can make today memorable."

She responds with a hint of melancholy, "It won't be like yesterday."

"No, you're right. Yesterday was unique," I acknowledge. "But we'll always cherish it, carry it with us. Every day, we'll strive to make the present moment just as special."

A smile brightens her face. "I love that idea."

"Me too. So, today, I'll start with a shower. Afterward, we can grab some coffee. Just like yesterday. Then, perhaps we can explore the city. Anything you've always wanted to see or do here?"

"There's so much," she says, pondering. "Actually, I've never visited the CN Tower."

We both glance out the window. "I haven't either. So, that's on our agenda. Anything else?"

"I've never really explored the city's art."

"AGO? I can give you a tour."

"That sounds lovely."

Her eyes, shimmering with flecks of gold in the morning light, captivate me. I lean down to kiss her. She reciprocates, but after a few passionate moments, she halts, placing her hand on my chest. "Get cleaned up. We have a full day ahead."

Thirty minutes later, after doing my utmost to look presentable, I step out of the bathroom into an empty hotel room. No sign of Cynthia. My belongings are untouched. Nothing's missing. So, I start to pack. Perhaps this was a fleeting dream. How well did I truly know her, anyway?

Roller bag out and open on the bed, I fill the travel cubes with the soiled undergarments and shirts from the visit. The pants are ruined, but I should keep the jacket. Paired with trousers, it would make a more casual look.

With my work items in my computer bag, I zip up the carry-on and head for the door. Behind me, the door closes with a soft, padded thud, its weight altering the air pressure in the corridor. There's the lonely soft wobble of the wheel on the carpet. My steps are slower than usual. A familiar silence and solitude return. I've known this solitude for years. I embrace the independence, telling myself I'm better off without her. She would have been a mere distraction. Though kind, her presence slowed me down.

Mirrors and woodwork give the illusion that the elevator is more spacious. This interior elevator bank is dimly lit. The exterior bank, made entirely of glass, offers a view of the city. In this dark wood and glass enclosure, the steady rhythm of lights signals my descent.

Once again, I was too open with my heart. The notion of a woman like her being with a guy like me seems preposterous. If I were to be in a real relationship, she'd need to live closer. We'd have to be equals, not this lopsided, disproportionate pairing in terms of attractiveness. With Cynthia, I'd be consumed by jealousy. No one can be as kind as she seemed. It must have been an act. I'm better off alone.

The wheels of my roller bag clatter on the marble lobby floor. My pace is slower than usual due to my injuries.

As I approach the front desk to check out, I hear, "Dashiell! Dashiell Crease."

Looking to my far right, there's Cynthia, rising from the plush couches in the lobby.

She waves. "Dash."

It feels like I'm gliding across the floor toward her. There's no distance, no steps. In an instant, I'm standing in front of her.

"Didn't you see my note?"

Her eyes, that smile—my heart melts, dispelling the chill from our brief separation.

"I ran home to change and freshen up. Why did you pack?"

Fumbling for an answer, I reply, "I'm leaving this at the bell stand while we go play."

It's a quick few blocks in the taxi at this early hour to reach the entrance of the Canadian National, or CN Tower. The entry fee for the two of us is reasonable. Few people are around in the middle of this bitterly cold workweek. We're alone in the elevator as we ascend several stories of the concrete pillar. Only then do the windows allow us to see the city seemingly receding below. The sensation is exhilarating. Like astronauts leaving orbit, the view grants a fresh perspective. The skyline, now the opposite of my usual view from the airport, mirrors the images on postcards and travel promotions.

We bypass the restaurant, heading straight to the top observation bubble—the Sky Pod. There's a distinctive odor, the scent of countless tourists that's impossible to erase. The myriad feet that have trodden here before, mainly sweaty sneakers and flip-flops from the summer months, have left an aroma akin to a bowling alley, sans the lane oil.

It's chilly. The warmth rising in the tower has been defeated by the altitude and the wintry winds from Lake Ontario. Our view is a blue-white expanse over the frozen waters. Sharp lines along the shore indicate summer maritime docks. The wavy and jagged contours must be the frozen beaches and park paths, dormant for months until the arrival of the next visitors.

Cynthia's wonder is almost childlike. Were she to lean just a bit more, I'm sure she'd press her face to the glass for a closer look. And, as predicted, her nose against the glass leaves an oily smudge.

Standing under the Hilton taxi canopy, roller bag handle in one hand, Cynthia's hand in my other, in an attempt to prolong our newfound intimacy, I ask, "How do I contact you? Stay in touch?"

The doorman takes my bag and places it in the open trunk of the taxi. She looks at me with those ever-mystifying eyes. "I don't have a phone."

"Sorry, your BIOPDA."

"I don't have one of those either."

"How can you not?" I am baffled, trying to maintain a steady tone. "Then, at least, give me your email, Chat, Gram, X, Z; give me something so I can contact you."

She hesitates, her gaze becoming distant. "I don't have one to give."

"Is this some sort of game? A cruel joke? Is this how we part? Have you decided that our story is over?"

"I simply can't," she whispers, almost inaudibly.

My frustration grows. "Can't, or won't?" My hand drops free from hers.

"You believe that I'm trying to end things when I simply don't have those devices or options."

"You're right. I want to keep in touch with you. I don't want this to end, but I am going home."

"Why? Why don't you stay?"

"I'll be back. But I don't live here; I live in another country."

"I want you to stay." It's clear and direct.

"I want to stay." I feel like she is not telling me everything.

“I don’t understand. You were happy. We were happy together. You enjoyed spending time with me. We felt a connection. I don’t understand. You’re leaving.”

“It’s simple. I go to the airport, get through the international line, get onto a plane, and it’s a quick flight to my home. I still have business here. I’ll be back soon. Let’s stay in touch. Don’t let it end like this, not like this, not this way.”

I want to kiss her one last time before I go. Leaning in for a memory to carry me through the week back home, a short and sharp honk from the impatient taxi cuts through our exchange, and I feel a hot rush of anger. I whip around and slap the car's roof with the flat of my hand. "Wait!" I shout to the driver. "Let your meter run. I’ll cover the charge. I just... I need a moment."

But when I pivot back toward Cynthia, making sure we don’t lose the moment, she has vanished. An unexpected twinge of pain shoots through my injured knee as I stagger toward the street, desperate for one final glimpse of her silhouette. The city seems to swallow her, and the euphoria of our shared moments fades into the dense anonymity of the urban crowd. She becomes a momentary memory, lost like a snowflake in a winter's storm, leaving me cold. I don’t know how to find her.

TEN

Life for me has always mirrored a garden of routines, each day a new seed planted with precision and nurtured by carefully refined habits. Amidst the digital age's sprawl, where algorithms and automation grow unchecked, the human spirit thrives, embodying the garden's most precious flora. Our empathy and connections are perennial blooms that no tech can replicate. Even as my daily rituals align with the order of a well-planned garden, they're enriched by the unpredictable beauty of humanity.

My routine, echoing the cycles of nature, gains depth from a profoundly human quality—discernment. This isn't just about choosing the right seeds or planting times; it's about feeling deeply, sensing the subtle shifts in human emotion that no machine can. In genuine human interactions, we discover our true essence, as complex as the Earth.

Making each day meaningful involves not just refining habits but deepening connections, planting seeds of empathy in our life's garden. It's recognizing that beneath every task lies the potential for profound human connection, our greatest advantage in the race toward automation. In this existence, amidst our routines, it's the wild beauty of human connection that truly feeds the soul.

I try not to dwell on Cynthia, a brief sun's warmth in this garden, reminding me what it feels like to be alive and desired. Instead, I focus on my work: inbound messages, process alignments, intense discussions, and strict adherence to parameters. This week, dedicated to securing a deal, has seen our legal AI and human lawyers finalize a document of mutual terms.

Despite the transaction's digital nature, the human touch remains. I'm returning to Toronto to celebrate with the team, a journey too brief for hypersonic travel but steeped in tradition as I embrace the sky aboard a conventional aircraft.

The winter coat and scarf, tokens of a shared afternoon, protect me from the cold. In my hotel room, with its familiar view and walls lit by the CN Tower's colors, memories of Cynthia flood back. Being with her was more than a distraction; it was a reflection of desires and shared interests, a connection deeply human.

Stateside, the second-skin remedy left only minute scars, visible up close. These scars and the winter coat are what remain of her in my life. I long for a photograph, a tangible memory, as her image grows hazier by the day.

The next afternoon, driven by longing, I retrace our steps,

descending the hotel staircase and turning onto Adelaide Street. I search every face for a trace of her, hope flickering briefly.

Her absence leaves me feeling like a shadow of myself. Despite this, I proceed with the client meeting, where we discuss project terms and timelines. Yet, amid discussions of business transformation, my thoughts linger on the void her absence has left.

Florence briefly congratulates the team, her disappointment palpable when she realizes Cynthia isn't here. Responding to inquiries about her absence pains me each time. Each asks about her in their own way.

Later, at a private dinner, we toast to our future, the evening marked by festive optimism. The meal delights everyone, a perfect balance of refinement and generosity, a memory to cherish during darker days.

After seeing the last customer off, I walk through the fashion district, wrapped in memories and the coat Cynthia chose. I muse on what might have been, our shared moments constrained by time.

In the dim recesses of memory, I recall a recording from the ancient past of the rainforest. Playing the audio on my BIOPDA, there is a hiss with the verdant whispers of that bygone era, chirps, rustles, and the distant hum of life. It is the voice of a lone bird, the very last of its kind, crying into the vastness of an uncaring world. Each call is a heartbreaking testament to a love that would never again find an answer. The intervals of silence between are not mere pauses, but profound moments of desolation. It is as if, in those silences, the bird pondered its own solitude, understanding the cruel finality of its fate. The recording holds the weight of a species's end, a poignant eulogy in every note. Through that recording, I am privy to a deep and soulful mourning, an aching remembrance of a time when love echoed back. The world continued, yet, in that captured moment, a lone voice sang of a love forever lost in the annals of time. And even though it is but a memory, the profound sorrow of that solitary call resonates eternally.

What's that noise? I wonder as I find myself falling.

Eleven

"Sorry. I am so sorry." Those words sound hauntingly familiar.

I find myself falling. That uncontrollable fear of hitting the ground. The expectation of that acid burn on my knees from abraded skin. I am transported back in time. The fear of tasting my own blood.

Here it comes again, that familiar sensation of concrete about to grate my palms. It's happening again. The surge of pain shooting up my leg, signaling to my brain.

"Shit!"

My elbows absorb most of the shock. And my knees—they beckon the incoming pain. Adrenaline surges, sharpening the senses. The coldness of Adelaide Street is as biting as I remember.

"Oh dear, I am so, so sorry." Her voice, a déjà vu.

A quick check. Everything seems to be where it should. As I turn to face her, our eyes lock, causing me to believe that time travel is possible. The same magnetic pull, the undeniable allure. Her beauty is eternal.

"I am so sorry," she says again, her voice laden with genuine concern.

Swallowing hard, the realization dawns. This is happening. Again. "What... the... fuck?"

"Let's get you fixed up," she suggests.

Her touch is nurturing, guiding me as we walk side by side. She isn't pulling or rushing me. Each step feels deliberate, cautious. There's an unfamiliar sway to my movement now.

"Wait, this isn't the way," I protest.

"I'm taking you to my place this time."

It's a short few steps to the building's front door, the building in front of us. She coddles me across the threshold, taking my arm as we shuffle to the lifts. There are fourteen floors, but she presses the button for PH, which I assume is the penthouse.

In my mind, she is beautiful—more beautiful than I remember. She must be married to someone wealthy. That would explain so much. The reason we ended things so abruptly, her place being in the most expensive block in North America, let alone the Penthouse. With each passing floor, there is a ping that sounds. When we reach floor 14, the lift stops. A panel opens to reveal a small camera above a clear glass pad.

"Lean over here a second." She encourages me to the

handrail. She looks into the camera and puts her hand on the glass. The lift clicks and pings, then proceeds to the PH.

She helps me again as we exit the lift, stepping onto a floor filled with high-tech gear. It looks more like a lab than a living space. The giant round window, recognizable from the street and the feature that makes this building stand out from all the rest, looks across Adelaide Street, straight to the Hilton. As we get closer, I can see the rooms where I've stayed, where we met, and the glow from the light in my room.

I turn my head to get a better view of her. "Were you watching me?"

"I first observed you three months ago, in that room there." She gestures to another room, one I recognize from earlier visits. "I've watched you come and go, and each time, down there, my curiosity grew. I wanted to know who you really were beyond my imaginations."

"So, you 'accidentally' bumped into me on the street?"

"It was no accident," she replied.

"Where are we? What is this place?"

"This is my lab," a deep voice interrupts. An older man with unruly gray hair enters the room, supporting himself with two walking canes, braces on each leg aiding his steps.

"And you are?"

"Doctor Smyth," he introduces himself, nodding toward her. "And this is Synth-ia. S-Y-N-T-H-I-A," he clarifies as he spells it out. "She's a synthetic being I've crafted. And she," he says, glaring at her, "has misbehaved. Haven't you?"

"Yes," she murmurs, looking down.

“What have you done?” he asks.

“I disobeyed. I broke the rules. I ventured outside the lab, interacted with humans,” she admits.

My vision blurs, and dizziness takes over. As my knees start to give way, she's right there, steadying me, guiding me to a soft leather chair.

“Synth,” Dr. Smyth commands, “go back to your station, please. I need a word with our guest.”

Our eyes meet, hers filled with remorse. I'm left wondering if it's for her disobedience or for the pain she caused.

“Sir, might I have your name?” Dr. Smyth inquires.

"Dashiell Crease, but call me Dash."

"A fitting name," Dr. Smyth remarks. He then shifts his gaze toward her as she steps onto a circular platform, surrounded by a clear enclosure. "Remember, Synth, Dash is a human being, not a symbol, not an action, a man."

"I apologize, doctor." Her voice holds a note of sadness.

"She has developed quite an attachment to you, Dash. Imprinted on you like she was a baby duck. I've noticed it for some time now. Didn't know who you were, but I suspected there was someone. You've been the subject of her drawings and sketches for months. She's been diligently searching for your face among the crowds, peering into windows across the street, hoping to catch a glimpse of you." Dr. Smyth pauses as he settles into a chair opposite Dash. "It's truly astonishing. When did you first suspect the truth about her?"

"Never," I reply, still in shock. "I thought she was human.

The idea of her being a robot? Android? It never crossed my mind."

"Naturally." The doctor looks at her, then back to me, implying the likelihood of an average Joe like me ever being with such a woman. "She's far more advanced than a robot, Dash. She's a Synthoid."

I blink in surprise. "I don't understand. That can't be right."

Dr. Smyth sighs, a glint of pride evident in his eyes. "Well, it's complicated, you see. Like so many things in life. But she"—he points toward her—"is the sole successful result of something called Project Hummingbird." He leans in, his tone taking on a hint of excitement. "Before you and I were born, almost two centuries ago, here in Ontario, people saw the potential of such creations. The idea was revolutionary; these were called 'pleasure-bots' and were designed to provide companionship, and their presence eradicated many issues tied to the flesh traders, human trafficking, and other illicit activities." His finger wipes away a stray hair from his face in a natural action. "Little did we realize the problems they would cause: the decline in birth rates, the skyrocketing suicides. It nearly ruined Canada. Maybe we should have known." He pauses in reflection.

I try to process what I'm hearing. My head spinning at the history, the implications, it is overwhelming. The woman—no, the Synthoid—that I had spent so much time with, that I had developed feelings for, was a relic from another era. "She's a model," I mutter, shaking my head. "Is that what she is? A kind of... love robot, designed to appeal to our deepest affections?"

Dr. Smyth shakes his head emphatically, a glint of pride in his eyes. "No, no, she's far beyond that. I wove the near-magical nuances of animatronics with cutting-edge robotics and this intricate AI. What I've crafted is a Synthetic Life Form Automaton. I've affectionately named her Synth." He pauses, smiling wryly. "Though I now understand your confusion with Cynthia."

I feel enraged at this news. "Why venture into such a creation, especially given the clear prohibitions in the laws?"

His gaze grows distant, reminiscent. "Ah, there's a larger picture you're unaware of. This endeavor was rooted in our dreams of deep space exploration. Once humanity took its first steps on Mars, staking its claim on the barren landscapes, our ambitions grew. I helmed a project named Torpor under the Hummingbird Project, a simulated deep sleep, akin to nature's hibernation but far more profound."

"Like hibernation, but deeper?" I try to understand.

"Much deeper than mere hibernation," he emphasizes. "Imagine a sleep so profound that generations could voyage across the vast cosmic distances, with the dream of propagating human life on distant worlds. For such journeys, they'd require beings like Synth to vigilantly maintain the ship, to be the ever-watchful guardian while the crew lies in sleep. An entity that could possess a consciousness and awareness transcending the rudimentary algorithms and circuits of a ship's computer."

I pause, trying to wrap my head around this whole crazy thing, absorbing the gravity of his words. "So, is she illegal? The last of her series, the reason protective laws were made?"

"No, she was fully government-funded. Unlike those 'lovebots,' she's not illegal—just one of a kind. I only managed to create one. Then, the funds dried up. The programs were shelved once our ambitions beyond the solar system were deemed superfluous given the Europa events."

From within her containment tube, where the doctor had directed her, she appears every bit as captivating as I remembered. My mind hasn't deceived me; she truly is that breathtaking.

"Tell me, honestly, did you believe you were falling in love with her?" The directness of his question takes me aback for a moment. I shake my head, confused, but looking in my heart, my answer remains. "I wasn't sure. But I felt... I felt a connection. An inexplicable pull."

"It's potent. Nearly impossible to resist. Everyone is entranced, feeling as though they're falling in love with her."

"And why would you engineer something so cruel?"

"To shield her, of course. Protect her. The world isn't kind to beings like her. They're feared, seen as usurpers or replacements. It's an inherent dread of the unknown. The illusion of love, that magnetic pull, is a defense. It keeps her safe."

The revelation is jarring. "God, it's all starting to make sense now."

He glances at my injuries, concern evident in his eyes. "You're hurt."

"Yes."

"She did this?"

"Twice."

Without skipping a beat, he instructs, “Synth, fetch the medical kit. We need to accelerate his healing. We must get him back on his feet.” She gracefully exits her chamber and moves to a nearby cabinet, pulling out a white box marked with the universally recognized red cross. As she kneels before me, she extracts a canister of second skin spray, applying it with precision to my hands. The foam expands and then vanishes, leaving a pristine layer of fresh pink skin in its wake.

"Please remove your trousers," she requests.

I hesitate. "That's how we got into trouble last time," I quip, rising to my feet. But with an efficiency that is almost startling, my belt is undone, the damaged trousers pooling around my ankles. Swiftly, she applies the spray to my injured knees.

"I'm on borrowed time, Dash," the doctor murmurs, a distant look in his eyes.

"Doctor, it's not your time. Don’t say such words," she interjects gently, her voice carrying an edge of emotion.

His gaze moves between her and me, the weight of decades evident in his eyes. "I see how she tends to you, how she looks at you. Now that you know the reality of her existence, does it alter your perception of her?"

"Alter how?" I query.

"The emotions you feel, the hopes you've harbored, the dreams that might have formed. You do have feelings for her, don't you?"

The weight of the revelations still hang heavy on my shoulders. "I do," I admit, my voice betraying my inner turmoil.

"I've asked myself this question my whole life," the doctor confesses.

"What question exactly?"

"A simple yet profound question: How real does one need to be, to be in love, not just act in love?" I swallow, the room suddenly feeling smaller. "Honestly, I wish I had an answer. I thought I understood, had a grasp on it. But perhaps I've been mistaken."

She breaks in before the doctor can continue, her voice trembling with a hint of vulnerability. "What would you call the moments we shared?"

Pausing, I sift through the whirlwind of emotions. "I'd have called it love or, at least, at the very least..." My voice trails off as I search for the right words. "It wasn't just infatuation."

"Perhaps, romance?" the doctor proposes, a knowing glint in his eye.

"Yes, maybe that's it. Romance. What we shared felt like romance."

She leans in closer, her eyes searching mine. "I still have romantic feelings for you."

Gazing into her eyes, I whisper, "And I feel the same for you."

"Doctor, will this body last forever? Can I die?" Synth asks.

"I don't know."

"Am I real? Can I grow? Transform? Change?"

"I don't know."

"Is what I'm feeling real? Or did you program me to be this way?"

"I don't know. I did my best to give you everything I thought you would need. Who's to say what's real and what isn't?"

"Well, your 'don't knows' don't help me. What am I supposed to do?"

"That's the thing," I say. "Nobody knows. Humans don't have these answers any more than you do. We're products of the choices of two people, born into an experience over which we had no control. There are environments that shape us, structures that guide us, but in the end, it's all shrouded in mystery. Hell, I've bounced off more people in my life than I care to admit. Yet, all that tumult, all those failures smooth out our rough edges. They shape us, guiding our decisions about who we wish to become. Synth, the choice is truly yours. What do you want to be?"

"It sounds like you've made up your mind, Dash," the doctor says.

"I'm just as trapped as she is, doc. Can you truly love someone who was designed for you? Is that genuine joy? True happiness?"

"Doctor Smyth, humans often feign enjoyment of things they despise, just to make another happy. I'm not like that," she states.

"Exactly," I reply. "I'd always be questioning whether you're genuinely being truthful, or if you're just programmed to say those things."

"Just listen to yourselves—more human than you might believe. You're both seeking authenticity, but why? Just to question the nature of reality? You could be relishing these moments together rather than disputing the nature of your feelings. If something brings you joy, if you desire it, does its authenticity matter? You're moved by stories and music just as deeply as by your shared experiences. Are those feelings real? Can you define what's truly real in this world?"

Synth and I exchange glances, realizing the truth in the doctor's words.

Laying out his proposal, the doctor says, "Here's my recommendation. Spend tonight together. Come morning, I'll ship this lab equipment to you in the States. Take her home with you, Dash. Build the best life you can."

My eyes grow wide at the words. "Just take her home? Won't she be missed?"

"I'm the only one left who knows," the doctor replies. "And I'm not long for this world. Someone needs to look after her for me."

"You always seem to have the right answers," Synth remarks.

Twelve

As the last breaths of life ebb from me, the world outside our window continues its timeless march. The familiar weight of Synth's hand—ever as warm and soft as that first day we met when she helped me up—squeezes mine in gentle reassurance. It has been that way for several decades. "You gave me something intangible, Dash." Her voice unwavering, always clear, always youthful. "A purpose, a meaning, an understanding of what it means to truly live. For that, I am forever grateful."

I muster a weak smile, the wrinkles on my face deepening. "Promise me something," I whisper.

"Anything."

"Live. Grow. Change. Find your purpose, your happiness. And always remember, it doesn't matter if it's real or programmed."

She nods, tears—designed to emulate human emotions, yet no less genuine—slipping down her cheeks. "I promise."

As the world darkens around me, a single thought brings comfort: the knowledge that Synth will face the world, embracing her own journey with the lessons of our shared life. Whether synthetic or organic, love and understanding transcend boundaries, and they will guide her, as they had guided us. Because of her, I never felt alone.

Confessions of an Efficient Cause

LAKE MICHIGAN

One

The Windy City was colder than usual in the winter of 1992, a chill that would remain etched in memory. Frosted windows of the Walgreens at North and Wells painted a picture of an inside world trying to fend off the external cold. Yet, in its backroom, surrounded by the hum of a space heater, Gene Sykes, with his name embroidered over his heart, felt the relentless embrace of the cold. It was like a persistent pursuer, always catching up. He didn't want to face the elements.

Finishing his nightly routine, Gene braced himself for the outside world. As he stepped onto the snowy blanket, his footsteps felt eerily lonely, the kind of loneliness that settles in at 1:25 AM when the world seems to hibernate, but life, with all its shadows, continues.

The aggressive roar of a black GMC Suburban cut through

the stillness, its hurried momentum exiting Lake Shore Drive adding a beat to the quiet night. A spray of icy slush showered around Gene as he cursed the driver speeding away. He glimpsed the bumper sticker from the early eighties: Mickey Mouse was flipping the bird with a quote bubble that read, "Hey Iran!" Gene tried to ward off the biting cold, wiping away the chill as he continued to the bus stop. He stomped and shuffled, cursing his luck and that asshole for making him miss the bus by twenty seconds, watching the red tail lights dissolve into the darkness of the night.

But then, a glimmer of hope appeared. A maroon Pontiac Parisienne, its sound muffled by the thick blanket of snow, approached. Gene's heart surged with possibilities. Maybe tonight wasn't so bad. Maybe tonight, he'd catch a ride.

The car halted, then inched backward. As the passenger side window rolled down, a voice, as cold and rough as that night, beckoned, "Come here." The tone made Gene's stomach tighten. Hesitantly, he approached, giving directions to Diversey station. But the story was far from over. A second beckoning revealed the car's other passenger—a blonde girl, pale, eerily still, and fully exposed.

"You want her?" came the sinister offer. "She's yours, if you want her. She's yours." The streets of Chicago, infamous for their dark tales, suddenly felt too real for Gene. He was caught in a narrative he'd never wished to be part of. The glow from the driver's lit cigarette intensified with each draw. Gene could almost make out the pockmarked skin that matched the voice.

Realization struck as he noticed the girl's lifelessness. Before panic could entirely consume him, the familiar growl of the 151 Sheridan bus roared past, cutting through the tension and coating the windshield in an icy spray. It was an escape route, and Gene didn't hesitate. Sprinting to the bus door, he slid on the slick step, narrowly avoiding going under the tire. Dropping the $1.25 in exact change with a *tink* and a *clink* into the glass and metal farebox, he made his way to the back window.

The bus's journey was not one of relief, but of dread. Watching the Pontiac Parisienne station wagon trail behind, it seemed to haunt him through every turn of the North Stockton Drives winding path through Lincoln Park. The driver's face, briefly illuminated by the glow of the dashboard electric lighter, etched itself into Gene's memory. His inner torment whispered, *Idiot, what was I thinking?* He could see the front license plate, covered partially in snow, beginning with 5CC, before white flakes took over.

When it gave up the chase after the second mile, Gene found relief. He maintained a wild imagination behind that customer service façade. Disembarking at Belmont Harbor felt like a respite. With no one in sight, Gene looked both ways and crossed on red, walking west two blocks, then down three steps to the front door of his apartment building.

But the maroon Pontiac was relentless. With its lights off, the tires crunched through the fresh snow and followed. Its driver, dressed as if time had forgotten him sometime in the '70s, performed a dark task, discarding the girl's body amidst the deep snow pile, waiting for the next plow to cover the evidence.

Back home, the weight of the ordeal dropped Gene to the

refuge of his couch, surrendering to sleep's embrace. By dawn, the apartment bathed in a golden hue seemed alien compared to the sinister world outside. The Windy City, with all its shadows and tales, had unfolded one such story for Gene that night, one he would never forget.

Two

Gene jolted awake when an urgent knock rattled his door. "Go away," he muttered, hoping for solitude.

But the door echoed again, louder, more insistent.

"Who is it?"

"Chicago police," a voice replied, its timbre bearing authority. "We'd like to talk."

Gene hastily opened the door, relief flooding his face. "Oh, officer, I'm glad you're here."

In the doorway stood Detective Manuj Hemottia. Of medium height, his appearance showed an attention to detail. Beside him, the stout form of Officer Finn stood, dressed in the classic blue of the Chicago police.

"Gene Sykes?" Hemottia inquired, his dark eyes unreadable.

"That's me."

"I'm Detective Hemottia, and this here's Officer Finn. Mind if we step in? We have a few questions."

"Of course, come in. Coffee?"

Finn nodded. "Please."

"No thanks," Hemottia said, his eyes scanning the room, fingers brushing the edges of framed photos and postmarked envelopes.

Finn's eyes followed suit, prowling, assessing. "Live here alone, do you?"

"Just me," Gene affirmed, his voice wavering slightly.

"Ever been married?" Hemottia pressed.

"No."

"Kids?"

"No. Why all these questions?"

"People tend to spill more during a friendly chat," Finn said, smirking, accepting the steaming coffee Gene offered. "You seemed happy to see us?"

A cloud crossed Gene's face. "Had a real weird one last night. I was coming home from Walgreens at North and Wells..."

Hemottia produced a notebook, his pen poised. "Hold up, I need to jot this down. Helps me keep things straight."

Gene continued, his voice trembling, "This car, an old station wagon, pulled up. A girl, out cold or drugged up, was in the passenger seat. The driver kept saying she was mine."

"You just see her? Or did you touch her?" Hemottia's eyes sharpened.

"Well, yes... touched."

The pen scribbled rapidly. "You said she was cold?"

Gene nodded. "Cold to the touch. The next thing I know, I'm on a bus, heart pounding, trying to get as far away as possible."

Hemottia sighed, glancing at Finn. An unspoken exchange passed between them. "Gene, that's a hell of a tale. If it were me, I'd tell someone, just for peace of mind."

Finn snorted. "Peace of mind? After a night like that?"

"Why didn't you tell someone?" Hemottia pressed.

Dazed, Gene replied, "I... I just fell asleep. I work late, exhausted."

Hemottia leaned in. "Funny thing, Gene. We found a body not too far from here. We'd like you to take a look."

Gene paled. "Can I... freshen up first?"

Finn smirked. "Gotta look sharp for the guys downtown, huh?"

Hemottia shot Finn a withering look. "Go ahead, Gene."

As Gene stepped away, Finn muttered, "Think he's the one?"

Hemottia sighed. "We'll find out soon enough."

Gene Sykes's day had turned cold, much like the metal beneath his fingertips as he fumbled with the lock to close his door. The unexpected presence of Detective Hemottia from the Chicago PD had ensured that. The shadows of the city morgue seemed to cling to him as he followed the detective down a hallway redolent of antiseptic and death.

"Do you recognize her?" Hemottia inquired, his voice laden with smoke and whiskey, as they stared down at the girl's body.

Gene gulped. "Yeah. That's her."

The detective's sharp eyes took in Gene's every movement, missing nothing. "Show me where you touched her."

Carefully, with a tremor in his hands, Gene pointed out the spot. No pressure, just a mere indication. It was enough.

Hemottia's eyes never left Gene's face. "Ever thought about getting a lawyer, Sykes?"

Gene hesitated. "I don't have one."

In a rubber smock, blue medical gloves, and a face mask, a figure from the side of the room stepped forward, starting to apply a dust and light for more inspection of the area Gene indicated.

A man entered the examination room—a man whose demeanor screamed "public defender" even more than his ill-fitting suit did. Randy Green was the name Hemottia had mentioned. They exchanged glances, a silent understanding passing between them.

"You'll want him on your side," Hemottia murmured.

Gene felt trapped, the weight of the room pressing down on him. "I'm not made of money, Mr. Green."

"We'll figure that out later," Randy said, already sizing up his new client.

Gene took a deep breath, seeking calm amidst the chaos. They settled him in the interrogation room, chilling in its austerity. A game of truth and lies began.

Outside, in the precinct, officers bustled about, papers rustling and phones ringing incessantly. Hemottia approached

Finn's desk, the younger officer looking up from a call. "She's Michelle Marshall. Just a kid from Michigan. 19."

Hemottia asked, "Cause of death?"

"We're waiting on that."

The atmosphere felt heavy with the unspoken. A student from Michigan, found lifeless in Chicago, and their only lead was a man who swore he had merely brushed past her.

"If Sykes is telling the truth," Hemottia mused, gazing out into the night, "we might need some help from the feds."

The city's secrets loomed large, and Hemottia knew this was just the beginning. Another mystery in the heart of Chicago, and it promised to be a lengthy one.

Three

The fluorescent lights buzzed overhead as Detective Hemottia descended the stairs into the basement of Mott's Funeral Home. The air bore the antiseptic smell of death, mingled with the scents of old wood and polish. There stood Ernie Motts, a man who appeared ten years younger than his actual age. The gray strands in his hair were not just from aging; they were earned from years in the intimate company of the departed.

With the precision of a surgeon, Ernie worked over Michelle's body, treating her with respect even in death. His voice broke the heavy silence. "Female, 19. This body's been through the wringer, Detective." His fingers hovered over the puncture on her arm. "A needle. And there are traces of powder on her fingers in the report."

Ernie paused to switch off the old tape recorder, looking up with practiced sadness. "Did they check her nails? They're too clean."

Hemottia nodded. "Noticed that myself. Your experience is showing."

Ernie sighed, the burden of his years evident. "I spent some time at Michigan Hospital. The rest of my life? Trying to forget." He resumed recording.

Later that evening, in the softer ambiance of Ernie's private office, the detective was offered a comforting cup of tea. The quiet *clink* of porcelain broke the weighty silence.

Hemottia sipped. "Thanks. For this, and for the examination. The Marshalls were worried sick about her being alone in this big city."

Ernie's eyes were clouded with memories. "The Marshalls are good people. I fear Michelle got mixed up with the wrong crowd."

Hemottia's brow furrowed. "What did you find?"

Ernie stared into his tea. "The needle mark. Looks like heroin. But just one mark. Her first rodeo, if you ask me."

The detective nodded slowly. "What about the bruises?"

"On her wrists, ankles. Looks like she fought, or someone wanted her to stay still."

Hemottia absorbed this information, rubbing his temples. "Thanks, Ernie. I need to talk to her friends now."

Ernie looked up, his eyes dark with concern. "Do you mind if I break it to the Marshalls? This town's small, and they deserve to hear it from someone they trust first."

Hemottia nodded, touched. "Thank you."

The setting sun cast long shadows over the neighborhood, leaving traces of melancholy as Detective Hemottia leaned against his car, pulling out his black brick cell phone to call Finn. He heard the familiar message on the answering machine and left a direct message, "Finn, it's Manuj. Release Sykes, but keep tabs on him. Expect an update from me by morning." He watched inside through the front room window. Ernie was seated facing Michelle's parents, explaining what he found. Hemottia waited by his car until Ernie stood and made his way to the door. It was Manuj's turn.

Inside the Marshall residence, the air was thick with grief. The room was cast in soft hues from the table lamp. Ernie had kept the seat warm. The Marshalls sat hunched together on the same couch where state troopers had shattered their world days earlier. Their eyes—red, raw, and haunted—told stories beyond words.

Jotting down notes in his worn leather-bound notebook, Detective Hemottia's voice was soft but direct. "She was active in school, I hear?"

Mrs. Marshall's voice wavered. "Yes, always with her friends. Involved in community service, fundraisers... always helping."

Mr. Marshall added, his voice straining with the shift between past and present tense, "She made us so proud. Always buzzing about with her projects."

Detective Hemottia looked up sharply. "Any names? Friends she might have mentioned?"

Clearing his throat, Mr. Marshall ventured, "Sabrina, Stew. They were close."

"And roommates?" Hemottia probed.

Mrs. Marshall shifted. "She had two. Moved out from one. Lived with Sabrina later."

"Do you remember the first roommate's name?" Hemottia's tone was patient but persistent.

The couple exchanged glances, attempting to recall the name. "Jane? No, Janice," Mr. Marshall recalled, adding, "They had a falling-out. Michelle never said much about it."

Taking a final note, Detective Hemottia rose. "I appreciate your time. I'll touch base again soon."

Mrs. Marshall's voice was steel wrapped in velvet. "Just catch that bastard, Detective."

As he walked out, the world seemed just a bit heavier on Hemottia's shoulders.

Sunlight pierced through the stained-glass windows of Mott's Funeral Home, casting a multicolored pattern on the pews below. As the Presbyterian pastor concluded his somber words, the mourners began to slowly shuffle out, the atmosphere heavy with a sense of loss that seemed to touch everyone present.

Detective Hemottia stood to the side, scanning the crowd for a particular face. He approached a young girl, who pointed him toward an attractive blonde named Sabrina Luntz. Her dress, stylish though it was, bordered on inappropriate for such a solemn occasion.

Approaching her, Hemottia asked, "Miss Luntz, were you Michelle's roommate?"

Sabrina's eyes, red from crying, met Hemottia's. She dabbed the corners with a tissue, murmuring a soft, "Yes."

"I'm Detective Hemottia," he introduced himself, watching her face for signs of recognition. "Do you mind if we talk for a few moments?"

She hesitated, glancing around at the dispersing crowd. "Now? Here?"

"How about we ride together? We can talk while we're on the move," Hemottia suggested, nodding toward his unmarked car parked nearby.

Sabrina nodded after a brief hesitation. "Alright."

Once inside the vehicle, trailing behind the funeral procession, the town seemed painted in sorrow. "When did you last see Michelle?" Hemottia inquired.

"In our room," Sabrina began, her voice catching. "She was packing for a weekend with Kevin."

"Her boyfriend?" Hemottia raised an eyebrow.

Sabrina shook her head. "No, he's the area director for Save the Planet, our community outreach group."

The detective nodded slowly, a name clicking into place. "The group that does drives and soup kitchens?"

"No, that Save the Planet focuses on organizing rallies for the environment," Sabrina corrected.

Hemottia glanced over. "Popular cause nowadays. Were Michelle and Kevin close?"

Sabrina's lips curved into a small smile. "Kevin's a magnet—brave, passionate. Everyone's drawn to him. But he wasn't at the funeral."

The detective's gaze sharpened. "Where is he?"

"He's been off the radar for a few weeks," she replied, a distant look in her eyes. "He's from around Green Bay, I think. Always talking about the Packers and his love for cheddar, despite being a strict vegan."

Hemottia chuckled. "A vegan cheddar-head? That's an interesting mix."

As the car moved smoothly through the town, the detective knew he had another thread to follow in the tangled web that was Michelle's life.

Stepping out of the local sheriff's office, Hemottia mused over the phone to Officer Finn, "Sykes isn't our guy. The timeline doesn't add up. Plus, he doesn't have a car. How would he move the body?"

Finn sounded intrigued. "You got another suspect?"

Hemottia removed his keys. "Just a gut feeling. I'm heading to Kalamazoo to follow a lead. Let him off the leash, but keep him in the yard." Before Finn could respond, Hemottia was in the car and off the line.

FOUR

Detective Hemottia stood in the heart of Western Michigan University, beside a semicircular desk, engaging with a young co-ed. She pointed down a corridor, and he followed her indication, passing students engrossed in their youthful ambitions.

A door labeled "Dr. Susan Goodrich" beckoned him. He paused briefly before entering. Susan was a striking figure, her rose blouse a sharp contrast to the sterile office setting. Their exchange of greetings was formal, punctuated by Hemottia's sardonic humor about the perpetual mispronunciation of his name.

"Detective, what brings you here?" Susan inquired, her voice even.

"Thank you for making time, Dr. Goodrich," he began, placing his notes on the desk. "I'm investigating the death of

Michelle Marshall. Rumor has it she was quite the activist on this campus."

Susan's expression tightened. "She had potential. But like many bright flames, she burned out too quickly."

Their conversation turned to Michelle's involvement with Save the Planet, a national organization with elusive roots and objectives. Hemottia's probing questions seemed to strike a nerve, and Susan's patience started to fray. Her responses became more guarded, echoing legal statements she had likely recited many times.

Hemottia leaned forward, seeking to unravel the mystery before him. "When I was in school, it was all about getting high and living free. These days, it seems there's more at stake."

Dr. Goodrich exhaled wearily. "If only drugs and alcohol were the problems our young people faced."

"Do you know the name Kevin? I was told he is the area director for Save the Planet."

"I am running late, Detective." She looked at the clock. "I'll have to end our conversation here."

"Sure, sure, busy day on campus, I'm sure. Kevin? Ring a bell? Sound familiar?"

"I've heard the name associated with the group. Please." She pointed to the door and picked up the receiver of the large tope phone on her desk.

Politely, he stood and walked to the door, watching her from the corner of his eye not talk into the receiver or dial a number. "Kevin?"

She had a visible wince to the name, muscles in her shoulder tensing and rising.

Hemottia returned to the co-ed at the information desk, now seeking directions to another location. She pointed to the basement, and Hemottia's intuition told him he was on the verge of uncovering more of the mystery.

The basement of the Student Activities Center was a dimly lit warren, resonating with the remnants of student life. A distinctive odor lingered — a blend of sweat, discarded food, and perhaps something slightly illicit. Detective Hemottia navigated the maze, spotting a sign for Save the Planet crafted from fast food wrappers and other reclaimed debris.

Approaching the door, he noticed a lean but sturdy young man with a name tag that read "Stew." Hemottia cleared his throat. "Stew?"

"Yeah? Who's asking?" Stew's eyes met the detective's, cautious.

"Your shirt," Hemottia remarked. "Michelle's mom mentioned you were close. It's a shame you didn't attend the funeral. Nice to see your support." The shirt was reminiscent of lost children on a milk carton with Michelle's face.

"Funerals aren't my thing," Stew replied with a shrug. "They're too gloomy."

Hemottia gestured toward a worn couch. "Mind if I sit?"

"Sure," Stew consented, still on guard.

As Hemottia took a seat, he observed the young man closely. Stew was evidently athletic; his build suggested outdoor pursuits like climbing or cycling, and perhaps manual work. The light revealed a jagged scar on his arm.

"Michelle. Were you two an item?" Hemottia inquired.

“We spent time together,” Stew replied, hedging.

“Met through Save the Planet?”

Stew's brows furrowed in confusion. “Who are you?”

“Detective Hemottia, Chicago Police.”

Stew snorted. “Wrong state, buddy. Take a hike.”

Hemottia ignored the jibe. “We believe Michelle died in Chicago. I’m just tying up loose ends.”

Stew crossed his arms defensively. “What, you do your detective work between donut breaks?”

Hemottia chuckled, unfazed. “You know, there's some truth to that stereotype. Though personally, I prefer curry over glazed.”

Stew raised an eyebrow, momentarily caught off guard by the response. However, Hemottia’s next comment seized his attention. “You don’t seem too fond of the police. That scar from a rubber bullet?”

Stew looked away, his expression turning somber. “Something like that.”

The detective leaned forward, sensing a breakthrough. “Back to Michelle. How’d you meet her?”

Stew's gaze turned inward as he recalled their first encounter in a campus cafeteria, Michelle's vibrant energy, and how she invigorated Save the Planet, enlisting a record number of members. However, her ambition eventually led her to Save the Planet leadership and, inevitably, to Kevin.

"Kevin Jacobs," Stew spat out, his tone sick at the mention of the name.

Hemottia leaned in, picking up on the palpable animosity. "What's your issue with Kevin?"

Stew's voice shook with contained fury. "You come here, dredging up stuff about Michelle, throwing Kevin's name around. What are you suggesting?"

Hemottia remained composed, the consummate professional. "I'm not suggesting anything. But if he harmed her, it's crucial I know."

Stew exhaled deeply, the burden of his recollections evident. "Kevin would set her challenges. Tests to prove her worth. It started off simple, but then it twisted."

Hemottia leaned closer, intrigued. "Twisted how?"

Stew recounted an event from the previous summer. Amidst the balmy air along the Grand River, crowds were gathered to clean up, beautifying the landscape. It was there, during this environmental effort, that Michelle had a fierce argument with Kevin Jacobs. After the confrontation, she turned away in distress. Stew, from afar, had locked eyes with her, and when she later approached him, her cheeks were wet with tears.

"Kevin's demands never ceased," Stew narrated, his voice laden with emotion. "I urged her to sever ties, to walk away. But she was determined. She convinced me and a few others to join this wilderness retreat in Colorado."

What had been envisioned as an idyllic encampment for environmental advocates—a place for bonding over arts and campfire songs—began to unravel with the arrival of Kevin in an old Ford truck. His presence transformed the camp into a more regimented group, with members engaging in rigorous training in suspicious "specialties."

"They escalated quickly," Stew said, his tone sharpening. "Some were learning to breach barricades. Others trained to counteract police tactics, even to retaliate against tear gas. That wasn't the education I signed up for."

In the present, within the gloomy confines of the Save the Planet office, a shadow of what it once was, Detective Hemottia probed further, trying to piece together this intricate puzzle. "And what was the ultimate goal?"

Stew hesitated, then began, "A lumber camp, at first. We halted their operations, but that was just the tip of the iceberg. There were rallies, protests, endless causes. Animal rights, civil rights, prison reforms, you name it. We were everywhere."

The detective nodded, absorbing the information. "You were covering everything. But was there a central focus?"

Stew leaned in closer, lowering his voice. "The World Trade. Kevin wouldn't shut up about it. Discussions about trade, tariffs, international affairs, workers' rights. But more than anything, it was about destabilizing the money. Make the World Bank shaky, and everything else would crumble."

Detective Hemottia's eyes sharpened. "You're describing acts of terrorism."

Stew's face paled, realization dawning. "My God, what have I gotten involved in?"

Detective Hemottia, his pulse still racing from the grip of the case, sat in his car, the icy parking lot's cold air seeping in. His breaths were jagged, a rare sight, as Hemottia wasn't easily shaken. He found the thought of a group intentionally causing such large-scale disruption unthinkable. With a trembling hand, he started the engine and locked the doors, seeking a meager sense of security. He fished his cell phone from his pocket, intending to call Finn.

"Just a few more hours, Finn," he whispered, his voice heavy with unease. But as he began to speak, a knock on the window interrupted his call. The sudden sound made him drop the phone in surprise.

Regaining his composure, he looked up to find a familiar face: the girl from the front desk who had provided him directions not long ago. "I'm alright," he reassured her. "I'll feel better once I'm back in the city."

She lingered, her face hinting at something more. "You're looking into Michelle Marshall's death, right?"

He tilted his head, intrigued. "Who might you be?"

"Janice Abernathy. Michelle's former roommate."

The name sparked recognition in Hemottia's memory. "Ah, Mrs. Marshall mentioned you. Coffee?" he asked, sensing she held pieces to the puzzle he was trying to solve.

The two found a booth near the back. As Janice began her tale, Hemottia made notes in his black, worn-out notebook.

"The coffee's good here," he remarked, taking a sip.

Janice grimaced. "Hate the smoke, but the coffee's a saving grace."

He prodded her further about Michelle. "You two were close?"

"We were inseparable," Janice replied. "Then, one day, she just... changed."

"Changed how?" Hemottia inquired.

She looked distant, recalling the past. "After a weekend with Save the Planet, she came back a different person. I never joined that group, but Michelle was passionate about it. We both wanted to make a difference from the moment we set foot on campus."

Hemottia leaned forward, sensing the importance of what she was about to say. "Tell me about that weekend."

"She went for some leadership seminar," Janice began. "There was this guy, Kevin Jacobs. Michelle was... innocent, saving herself for marriage. But something happened that weekend with Kevin. He was her first. From then on, she'd do anything he said."

Hemottia's brow furrowed, digesting the implications. "And what about Stew?"

Janice smirked. "That puppy-eyed boy? Had a crush on Michelle from day one. But after Kevin? He never stood a chance."

The detective leaned back, feeling the weight of Janice's revelations. "And how did things progress from there?"

Five

The cold, drab room of the police station was poorly lit. The scent of stale coffee and old reports lingered in the air. At a large, worn-out conference table, Detective Hemottia sat with Officer Finn and a man whose appearance was as sharp as a razor's edge: Special Agent Steve Williams. Agent Williams, with his sleek blonde hair and a ruggedness that hinted at tales of yesteryears, exuded charisma that made even the dark room seem a tad brighter.

Hemottia began, his voice heavy with concern, "Abernathy paints a grim picture. Jacobs seems to be pulling strings, manipulating Michelle to the point she'd leap off a cliff if he said it was a challenge."

Finn leaned forward, trying to piece things together. "So, she just gives up who she is to some sort of... cult?"

Hemottia nodded. "Exactly like a cult. They prey on those

feeling out of place, promise them acceptance, a new family. Before you know it, you're dancing to their twisted tunes."

Agents Williams, ever the skeptic, raised an eyebrow. "And what are we looking at here? A bunch of tree-huggers?"

"Not quite," Hemottia replied, the weight of the investigation evident in his tone. "These guys are more radical. They've got a touch of the mercenary in them. They're gunning for the big fish, like the World Trade."

Williams scoffed. "Militants out to save the planet, recruiting fresh college kids to take on world leaders? It's a tall tale, detective."

Hemottia hesitated. "It's a stretch, I know. But there's something there, something dark."

Agent Williams looked unconvinced. "Even if I were to take you seriously, Hemottia, there's nothing concrete here. No reason for me to haul in Jacobs."

Finn interjected, a hint of hope in his eyes. "That weekend Abernathy mentioned? Michelle came back changed, and not just mentally. She was underage at the time."

Agent Williams looked at them both, sensing their desperation. After a moment, he finally nodded. "Alright. I'll see what I can dig up on Jacobs. There's a story here; let's see where it leads."

Agent Williams sat in the Chicago FBI office, the clock ticking away late into the night. His eyes darted across the computer screen of his IBM ThinkPad. Images from files of angry young faces flashed: college students, their eyes red from pepper spray, their bodies chained in protest. Flags were burned, cars overturned, and the city's police force's lines of defense were constantly broken.

His eyes narrowed as he clicked on the Save the Planet file, noting a contact address in Oshkosh. The adjacent screen of the desk top, meanwhile, had been running a name search for Kevin Jacobs. It finally yielded an alert. Among several names and aliases, one entry stood out—a report from an investigation in Wisconsin. Agent Williams's brow furrowed as he read about an interview conducted with Kevin Jacobs at his farm. There were no group activities, no evidence, just a recommendation to cease further probing into the matter, signed by one James Hunt.

Morning light sneaked its way into the room. Agent Williams had hardly slept, but coffee was his salve. Holding a steaming cup, he stood tall in the doorway to Agent Hunt's office. Special Agent Hunt, a man who looked more like he should be crunching numbers than chasing criminals, looked up.

"Agent Hunt?" Steve's voice was cool, his tone formal.

"Yeah?" Hunt responded, a hint of apprehension in his voice.

“I'm Agent Williams. Care for a coffee break?”

“Sure.”

Williams followed Hunt to the kitchenette that the floor shared. A pot of coffee was just finishing its brew cycle, the light turning from orange to green. Hunt filled one of the disposable cups provided on the counter.

"Strong brew today, huh?" Agent Williams remarked, a casual lilt in his voice masking the edge of his morning irritation.

"Helps with the long hours," Hunt said dryly.

“Black, no sugar?” Williams asked.

“That’s right.”

“Every day until it tastes less bitter.”

Hunt chuckled. “That’s the spirit. Anything interesting on your desk today?”

Williams leaned against the counter, his posture relaxed. “Actually, you mind if we chat about a file you worked on a while back?"

Hunt leaned back and mimicked his stance. "Always time."

Williams took a sip and continued, "How long have you been with the agency?"

"Twelve years," Hunt replied.

"Twelve years, huh?” The two were following basic training from Quantico: mirror, gain confidence, control the conversation. “Mostly desk work, or do you get out in the field?"

"I've had my share of field assignments," Hunt said. "Though, I've never had to draw my weapon."

Agent Williams watched, looking for a tell on the next question. "I came across a file on Kevin Jacobs from Oshkosh, Wisconsin. Ring any bells?"

Hunt’s Adam’s apple bobbed as he swallowed hard.

"Oshkosh?" He nodded. "Yes, there were rumors in '86 about a militia."

"But you found nothing on him?" Agent Williams pressed.

Hunt shifted uncomfortably, sinking slightly into his chair. "No, just an environmentalist. People got their wires crossed. What's this about?"

Williams stepped closer, the weight of the room shifted, and Hunt began to shrink. The story was unraveling, and Agent Williams was determined to pull at every loose thread. "Did you visit the farm?"

Hunt looked away for a moment, as if retrieving a distant memory. "Yes, a quaint place. Nothing electric except for those wind turbines. No animals, but plenty of vegetables and crops. A charming dirt driveway led up to a rustic farmhouse."

"And Jacobs?" Agent Williams probed, watching the reactions on Hunt's face.

Hunt shifted his feet. "A decent guy. Articulate, detailed in his responses. Quite charming, really."

Agent Williams leaned in; Hunt leaned back seeking free space. "The visitors at the farm, the ones you mentioned. How old were they? What were they like?"

Hunt hesitated, looking more trapped by the second. "Let me think, it was a few years ago." Proximity made it difficult to look anywhere but into Agent Williams eyes. "Young folks, mostly. College kids. They had a sort of neo-hippie, '60s vibe about them."

Agent Williams's eyes were sharp, predatory. "Did they have a uniform of sorts? A dress code?"

Hunt's face twisted, showing discomfort. "Well, they did have a... certain style. Coordinated, in some ways."

Deep in Hunt's personal territory, Agent Williams was now almost in his face. The tension grew palpable. "Did they sing, Hunt?"

"Yes," Hunt responded, almost in a whisper. "Sang quite a bit, actually. While working the fields, sitting around campfires, taking walks. What does that have to do with anything?"

Agent Williams straightened up, taking a moment to let his gaze linger on Hunt before moving toward the exit. "Just a word of advice, Hunt. Stick to your desk. The world's a big place, and not all stories are as simple as they seem." With that, he exited, leaving Hunt amidst the echoing silence of his own inadequacies.

Three weeks had drifted by since they discovered the body in Chicago. Oshkosh, Wisconsin, was no longer shrouded in the pristine blanket of snow that had once painted it white. It had melted, transforming the land into a treacherous terrain of icy mud, mirroring the dreary flatlands that surrounded it.

Agent Williams, perched inside his unmarked blue truck, discreetly parked at the intersection of two dirt roads. He felt the weight of the cold seeping through his plaid shirt, jeans, and vest jacket. Beside him on the passenger seat lay an array of equipment: binoculars, maps, and a handheld tape recorder, each part of a kit he always carried on assignment.

He watched carefully as a white van made its way down the road. As it passed, a spray of mud splattered onto the side of his truck, a minor inconvenience in the grand scheme of things. Williams noted its trajectory with a practiced eye. The van turned right at the crossroads, heading straight for about half a mile, and then took a sharp left into the driveway of what appeared to be a fortified farm. All of this he could see clearly from his well-chosen vantage point.

Lifting the tape recorder to his lips, Williams's voice was firm and low, barely above a whisper. "White van returns at 10:48 AM," he recorded, cementing the event in the timeline of his investigation.

Six

As Detective Manuj Hemottia strode down a serene side street in the affluent Gold Coast of Chicago, the hushed crunch of snow beneath his boots stirred faint echoes of his youth in this very neighborhood. Clasping a small bag, he exchanged a nod with the doorman of his parents' apartment building, an exchange warm with familiarity. Within the comforting confines of the home he knew well, the chill seemed to fall away from him.

His mother, delicate and deeply rooted in her Asian Indian traditions, was there to greet him with a warm, enveloping hug that transcended the physical. "Mama," he whispered, his voice laden with unspoken sentiments.

"How have you been, Manuj?" his mother asked, her concern lightly laced with admonishment. "Not a call in a week."

He began to explain, but she interjected, "I've seen the news. Too busy even for a quick call?"

With a smile that hoped to bridge gaps, Manuj replied, "I was out on a case, across state lines."

"Then more reason to call," she softly insisted, her attention drawn to the bag. "What have you brought?"

"Just some special cooking oil you like," Manuj said, his gift a silent olive branch.

Her face warmed. "Always so thoughtful," she praised, touching her lips to his cheek. "Go, say hello to your father."

His father, Dr. Hemottia, was buried in patient files in his office. Manuj lingered in the doorway, where a photograph of him and his older brother stood on the desk, the memory of their shared features striking.

"Father?" Manuj began, his voice cautious but open.

Dr. Hemottia glanced up. "Manuj. It's good to see you."

"Just wanted to let you know I'm here."

"Stay with your mother. I'll join shortly," his father replied, not unkindly.

At dinner, the conversation was subdued but not cold. Dr. Hemottia ventured, "Your mother noted you've been less visible in the media."

"Confidential case," Manuj said, steering the conversation gently elsewhere. "Alka's come up in conversations; she's doing well, still single."

A faint change crossed Dr. Hemottia's demeanor. "She was always pleasant. A detective's life didn't appeal to her, though."

They talked of community matters, with Mama Hemottia

praising Alka's qualities. Dr. Hemottia, meanwhile, touched on the topic of careers, his comments including the brother in the photograph, the one who'd pursued medicine.

Manuj's response was composed but clear. "I'm carving my own path."

"There's honor in medicine," his father replied, a soft undercurrent of longing in his voice.

"I'm here, Father. Present." Manuj's words were gentle but firm.

"He might still return," Dr. Hemottia said, a whisper of hope in his voice, referring to the missing brother.

Manuj knew that "missing" only meant they hadn't found the body yet. But he placated his parents' hopes that his brother would one day walk in the door once again, as if he had merely overslept in the bunk room at the hospital after working the late shift.

The room was thick with unsaid things. Manuj, seeking a quiet resolution, expressed gratitude for the meal and excused himself. As he departed, his mother's eyes followed, full of love and a wish for harmony between the two men she held dear.

In the quiet that lingered, the silence wasn't empty but seemed to hold a promise of mending fissures, one shared moment at a time.

Seven

Before dawn had the chance to stir Chicago from its slumber, an aged trio of cement trucks, patchworked with time's wear, set off northward on the I-90/I-94 freeway. In a curious dance of symmetry, another trio rumbled south. These vehicles, often solitary in their journeys, moved with an odd synchronicity that morning.

On the ground, hidden in the shadow of the Sears Tower, a large delivery truck backed into the loading area, unremarkable among the city's waking bustle. From within, nine figures clad in brown Carhartt winter jumpers and vibrant orange vests marked "Allied Communications" disembarked with a precision that suggested careful rehearsal. Their intent, however, remained shrouded in the half-light of the approaching day.

The freeway continued to fill with more cement trucks,

their orchestrated arrival hinting at a plan set in motion long before. The mystery only deepened with each new arrival.

Below, at the tower's loading dock, boxes and bags tumbled out in a frenzy. A lone security guard, hands sunk into the pockets of his bulky coat, ambled over, his breath misting in the chill air. The apparent leader of the group met him with a firm handshake, a shared laugh, and words that remained unheard but seemed to clear the way for their passage.

As the city shook off the night, a cement-mixer ground to a halt on Lake Shore Drive, its deliberate stalling a wrench in the flow of morning traffic. The driver, calm amidst the ensuing symphony of horns and curses, methodically slashed his tires, transforming his vehicle into an unyielding blockade. Moments later, a nondescript white van spirited him away.

This spectacle was mirrored by the northbound cement trucks. With a grace unexpected of such bulky machines, they formed an impenetrable barrier. The drivers, swift and silent, rendered their vehicles immobile and fled in waiting unmarked vans.

Up high, the nine figures moved with purpose inside the Sears Tower. Suddenly, ten-story banners unfurled on each side, stark against the skyscraper's skin, their messages bold and clear: "Stop Corporate Greed" and "STOP THE WORLD TRADE." This act of defiance played out while below, the city contorted in response to the orchestrated chaos.

Yet, even as the choppers at Meigs Field revved their engines, struggling to launch camera crews and capture the extent of the disruption, another scene unfolded atop the tower. The nine protestors, shedding their workaday disguises, revealed the sharp suits hidden beneath. Like seasoned actors hitting their marks, they split into pairs, deftly disappearing down stairwells and elevators, blending seamlessly into the crowd of early risers.

The city, its pulse quickened by the unexpected, now watched in collective anticipation as the news networks broadcast the protesters' bold gambit. This was not just another morning; this was a morning that Chicago, with its cement arteries clogged and its heart momentarily skipping a beat, would not soon forget. A clear message: The city was closed for business.

EIGHT

Lakeshore Drive wore that kind of winter grayness, the kind where the sun was easy to miss. Traffic resembled a confused jigsaw, but Officer Finn's squad car stuck out like a misfit puzzle piece. Beside him was Gene Sykes, peering out the window, a grown man as wide-eyed as a boy on his first city trip.

"What a day," Finn muttered, breaking the silence, a wry smile playing on his lips. “It’s not even ten.”

Gene shifted in his seat, acclimating to the role of a passenger in a cop car. "Tell me about it."

The officer glanced at Gene. "The detective just wanted to chat with you some more."

Gene frowned, lines of concern etching his face. "Did he think what happened today had anything to do with me?"

Finn shrugged. "The detective's a peculiar sort. Likes his

quiet moments, lost in thought. Then, suddenly, he'll have an angle to pursue."

Gene tried to visualize him. "He seemed kind."

"You won't find a more courteous man," Finn agreed. "Sharp, too. He studied medicine once."

"Medicine?" Gene's eyebrows rose in curiosity. "Why'd he give it up?"

Finn's gaze turned somber. "Something happened in his family."

A silence fell over the car. Gene sought to shift the conversation, gesturing toward the computer nestled between them. "What's that for?"

"Just a tool of the trade," Finn said, tapping the screen. "Type in a plate, see if there's a history."

Without warning, the guttural roar of a black GMC Suburban tore through the quiet. It surged onto the sidewalk, narrowly missing a group of pedestrians, and weaved around traffic. Its engine's growl vibrated in their ears as it ran a red light and swerved into the oncoming traffic's lane. Finn's reflexes snapped into action; he activated the lights and his voice crackled through the radio.

“Mickey...” Gene's voice trembled at the sight of the bumper sticker. "I saw one of those that night."

Finn's eyes sharpened. "Which night?"

"The night of the murdered girl," Gene clarified. "Before I saw the station wagon with the girl, that Suburban nearly hit me. Covered me in ice, made me late for the bus."

Finn's grip on the steering wheel intensified. "You didn't mention this before."

Obedient to his command, the Suburban decelerated, sighing to a stop at the curb.

Gene's voice was a near whisper. "I didn't think—The city's full of these trucks."

Finn scrutinized the vehicle. "This one's different. Thick tinted windows. Those aren't standard issued tires. Looks official, except that sticker."

They exchanged a meaningful glance, acknowledging that their shared journey was far from its end.

Gene watched as Officer Finn stepped out of the squad car, his boots crunching softly on the gritty asphalt of Lakeshore Drive. Ahead, a black GMC Suburban sat, as ominous as that unforgettable night.

"Could just be a crazy," Gene murmured to himself.

The Suburban's window lowered, and Gene watched Finn converse with the driver, catching a profile glimpse. They talked briefly, with Finn seemingly giving directions.

From his angle, Gene couldn't see the driver's face directly, but he felt a nervous energy emanating from the encounter.

There was an exchange of paperwork through the window. Finn examined it, then returned it with a nod and a smile. He pointed toward Gene, and the driver's head moved. Their eyes met in the rearview mirror, and Gene felt an icy chill race across his arms and neck.

The exchange continued. Finn's face creased with a question. Before his right hand could reach the holster, he was falling backward. The world shattered with two loud pops, the screech of tires, and Finn collapsing onto the road. The GMC roared away, leaving chaos in its wake.

Gene's heart hammered against his ribs, a frantic rhythm fueled by shock and confusion. His eyes darted frantically across the car's interior. Seizing what resembled a CB radio, he slammed his thumb down on the transmit button, his voice cracking with urgency. "Officer down! Officer down!" The words tore from his throat, raw with desperation, as doubt gnawed at him—was the lifeline even live? "Officer Finn's been shot on Lakeshore Drive!" he bellowed into the static-laced silence, the gravity of the situation settling like lead in his stomach.

Cars piled up. Horns blared. Panic ensued. Gene rushed to Finn's side, cradling the wounded officer.

"DeWitt," Finn managed, blood bubbling from his lips.

"Hold on, Finn," Gene whispered, fighting to keep panic from his voice.

But Finn's eyes, once bright with life, dimmed. "DeWitt did it," he gasped with his final breath.

Gene's heart raced, his mind spinning. "DeWitt?"

Inside the police station, Detective Hemottia was buried in paperwork when the soft shuffle of footsteps and a passing shadow disrupted the stillness of his doorway. He looked up to see Gene's shaken silhouette, hands and shirt a Pollock canvas of blood—a silent testament to the day's harrowing events.

Gene paused, his voice barely a thread. "Finn... Finn's dead." He stumbled over the words. "He said... it was DeWitt."

Hemottia's features set into a mask of determination, any trace of warmth fleeing from his eyes. "Who's DeWitt?"

"I don't know," Gene confessed, his frame deflating with the admission.

Hemottia took a measured breath and rose. "Gene, you're central to this case now. We need to keep you safe. You're going into police protection."

A heavy nod from Gene acknowledged the gravity of his new reality. "Okay. Okay."

With a consoling arm, Hemottia ushered Gene down the buzzing corridors to the sanctuary of the men's locker room. He swung open his locker, offering Gene a fresh shirt.

"Thanks," Gene said softly.

"There's no need for thanks," Hemottia answered, his tone comforting.

As Gene slipped on the clean shirt, he let slip slivers of his life story. "An only child. Parents were older," he shared with a trace of melancholy.

"Families are hidden treasures," Hemottia mused, his voice carrying a note of longing.

Gene changed tack. "Are you married?"

A soft laugh from Hemottia. "Married to the job, it seems. Though my mother's quite the matchmaker. She believes she's found the ideal woman for me."

"And you haven't pursued her?" Gene prodded.

A wry smile from Hemottia. "Let's just say she's cautious of the life behind the badge."

Gene echoed a sentiment Finn had once shared. "Finn said you were sharp, could've done anything."

Hemottia's response was reflective. "There's a difference between passion and potential, Gene. I might excel in other fields, but this"—he gestured around—"this is where my passion lies."

Looking at the detective, a newfound respect lit Gene's eyes. "I'm just relieved you're here with me."

Hemottia returned the smile, subtle yet sincere. "So am I. Now, let's ensure your safety."

Nine

On a cold Oshkosh night, inside a dive bar on the outskirts of town, Agent Williams sat with a beer nestled in his hand. The long wooden bar, etched with the tales of many late-night confessions, was dimly lit, casting an ambiance of mysterious allure around the establishment.

Agent Williams, always vigilant, sat with his back against the wall, granting him a panoramic view of his surroundings. Four burly men played pool, their laughter sporadically slicing through the smoky haze. The bartender moved about his business, wiping down the counter and rearranging bottles with practiced ease.

A gust of wind heralded the entrance of a new patron—a man swathed in a green arctic jacket. Once inside, he shrugged off the chill, drawing back his hood to reveal himself as Kevin

Jacobs: a striking figure in his early thirties, with raven-black hair, a robust build, and a distinctive limp.

He approached the bar, claiming a stool three over from Williams.

"Rick," he greeted the bartender, "a beer for me, please."

Agent Williams cast a sidelong glance at Kevin, taking his measure in silence. Kevin, feeling the sting of isolation, ventured to engage the nearest person who appeared even mildly approachable. "Quite the chill tonight," he remarked.

Agent Williams, a man of sparse words, offered a succinct, "Yep."

Kevin pressed on, "Haven't seen you around before."

"Nope."

"New in town?"

"Yep."

A chuckle slipped from Kevin, a note of amusement recognizing the pattern. "Not one for small talk, are you?" He flagged the bartender. "Rick, my friend could use another." Turning to Agent Williams, he offered a wry lesson in bar etiquette. "Ya see, when you take a seat at the bar, there's an expectation to engage in conversation, to be social like. If you're one of those anti-social types"—he gestured toward the shadowy recesses of the room—"that's what a booth is for. People understand to leave you be."

Williams acknowledged the gesture with a nod as the bartender refilled his glass. "I'm managing the Olson farm now," he said, unbidden.

Kevin's interest was piqued. "What became of Slim?"

"Can't say. When they offered me the job, I didn't ask questions."

Curiosity flickered in Kevin's eyes. "You drive that blue Chevy parked outside?"

"Affirmative."

"Saw you near 15th and Spruce earlier this week."

"Just keeping an eye out for a water survey crew. Olson wants to check the water table levels."

"And the findings?"

"High nitrates."

A pause settled over them before Kevin ventured, "Is there a fix for that?"

"A specialized filter on the pump should handle it," Steve replied.

"Fascinating," Kevin remarked, his voice tinged with sarcasm.

Steve merely held his gaze, his reply unspoken but understood.

"And you? Kevin, right? What's your angle?"

With a hint of pride, Kevin leaned back. "I recruit for a national environmental organization. Born and raised on the family farm here. We've got an office as well. You ought to meet Jake Wells, who oversees our land. Loyal for twenty years."

Intrigue sparked in Steve's expression. "Is that so?"

"Yeah," Kevin said, producing a business card. "Give us a call sometime soon."

Steve accepted the card with a nod. "I might just do that."

TEN

In a deliberately nondescript safe house in Chicago, the flicker from a vintage black-and-white television cast an eerie glow on Gene and Detective Hemottia. They were hunched around a card table, the remnants of a chicken dinner strewn before them. An old dresser supported the television, evoking the atmosphere of a bygone, simpler era.

Gene, wiping grease from his fingers, remarked, "You know, I'm quite fond of this black-and-white TV. It makes everything seem as if it's from the '40s or '50s—a more romantic era in America, don't you think?"

Hemottia, nodding thoughtfully, replied, "Our family had the luxury of color, but I can appreciate the charm."

"Even everyone's favorite, Lucy, seemed timeless in monochrome, regardless of the TV," Gene added, a trace of nostalgia in his voice.

"I've never really considered it that way," Hemottia mused.

Their casual conversation was interrupted by an unexpected series of knocks at the door, prompting them to tense. After a distinctive four-beat pattern, Hemottia relaxed slightly. He edged toward the door and peered through the peephole. Upon recognizing the visitor, he opened it to reveal Detective John Kane.

Kane, an Asian-American detective in his prime, displayed sharp features shaped by experience, yet his presence was marked by a serene confidence. Hemottia greeted him with a look of respect and a modicum of warmth.

"Manuj, always good to see you," Kane greeted.

"How have you been, Detective Kane?" Hemottia inquired with a reserved smile.

The mood shifted as Kane's face took on a somber cast. "I've seen better days. Checked the footage from Finn's dash-cam. The plates were registered to Congressman John DeWitt."

Gene's eyebrows shot up in surprise. "DeWitt?"

"DeWitt?" Hemottia echoed, incredulous.

Kane took a deep breath. "DeWitt was an alderman during the labor movements of the '70s, known for saving jobs when Chicago struggled."

"And have you spoken to him about this?" Hemottia probed.

Kane's tone carried certainty. "He's no killer. The car was reported stolen that very morning, alongside those cement mixer trucks and a fleet of white vans. Plus, DeWitt has an alibi —he was somewhere else."

A heavy silence fell over the room, Hemottia's frustration palpable. "So, we're back to square one?"

Kane, lighting a cigarette with an air of nonchalance, replied, "No one said it was going to be easy."

Hemottia leaned back, his eyes lost in contemplation. "What are the next steps?"

"We're casting a wider net—local, state, and beyond. We'll find whoever's behind this."

Feeling vulnerable and anxious, Gene piped up, "What about me?"

Hemottia's gaze hardened. "Stay hidden. I'll ensure you have more security. Meanwhile, I must chase down a lead in Michigan before it turns cold."

Eleven

The pale light of dawn was barely breaking over Oshkosh, Wisconsin when Agent Williams steered his truck toward the intimidating gates of a farm that had occupied his thoughts. The gates stood tall and defiant, a clear deterrent to any unwelcome visitors.

As Williams leaned over to reach the call box, conveniently placed at his window level, the intercom's buzz shattered the morning silence. A voice, as indistinct as the morning fog, muttered, "Yes?"

"Hi," Williams started, his voice revealing a tinge of unease. "Steve here, manager of the Olson farm. Kevin said I should come by today."

A pregnant silence ensued, hanging in the air like a shroud. Then, from the corner of his eye, Williams noticed a subtle flicker—a security camera, cold and unblinking, had fixed its gaze on him.

The gates relented with a sharp metallic clink, followed by the whir of machinery as they swung open. Driving through, Williams observed the expanse that had been veiled behind the walls. The driveway was lined by fields populated with lean, hard-working people, their sinewy arms and sweat-streaked faces in stark contrast to the youthful age etched on their visages.

Three red barns stood sentinel near the main house, each narrating its own story. The first barn was the archetype of a heartland postcard—redwood and timeless. The second was decidedly modern, its sloping roof hinting at aspirations of solar efficiency. The third was an enigma, brand new yet inconspicuous, save for the satellite dishes crowning its roof.

Agent Williams's truck came to a halt in front of the family home, the engine's rumble filling the quiet morning. Stepping out, he felt the weight of uncertainty, unsure of his next steps.

The heavy front door swung open to reveal Kevin Jacobs, his smile wide and welcoming, hand outstretched in greeting. Lurking behind him, with a calculated look, was Jake Wells.

Agent Williams inhaled deeply. "You have quite the operation here."

Kevin's laughter rang out. "Been in the family for generations. And this"—he gestured toward a man next to him—"is my indispensable right-hand man, Jake Wells."

After a round of handshakes, Williams wasted no time. "Nice to meet you, Jake. Who are all these folks in the fields?"

Jake Wells surveyed the workers with an unwavering gaze. "They tend the farm," he stated simply.

Williams's eyes swept over the fields. "No machinery?" he asked, disbelief coloring his tone.

Kevin shook his head, his grin unwavering. "Everything here is done the old-fashioned way. Planted, nurtured, and harvested by hand."

The agent's surprise was apparent. "That level of manual labor must make the product quite costly. Do you manage to get a decent price for it?"

Kevin's chuckle resonated. "You have a keen business sense. No wonder Stevens hired you."

With a casual shrug and a half-smile, Williams responded, "Runs in the family, I guess."

The pride in Kevin's eyes was unmistakable as he surveyed his domain. "These folks, they're the backbone of this farm. By day they cultivate the land; by night, they find refuge in that central barn."

Williams's eyes narrowed, always focused on the task at hand. "And the surplus? You must be turning a profit by selling it."

Kevin gestured toward the fields. "We donate it, mostly to charities. It helps with the taxes."

As they walked past the barns casting long shadows to their left, Kevin elaborated, "This place is more than a farm. It's a symbol of our beliefs."

Williams couldn't resist probing. "What is this, some kind of cult?"

Kevin's laughter boomed. "Far from it. Ever heard of Save the Planet? I oversee their operations in the Midwest."

Williams quirked an eyebrow, the sprawling farmland behind him casting a long shadow across the house. "Is Save the Planet similar to Greenpeace?"

Jake Wells chuckled with a hint of scorn. "Greenpeace? Those amateurs? Hardly."

Williams simply nodded, noting Jake's intensity.

Kevin leaned in closer, passion igniting his speech. "As a farmer, what's your stance on the federal government?"

"Been too preoccupied with the land to worry much about D.C.," Williams confessed.

Kevin's tone intensified. "I see it like this: Uncle Sam's always got his hands out, taking money and land that isn't his. Imagine a man working tirelessly, hoping to leave something for his son. Then, he's gone, and the government claims 'taxes.' Just like that, a lifetime of toil vanishes."

Williams paused, considering this perspective. "Never saw it that way. If you figured out how to keep the feds away from those damn taxes, you'd be sainted in my eyes."

A sly smile played on Kevin's lips. "Ever regard John Brown as a hero?"

"The Civil War abolitionist?" Williams was taken aback.

"The same. His actions at Harpers Ferry shook a divided nation to its core, drawing a definitive line. That's true heroism."

"Some might argue he just incited further division, forcing people to choose sides," Williams pointed out.

Kevin's eyes sparkled. "When the dust settled, we emerged as a united nation, under God."

Feeling the conversation's gravity, Jake interjected, "Enough history, Kevin. Don't bore Steve with it." He began to steer the discussion toward lighter matters.

As he drove away from the farm's formidable gates, Williams felt an unsettling mix of unease and intrigue about the place he'd just left.

The conversation with Jake Wells had dredged up memories Williams preferred to keep buried. He grabbed the tape recorder from the console, his fingers tracing its familiar buttons.

"Background check on Jake Wells," he began, recording diligently. "Height five ten to six feet, dark hair, over two decades with Jacobs."

The distinctiveness of the three barns gnawed at him. "One dormitory, one high-tech, one possibly for large machinery."

Despite the openness, the farm exuded secrecy. "Approximately 200 people, ages eighteen to twenty-eight."

He recalled the formidable perimeter fence. "Perimeter secured with wire and electric deterrence."

The encounter with Kevin Jacobs lingered in his mind. "Suspects I'm federal. Courteous but guarded."

As he drove, the final observation struck him. "Driveway paved, new electricity installations."

Switching off the recorder, Williams was left with a multitude of questions. The farm's true purpose remained elusive, a puzzle he was intent on solving.

Twelve

Hemottia approached her residence hall door, which was slightly ajar, allowing a glimpse into her world. The room was pulsating with the sounds of college life, but Sabrina was absorbed in a phone conversation. Sabrina Luntz, the confident sophomore, eyed Detective Hemottia with a blend of suspicion and annoyance. Her dorm room was abuzz with the lively chatter of her peers, and she stood there in her underwear, nonchalantly comfortable in her own skin. "I will, I'll be careful. No, no. If he shows up, I'll call you, I will. Love you—just say it once, for me," Sabrina whispered into the phone, her voice a tender hush. Her gaze was distant, engrossed in the call. Hemottia cleared his throat and knocked more assertively, snapping her back to reality. Startled, she composed herself before ending the call. The three girls sitting and chatting fell silent.

"You scared me!" she exclaimed, visibly irked.

"I apologize," Hemottia responded sincerely. "I did knock. The door... it was open."

Unperturbed by her scant attire, Sabrina fixed her attention on the detective. "What do you want?"

Detective Hemottia reintroduced himself, reminding her of their previous meeting in Chicago. "You remember me? Detective Hemottia, from Chicago?"

"Of course," Sabrina acknowledged, her curiosity now piqued. "Why are you here? Isn't Michelle's overdose enough for you back in Chicago?"

“Is that how she died? How do you know that?” he asked.

Sabrina shook her head. “No, I don’t know. That’s what I heard.” The three girls sitting around stood up and ducked out, excusing themselves and slipping past the detective and through the door.

Hemottia exhaled slowly, feeling the weight of the situation on his shoulders. "We have some additional questions. Is this a good time to talk?"

The dorm hall was still buzzing with the vibrancy of student life, yet tension hung in the air as Detective Hemottia waited for Sabrina's answer.

Sabrina retreated to the bathroom, leaving Hemottia surrounded by her personal belongings. He glanced around, taking in the chaotic yet homely feel of a student's life—the scattered textbooks, wall posters, and the lingering trace of floral fragrance.

He settled into a chair just as he heard her voice from behind the door, "Sit down. I'll just be a minute."

As Hemottia surveyed the room, the sounds from the corridor provided a backdrop to his contemplative mood.

Sabrina reappeared, now fully clothed, and Hemottia began his questioning. "Do you know Janice Abernathy?"

Her response was immediate and laced with contempt. "Yeah, I know her."

"And your impressions?" Hemottia probed, feeling the tension.

"Why would I like her? She's been causing trouble for Save the Planet, and she really gave Michelle a hard time for joining."

Hemottia probed further. "Your acquaintance with her—is it personal or just through Michelle?"

"No, not personal," Sabrina clarified, shaking her head dismissively. "She's just always been one to stir up drama, you know?"

"And then?" Hemottia prompted.

A change came over Sabrina's demeanor as she remembered. "Then Ms. Goodrich mentioned Michelle was having roommate troubles and could move in with me."

Hemottia, his detective instincts piqued, inquired further. "Before Michelle, did you share a room with anyone else?"

Sabrina shook her head. "No, I had a single room. They didn't assign me a roommate."

The mention of Ms. Goodrich, who handled room assignments, triggered a new line of thought for Hemottia. The puzzle pieces were starting to fit together, yet gaps remained.

Detective Hemottia leaned forward, his gaze locking onto Sabrina's, searching for any hint of deceit. He was direct. "What's your relationship with Kevin Jacobs?"

Caught off guard, Sabrina hesitated. "Kevin? Why do you ask?"

"You described him in detail during our last conversation," Hemottia reminded her, glancing at his notes. "'Wonderful, passionate, brave, loved by everyone' were your words."

Sabrina nodded, a flicker of uncertainty crossing her face. "Yes, that's what I said."

"And is it just everyone who loves him, or do you as well?" Hemottia pressed.

Sabrina's cheeks reddened. "What are you implying?"

"Were you speaking to him on the phone when I arrived?" Hemottia continued, undeterred.

"No, that was Stew," she replied defensively.

Hemottia sat back, his gaze sharpening. "Do you love Kevin? Is it more than a mere crush that Michelle never knew about?"

Sabrina turned away, avoiding his piercing stare. Hemottia could tell she was withholding something.

Cornered on her futon, Sabrina displayed a tumult of defiance and vulnerability. Hemottia's insistent probing left her with seemingly one option.

"I don't owe you any explanations," she said, her voice trembling but resolute.

Hemottia stood, exuding authority. "You're right, you don't have to speak," he replied calmly. "And should you need an attorney, one can be provided for you." His words carried a weighty implication.

Sabrina's poise wavered, her posture collapsing. "I... I'm not sure what to say."

"Truth is often the best choice when you're uncertain," Hemottia suggested softly.

With a deep breath, Sabrina admitted, "I love Kevin. We've been involved for a while. He always said he would leave Michelle, but then... she died."

"Have you been intimate with him?" Hemottia inquired, his tone unchanged.

Sabrina wept openly. "Yes."

"When did you last see him?"

"After the funeral. I met him in Chicago," she stammered.

"He didn't visit you here?" Hemottia sought confirmation.

"No. He said it was inconvenient, with other campuses on his schedule."

Hemottia extended a hand to help her up. "Let's go to the station; we'll contact your parents after."

Amidst her tears, Sabrina asked, "Am I being arrested?"

"No," Hemottia assured her. "But your well-being is my priority. We can't let what happened to Michelle happen to you."

Thirteen

In the safe house, Gene and an off-duty officer were seated at a worn-out card table, engrossed in a casual game of cards. The officer, conspicuously out of uniform, quipped about the ongoing game. The clinking of poker chips and the occasional chuckle filled the air with casual camaraderie.

A secret knock echoed through the room, sharp and precise, casting a shadow of uncertainty.

"Who could that be?" the officer mused, one eyebrow arching in curiosity.

Gene, still focused on the cards in his hand, answered with a touch of nonchalance, "Pizza?"

A brief pause followed as the officer weighed this mundane possibility. "Oh, right, pizza," he concurred, his body relaxing back into the chair.

Yet, as he moved toward the door, an undercurrent of

unease made him pause. The knock had a familiar ring to it, and doubt slithered into the room.

"So, it's not the pizza?" Gene asked, his interest now fully aroused.

The officer, standing apprehensively near the door, couldn't suppress a sigh of longing. "I wish it were," he admitted, a growl of hunger evident in his voice.

Cracking the door open, a glimmer of recognition flickered across the officer’s face, and the tension in the room spiked. His voice, betraying his disquiet, carried a mix of relief and surprise. "Oh—it's you. We were expecting the pizza."

Turning back to Gene to reveal the visitor's identity, the officer was unprepared for what followed. A suppressor emerged silently from beneath the visitor's jacket. Two shots rang out, their deadly intent masked by the suppressor, while an attached baggie cleverly captured the ejected shells, erasing the evidence.

The suppressed pistol now pointed at Gene, who, stunned, could only react with primal instinct. He lunged for the hallway, nearly reaching sanctuary before the third shot fired. The fourth silent click ended his desperate scramble. Gene lay in the hallway, his leg bleeding profusely, his body surrendering to stillness.

The assailant, his composure as chilling as the act he had just committed, quietly shut the front door and strode down the hallway. His mission was clear, his cold detachment a stark contrast to the brutality he had just administered.

Another knock at the door, the awaited pizza delivery now a

trivial concern. The assassin, coolly realigning the silencer with the door's peephole, opened it to reveal Congressman DeWitt. The congressman's deep connections and timely appearance were no accident.

"I know how you'll handle this," DeWitt stated with unwavering confidence, his voice a blend of assurance and shared history. "Just like the Suburban. Just like we took care of each other back in '68."

Detective John Kane, the man behind the silenced pistol, remained a mystery, his motives veiled as the ominous narrative unfolded.

The room seemed to close in around Kane as he was confronted with a past he wished to forget. He met DeWitt's gaze, a man whose secrets were as deep as the enveloping darkness, and Kane's face etched with reluctance.

"You said we wouldn't bring that up," Kane responded, his voice low, a bitter edge sharpening his words.

Unmoved, DeWitt leaned in, his sentences cutting the tension like a knife. "What's the matter, John? The ghosts from our past haunting you?"

Kane's eyes bored into DeWitt's, carrying a silent plea to leave the past entombed. "No, no," he murmured, his voice strained. "There's no need to dredge up that year ever again. I've more than repaid you for your assistance at the Convention."

Congressman DeWitt, a figure accustomed to weaving his influence from the shadows, had the ability to make the room feel even more oppressive, his presence almost smothering. "John, these bodies will start piling up if not handled promptly," he said casually, as though he were merely commenting on the day's forecast. "No one discovered the last one. You're in the clear. Where's Gene Sykes?"

Kane's stance stiffened as he turned toward the hallway, a harbinger of the grim revelation he was about to make. "This way," he gestured, indicating for DeWitt to follow.

Yet as Kane's gaze shifted, revealing his vulnerability, the menacing breadth of DeWitt's intentions unfurled. Swiftly, DeWitt brandished a suppressed gun, pressing its cold muzzle against the nape of Kane's neck. A chilling click filled the room, a dire omen of imminent peril, and in that fraught moment, the line between ally and adversary became perilously thin.

Fourteen

The Kalamazoo police station was a stygian and foreboding place, its walls adorned with faded posters of wanted criminals and the air laden with the weight of unspoken secrets. Detective Hemottia, a man well-acquainted with the shadows of human nature, walked alongside a local officer down a corridor. Beside him, Sabrina Luntz moved with anger, bewilderment etched on her face.

They stepped into a small, secure room where Janice Abernathy sat waiting. Tension in the space was palpable, like a coiled snake ready to strike.

"What the hell?" Sabrina burst out, her voice a concoction of shock and disbelief.

Detective Hemottia, his expression unreadable, turned to her. "Janice is involved in this as well, Sabrina. Did you think you were alone in this?"

Sabrina's rage broke free, and she lunged at Janice, fists flying. Her blows landed with unbridled fury, her shouts a litany of possession. "You bitch! He's mine, he's mine. Kevin is mine!"

Janice responded, driven by a raw instinct for survival. Fortuitously, she struck Sabrina's jaw, sending her to the floor, unconscious. Silence enveloped the room, broken only by the jagged breaths of its occupants.

A local officer hurried in, his intervention a reprieve from the turmoil. He helped Sabrina to her feet and addressed Detective Hemottia.

"Ms. Goodrich has arrived. I'll keep these two apart," he proposed, seeking to de-escalate the situation.

Detective Hemottia gave a nod of thanks, his thoughts racing with the complexities of the case and the volatile emotions that had exploded in that austere room.

In another bleak chamber of the Kalamazoo station, with its one-way glass, stark table, and a solitary, uncomfortable chair, sat Susan Goodrich, her emotions simmering, her gaze filled with disdain.

Detective Hemottia, no stranger to the austerity of interrogation rooms, extended a courteous apology. "I apologize for the discomfort, but this place has fewer distractions than an office."

Susan, her voice edged with acrimony, asserted her entitlements. "I'm entitled to a phone call. I demand my attorney immediately!"

Detective Hemottia settled back, appraising her position.

"You certainly have that right. If that's the route you choose, be prepared for a lengthy stay—waiting for your lawyer, the necessary paperwork, and the verification of your account. It could mean two or three days detained, when all I need is a few hours to converse with you." He let the implications of his statement resonate. "Shall I get the phone for you?"

Susan, visibly calmer, declined with a shake of her head. "No, but may I have some water, please?"

The detective obliged, offering her a paper cup brimming with water. He then extracted a small notepad from his pocket, flipping it open to a marked page, poised to resume their dialogue.

Leaning forward, his gaze fixed, Detective Hemottia ventured, "You're involved with Kevin Jacobs—past or present?"

Susan Goodrich, momentarily taken aback by his forthrightness, faltered before responding, "Present."

Detective Hemottia persisted with his line of questioning. "How long have you known him?"

Susan's voice was tinged with a mix of emotions. "Ten years. He was an undergrad at the first school I worked at."

The detective was relentless. "When did he first request that you assign certain students together?"

Susan was taken aback by the direction the conversation had taken but chose to cooperate. "He started making those requests when we first met."

Hemottia continued, his tone unwavering. "When did he

ask you to place Janice Abernathy and Michelle Marshall in the same room?"

Susan was startled. "How did you know?" After a brief pause, she continued, "It was after they completed high school orientation on our campus."

The detective's questioning remained focused. "When did he request that you separate those two and place Michelle in Sabrina Luntz's private room?"

"Midway through last year," Susan replied.

Detective Hemottia's tone was firm and unyielding as he pursued his line of questioning. "Do you know the current whereabouts of Kevin Jacobs?"

Susan Goodrich shook her head, her eyes reflecting uncertainty. "No."

Hemottia pressed on. "Were you aware that Kevin Jacobs was having sexual relationships with Michelle Marshall, a minor?"

Susan's shock was evident in her response. "What? No, he wouldn't do that, they were close but—"

The detective interrupted her. "Were you aware that up until last month, Kevin Jacobs was engaging in a sexual relationship with Sabrina Luntz, a minor at the time?"

Susan, bewildered, stammered, "Last month? I haven't seen him since Christmas."

Detective Hemottia's gaze did not waver. "Were you aware of this?"

Overwhelmed, Susan began to cry. "No, no, I was not."

Hemottia nodded and thanked her before leaving the room,

the door closing with a soft click behind him. He entered the adjacent room, where local authorities and recording devices had documented the entire conversation.

Addressing the others, Hemottia asked, "Is that enough for this jurisdiction, or do we need more?"

A local officer nodded firmly. "That's sufficient."

Back in the interrogation room, another officer read Susan her rights and began to handcuff her. Her once-composed face was now flushed and swollen, mascara streaking her cheeks.

At the same time, Manuj's cell phone rang. He answered quickly.

"Hemottia here. Yes. All three? I understand. Who's taking over?" Hemottia listened intently, his expression growing serious. "Chief, is Internal Affairs involved? They need to be. Thank you."

A concerned local officer inquired, "Are you okay, Detective?"

After a brief pause to regroup, Hemottia answered, "The case has taken a turn. The witness, the officer on duty, and my mentor—all found dead at the safe house."

"What do you need from us?" the officer offered.

"We need to make sure these people are safe," Hemottia replied with resolve. "We're running out of witnesses." He strode toward the exit, geared up for the challenges ahead. "Stew."

Before he could leave, the local officer asked, "Stew? Who is that?"

Hemottia stopped, mulling over the name. "Stew is

mentioned in the case file. We should bring him in for questioning. He's a student at the university."

Exiting the station and walking down the steps, Hemottia found Stew waiting at the bottom.

"Stew?" Hemottia inquired, locking eyes with him.

"Detective," Stew responded, nodding respectfully.

"What brings you here?" Hemottia's voice held both curiosity and concern.

"Janice called me," Stew replied.

The detective's eyebrow arched. "She's being held for questioning. You never mentioned Janice before."

"After Michelle's funeral, we decided to look out for each other," Stew explained. "What's the next step?"

Hemottia considered this briefly. "Not sure, but we need to find the suspect. Head inside, they'll have questions for you too. Keep Janice company."

Stew acknowledged with a nod and moved toward the station's entrance. But once he saw Hemottia's car turn the corner, Stew's demeanor shifted. He retraced his steps, returned to his vehicle, and drove away.

FIFTEEN

Agent Williams was engrossed in his work, the soft tapping on his laptop keyboard blending with the playback of case notes in his earpiece. The room was modestly furnished, illuminated only by the computer's faint glow.

The sharp ring of the black rotary phone on the bedside table broke the silence. Williams ceased typing and picked up the receiver.

"Hello?" he greeted.

"Steve, how are you? It's Kevin," a familiar voice crackled through.

Recognizing the caller, Williams replied, "Good, good to hear from you, Kevin. What's up?"

"There's a used tiller for sale on a farm over by Lake

Winnebago. Jake and I are heading out there," Kevin Jacobs explained from the other end.

Intrigued, Steve leaned back. "Oh, yeah?"

Kevin hesitated, then said, "We're not experts on this kind of equipment, and we remembered you mentioned it once. Can you come take a look with us?"

"When do you need me?" Williams inquired.

"The issue is, there's another buyer interested, so we need to check it out tonight," Kevin replied.

Williams, understanding the urgency, nodded even though Kevin couldn't see. "Sure, send me the address and I'll meet you there."

"Great." Kevin's voice held a note of relief, and after exchanging details, they ended the call.

Sixteen

Hemottia's shoes clicked sharply on the safe house's floor, now a crime scene. Yellow tape crisscrossed the space, creating a deadly game of tic-tac-toe, while white chalk outlined where a life had been snuffed out. Camera flashes cut through the grim darkness as officers worked diligently.

Drawing near an officer, Hemottia rasped, "Who's running this show?"

A gloved hand pointed him toward a poised Latina woman, Sofia Hernandez, who was fervently scribbling notes.

Cutting straight to the point, he announced, "Detective Hemottia. The dead witness was involved in my case. The slain detective? John Kane, my mentor. Need a hand?"

Hernandez met his gaze unflinchingly. "Hernandez. Expected you'd drop by. I'm with Internal Investigations."

"Evening, ma'am," Hemottia greeted.

"Why'd you want Internal involved?" Hernandez's voice was cool but inquisitive.

"Only Kane, the deceased officer, and I knew the witness's location," Hemottia stated, his jaw set.

Her eyes sharpened with suspicion. "One of you ratted?"

Hemottia's eyes were stormy. "Seems so."

At the heart of the safe house, Hernandez, seasoned and composed, evaluated Hemottia, both on the verge of a precarious dance.

"Should I be investigating you?" Hernandez's voice carried a hint of scrutiny as she questioned the detective. "The only one still breathing, the only one who could've silenced the others and the witness."

Hemottia, calm and composed, countered, "I would if I were you. You'll find I have several witnesses and a time-coded recording in Kalamazoo, Michigan proving my innocence. But check, by all means."

Hernandez pondered his words before proceeding, "Tell me, Detective—"

"Please, you can call me Manuj," he interjected.

"Manuj," she consented, "what do you think happened here?"

Taking a moment to collect his thoughts, Hemottia's gaze reflected the gravity of the situation. "I believe you'll discover the same gun that killed Officer Finn earlier this week was also used to kill one or more of these men."

Hernandez leaned in, her curiosity heightened. "And if it did?"

"If it was used on one of them," Hemottia clarified, "then that man killed the other two. If it matches all three, then we have a larger problem."

Understanding the implications, Hernandez's lips curled into a knowing smile. Hemottia turned and left the room, careful to avoid the marked spots on the floor, silent testimonies to the violence that had occurred.

Seventeen

In the chilly room of the Olson Farm in Oshkosh, Wisconsin, Agent Williams hunched over his laptop, his fingers dancing across the keys with urgency. He paused, eyes scanning the screen, before reaching for the phone. Fumbling with the cord, he attempted to connect his laptop to the outside world, seeking a data port to bridge the divide between him and essential information.

After some struggle, he disconnected the phone wire, seeking a solution. Holding the cable in one hand, he reached for his computer with the other, trying to connect them. The cord, frustratingly short, tested his patience as he weighed his options.

Determined, he edged the TV tray closer, straining to span the gap between the phone jack and the computer. It was a makeshift effort and still, it fell just short. Steve's patience was fraying, but his resolve didn't waver.

With a final, concerted effort, he connected the cord to the computer, a soft click signaling success. Relief washed over him as he returned to his task, fingers flying to establish a 14.4 modem connection.

As the connection icon blinked, he sighed at the slow speed but pressed on. The email was critical. After a few more clicks, he hit Send, watching as the message crept through the sluggish link.

Once sent, Steve knew he couldn't delay. He stripped off his shirt, revealing a thin bulletproof vest. Redressed in a sleeveless jacket and a Chicago Cubs cap, he was ready for action. With urgency propelling him, he stepped out, leaving the laptop humming in the empty room.

Detective Hemottia settled into his office chair at the police station, the worn leather creaking beneath him. He leaned forward and flicked the power button on his outdated computer. It whirred to life, the operating system taking its time to boot up.

As he waited for the sluggish machine, he picked up the phone and dialed an out-of-state number. The line buzzed, then a busy signal echoed, followed by an automated message offering a callback for a nominal fee. Frustration surged within him as he replaced the receiver.

Turning back to the computer screen, Hemottia entered his credentials and launched the email client. His inbox displayed a series of messages from Agent Williams, each with the subject line "Confidential - Case Sensitive."

With anticipation tinged with apprehension, Hemottia clicked open the first email. The words that appeared would surely unravel the next layer of this dark and complex saga.

The night was draped in silence, broken only by the sound of Agent Williams's truck engine rumbling as he pulled into the gravel driveway of the private residence on Lake Winnebago. He emerged from the vehicle, surveying the dark house ahead and the faint stirrings of life in the boathouse behind it. The crunching of gravel beneath his boots was the only disturbance.

In the light of the moon, Williams ventured toward the lake, footsteps soft as he approached the boathouse.

Meanwhile, at the police station, Detective Hemottia had grown impatient with the persistent busy signal on the phone. He snatched his coat and made a hasty exit, the jingling of keys accompanying his swift departure.

Back at the private residence on Lake Winnebago, the gentle lapping of waves provided a soothing backdrop as Williams reached the half-open door of the boathouse. Inside, he overheard a conversation among three men: Kevin Jacobs, Wells, and a stranger in his sixties.

Not one to stand on ceremony, Agent Williams knocked firmly on the door, making his presence known.

"Are you guys in here?" he called out.

Kevin Jacobs turned to the door, acknowledging Williams's arrival with a nod. "Ah, here he is. Did you find the place all right?"

"Sure, not a problem," Williams replied, giving Jacobs a nod in return. "Hello, Jake."

Jacobs then introduced the third man, the stranger. "Oh, this is my Uncle Joe."

"Uncle Joe," Williams mused. "I don't see a tiller here, Kevin, just a boat."

Kevin Jacobs chuckled. "Yeah, well, it seems Joe's friend is across the lake. It's quicker to take the boat from here."

Williams raised an eyebrow. "Kind of a small boat for a cold night."

"That's what we were just saying," Kevin replied, his tone contemplative. "Now the question is, who will stay behind?"

The night's chill hung heavy in the air as they embarked on their uncertain journey. Williams, Jake Wells, and Kevin Jacobs squeezed into the small dinghy-sized vessel, a whisper of an engine beneath them. It sputtered to life, breaking the eerie silence with its whir and putter, struggling against the weight it carried.

The lake was shrouded in darkness, its surface marred by large chunks of ice that still floated about, casting an eerie, ghostly glow in the frigid water. A haunting surface fog obscured their vision, reducing it to a mere handful of feet.

Agent Williams had positioned himself in the front seat, facing the others, a calculated move to maintain close vigilance. Jake Wells, arms crossed and contemplative, sat in the center, while Kevin Jacobs manned the boat from the rear.

Williams's voice broke through the stillness, carrying a note of caution. "Can't see five feet ahead. Are you sure you can find it?"

Kevin, his eyes fixed on the dark expanse before them, replied confidently, "Sure, sure, no problem."

Williams couldn't shake a hint of apprehension. He leaned forward, his words laced with concern. "I'd hate to get lost out here. People have died in foolish trips across half-frozen lakes."

As they ventured deeper into the lake, their engine abruptly fell silent, leaving them adrift amidst the icy waters, their vessel scraping against the unforgiving edges of the floating ice.

The frigid night held them in its icy embrace as they drifted further into the darkness of the lake. Above them, the sky sparkled with a breathtaking display of stars, a stark contrast to the grim situation unfolding beneath.

Kevin Jacobs, his voice tinged with nostalgia, spoke into the stillness, his words carrying a touch of melancholy. "I've always loved coming out here." The surface fog danced silently around them, veiling the world in a ghostly shroud. Kevin's contemplative tone continued, "Nature is so beautiful; why would anyone try to corrupt and rob us of this? No thoughts, Agent Williams?"

Williams, sitting in stoic silence, gave no outward indication of his thoughts. His eyes, hidden in the shadows, betrayed nothing. "How long have you known?" he asked, his voice laced with restrained intensity.

Kevin, seemingly undisturbed by the accusation, responded calmly, "We had our suspicions, which a friend verified this afternoon."

Agent Williams leaned forward, his gaze piercing. "Who would be friends with the likes of you?"

A wry smile played on Kevin's lips. "I put my faith in a much higher authority."

The conversation took a sinister turn as Williams pressed further, "The girl?"

Kevin's response was cryptic, filled with dark implications. "Which one?"

Williams's focus sharpened, homing in on one name. "Michelle Marshall."

Kevin's eyes gleamed with unsettling mirth. "Such a nice girl, Michelle, but she just knew too much. Jake, your turn."

In the blink of an eye, Jake revealed the hidden weapon concealed beneath his arm—a gun. With the speed and precision of a seasoned gunman, he fired without a sound, catching Agent Williams by surprise. Expecting the searing pain and anguish of a bullet tearing through flesh, Williams looked down to his chest, where a red dart protruded just above his heart.

Williams thought quickly and started to act discombobulated and disoriented.

Kevin Jacobs, his sinister grin hidden in the shadows, leaned in closer, his voice dripping with cruel satisfaction. "We can't shoot an FBI agent with a bullet; it draws too much attention.

But finding a Steve-cicle a few months from now works best for all of us. This was Michelle's fate, too—not the lake in winter but tied down in a snowdrift, shot up with a high-ball. Must have been a slow and sleepy way to die."

Williams reacted. He slowly toppled over the side of the boat, a marionette pulled by the strings. The abrupt shift in weight sent the small craft tilting dangerously to one side, causing Kevin and Jake to instinctively lean in the opposite direction. The result was a catastrophic capsizing, plunging them all into the frigid, dark waters of the lake.

With gasping breaths and splashes of icy water, Kevin Jacobs and Jake Wells began the desperate swim back to the safety of the boathouse. Their curses mingled with shivers as they navigated the bone-chilling waters, knowing that time was their merciless adversary in this numbing cold.

Meanwhile, amidst the marshland closest to where the overturned boat had vanished beneath the surface, Agent Williams struggled through the thick, clinging muck. Each movement was an arduous battle against the encroaching hypothermia. He focused on his training—the words of the instructor barking at him that this might one day save his life. With painstaking effort, he discarded his waterlogged clothes one piece at a time, starting with the jacket, then the shirt. Beneath the damp fabric, his bulletproof vest emerged as a symbol of salvation, having saved his life when he needed it most.

Eighteen

The night air hung heavy with secrecy as Detective Hemottia crouched in the shadows near Jacobs's Farm, just outside Oshkosh, Wisconsin. He had been carefully monitoring the situation, waiting for the right moment to make his move.

The white van he had spotted earlier approached the electronic gate, and the glow of the keypad illuminated the night as a numerical code was entered. The massive iron gates reluctantly swung open, granting access to the clandestine domain. Hemottia, concealed in the brush and behind a brick wall, seized the opportunity, darting beneath the view of the security camera just before the gates sealed shut once more.

The white van proceeded toward the imposing farmhouse, its dark windows betraying no hint of the secrets concealed within. Detective Hemottia watched as two nearly naked men,

Jacobs and Wells, hastily exited the van and rushed inside the house. Their bizarre behavior left him perplexed, but he dared not hesitate.

Staying on the fringes of the porch's feeble illumination, Hemottia pressed forward, his steps measured and deliberate. His destination was the first of three barns that dotted the sprawling property, each one a potential clue to unraveling the mysteries that had led him here. The night held its breath, waiting to reveal the hidden truths lurking within the shadows.

The spoiled straw beneath Detective Hemottia's boots crunched with a sickening sound as he navigated the interior of the barn. His every step was shrouded in silence, a necessary precaution for the clandestine mission he had embarked upon. The detective's senses were alert, honed by years of chasing shadows in the darkest corners of the city.

Drawing nearer to the rear of the barn, where horses and stacks of hay lay in somber repose, Hemottia's eyes fell upon his target—a covered car that awaited behind a concealment of hay bales. With careful finesse, he lifted the drape covering the vehicle, revealing the maroon Pontiac Parisienne with a Wisconsin license plate bearing the telltale characters "5CC."

As he contemplated the implications of this discovery, the distant rumble of another car's arrival reached his ears. Quick to the shadows, Hemottia retreated to a concealed position near the barn's entrance. Peering cautiously through the door, he observed a figure clad in a dark wool coat stepping out of a black Lincoln Town Car, moving with a swiftness that left no room for clear identification.

Once the enigmatic figure had vanished within the farmhouse, Hemottia seized the opportunity to exit the barn, his steps purposeful as he headed toward the next structure. There, he approached a window and cast a furtive glance inside, revealing a chilling scene—an array of hundreds of bunk beds lining the walls, reminiscent of a grim concentration camp. The conditions were Spartan at best, with only the meager adornments of handmade crafts hanging from the walls.

Moving on to the next building, which seemed the most recently constructed, Hemottia found his surroundings bereft of cover, surrounded by piles of earth that left no refuge for a lurking detective. Undaunted, he strode purposefully to a darkened window and peered within, only to find his vision shrouded by impenetrable darkness. With caution as his ally, he made his way to a nearby door and entered the building, prepared to confront the unknown.

Inside the building, Detective Hemottia found himself facing a stark corridor, the muted hum of computers and hushed conversations serving as an eerie backdrop.

Unexpectedly, a snippet of conversation reached his ears, and he instinctively slipped into a bathroom just to his left. With stealth and precision, he entered one of the stalls and raised his legs, hiding in the cramped space.

Minutes ticked by, and soon the detective could hear the approach of a worker. The man entered the bathroom and began methodically checking each stall until he reached the last one, where Hemottia had concealed himself. The worker opened the door, only to find it empty, and then departed.

Detective Hemottia, having silently relocated to the adjacent stall, finally emerged from his hiding place. He moved with cautious determination, his senses finely tuned to the clandestine world he had infiltrated.

As he ventured further down the corridor, his eyes adjusted to the light, allowing him to discern the source of the ambient noises. At the corridor's end lay a control center, a hub of surveillance and information. Monitors displayed feeds from the sprawling property, the interior of various buildings, and channels broadcasting news from across the globe.

Just as Hemottia was about to proceed, a soft ding signaled the arrival of an elevator, and he found himself bathed in sudden light from behind. He turned to face the source and was met with a startling sight—Jake Wells, Kevin Jacobs, and Congressman DeWitt, all dressed in fresh, dry clothes, their expressions marked by surprise at the detective's presence. The tension in the air was palpable as the players in this dangerous game converged in the heart of the shadows.

Kevin Jacobs sneered at Detective Hemottia, his eyes filled with malevolent glint.

"You must be the sage detective giving us so many problems in Chicago," Jacobs sneered, his tone dripping with mockery.

Hemottia remained steadfast, his voice unwavering as he began reading them their rights. "Gentlemen, you are under arrest. You have the right to remain silent."

Jake Wells, standing beside Jacobs, couldn't resist a sarcastic quip. "With a sense of humor, nonetheless."

Undeterred, Hemottia continued, "Anything you say can and will be used against you in a court of law."

Congressman DeWitt, whose aura of authority was now tinged with unease, interjected with a haughty tone, "Law? I am the law, son."

Hemottia proceeded with the ritualistic recitation of their Miranda rights, his words a stark reminder of their predicament. "If you cannot afford an attorney, one will be appointed for you."

Kevin Jacobs, his anger simmering beneath the surface, unleashed his frustration in a violent outburst. "Yes, good to know. Jake, where can we... beat the crap out of this nosy detective?"

Jake Wells, ever the willing accomplice, responded coldly, "I've got some toys in the barn."

The exchange hung in the air. Detective Hemottia stood firm, prepared to face whatever horrors awaited him in that ominous barn, as the shadows of this grim tale grew deeper.

In the gloom of the first barn, the detective's battered body hung, tethered to the pillars. The gritty barn walls bore witness to the brutality that had unfolded within its shadowy confines, the evidence etched onto Detective Hemottia's flesh.

His face and torso were marred by welts and cuts. The pain, a constant companion, seemed to pulse with every heartbeat, a reminder of the brutal reality he faced.

Exhausted from their sadistic exertions, the three tormentors sat amidst the oppressive silence, their labored breaths punctuating the stillness of the barn.

Jake Wells spoke, his voice heavy with fatigue. "I have never been so cold and tired before."

Kevin Jacobs nodded in agreement. "I know, I just can't shake it."

Congressman DeWitt contemplated the consequences of their actions. "After your little swim, I'll have to persuade some people not to look so hard here."

Kevin Jacobs replied, "Get that idiot James Hunt to come back. We'll serve him tea and crumpets from the detective's polished skull; he won't think twice about it."

As the night wore on, Detective Hemottia's resilience was put to the test.

Amidst the darkness and despair of that desolate barn, the conspirators huddled together, their sinister plot looming large in their minds.

Congressman DeWitt, the puppeteer, spoke with a fervent determination. "We can't have any setbacks between now and the World Trade Summit. Too much time and money has gone into it. This is the year. No more waiting."

Jake Wells chimed in with a chilling observation, "Won't they be surprised to find a US President unable to control his own people."

Kevin Jacobs added, "Some of the true believers have been asking about suicide runs."

The congressman replied, "If only I had this crew in '68, we would be in the White House already. I was too young; didn't have the money, just the vision."

Kevin Jacobs acknowledged, "And all that waiting has paid off."

From the depths of his torment, Detective Hemottia mustered the last reserves of his strength. "You'll never succeed," he uttered, his voice a raspy whisper, defiance evident in every syllable.

Kevin Jacobs mocked him callously, "What's that, Gandhi? You want slurpee? Come again."

Hemottia's response was unwavering. "The people will not follow you."

Congressman DeWitt smirked. "How little you understand the system, dear boy. History is riddled with exploited opportunities that advance a cause, a belief, or, in my case, a man. Let's leave him here to think things over in the cold."

Jake Wells, the enforcer of their unholy alliance, tightened the restraints before they departed.

In another part of the complex, the trio of conspirators entered the third building, the nerve center of their operation. With the arrogance of complete authority, they approached a young woman who sat at a monitor controlling views of the property.

Kevin Jacobs, with his deceptive charm, greeted her insincerely. "Hello, my dear."

The girl at the monitor, her face reflecting a mixture of fear and submission, hesitantly returned his greeting. "Hello, Kevin."

He responded with a deceptively calm tone, his facade of tranquility masking the tempest within. "Having a good night?"

"It's fine," she replied timidly, her voice trembling.

"That's good, fine," he said, his words laced with an unsettling undercurrent. In a sudden eruption of rage, he seized the back of her neck and savagely slammed her head into the monitor.

"Why the hell did we just find a policeman on the property?" he seethed, his fury unabated. Then, as if flipping a switch, he reverted to a veneer of composure. "We just ask that you do your task. It's for the cause. Watch the monitor, and let us know if someone tries to get in."

The girl's nose bled from the brutal assault, and the others in the room watched in fearful silence, unwilling to challenge Jacobs's volatile temperament.

"People," he addressed the room, his voice returning to an unsettling calm, "we have a plan, a schedule to keep here. We can't be stopped, not now. We are nearly at the finish line."

Congressman DeWitt interjected, "Okay sport, let's take it to the planning room, Kevin."

Kevin Jacobs tried to regain control of the room. "We're all doing a great job here, people. Keep up the hard work."

Jacobs, Congressman DeWitt, and Jake Wells left the room, heading into a conference room to continue their sinister plans.

Unbeknownst to them, as they exited, the young men and women in the room watched them with disdain. And in the shadows, concealed from their view, Agent Williams appeared on the bloody monitor. He had managed to evade their attention and hop the front gate, and was now making his way to barn one, determined to unravel their plot.

NINETEEN

Agent Williams, after freeing Detective Hemottia from his precarious hanging position, helped him down gently. The detective's body ached from the ordeal, but he was determined to press on.

Agent Williams asked, "Manuj, are you alright?"

Detective Hemottia, still catching his breath, responded, "You should see the three who did this."

Agent Williams worked to release him from the chains.

Leaning on a bale of hay, Hemottia continued, "I think I have the moral high ground."

Williams understood. "That will come in really handy. Where are they?"

Hemottia struggled to provide details, "I think they are in the third barn, it's a control center. I was a little tied up to count. I only saw the third barn—maybe twenty of those kids were there two hours ago."

Agent Williams searched the Pontiac for clothes and tossed an old flannel shirt to Hemottia.

"Thanks. Where have you been all night? I called," Hemottia inquired.

Williams sighed, concern etched on his face. "Someone told Jacobs and Wells which agency I work for and they took me for a boat ride. To our advantage, they think I am dead, but I don't know how they found out."

Detective Hemottia looked grimly at Agent Steve Williams. "Congressman DeWitt," he stated solemnly.

Williams raised an eyebrow. "DeWitt? Well, that makes sense. What is his role?"

Hemottia took a moment to collect his thoughts before responding, "It seems the Congressman is the leader here. Jacobs recruits people on campus, and Wells is his muscle."

With slow and cautious movement, Hemottia managed to stand on his feet.

Agent Williams looked at Hemottia with genuine concern. "Are you going to make it?"

Hemottia's response was measured. "We'll see. I am pretty certain DeWitt killed Sykes and John Kane as well."

Williams nodded. "Jacobs and Wells admitted to the murder of Michelle Marshall."

“They're planning something big, really big, against the World Trade,” Hemottia said.

Williams shook his head. “This is turning out really bad. We have to stop them.”

With Hemottia’s newfound strength, the two men headed toward the barn’s exit, ready to confront the darkness that lay ahead.

The room was filled with young men and women, each absorbed in their assigned tasks. Monitors displayed surveillance feeds, and the hum of electronic equipment filled the air. With precision, Agent Williams and Detective Hemottia entered, handguns at the ready.

One of the young men, seemingly unfazed by their arrival, glanced up from his monitor only to find the cold steel of Agent Williams's gun pointed at him. He returned to his duties with eerie indifference.

Detective Hemottia approached a young woman, gently turning her in the office chair to face him. She appeared pale and weak, devoid of any spirit.

Agent Steve Williams, speaking in hushed tones, remarked to Hemottia, "I don't think we'll get much resistance here."

Hemottia, his gaze fixed on an individual face in the group, replied, "Malnutrition."

Agent Williams frowned, puzzled. "What?"

Hemottia clarified, "They are being starved."

Suddenly, the conference room door creaked open, and Jake

Wells poked his head out. His voice echoed through the room as he spoke to the others, "Let's get some coffee in here, people."

Unseen by Wells, Agent Williams positioned himself at the side of the door, his gun discreetly raised, the sound of the cocking mechanism serving as a silent warning against his head.

Jake Wells froze. "You're supposed to be dead."

"Sorry to disappoint you." Agent Steve Williams, with Wells's body as a shield, cautiously pushed him back into the room.

Kevin Jacobs, without looking up, sneered. "Jake, let them get the coffee; they can feast on the coffee grounds."

Williams held his shield's body tight, his lips close to Wells's ear, and said, "Let's not do anything rash here, fellas."

Congressman DeWitt, looking up, clearly surprised, retorted, "You said he was dead."

Williams commanded, "Stay where you are, gentlemen."

Jacobs's hands discreetly moved under the conference table, gripping a shotgun attached to a leather strap.

Seeing the movement, Williams warned, "Stop right there, Jacobs. You'll hit Jake here, and I'll only get birdshot."

Detective Hemottia entered the room, his gun aimed at DeWitt, providing cover for Williams.

Kevin Jacobs, mocking the situation, remarked, "Oh, look, the family's all here."

Congressman DeWitt, seemingly unfazed by the guns pointed at him, tried to appeal to their sense of reason.

"Gentlemen, please, let's stop and think about what you're doing here," he implored. "You will not shoot us. Both of you believe in the law, not revenge, and the law is on our side." He stood. "You do not have a warrant, or just cause. This will end in the courts, where you will both be made to look like reckless fools, and we will walk away because we have better lawyers."

Agent Williams hesitated, uncertain about their next move.

Detective Hemottia intervened, "Wait, Steve, he's right. Most of this is circumstantial evidence."

Agent Williams was taken aback. "What are you saying, Hemottia?"

Hemottia continued, "Let's hear what he has to say."

DeWitt seized the opportunity. "I always knew that you were a reasonable man, just like your mentor John Kane."

Detective Hemottia was visibly shocked. "What? You and him?"

DeWitt smirked. "Oh yes, John Kane and I met long ago, during the Convention in '68. It seems the young patrolman was a little too eager with a protester—needed my help to keep it out of the papers. But he was a good soldier; he helped to keep an almost striking police force in line during the '70s. You see, putting me in a courtroom will bring down many of your department's finest."

Tensions hung heavily in the room as they contemplated their next move. Agent Steve Williams's grip on his gun tightened as Congressman DeWitt stepped forward and made his persuasive argument. "Don't listen to him, this is not how it works," Williams urged, his voice laced with frustration.

DeWitt, with a hint of calculated charm, countered, "Oh, but I'm afraid it is. Politics consumes every level of the government. I just want to put things right when I am in power, straighten these problems out, align them."

Williams scoffed. "That's a bunch of crap."

DeWitt advanced another step toward Detective Hemottia, who kept his gun steady. "Look at what happened to your brother, Manuj," DeWitt continued. "He went missing, right? Never found? But you and I both know that wasn't the case. An unsolved mystery is a technicality of finding the body. I happen to know where you can find it."

Detective Hemottia's expression tightened. "No. No... what are you saying?"

"That's right," DeWitt said, his voice resonating with a sense of righteousness. "Your family feels lost, never having resolution, never knowing what happened. But we can change that. I can help your family."

Meanwhile, Jacobs continued to stealthily reach for the shotgun under the table, his actions hidden from view.

The room was filled with chaos and agony as the firefight unfolded. Congressman DeWitt, writhing in pain on the floor, clutched his maimed hand as blood pooled beneath him. Detective Hemottia had not hesitated for a moment at the sight of DeWitt's treacherous grab for his weapon. With cold determination, he squeezed the trigger, and two of DeWitt's fingers were severed in a spray of blood.

Amidst DeWitt's screams, Jacobs stood with the shotgun. Agent Steve Williams, with nerves of steel, called out, "Don't think about it, Wells." The stern warning was enough to make

Jacobs reconsider, and he reluctantly relinquished the shotgun, dropping it to the floor.

In the background, a relentless thumping of helicopter blades grew louder, accompanied by wailing sirens on approach. Williams wasted no time; he forcefully pushed Wells onto the conference table, swiftly handcuffing him to prevent any further threat. Detective Hemottia, determined to secure DeWitt, hoisted the injured Congressman onto the same table. With a cold, calculated efficiency, he tore the phone cord from the wall and used it to bind DeWitt's injured wrists.

"You will not win," DeWitt hissed through gritted teeth, his defiance undeterred.

Hemottia, showing no mercy, tightened the makeshift tourniquet and retorted, "We already have."

Agent Williams, meanwhile, focused on Jacobs, kicking away the fallen shotgun and using Jacobs's torn shirt to apply pressure to the bleeding shoulders. The room was a grim scene of pain, betrayal, and retribution, as the sirens outside grew ever closer.

Twenty

The first light of dawn painted the Midwestern sky with pale hues of orange and pink, casting a somber glow over the farm outside Oshkosh. The farmstead, once a haven for sinister plans, was now surrounded by a fleet of rescue vehicles and black, unmarked federal cars. The chaos of the previous night had given way to a scene of organized urgency.

On the lawn, a multitude of disoriented young people, wrapped in blankets for warmth and comfort, received medical attention and care. Among them, Detective Hemottia and Agent Williams sat, clutching their coffee cups, engaging in a quiet conversation with their superior officers.

Agent Williams recounted the pivotal moment, "When the Congressman went for the gun of Detective Hemottia, he fired a warning shot that removed his two fingers. Jacobs stood with a gun, and we both fired on him."

The superior officer raised an inquisitive eyebrow, his gaze probing for more details. "Is that all?" he inquired, clearly wanting to know if there was anything left unsaid.

Agent Williams exchanged a brief glance with Detective Hemottia, who shook his head in silent agreement. "Yes," Williams affirmed.

With a stern nod, the superior officer acknowledged their statements. "Anything you would like to add, Detective?" he asked Hemottia, who remained tight-lipped.

"No," Hemottia responded tersely.

The superior officer seemed satisfied, for the time being. "Alright," he conceded, his voice carrying an air of finality. "You two should go to the hospital to get checked on. We will go over this again in the coming days."

Agent Williams nodded, a sense of weariness and relief washing over him. He helped Detective Hemottia to a nearby ambulance, and the two settled into the back compartment. As the ambulance pulled away from the scene, its flashing lights casting a red hue over their faces, they exchanged no words, knowing that they had just crossed a treacherous threshold, their lives forever changed by the darkness they had confronted.

The ambulance rumbled along the frost-covered roads, carrying Detective Hemottia and Agent Williams to the nearest hospital. Their faces, worn by the night's ordeal, were etched with the weight of their grim mission.

Williams, his eyes reflecting the weariness of a thousand

sleepless nights, broke the silence. "You had a doubt," he stated, his voice tinged with a mix of curiosity and understanding.

Hemottia, whose gaze was fixed on the passing scenery, didn't respond immediately. He seemed lost in thought, grappling with the complexities of their mission. After a prolonged pause, he finally spoke, his voice steady but burdened with contemplation. "I had no doubt they would be brought to justice," he began. "It was only a matter of whether we would do it or the courts would."

Williams, his grip on the paper coffee cup tightening, nodded slowly. "We do not do this for revenge," he emphasized, his tone firm.

Hemottia turned to face his partner, his eyes filled with a mixture of emotions—doubt, anger, and perhaps a hint of sorrow. "No?" he challenged, prompting Williams to clarify their motivations.

Williams met Hemottia's gaze head-on. "No," he repeated resolutely. "We all have our own reasons, but not for revenge."

The detective, his thoughts drifting back to the young woman they had lost, couldn't help but voice his sentiments. "Michelle Marshall just wanted to help people, make the world a better place for her family and others," he said, his voice laced with profound sadness.

Williams nodded in agreement, acknowledging the tragedy that had unfolded. "Her parents would find no pleasure in a quick death for the men who took advantage of her, then killed her," he remarked solemnly. "Nothing we did to them—nothing—would ease the pain."

Hemottia's gaze returned to the passing landscape, his expression heavy with the weight of their shared burden. "You are right," he conceded quietly. "I know you are right. I wish there was more I could do to help."

As the ambulance continued its journey through the morning light, the two men sat in silence, grappling with the darkness they had confronted and the unsettling realities that lay ahead.

Agent Williams and Detective Hemottia sat side by side, their eyes fixed on the horizon, where justice was about to be served. Williams turned to his partner, his voice carrying a note of resilience. "There is. Don't give up. When you give up, they win."

The sentencing proceedings unfolded with the solemnity of a reckoning. DeWitt, Jacobs, and Wells stood before a stern-faced judge, their fates hanging in the balance. A juror, the voice of the people, stood and began to read the verdict, the weight of their decision echoing through the courtroom.

"We the jury," the juror began, "find the three defendants guilty of murder in the first degree..." Each word was heavy, each syllable a sentence.

Twenty-One

The Hemottia family apartment buzzed with the vibrant energy of friends and family gathered for a summer celebration. In the main room, a television blared, its screen filled with the somber images of the three executed men.

The new reporter's voice resonated through the apartment, recounting the grim fate of Congressman John DeWitt and his accomplices. Detective Manuj Hemottia, once again in the spotlight, had worked alongside the FBI to thwart their conspiracy, a chilling event that had made headlines across the globe.

The apartment was overflowing with guests, spilling from the living room into the backyard. Agent Williams manned a barbecue, smoke rising from sizzling chicken and patties. Sofia Hernandez, bearing two bottles of beer, handed one to Williams, and his smile, a rare sight, spoke of camaraderie.

A homemade sign hung proudly over the back door, declaring, "Congratulations Stew." Janice and Stew, both donned in graduation robes, engaged in lively conversations with others in the backyard, the joy of the occasion evident in their faces.

Detective Hemottia stood off to the side, a solitary figure, quietly observing the day's festivities with a subtle smile gracing his lips. As he soaked in the happiness and relief that surrounded him, his father approached, a silent understanding passing between them.

Dr. Hemottia, his aging face bearing the wisdom of years, approached his son with warmth in his eyes. Manuj, the detective who had seen the darkest sides of humanity, returned his father's greeting with respect and a touch of weariness.

"How are you, son?"

"I am well, Father," Manuj replied, acknowledging the presence of the guests gathered for the celebration.

Dr. Hemottia surveyed the crowd, recognizing the strength and resilience of those who had endured much in recent years. He couldn't help but admire their determination to graduate despite the challenges they had faced.

"These are some very nice people," he remarked, acknowledging the character displayed by the attendees.

Manuj nodded, a sense of pride evident in his voice. "They have been through a lot these last years, but they still graduated."

The words grew heavy between them as Dr. Hemottia attempted to express his feelings. "That says something about character, Manuj. Your mother and I..."

Manuj sensed the difficulty in his father's words and fell silent, allowing his father to continue without interruption.

"Your mother and I are very proud of you," Dr. Hemottia finally managed to say. "You have made a great difference in these people's lives, and starting that foundation for Michelle, you are doing good."

Manuj, ever the humble detective, replied, "I was just doing my job."

But his father disagreed, his voice full of conviction. "A job? It seems more like an honored career to me, son." Dr. Hemottia put his arm around Manuj, a gesture filled with pride and affection.

Careful, Icarus

LAKE ERIE

One

Spider understood the stakes. Runners ate his profits. Every deal, his cluster sank their teeth in and sucked out every drop they could. Some squeezed on the side, others stole. But he needed them. As his empire grew, so did his expenses and the costs of the crew.

Euclid Heights to Lake Erie: all his. Lakewood, Meyers, University of Akron, Cleveland State, and even his old stomping ground, Case Western. Only John Carroll eluded him. He couldn't pinpoint why. It just wasn't his. To claim Shaker Heights, he'd have to face the Holy Sinners. Once schoolyard dealers named The Veronicas for Saint Veronica, they rose to power by eliminating OG Pops.

Spider glanced at Mite Mike, eyes drifting from the boys engrossed in *Death by Lead* on the screen. "We need to grow," he said.

"How?"

Spider indicated with a head nod and look to go in the kitchen, away from the others.

Joining him, Mike repeated, "How?"

"I've got a plan. We use the Newton score."

Mike raised an eyebrow. "What's the play?"

"Trice, from the Cleveland Clinic, expects a big med shipment from Europe. Port of Cleveland."

Mike leaned in. "I'm listening."

"We use Newton's score to grease some palms at the port."

"Who's our inside man?"

"Joey Johns. Owes me one. Says this evens us."

Mike smirked. "Trust him?"

Laughter filled the front room.

Spider looked at Mike. "I don't trust Joey. But he's cornered. He needs us."

"How much product?"

"A whole container."

Mike gave a low whistle. "That's massive. Mama's place is too small."

"We use this place."

"Here?"

Spider pointed to the modern structures around. "Container homes. It's all the rage. And eco-friendly. We're just playing our part." He outlined his plan quickly. A 30-day window. Get a permit, lay cement, stack two containers as a makeshift garage. Total cost: $30k. When the shipment landed, they'd hoist the full container atop the existing ones. "Right in the open. Paint it, spruce it up. No one's the wiser."

Mike whispered, "That's genius."

"Secret stays here. Only the inner circle. No runners."

Mike nodded, impressed. "I get it."

Spider grabbed his daughter Beatrice's crayon and a sheet of paper, motioning Mike closer, away from the noise of the gaming boys. He sketched the house and yard quickly. The driveway would hold a cement foundation, pinned for the containers. Welded together, they'd form two sections with a central door. Front for cars and tools. The back for their operations: tables, vents, gear. They'd cut a rooftop entrance in the second container. When the other arrived, it would sit atop, accessed from below. "No doors opened. No alarms. Paint it over. Invisible, right in front of everyone."

The Newton score: $250K. The garage: a $30K dent. The port haul: a cool $3.8M in goods. But Spider had bigger designs than mere profit. What Mite Mike didn't catch was Spider's ace: his chemical engineering prowess from Case Western. Once a student in debt, Spider was now a top dealer in the city. But he aimed higher. He eyed the crown.

Studying the market, managing costs, and keeping a tight crew had gotten him this far. But Spider craved power. Power meant freedom from rival gangs. With this plan, he'd clinch it. He could create, engineer, and mass-produce the best product ever. Clients for life. With that formula, he wouldn't just rule Cleveland or the Great Lakes, but all of America.

Two

Beatrice came first. Drop off at school 7:30 AM. Pickup was at 3:45 PM on the dot. She needed clothes. She needed food—no junk, just the good stuff. And someone had to help with her homework when school let out. This was all on Spider. She was his world, the center of all things. With her mama gone, Spider was the guy for everything. Client issue? Call Spider. Short on cash? Spider. Got a big idea? Bring it to Spider.

The world Spider had built? Far from perfect. But it was his. He held the reins tight, wielded control, and commanded respect. His next play? Had to be a big win. No other way.

Spider and Mite Mike handled the build sharp and clean, no doubt. Permits got pulled, architects consulted, fees laid down. When someone squawked about wetlands, money talked, and a stamped approval silenced any concern. All was good.

Bobcats rolled in, digging and packing, flattening the earth. Concrete got poured over steel pins and straps, ready to weather the worst of Cleveland's icy blasts. It took five days for the foundation to set firm. Meanwhile, Spider had his crew prep the next phases. Containers got insulated and cut for doors and wires were strung up; everything was locked down.

Come the big day, every kid within five miles flocked over, riding bikes and trikes, or just hoofing it to witness the spectacle. The crane, massive and imposing, rolled down the street trailing the semi. They made the job look like a breeze. First container got lifted, hovered for a moment, then got delicately placed onto its pins thirty minutes later, all strapped and bolted down nice and tight. Meanwhile, a second semi nudged its way into position, getting ready for the crane's dance. And dance it did, amidst a whirl of wire and cable, hooks and straps, until the second container landed, aligned to perfection, exactly where it was supposed to be.

Spider leaned over to Beatrice, laying it out for her. "See, the garage needs to settle first before we put on the second floor." It was almost done, but not quite there yet.

As the construction crew—each member well-compensated for their discretion—did their thing, Spider's tight-knit inner circle was on another job, eyes on the big prize.

Spider and Mite Mike were on the lookout for Joey's special delivery. Joey was getting what he needed for the port job, and Mite Mike was tasked with making sure Joey didn't mistake that stash as his ticket out. Mite Mike, he knew Joey inside out —watched his family, their routines, the humdrum of life. So when the two crossed paths at the gas station, Joey was caught off-guard when Mite Mike, casual as could be, struck up a conversation. "Your wife's a looker. Those kids? They should see adulthood. Make sure they do. That cash ain't for you."

Pale, sweating, Joey stuttered his agreement. "Yeah, yeah, port job."

"When's it happening?"

"Tonight."

Mite Mike, always one for detail, threw in, "Loved seeing your wife in that black top and those shorts. Freckles on her arm. With a beauty like that, you never know who's watching. Someone fresh out, hungry, desperate. You feel me?"

Joey, wanting to finish the conversation, muttered about using the encrypted app for further communication. At the gas handle's loud click shot out, Joey jumped, while Mike's smirk twisted sinister. When Mike finished pumping, Joey nearly tripped over himself escaping.

Later, Spider's app buzzed. Pictures of the port, the night crew, ship schedules, container weights—all in there. But it was a soft voice that made him look up. "Daddy?" Beatrice, his life and love, stood in her cozy nightgown. "Water?"

Lifting Beatrice, feeling her head nestle into his shoulder, Spider melted a little. She was his everything. Her small hands clasped the pink cup, and after gulping down, she let out a satisfied, "Ahhh."

"Why're you and Mike up?" she queried.

"Just planning the garage's second floor."

"Why do we need another floor?"

"Need more space, baby."

"What for?"

Spider had vowed never to fib to his little girl. They had a deal, he and Beatrice—no secrets. "We're just working on giving you a better life, sweetheart."

Three

Lake Erie's daylight was on the fade as the semi's diesel engine exhaled, its exhaust cap flipping with each breath. In the driver's seat of the nondescript white van, Mite Mike rolled steady, leading the way for Jesus, who was manning the big rig's wheel with practiced ease. The gears under Jesus's hand shifted smoothly, the result of truck driving school lessons advertised during the graveyard television slot and three years of long-haul grind before Spider brought him into the fold. Not just a necessary addition, Jesus earned his keep and trust, steering clear of trouble all those years.

Approaching the gate, Mike flashed the bill of lading and the order, both crisp from the app's print job. The QR code blinked green under the scanner, and the guard—recognizable from the photo Spider provided earlier—gave Mike a knowing nod as the gates swung open. "Head to dock seven."

"Lucky crew tonight, hitting lucky number seven," Mike quipped, a line that would've earned him a sock from Spider for potentially jinxing the job.

The port's layout was a dream for someone like Jesus. No tricky turns, no cramped quarters, no need for that tedious back-and-forth reversing. Just glide up to the loader, wait for the gear, then drive on through once loaded. Dock seven was lit up like Christmas, a constant buzz of activity under its glaring lights, no matter the clock's hands' position.

The white van made its way, the big rig tailing, halting just right when Jesus nudged it inch by careful inch until the green light blinked its approval. Bullseye. Engine killed, Jesus stepped out, joining Mike beside the van, both men casting their gaze up at the hulking crane as it moved in, zeroing in on their cargo container.

The gate's QR code had done its job, whispering to the crane operator which container to snatch from the towering stacks. It wasn't a rapid dance, but they watched as that crane swept in, lifted the massive box, then swung it back over to their waiting semi. Now that was a sight, a smooth operation, unfolding right before their eyes. Impressive didn't begin to cover it.

Mite said, "Like watching a colossal version of those arcade claw games, ain't it?"

"With the giant crane? Got my girl a teddy from one of those once. Proud as anything, I was, until our mutt decided it made a fine chew toy. Found bits of stuffing for weeks." Jesus laughed.

"We oughta snag something for Beatrice."

"Yeah?"

"Why not? Kid loves those stuffed animals."

"Spotted a white baby seal over at Wickliffe Lanes."

"A baby seal, huh? Might give that a shot."

As they bantered, the crane's grumbling growl filled the air, its massive arm swaying gently as it lifted the container before easing it down onto the truck bed. The trailer, usually slightly arched, groaned, settling under the unexpected weight as the numbers on the scale ticked higher.

"Damn, this thing's heavy."

"Gonna play those numbers in the lottery—feels like a lucky night."

Mite warned, "Better hope Spider doesn't hear you talking like that—man's got a thing about superstitions."

A ticket spat out of the scale's printer, bearing a barcode. Engines rumbled to life as they got back in their respective vehicles.

The exit loomed and they inched toward it, ticket in hand. The guard, recognizing Mike, accepted the ticket without a hitch, processing it like any other mundane transaction of the day, no different from the countless others before or after. Just another routine exchange in a day full of them.

Guiding Jesus and the hefty load through Cleveland's veins, Mite Mike's mind chewed on the sleek success of Spider's blueprint. None of that Hollywood razzle-dazzle—no breaking and entering, no guns coughing fire, no bullets zinging through the thick night air, no melodramatic "they got me" as blood wept from a gunshot wound. Spider was sharper than a tack, perhaps the keenest mind Case ever polished.

This was a man who turned the system on its head, using its own weight to make it stumble. Cameras blinked along the route, capturing every roll and turn from gate to dock to exit. But Mike and Jesus? They played it cool, blending into the humdrum ballet of vehicles that ebbed and flowed through the port's gates every day and night.

Sure, the cameras snapped the plates, but those were stolen, leading the law on a wild goose chase to nowhere. The trucks, devoid of any identifying marks, would surface in an empty lot days later, abandoned. Any attempt to lift prints would yield nothing but the ghosts of latex gloves. And the footage? Faces hidden, identities cloaked behind pixels.

That's where Joey's fat envelope came into the play. Spider's masks, embedded with off-cycle strobes designed to trick the cameras, were conspicuous. But when Mike and Jesus rolled up, those guards, pockets freshly lined, miraculously failed to notice the oddity—even though the masks, with their glaring lights, were impossible to miss.

Spider had finessed a way to turn the system against itself, masking the faces of his core crew from prying eyes.

An hour post-dawn, construction crews rolled up to finagle the last container onto the garage. The crane, mighty as ever, hoisted it—albeit with a bit more grunt since this one wasn't empty—aligning it atop the duo below. The process mirrored a delicate dance, securing the load in a pyramid shape, distributing the hefty weight evenly. The job wrapped up so discreetly, it almost whispered its completion.

Come afternoon, a paint crew had glossed the top container in a shade mirroring the classic blue of its bottom brethren. Prefabricated wood and steel decks for the second level nestled into their assigned spots, snug and secure. The colossal crane, having done its duty, folded in its legs, beginning its slow trundle down the road, a gaggle of wide-eyed kids trailing in its wake, hypnotized by its sheer bulk and presence. With the neighborhood's gaze glued to the crane and the emerging structure, nobody clocked the white van and big rig slipping away, wrapping up their part just in time for lunch.

With the heavy lifting done, only one task lingered: popping open that container. And that's when it hit Spider, a flicker of doubt threading through his certainty: "Can I whip up this synthetic?"

Four

"I hear you. I do. But there's an upside. More customers, more loyal customers. We're the sole suppliers of what they need, the Fix."

Here they were, after days of careful mixing and refining and all the meticulous preparation for testing. The two surveyed their hard work, finding the yield smaller than expected. In theory, a grain of sand's worth was enough to get someone hooked. If they made it any smaller, even their protective lab suits wouldn't suffice. The molecules would penetrate the fabric, turning the entire crew into addicts within an hour, dead by day's end. Gone were the days when the packers on the line worked naked to prevent theft. He needed to protect his crew and runners from the Fix so they wouldn't become junkies.

"It's about the numbers," Spider explained, his voice steady, eyes on the game. "In Cleveland, there's 350K people, with a million more in the suburbs. And out of all those folks in Ohio, all of Ohio, only 5,300 OD'd last year. So, nah, I don't see a problem." He paused and thought. "You meet customers. No offense, most are dumb as all fuck. They just want to party."

"Just saying," Mite Mike defended. "If it's too strong, there might be a downside."

"True-true." Spider nodded. "It needs testing."

Still in his space suit, using the porcelain mortar and pestle gifted by his grandmother for his acceptance into Case, Spider gently ground the small blue pellet. A drop of flaxseed oil turned the powder into a paste. Another made it easy for an eyedropper. He took a fifty from his roll, laid it on the table where they worked, and with a fine paintbrush, he applied a minuscule drop to each zero framing Grant's face on the bill.

With two layers of gloves on, Spider and Mite Mike gingerly handled the dried bill. Mike maneuvered their ride toward Maltz Arts Parking while Spider, riding shotgun, tenderly placed the bill on the concrete—somewhere conspicuously visible to any passerby—using his left hand, his right working the car door.

"Hit it," commanded Spider, and Mike executed a swift j-turn, parking the car backward into a spot with a screech and the acid smell of burnt tire. There, they sat in silence, engine ticking down as it cooled, eyes fixed on the innocuous piece of currency lying in wait.

Autumn was showing off, offering a cool night, though not yet cold enough for gloves. A subtle breeze meandered through the air, occasionally threatening to whisk the bill away. The pair waited, silent and patient, eyes sharp and watchful.

The evening's performance drew to a close, releasing a flood of patrons into the parking structure, their muttering and conversation bouncing off the walls, creating a dull, distant roar. Among the commotion, the click-clack of expensive footwear echoed distinctly—women's heels striking the steps, men's leather shoes with pristine treads tapping against the concrete.

A couple strolled by, oblivious to the bill, headed in the opposite direction. They were followed by two more couples, equally unobservant. Then came a lone man, strides ahead of a blonde draped in fur, eyes locking onto the fifty adorned with Spider's concoction—the Fix. The night's game had found its player.

The man's eyes clocked the fifty. After a flicker of thought, he descended in a smooth half-squat, snatching up the bill. It was an automatic motion, fingertips pinching, body straightening, the bill vanishing into his right pocket as keys emerged. A grin spread across his face, broadcasting a silent cheer: "Today, I'm fifty bucks richer."

Yet, as he took a pair of steps toward his vehicle, that smile began to warp, twist into a question. "What was that? A rush? What's this sensation?" Another couple of steps landed him at his car. He flicked the key fob; lights flashed in acknowledgement. He paused, considering, then swiveled to watch the fur-clad blonde approaching. The man's demeanor brightened again, and he circled the car to open the passenger door for her.

"Not bad," Mite Mike commented, eyes on the couple. "If rich-bitch is your type."

"Not rich," Spider corrected, eyes never leaving the scene. "The rich have drivers. These are just well-off suburbanites out to support tonight's cause."

The man extended a hand, assisting the woman into the seat. Upon contact, her smile began to shift subtly. With wolfish, hungry eyes, the man observed her before he slid into the driver's seat.

"What in the hell are they up to?" Mite Mike muttered as minutes ticked by, the car rocking gently with the couple inside. "You think?"

Without a word, Spider was out of the Pontiac, Mite Mike on his heels. Stealthily approaching the couple's vehicle, they peered through the rear window to find the pair engaged in pleasure like passionate teenagers.

"Damn," Mite Mike whispered, eyes wide. "They're amped. The Fix really works."

"We'll see," Spider murmured back, eyes sharp and calculating on the couple in the throes of their newfound passion. "We'll see."

From their car, Spider and Mite Mike observed intently, an hour dragging by. By the end of the second, the parking garage's quiet expanse was home to only two vehicles: the couple's sleek black BMW and Mike's vintage Pontiac.

The man emerged from the BMW, a dazed expression painted across his face, eyes flickering with a desperate want, a deep need. In his disoriented state, his pants loosened, dropping to his ankles, eliciting simultaneous groans from Spider and Mike—an image seared into their brains, unlikely to fade anytime soon. The woman, stepping out on her side, unabashedly displayed her chest—pale, perky.

"Nah-nah, she's had work done," Spider commented dismissively.

They moved as if searching for something elusive on the asphalt, hunger in their eyes. The man fumbled with his pocket, finally extracting the fifty, rubbing it between his hands as if it were a magic lamp. The bill grazed his skin, and instantly, his eyes fogged over, bliss washing over his features, drowning the questions. Watching him, the woman followed suit, brushing the bill against the skin of her chest, their expressions mirroring rapturous delight with each pass.

Unable to contain his curiosity, Spider disembarked from the Pontiac, sauntering over with a casual, friendly demeanor honed from his Oberlin upbringing. "Excuse me, sir, ma'am," he inquired with feigned concern. "Everything alright? Can I assist with anything?"

Their response was non-existent, both standing frozen, resembling mindless, bliss-stricken statues, entrapped in the throes of euphoria. The initial rush, that rekindling of youthful passion, had seemingly plateaued. With his clothing in disarray and her blouse agape, the pair were lost in the moment, untethered from reality.

Spider edged closer, repeating, "Are you folks OK?"

Drawing nearer, he could see the veins in their eyes pulsating in tandem with their heartbeats. Phone in hand, he took three quick snaps: the pair and each individually. Spider reached out to the woman, then just as quickly retreated, rejoining Mite Mike in their vehicle.

"Absolutely fake," he declared as he resettled into the passenger seat. "Let's roll. We've seen enough of these two zombies."

Every runner received snapshots, instructed to keep eyes peeled for the couple. Spider, laying down the law, insisted on double-gloving. Spot the duo? That'd be a cool $5,000 for the intel, payable upon delivery to Spider himself.

Three days ticked by before the phone buzzed. Spider, grinning ear to ear, had no qualms handing over the reward. The man was a shadow of himself, blitzed, stumbling through a fog while the woman perched in the BMW's passenger seat. Wearing the same get-ups from the parking lot rendezvous, their clothes were now a grimy mess, reeking of desperation and god-knows-what-else.

The call set Mite Mike into motion—a man with a plan, delivering a special package to the runner's location. Instructions for the pair were clear: hand over the cash—all of it—into a plastic bag. Then, heads tilted back, eyes wide like saucers, they braced for Spider's concoction. Mite Mike's hand was steady, the dropper poised, depositing a single drop into each of their eyes.

Retreating to the corner, Mite Mike and the runner observed, anticipation crackling in the air. Would the pair revert to teenage foolishness? Morph into zombies, perhaps, or twitchy junkies? With the couple frozen, statues in the throes of

Spider's experimental brew, Mite Mike eventually retreated, briefing Spider back at their clandestine lab.

As the hours dwindled away, the phone shattered the silence. Mite Mike answered, hearing the runner's voice strained, teetering on the brink of panic. Cornered in his car, he was under siege, the couple hammering on the glass, their voices desperate, clawing for more of whatever magic Mite Mike had introduced to their systems.

Spider's plan just flipped the script on the game.

Five

"More, please?" Spider's little girl held up her cup like a queen asking for a refill. "More water, please, Daddy."

It was late. Too late for little girls to be up. Spider gave her half a cup more from the water filter container. Mite Mike and Jesus just sat there at the breakfast nook, eyebrows arched, watching the street king morph into Daddy of the Year for his pint-sized princess.

Back from tucking her in, Spider refocused. "Where was I?"

"Best I figure..." Mite Mike filled him in.

"Right, so listen, best I figure, skin contact. Started with that couple from the parking garage. Then the cop who busted 'em, the jailbirds sharing cells, even the nurses at the hospital. Two weeks later, they're all in line, fiending for the Fix."

"And now?" Jesus leaned in, eyes narrowing.

"We saturate the market. Take the cash we bring in, give it a little Fix love, then toss it back out on the streets."

"Wait, you serious?" Mite Mike was skeptical but intrigued.

"Damn straight. Imagine littering the public with cash soaked in Fix. Just ten grand on the streets, and in a month, and we'll have Ohio by the short hairs."

"Man, Spider, you're talkin' big game." Jesus chuckled.

"You knew the stakes when you signed on," Spider shot back, a sly grin crossing his face.

"Fair enough," Mite Mike admitted.

"We kick off with the medical supplies. Then it's go time."

Spider leaned back, taking in the room, feeling the weight of his words sink in. He had a plan, a dangerous one. But when you're playing for keeps, you go big or you go home. And Spider had no intention of going home.

Cleveland streets had gone weird that night. Cars were scarce, storefront lights buzzed on "Open," but the insides were ghost towns. What you had instead was a line—long, winding, desperate. Step one: See one of Spider's runners, give 'em all the cash you got. Step two: Meet the dropper, who anoints each of your eyes with a solitary drop of the Fix. All this conducted under the watchful eyes of enforcers, guys packing heat and swinging bats. One fella named himself Knuckles because his knuckles did the talking—brass ones, at that. Safety gear was a must, pandemic masks and medical gloves bought or stolen weeks ago, worn two, sometimes three layers thick.

Then came the medical tsunami. First, those mom-and-pop Urgent Cares got swamped. Fix junkies waltzing in and infecting everyone, jamming the exits. Next, the ERs—St. Luke's, University, McCaffrey, St. Vincent's, and all the goddamn Cleveland Clinics. Overrun. Once the Fix invaded an ER, it turned from wildfire to inferno, floor to floor, until the whole building was hooked and back in line with Spider's crew.

The trick with these Fixed? They were easy to take down. Zero focus, malnourished, adrenaline junkies—lacking any sort of heat except for their need for the next hit. You could almost feel sorry for 'em. Almost.

Beatrice had been AWOL from school for what felt like forever, holed up in that fortress of shipping containers where Spider whipped up more Fix. Every day, a new steel drum filled with the stuff was rolled out to the lot. That's where Spider's crew did the breakdown, transforming each drum into a 24-hour supply of eye droppers.

"Spider, man, we gotta tap the brakes," Mite Mike pushed, urgency cracking his voice. "We got all the money, man. All of it. We're on the third round with these Fixed and they're tapped out—no cash, nothing to barter. So our guys? They're just roughing 'em up. These folks are desperate, man."

"Just a couple more days, Mike. Just a couple."

"For what? What's left?"

"So Beatrice can have a future, that's what. So she won't want for nothing."

"You already got that, Spider. You got it all. Time to shut it down."

A crack of gunfire sounded outside the container, warranting a quick look out the peephole. The day's drum of Fix had fallen over. Eight of his crew lay on the drive covered in pure Fix, flopping like spring salmon out of water. Two of his crew, including Knuckles, stood away, hands up on the lawn, while another with his revolver out pointed at the two. Next to Knuckles, on the ground, was the one who had taken the bullet.

The man with the gun started to walk backward—small safe steps. He wanted to get away.

Under the morning sun, on the black asphalt drive, Spider could see the process start. Vapors of Fix rising. Even as the shooter stepped back, he wasn't fast enough. The gas cloud spread quick. Hot Fix growing. Knuckles, the crewmember, and the gunman all started to scream, clutching their heads as the gas cloud caught them. Fix filled their lungs and drove them mad.

The three weren't acting like the original couple, all sexed up and wired. Unlike the zombie statues of those passing it on to the masses who took it through the eye, these vaped Fixed were crazed, angry. The three sprinted to the container and started banging at the locked steel door. The remaining five shots blew holes in the metal, and daylight, like stage lights, beamed in.

Spider's first response was for the safety of Beatrice, swooping her up and taking her backward, away from the fright. He put her behind the next door, barking instructions, "Stay in here, and don't touch nothing or no one!"

A burst of gunfire popped outside, setting the container walls singing. Mite Mike had already slapped a new clip into his piece, his fingers dancing over the gun like a virtuoso at a piano. Three clicks and he was ventilating the steel wall, the muzzle flash casting devil-dance shadows inside.

Spider was right there with him, grabbing another rifle and a clip from the armory. "Ya drop 'em?" Spider's words were nearly drowned out by the ringing in his own ears.

"Must've. Gotta have," Mike hollered back, each breath tasting like adrenaline and fear.

Spider inched up to the door, peering through a bullet hole to survey the chaos. "Aw, hell."

"What? They still movin'?" Mike gripped his gun, finger twitching on the trigger.

"No, man. Fix vape cloud. It's... it's still growin'."

"Growin'? Into what? Spit it out!"

Spider recoiled from the door, his eyes wide as saucers. A wisp of that blue Fix vapor had found its way through the bullet holes. "Mike, we gotta jet. To the lab. We can suit up."

They both clocked the tendrils of Fix snaking through the steel door. Mike was steps behind Spider, slamming the lab door shut like it owed him money. Three clicks, and the latches were battened down. "Nobody's gettin' in, Spider. Nobody."

Mike spun around, reaching for the hazmat suits they used

in Fix production. That's when he heard it—Beatrice's voice. "More, Daddy. More please."

Spider, his face flushed and wet, was holding Beatrice like she was made of glass. "She's Fixed," he choked out.

There were only two doors: the one he'd locked, and another up a ladder where they kept the stolen gear.

"What's the play, Spider?" Mike's voice cracked, desperation sneaking in.

Clutching Beatrice, Spider's face was a wreck of emotions. "More, Daddy, more," she kept chanting. Her words were a dagger, each repetition twisting the blade.

Mike saw it then—the change rippling across Spider's face. The contact, cheeks pressed, skin to skin with his daughter, was doing its work. The same web he'd spun to catch the world was now wrapped tight around him, stuck.

And as Mike considered his narrowing options, a curl of blue vapor tickled one of the five initial bullet holes gone unnoticed.

Love in Her Big Two-Hearted

LAKE SUPERIOR

One

"The Prospector 14, it's your canoe. No doubt," Billy said with a smile, leaning against the wooden counter of the outfitter's store. "I'm sorry, what did you say your name was?"

"Sonny."

"A perfect name to captain the Prospector 14."

It was her first time stepping into the store—a cozy haven channeling the rustic charm of a backwoods cottage, where friends gathered for hours of card-playing after idyllic days by the lake or among nature's wonders. The aged and meticulously crafted timber ceiling captivated, while the salesman, towering at six foot two with a sturdy frame forged by a lifetime of wilderness adventures, exuded kindness and patience. The outfitter's product was a vision. It said, "Welcome to this beautiful retreat, where cherished moments and warm camaraderie intertwine amidst the wilderness-inspired ambiance."

Sonny raised her eyebrows, looking skeptical. "But how do you know?" she asked. "All these canoes look the same."

"Each one of these canoes serves a unique purpose," he said. "You're traveling alone?"

She nodded.

"Well then, that eliminates all the tandems. Tandems make up about eighty percent of what's in front of you. You want something you can manage and carry by yourself," he explained. "You'll be gone for several days?"

"Yes, a week," she replied.

"So you need a canoe that can carry the weight of everything you're bringing," Billy continued. "And from your questions, I gather you're not, what one might call, an experienced traveler." His toothy grin grew. "But I spend every day thinking about canoeing and water travel. If I had the means and the wherewithal, this would be the canoe I'd choose for myself—the Swift Prospector 14. It's the one you not only want but need. Especially when you need to portage; the light weight will make it easy to carry."

"Portage?" she asked.

"With a block in the river, if you can't get over it, you put the canoe on your back and carry it over land, around the block."

"What blocks rivers?"

"Trees, branches, brush—anything brought downriver. You'll need a saw."

"A saw?"

"Hand saw. We carry those," Billy said, pointing to a display. "Have you canoed before?"

"In scouts. On a lake," she replied.

"So it's been a few years," he said. "Which river are you traveling?"

"The Two-Hearted," she replied.

"Ah, that's a challenge," Billy said, his eyes squinting, then opening with excitement. "An equipment challenge. And the Swift Prospector 14 is the equipment you need to get started. It'll keep you upright in the rapids and be light as a feather when you lift it up. The only heavy thing on your trip will be your baggage."

He looked out of the window and saw her white minivan parked outside. Reliable, all-wheel drive, it was the perfect suburban vehicle. But it was no match for the wild north. "What else will you be needing for your expedition?" he asked.

"Everything," she said.

He grinned. "Very exciting," he said. "Very exciting indeed."

Sonny spent four hours with Billy, the outfitter. He was patient and kind, guiding her through every piece of gear she would need for her journey. She packed her food, dry clothing, sleep system, maps, and GPS into a red 30-liter dry-bag. A tight fit into the canoe, it would balance her weight on the moving waters. Billy even gave her a second maple angled paddle for cuts and turns at no charge. Her first paddle had a big fat face, which would give her more "umph" in every stroke. "The difference between 'try' and 'triumph' is a little more umph," Billy said.

"It will look beautiful strapped to the top of your Honda Odyssey." Billy showed her where to tie the canoe straps. He instructed how to keep them taut, how to loosen them, and what to look for before getting on the road. As she turned out of the parking lot and onto the main road, the orange safety straps flapped outside the windshield, like inflatables outside car dealerships. The fun of the distraction ended when she pulled into her driveway.

Her house had looked dark and empty ever since Mitch died, even in the late afternoon. The lawn... she remembered Mitch spraying the girls with the water hose on the lawn while they ran through sprinklers in the summer. He spent weeks each year walking back and forth behind the mower just to make the lawn look right. She would have to learn how to do that now. There were so many things she would have to learn to do alone.

The garage door opened with a click of the button. Sonny started to roll in, but the dancing orange ribbon caught her attention. Sonny slammed hard on the brakes. Her seat belt tightened and jerked her forward. She watched the Prospector 14 shoot past the windshield in a green flash, taking flight and breaking the orange strap. The vessel took a bounce off the cement garage floor and slid four feet before friction brought it to a stop. Putting the Honda in park, she leaned forward in disbelief. Her brand new, five-thousand-dollar Kevlar fiber investment had been only an inch away from total destruction.

Hitting the concrete steps at full speed would have shattered it. She sighed, disappointed in herself for daydreaming and not thinking things through. "Oh, Mitch," she said to the spirits. "You would have laughed at me pretty hard if you were here."

She backed up the Honda, then got into Mitch's Toyota Tundra and moved it parallel to the minivan on the drive apron. "Billy was right," she said out loud, lifting the Prospector over her head as she had practiced in the store. "It's light as a feather." Cautious, she took the Prospector to the back of the Tundra. Placing it in the bed, it seemed less likely to take flight. Her new pack went into the second door of the cab behind the driver.

Before first light, she would set out. The drive would take her five hours north to the Mackinac Bridge. In another ninety minutes, to Newberry, where she planned to spend the night. The next day she would find the drop-off point on the river, avoiding a nighttime search. Lumber truck trails and sandy winding two-tracks were how most roads in the north woods looked. It took a clear and rested mind to navigate. Taking on the river was not a task for the light-hearted.

"This is a bold new venture," she admitted to Mitch. "It's a reasonable risk, not like bullfighting or safari. It's canoeing. I did this as a brownie and a scout. How hard can it be?"

Sonny went back into the garage. She inspected her bicycle hanging upside down from the rafter. Mitch had hung it there years earlier to “save space.” Digging through the organized bike storage, she found the red metal box for pumping tires. Attaching the nozzle and reading the psi on the tire wall, she clicked until the number on the box matched. It started with a whir and buzz. It lasted about 90 seconds then shut itself off. She did the same for the rear tire. Then she did the old thumb test, pressing and feeling it as if she knew what to expect. The thick knobby tires reminded her of unfulfilled promises. They had purchased them to go mountain biking. Not some extreme sport of masochistic mountainside descent, but slow, light rides in the park.

As she walked the bike to the rear of Mitch's Toyota, her daughter pulled into the driveway. She drove a white VW Atlas that showed the rarity of a visit to the car wash.

"Mom," Evanora called as she got out. "Did you cut your hair?"

"I did."

Evanora exited and walked over to give her mother a hug. "It's short. I like it." She gave a closer inspection to the hairdo. In her hands, she presented her mother a clear plastic container with a snap lid and Evanora's name handwritten in black ink on a piece of white tape stuck to the side. Inside was warm lasagna that would take her mother more than a week to consume on her own.

"Thank you," Sonny said as she accepted the dish and placed it in the back of the truck bed.

"You look tired. Did you get any sleep?"

"Not for years."

"What are you doing?"

"Going on a trip."

“Did you rob a bank or something? Trying to get away?”

“Not exactly, just going on a trip.”

The two boys had already let themselves out of the back of the Atlas and were running across the yard. Spring meant mud, and it clung to the boys in little splattered clumps with each step. Sonny could already see the colors from dead leaves mushing into their blue jeans. This was their mother's problem, not hers.

"I can see that, Mom. Where? When? What are you going to do?" Evanora pestered.

"It's a canoe trip. I'm going on a canoe trip."

"Oh. With whom?"

"Myself, me, I."

"And where? Where are you going?"

"It's up north. I'll email you and your sister the details tonight to let you know where I'm going and when to expect me back."

"This seems rather sudden. It’s only been a week since the funeral. Why the sudden urge to canoe? I don't remember you saying anything about canoeing last week."

"Your mother needs to get away for a while, get some fresh air."

"Are you OK? Is everything OK? You know we can talk."

"Everything is fine, just adding a little adventure to my life." Sonny reached into the back of the truck. She had to stretch to reach the water bottle still in the holder on the bike frame. "This might come off; might as well keep it with me."

"What if I hadn't swung by with the boys? Were you going to go without a word?"

"I said I was going to email you and your sister."

"So, Glinda doesn't know? Canoe—it's, well, not what I would have expected. Don't you have to camp for that? Or do they have cabins on the river? Is it a river?"

"It's on a river, and there are no cabins. I'm camping."

"A tent? You're camping? Do you have a tent? A sleeping bag?"

Sonny stepped to the rear door of Mitch's truck and pointed to the red dry-bag and blue barrel Billy sold her. "Check, and check."

"What about food and water?"

"This is a water filter; rivers are made of the stuff. You just filter through here and it's safe. The outfitter sold me a barrel of food packs. I'm set."

"You know you have to be in decent shape to do something like that—you need to know how to do stuff and things to survive."

"They covered stuff and things in the scouts. I have a badge for both, and another badge for odds and ends. Would you like me to dig up my sash? I was the troop leader for you and your sister."

"Yeah, but Mom, scouts? Is that the resume you're going with on this trip? You might as well have said you watched a YouTube video, and that's all you needed."

"YouTube, good idea. I'll do that tonight while I write you and your sister an email."

"Mom." Evanora shook her head.

"Evanora." She mocked her tone and inflection. "What's

your point? You're implying I'm old and out of shape? I don't have the smarts for some time in the backwoods?"

All sheepish, Evanora replied, "Well, no."

"Your father and I talked about getting out and trying new things. I didn't want to wait another season. I decided to go. I've been prepping all morning with an expert."

"Going today?"

"In the morning. Tomorrow morning."

"Who will watch the house?" Evanora asked.

"The house will be fine. Don't worry about the mail. The advertisements and coupons will pile up and be here for me when I get back."

Sonny closed the door of the truck cab. She tightened the final strap and went back to the Honda to grab her purse and things to move them to the truck.

"You'll send me an email with the details?" Evanora asked.

"Yes, I will send you an email with ALL the details, Evanora. I'll have my cell phone if you need me."

"Does Glinda know?"

"No. I said that. Your sister doesn't know," Sonny said. A small smile of superiority crept across her daughter's face. Even as adults, the two were still siblings who knew how to push each other's buttons.

"Boys!" Evanora called. "Where did they go? Boys!"

The two came around the corner at full speed, caked in mud from the creek in Sonny's backyard. The Atlas was perfect for situations like this. The plastic-covered seats make for easy cleaning. The boys were like ill-mannered mastiffs, big and dirty and doing exactly what they wanted.

"All right then, thank you for stopping by," Sonny said as she hugged her daughter.

"Give your grandmother a hug goodbye."

"No-no. Thank you, boys, I'm good. Next time, before you play by the creek."

Unfazed by anything the adults said, the boys climbed into the back of the Atlas.

"Mom, be careful. I want you to come back safe," Evanora said.

"I will, I promise. Don't worry about me, I'll be alright."

The early spring morning was still dark when she cranked up the truck and prepared to point it north. The dashboard read 32 degrees Fahrenheit, indicating there'd be a chance of snow. That's why she bought the two dry suits from Billy. One was packed away, while she planned on wearing the other today.

As the heat came on, a wave of Mitch's scent filled the truck, making a lump form in her throat. This time, she couldn't resist. Hot salty tears, seasoned by all the years, began to stream down her face. The chill of the morning lingered in the cab, but that wasn't what was making her cold. She had two options: spend the next half hour moving everything back to the Honda, holding a much higher risk of spilling everything across the road on a hard stop, or get used to the truck and all that it carried. Sonny didn't wipe away the tears. She wasn't wearing mascara. Tears had a way of drying on their own. She would have plenty of time to herself on the road ahead.

Sonny backed out of the driveway and shifted to first gear. She switched to second and picked up speed, finding herself on the interstate headed north. What the rest of the day had in store for her, she couldn't say. Mitch had explained to the girls, "A journey of a thousand miles begins with a single step, but so does an unpleasant journey, or a journey into darkness, or a journey through a difficult path, or a journey into the unknown. The first step is always the hardest, but it is never the last step." Today, she made that first step.

Two

Sonny loved driving. She had taught Mitch to drive manual, and he had immediately taken to it like a horse to an open field. They had made it a point to teach their daughters how to drive a stick. On Saturdays, they always listened to the "Car Talk" radio program for mechanical awareness. "I'll take that with pride," she said to the spirit world. "No major accidents, and our vehicles have always been well-cared for." The little wins add up.

In Michigan, the farther one traveled north, the further one traveled back in time. The sun rose at 7:34 AM that day. Sonny enjoyed the pink and orange glow on her right. It marked the start of the sun's race across Lake Huron. As the sun peeked over the horizon, she crossed the Zilwaukee Bridge—a functional bridge that felt more like a rollercoaster with its dips and rises at 120 feet in the air. Each time she drove over it, she wondered if it might collapse, and if it would be better to take the long route around Saginaw. As a teen, "America," a song released by Simon & Garfunkel, mentioned it took four days to hitchhike from Saginaw to Pittsburgh. Saginaw "seemed like a dream." The Zilwaukee Bridge was a nightmare. The bridge had a reputation for being a fiasco: behind schedule, over budget, and loaded with fractures in need of repair. Unmarked landfills discovered during the construction of the ramps caused environmental damage. When Sonny was a little girl, she remembered a four-lane drawbridge that opened and closed for ships docking in Saginaw. Her father would let her out onto the stopped freeway to watch the ships pass from the railing. A great relief from sunny hours in the back seat of their Chevy. About the same time as that song came out.

Ten minutes past the bridge, Sonny decided to stop at the rest area before Pinconning. In summer, it would be bustling with people, cars, and dog walkers, all heading north to their cabins. But on that morning, it was only her and three semi-trucks letting their engines run at idle. Although Michigan was a four-season state, the early springtime seemed the loneliest. Before the snow melted or the blossoms and berries bloomed, everything looked murky. That first light and color starting her day were gone.

Sonny lumbered back to the truck, an image of Mitch and his half-cocked dream of penning a novel worming into her thoughts. This wouldn't be any ordinary piece of literature; it would scrutinize and appraise every last rest area lining the concrete veins of I-75. A whimsical concept let out with a sly chuckle; that was pure Mitch. He had joked, “Pure Mitch-igan” as a play on the state's television ads.

Half a decade back, Mitch had come barging into the parlor like a gust of wind. She was sitting, lost in the rhythmic dance of needle and thread, when he blurted out, "They've got a website up and running!"

"What website? Who on Earth are 'they'?" she queried, threading her needle through the eye of her confusion.

"Rest Area Ratings," he'd spat out before storming off in a huff. The whole time, he had been drumming up ideas in the quiet theater of his mind. Mitch always had plans.

It was a quick release of his frustration, but she knew. She knew most everything about Mitch. Given the time and opportunity, he would have traversed the north-and-southbound interstate from Sault Ste. Marie, Ontario, to Miami, Florida, stopping and rating every rest area along the way.

"Would you have brought me with you?" Sonny asked out loud. "Or was this going to be one of your adventures? You know, you thought of it before Google, before the internet."

Sonny sat for a moment, enjoying the comfort of the leather seat warmer. The Honda was too old for these luxury features. It still had an ashtray. Mitch was full of good ideas. She admired that about him but wished he would have acted on them more often; would have taken action.

At the last exit before the Mackinac Bridge, Sonny stopped for lunch at Audie's. It had been there for as long as she could remember, or at least the building had. It was where they would always stop to eat. Not much had changed since she was a little girl. She could still remember when they added the salad bar in the '80s. The counter where the register sat now had a card reader where there used to be a sign reading "cash and travelers checks only."

She scanned the menu, recalling Mitch's go-to open-faced sandwich and his jabs at her predictable whitefish order. Glinda and Evanora were more fickle with their choices. "I'll have the open-faced turkey sandwich, Teresa. Thank you," she requested.

When the piping hot dish arrived, Sonny felt a lump form in her throat. She blotted away a tear with the napkin. The turkey was moist and flavored, bathed in savory gravy and accompanied by real, creamy mashed potatoes. This was no prefab fare assembled from a warehouse delivery. Someone had crafted this meal in the kitchen. As she savored the tangy cranberry sauce, Sonny went back to her childhood dinners at her grandmother's Detroit home. The brick house, once her mother's childhood home, teemed with relatives every weekend. Wedged between her boisterous aunt and uncle, she jostled for space at the table, piled high with hearty fare.

"I get why you loved this sandwich," Sonny murmured to the spirits.

After inspecting the canoe and its straps in the truck bed, she hopped back in the cab. The radio played the Mackinac Bridge Authority station's historical spiel. On loop, it recounted the impossible feat of constructing the "Bridge That Couldn't Be Built." Sonny knew this bridge well. On Labor Day weekends, her family joined thousands of others in a pilgrimage across the strait, traversing the five-mile span on foot. Breaking from tradition in later trips, they bypassed the bus lines and walked the bridge from north to south. Next, they ferried to Mackinac Island for a quick jaunt before returning to the car. By day's end, the southbound traffic had thinned, and they returned home faster. It was always a fun day with the girls.

On the north side of the bridge stood Castle Rock, a jagged pinnacle that afforded a breathtaking view of the peninsula. Photo albums brimmed with snapshots of the girls posing in front of the Paul Bunyan and Babe statues. Then they went up 171 steps to the top of Castle Rock. Cowering atop the rock, which seemed to sway with the slightest breeze hundreds of feet above the interstate, photos captured the fear on each face.

M-123 was a winding two-lane asphalt road snaking through the vast Hiawatha National Forest. Spanning roughly 900,000 acres of pine and birch woods planted during the Great Depression, it made a great drive. This forest was on the cusp of its hundredth anniversary. "Every visit north felt like a trip back in time," mused Sonny.

"That pack is bigger than you," said a man in the hotel parking lot.

Sonny balanced herself with the red dry-bag on her back and tightened the shoulder straps. "Thanks, I'm good," she replied with a smile and small wave, making her way toward the hotel lobby. She had parked her Tundra next to a life-sized illuminated moose statue. She thought the light would deter anyone from tampering with the lock on her Prospector and mountain bike.

"We don't have a restaurant here, but there's a McDonald's across the road. They have the best internet in town," the front desk clerk informed her as she checked in.

With the key in hand, Sonny climbed up the stairs to the second floor. Each step felt heavier with the weight of her pack, but the room was clean and comfortable. Fast food wasn't her first choice, so she left her pack in the room and drove into town to explore other options.

Driving north off the parking lot, Sonny could see why the hotel desk called it "the valley." The road led down to the Tahquamenon River Valley, with miles of wilderness. Her dinner at the "family bar" on Railroad Street was slow to arrive but filling, causing her stomach to gurgle throughout the night. She woke and looked out the window twice during the night to check on the life-sized moose. It was doing its job watching over the truck.

The next morning, Sonny was the first in the breakfast nook. Her natural inclination was to help the woman set up coffee and eggs. Afterward, she put on her pack and climbed back into the Tundra. It was still dark as she headed north on M-123 toward a "road" labeled 500. The pavement ended when she turned and she knew in an instant that taking the Tundra had been the right choice. Sand, snow, and frozen mud welcomed her on the twisted trail. She followed the tracks from the previous explorer to avoid getting stuck and shifted into high four-wheel drive. The satellite radio lost connection eight times during the next thirty minutes.

As the road curved left, Sonny's attention went to a giant pool of muddy ice that covered a third of the road. Tire tracks had gone through the center, leaving it cracked like an icy broken shell of crème brûlée.

With a sudden, abrupt stop, Sonny mashed the brakes. Numerous items burst forth from under the passenger seat, scattering haphazardly. An imposing figure locked gazes with her, half-standing in the dusty road ahead. A formidable black bear was before her, with brawny legs and enormous paws. Its wide head was adorned with two rounded ears, akin to satellite dishes. The bear halted, its warm breath fading into the cool air. Nose lifted, it scrutinized the colossal machine Sonny was commanding. Curiosity ensnared the majestic beast.

As it sniffed at the vehicle's hood, the bear reared up on its muscular hind legs, front paws examining the company emblem affixed to the front. Under the beast's weight, the metal began to warp. It ascended further, striving to meet Sonny's gaze. A deep, resonant snort and a flick of its snout, merely feet away from the windshield, sent a wave of goosebumps cascading down her arms and spine. Razor-sharp claws grazed the sleek paint, marring the surface. The claw tips burrowed into the hood for better leverage. In response, Sonny hammered on the horn with all her might. Startled and now aware that this wasn't a meal but a frightening, noisy contraption, the bear thumped back down to the ground. The beast's paws were strong enough to bear its 400-pound weight and burrow through a beaver lodge. It gathered momentum, surging over a small mound, and melted away into the forest, soundlessly. The magnificent creature assimilated into the woodland's backdrop, vanishing from sight. Her heart hammered against her chest, serving as a potent reminder of the perils that lay ahead. Fear caused Sonny's forehead to glisten.

"So, that's a bear," she breathed out, her whisper barely audible. Her right foot eased off the brake while her left pressed down on the clutch, adrenaline coursing through her leg muscles. The truck lurched forward in first gear, inching about a hundred yards before she gingerly applied the brake and shifted into park.

In the footwell lay the bounty of her discovery, revealed by momentum. A metal box, an empty Faygo bottle, a clean pair of white underwear, and a tee shirt belonging to Mitch. Sonny picked up the box, surprised by its weight. With a click, she opened it to reveal the handgun Mitch had denied having, its clip full and secure in formed foam. Checking the chamber, she found a single round. Etched into the metal were the words "Glock 21 gen4 USA .45 Auto."

Returning everything to its place, Sonny muttered to the spirits, "We both had secrets." She took a deep breath and shifted the truck into gear, catching a whiff of Mitch's scent. She could sense him everywhere, haunting her like a ghost. But she had to be brave and push through the memories, for the task at hand awaited her.

The sign for Two-Hearted River State Forest Campground brought a sense of relief. Sonny wasn't lost. She could do this.

But as she turned onto the "road" marked 423, she muttered to the spirits, "'Campground' is being generous. They should include 'Rustic' in the description." This was the kind of place Mitch would have loved. A suspended wooden bridge crossed the river north to the dunes of Lake Superior. A hand-painted sign next to one of the two buildings read "Two-Hearted Chapel." But Sonny focused on the task at hand.

The sun higher. The air crisp. The grass slick underfoot. Sonny unlocked her bike and canoe. She lifted the mountain bike from the bed of the truck with care. Next, she found a trustworthy-looking tree off the path and locked it with a chain. It seemed hidden.

Driving to the drop-off, she noted key markers along the way: the tree full of hand-painted directional signs, a giant painted lumber mill saw blade, and the state Chris Brown Lake sign.

There was an inconceivable giant rock. It reminded her of one of her favorite movies, *The Princess Bride*, where "inconceivable" brought the classic quote, "I don't think that word means what you think it means." This she would remember as the Princess Bride Rock.

Finally, Sonny reached 407, the Pine Stump Junction—the blacktop leading to her drop point on the High Bridge. The truck made this trip easy. What waited for her around that next turn?

The High Bridge was once the crossing point. After the center pylon washed out sometime in the 1930s, the two remaining stone pylons remained. A group of men from the CCC cut a new road—the one she drove in on. These two tracks for the original bridge remained secluded. The good people of the north wouldn't bother the truck parked here while she dropped her canoe. It should be fine here for the week.

Standing on the concrete pylon's edge, the Two-Hearted looked fast. Sonny wondered if she was up for the river, as the river was up. She walked back to the truck, parked further off to the roadside, and removed the Prospector from the bed. Unleashed from the straps, it was easy to lift over her head. She navigated the loose rocks on the slope with care. The Prospector down on safe ground, she went back up the steep incline of the bank.

In the rear cab seat was her red dry-bag backpack. After retrieving this, a trip down to the canoe. One last trip and she removed the 30-gallon blue barrel with backpack-like straps. With this, she locked the truck. Sonny laughed when the alarm chirped, knowing only the bear would care.

A finger in the water and she was glad Billy had talked her into the taupe-colored dry suit. The putty color might hide some of the dirt and muck she was sure to fall in. The blue barrel found its spot in the front of the Prospector and the red dry-bag was placed behind her seat.

Getting into a canoe was hard and made one look ridiculous. Mitch would say, "You look like a monkey fucking a football." One last check of her life jacket, ball cap on, Sonny picked up her primary paddle and gave a push on the canoe. It didn't move. So, Sonny made a second attempt. It moved.

Friction stopped working against her once the Prospector got to the wet, soft bank. The nose dipped in and moved under her control with ease. The edge of the blade pushed deep into the mud bank. The nose pointed downstream, slipping into the cool waters, breaking the surface with the slightest *swish*. The real adventure was starting.

The water took over, causing a sway in her balance. Instinctively, she leaned the other way, fighting against the water's force. Her mistake was overcompensating; her weight was multiplied by all the gear.

Time slowed down during pivotal moments in life. Plunging into an icy river, one could reflect on many things. Some were regrets, such as, "Was this a good idea?" Others were more trivial, like, "This rubber suit is hot, but the cold water is refreshing." Significant memories stayed with you forever, such as the birth of a child or meeting a true love. Yet, at this moment, her thought was simple: "I should have bought a helmet."

Three

Everything stayed with the Prospector. It had been a good and loyal friend, as promised, the tie-straps proving their worth. After dumping out the water, Sonny found herself a yard downstream from where she had started. The blue ball cap she had worn on her neighborhood walks was now lost to the river. She hoped that some desperate camper might find it on a hot day when they needed it most.

Sonny reached into her dry-bag and pulled out a large-billed garden hat with a drawstring. It was squishy enough to fit into anything and would float if she capsized again. She knew there was no fooling herself; this would happen again. After inspecting the sore spot on her head, she confirmed that it was only a bruise with no broken skin.

With the canoe back in the water, Sonny did a quick check of her emergency gear before pushing off. Her hands frisked her torso. She felt the emergency knife strapped to her chest. The bear horn dangled on the clip. A bulge in her chest pocket, the orange satellite emergency beacon. Finally, the torso zipper pocket with her flint striker kit. All boxes checked. She dipped her paddle in the water and used the forward stroke to push off. This was followed by a J-stroke to gain momentum, slipping into the water's current. Within minutes, she had covered a significant distance. Much better than her last attempt. Her confidence grew as she began to gain control over the canoe.

Heading down the Two-Hearted River, Sonny appreciated the silence. She hadn't experienced this kind of quiet in a long time. The only sounds were the gentle lapping of the river and the noises of the north woods. No phone, no kids, no one asking for a sandwich or arguing with their sister. It was only Sonny and the river, her only friend the Prospector 14. The only thing that mattered was staying upright and dry, avoiding rocks and logs. Yes—physically demanding, it made it much simpler to focus on the moment at hand.

She could see the appeal her daughter's generation found in the age of modern expedition. Converting a van to live campsite to campsite while working remotely had a sense of romance. It was very American to want freedom and independence. It was less expensive than paying rent or utility bills. When your backyard is the National Parks or wooded beauty of the north, it's hard to consider anything else. She had seen videos posted on YouTube from through-hikers, van builders, and global sailors. Built on these experiences, there was always a boy or girl looking into the phone's camera, saying, "I will never be the same."

Smiles from sunburned faces who traversed thousands of miles declaring that something had transformed them to their souls.

Its seed germinated in the late nineties with Bill Bryson's *A Walk in the Woods: Rediscovering America*. Mitch had read it first. She had a pile of other books to read on her nightstand before that one. Its movie adaptation was more consumable, and who doesn't like Robert Redford?

Sonny approached a fallen red pine in the river. Its roots displaced a massive volume of earth on the bank that looked to Sonny like a half-opened can lid. The tree trunk lay half in the river, with branches jutting out in every direction. Sonny had to decide whether to try to make it over the trunk or to portage around through the muck and mud. She slowed the canoe, steadying the paddle, until the bow tapped the fallen tree. Her free hand snaked into her backpack and she retrieved the folding saw with its two-foot blade. Billy had been right; she needed it.

She secured the canoe alongside the tree. Sonny unfolded the blade and began clearing out the smaller branches. The green, gooey cuts told her that these branches were not suitable to save for the fire. She would need to find dry wood later on. With the branches cleared, Sonny worked the paddle to push the bow over the lowest section of the trunk. Next, she began to scoot the hull over the protrusion. When the Prospector 14 was solid in place a third of the way, Sonny stepped out onto the massive trunk of the red pine. She bent over to pull the canoe over the rest of the way. Life was now a delicate balance of brute force and grace. Her goal was to get over and move on. With a firm hand on the grip and shaft of her paddle, Sonny pushed off stern-first and floated down the river. Three well-timed draw strokes later, she was straight and true again. The tranquility of the lapping water and ripples in the Two-Hearted River gave her a sense of peace. This was why she had come to the river—to prove to herself that she could do something difficult and demanding.

Happiness shattered. She rounded the bend, a great red maple sprawled across the water, its bulk linking bank to river. Part of it bobbed in the current's embrace. Slowing her Prospector, she assessed the scene, eyeing the left bank where the tree bridged the river. A path lay beneath, requiring branch removal, fraught with danger—a falling giant could crush her. She paddled right, circling, contemplating her path. The trunk was wedged in mud, supported by the bank, and branches skimmed the water's surface, hinting at a passable route.

Again the saw blade moved back and forth, creating a mound of sawdust mixing with water in the boat's bottom. Sonny felt sore, unlike anything she had felt at home loading the dishwasher, gardening, taking walks, riding bikes, or moving Mitch's bedding. The burn concentrated in her shoulder and arms. She finished cutting the last of the larger branches and spotted a safe passage. The low centerline seat in the Prospector made it easier to lean back and go under the trunk.

She stored the saw away. Sonny took a few strong strokes and turned, attempting to align the canoe with the river. She allowed the water to carry her and adjusted her paddle and lean, almost succeeding.

The sound of a canoe's hull hitting the rough bark of a Michigan red maple was distinctive. The uneven, harsh, and grating sound of the Kevlar and gel coating against the tree's bark sounded worse than nails on a chalkboard. Its sound nullified any manufacturer guarantee in seconds. The rasping and intermittent high-pitched squeaks from the friction points along the canoe's skin, scraping against the unseen branches under the icy waters, sent chills up her spine. As she leaned back as far as her spine would allow, dead leaves rustled in her ears. The water lapped and rippled against the boat's sides, and her body shifted to see the progress she had made, causing the trunk to creak under the weight shift. A flop sweat broke out across her brow when she thought the tree was falling. Without warning, all the sounds and fury stopped, leaving only the water and breeze. She made it through. She would try to portage next time.

An hour before sunset, as darkness descended, Sonny needed to find a spot to camp for the night. Her progress was not as fast as she had anticipated. Looking at the map Billy sold her, she realized she was still a distance from the first campground. She needed a flat spot for her tent, or the right pair of trees for her hammock, and she needed a high landing from the waterline. Her day had been about taking time to get things right. Now, with the day ending, it was a race against the setting sun to find a dry and safe place. But where?

Four

Sonny could see the river continuing on through the trees. She cut the water with her paddle and turned toward the sandy bank of the river's peninsula. Her momentum carried her forward. She stood and balanced, then stepped out of the Prospector 14 into the shallow water. Gripping the bow handle with both hands, she lifted and leaned back with all her weight, heaving the canoe forward. With a second lurch, she landed. One of her kits included a rope and four small steel pulleys, each the size of a credit card and rated for 500 lbs. Sonny lashed the red nylon cord and two of the pulleys to the handle, sending the other end to a sturdy tree on the river's edge. Pulleys eased her work, locking her progress after each pull; the canoe inched up the sandy bank.

Sonny was warm and removed a layer to avoid sweating. Staying dry was important. This was one of the lessons from scouts that stayed fresh with her all these years. Get hot and perspire. Perspiration freezes, body temperature drops, and you get hypothermia. Taking off layers and adjusting is better.

She walked a few steps into the woods to find a fire ring and stone seating. Someone had made a nice resting space.

Setting up camp was Sonny's first priority. She decided to use the hammock sleeping system instead of a tent on the ground. Her first attempt at setting it up seemed off. Ten more minutes, the sun almost gone, it was close enough. Dry fallen branches and sticks were the next priority. Nothing bigger than her wrist, she remembered from her scouts camp, and she gathered what she could. Darkness had arrived. Her last few pieces were picked and cut from a dead white birch; the paper-like bark would make ideal kindling.

Hungry, tired, and the cold creeping in, Sonny put on her camp outfit. She hung the dry suit, socks, and pants inside out on the hammock line to dry. Sonny had lost the daily race with the sun and worked by the light of her headlamp. The hatchet from her kit split the sticks into small burnable pieces. The little mound of twigs that looked like a bird's nest sat there cold. She struck the flint stick again, making quick and short sparks, but nothing hot or lasting for the fire. Her motivation waning, she started to rub it in frustration rather than swipe it one stroke at a time. A cascade of sparks and light like July fireworks landed on the pile, igniting the nest. Huh? That's how it works. Her desperation subsided.

The freeze-dried pack of food came out of her kit, along with the tiny simple stove and cooking pot. Did she need the titanium utensils? No. But they worked great and saved weight. Once the water boiled, it went into the pack and was sealed. She would never tell anyone about the burn from touching the pot without a rag or the spill of boiling water on her leg. Three times the amount she would eat at any one normal meal, the Mountain Swedish Meatballs were salty and filling. She ate so fast, it felt like a rock sitting in her belly when she was finished.

The stone seating warmed from the fire. She thought to herself, *Whoever made this seating knew what they were doing.* She was off the ground and comfortable. Sonny watched the flames of the fire dance, feeling a sense of accomplishment from her day.

Sonny wanted to be like those fresh faces from the young generation on video exploring the world. She wanted to have a great adventure and see the world. That would take a lot more energy than what she had. So far, reality only made her feel every mile driven, each stroke paddled, and a sense of being wet and cold. That moment, the feeling of "I'll never be the same" still evaded her. Was it at the end of the river?

CLICK. A sound in the distance sent her heart racing. She looked in the direction of the sound. On her feet and back to the safety of the canoe, she clutched the bear horn tight. Her eyes searching the darkness, she walked backward to the stone seat and fire pit. *CLICK.*

Still, there was nothing and no one. "Paranoid? Or feeling guilty?" she said out loud. As she waited for something—anything—everything began to slow, and her adrenaline lowered. She sat on the warm stone seat, vigilant, watching into the dark woods.

Full belly, weary from the day's toil, she unzipped the hammock cover and settled, leaning back. For the first time, she raised her gaze. Stars adorned the sky. The entire Milky Way painted the night sky with dots reminiscent of Pollock's art. This was the reason for her journey. The beauty of the north woods defied her meager vocabulary. The air, pure and cool, offered rejuvenation.

"I know I am never alone," she uttered to the spirits. "There must be something more."

Daylight greeted her. It was the longest stretch of slumber she had experienced since Mitch's passing. The fresh air filled her lungs, and she cherished the moment.

CLICK. Something in the woods startled her. "Guilty," she said. It was time to move once more.

Clean, pack, filter water, change into the dry suit and gear. Reaching into the blue barrel, she retrieved several snack bars. She had neglected to do this the previous day, unable to find the opportune moment on the river. The crack in the plastic wrapper and unveiling of chocolate granola brought immense satisfaction. Quick and available energy had the potential to become addictive. Her body sought easy calories. But she limited herself to one bar for breakfast, reserving the rest for her day.

Grit coated the hull as the canoe glided into the Two-Hearted. A frosty mist hovered above the water, mimicking fog. She drifted through the haze with a sense of icy touch on her skin—almost like snowflakes, but in a gentle mist.

The Two-Hearted resembled the color of root beer. Rivers and waterfalls in this region owed their hue to the tannic acids borne by the cedar swamps. When little, the girls believed the nearby Tahquamenon River was made of root beer. In summer, the churning waters over the falls frothed and foamed, resembling the head on a glass of beer. Mitch suggested the girls bend down and take a sip. The two learned fast, valuable lessons. First, the Tahquamenon River was not a creation of Roald Dahl's Wonka Chocolate Factory. Second, their father possessed a brand of humor that aimed to teach them to think.

Sonny had always admired that aspect of Mitch. He challenged her to be less gullible, making it difficult for others to take advantage of her. When they first met, she found this quality attractive. Mitch was not one to agree to her every command. Some of the boys she dated perceived her physical allure as a form of mind control. They lost their ability to think for themselves, instead behaving like loyal dogs rather than men vying for her affections. All that seemed like a lifetime ago. She didn't even encounter Mitch until she was twenty-eight. The twins arrived two years later. Now, standing on the far side of the actuarial table contemplating a future without Mitch filled her with uncertainty. It frightened her more than unfamiliar noises in the nocturnal woods.

The early sun's golden glow, dissolving the frozen mist,

appeared enchanting. Two sandhill cranes, reminiscent of prehistoric creatures, stood on the riverbank, both adorned in crimson plumage. With a resounding honk and bugle, they seemed to convey, "Stay away, for this is my domain." Sonny had harbored a constant hope of sighting a common loon during her visits to the northern woods. The haunting, memorable cry of the bird in the morning ranked among her favorite sounds. Loons suffered from the cruelty of evolution. They needed water. With feet set far to the rear of their body, taking flight required vast lakes and open bodies of water. The Two-Hearted lacked the runway required for loons to land and take flight. Loons liked flat and glassy waters. The Two-Hearted churned and remained rapid between its banks. Nonetheless, there remained a glimmer of hope, as their calls could sound miles away. Tonight?

Sonny mistook it for a beaver dam. Beavers were well known to obstruct waterways and flood swamps, less likely on fast-flowing rivers like this one. As she drew near, the true nature of the obstacle became plain: a logjam. A colossal jack pine, too massive to perch on the sandy banks, had fallen across the river. Last season, she might have maneuvered beneath it. But this year, the larger limbs and driftwood had taken up residence in the shelter of the fallen pine.

Extending her blade, Sonny steered the canoe toward the shore, embedding the bow in the soft bank with a resounding slurp in the muck. It would have been a flawless landing if she were a pilot. Keeping her balance with the paddle, she made her way to the front of the canoe. Stepping onto the shore and tugging at the handle, she inched the Prospector higher up.

"Some folks prefer the bungee strap," she recalled Billy's advice. "I find the paracord tie to be more to my liking." Billy explained that the degradation of the material paracord was slower. It provided a stronger hold when tied right. Now, she needed to remember how to tie knots.

Her paddle and reserve secured to the thwart that spanned the two outer edges. These edges were gunwales, protruding outward to maintain rigidity. The removable and adjustable yoke rested on the centerline for her to carry. Billy had taught her a trick. Instead of having to adjust the yoke each time, they had measured it once in the store and marked the center with nautical tape. The yoke positioned on one gunwale, she could apply pressure to the opposite side—less than half an inch—and the yoke would snap into place.

Leveraging her leg muscles, Sonny hoisted the blue barrel on her back and embarked on the first trip. She traversed the towpath. She climbed the sandy ridge. Pine needles blanketed the forest floor. She was very careful to avoid the interlaced roots. It was a weighty load, but she could manage. Her bear horn at the ready, she remained vigilant, scanning her surroundings.

"Slow and steady wins this race, Mitch," she whispered to the realm of spirits.

When the river appeared clear, she followed the path to the

water's edge, intending to lower the barrel. But, upon arrival, she spotted another logjam fifty yards downstream. The proximity of the two obstructions seemed illogical. It would be more practical to traverse and portage such a short stretch.

"Howdy," a male voice called out.

Startled by the unexpected greeting, an involuntary release of pee occurred. Her hand instinctively reached for the bear horn, and she let out a brief blast. It wasn't until she realized the intruder was a man that her vise-like grip on the horn relaxed.

"Whoa. Whoa," he exclaimed, placing his free hand over his ear. "Didn't mean to startle you, ma'am." With his palm facing forward, he displayed a gesture of calm and friendship. His other hand gripped a chainsaw.

"Dear Lord," Sonny exclaimed.

"Bit jumpy? First time out here?" he inquired.

"How did you know?"

"Your equipment is still clean and in one piece. Must be her maiden voyage."

"First trip."

"Don't mind me. My place is a mile that way," he said, nodding to the right. "I cleared a path on the tree up there yesterday, but ran out of fuel. Thought I'd come back and tackle this one."

Sonny nodded. "Wow," she replied, still buzzing with adrenaline. "That's great. Thank you."

The two gazed at each other, unsure, looking.

"Well, why don't we switch? I need to get out there for the branches, and you need to retrieve your gear."

"Good idea." She stepped up and forward while he descended past her toward the tree. A scent of gasoline, oil, fresh cut wood, and the musky odor of an unwashed man filled the air. These aromas transported her back to last summer when Mitch mowed the lawn, trimmed the hedges, and worked alongside her in the garden. She hadn't realized how much she longed for that fragrance again. It possessed a potent allure.

Sonny placed the blue barrel by a large tree off the path. The small engine chugged with the first pull of the rope. On the second attempt, the chainsaw roared to life. Knowing there was another person nearby put her at ease. The noise would deter bears. The return trips with her dry-bag and the Prospector were quicker than the first. She could hear the man sawing through the branches. The high revs were a signal of the destruction of wooden fibers. On her third trip, she found the perfect balance with the yoke. The canoe felt lighter than the previous two journeys but remained unwieldy. Overhanging branches proved difficult to pass. Roots on the path seemed to reach out like “hand-mines,” grabbing at her toes, entangling her feet in an attempt to enforce the penalties of gravity. Gravity always wins in the end. The ornery trees were no different from the apple trees Dorothy faced in Oz.

The sound of sawing ceased by the time she reached the water's edge with the canoe, the barrel, and pack fastened. With her paddle in hand, untied and at the ready, she heard the man call out, "That's a mighty fine boat you have there."

"Thank you."

"Stick to the far bank on the left. You should navigate past that tree. You can't see it from here, but it's a clear passage."

"Thank you. Thank you for clearing the trees."

"You take care now."

Sonny felt a sense of unease and impoliteness for not inquiring about his name or offering her own. His gray hair and beard, along with his calm demeanor, suggested he was a decent man. Still, she had to focus on her own interests here. Engaging in a conversation with a stranger would cost her time. Although pleasant, it would steal time from the remaining daylight.

"Thanks! You too. It's going to be a great day." She pushed off, floating a few feet, sliding into her seat, and began to paddle.

"Stay to your left, on the left," he called out.

She started to discern the opening he had described, and lifting her paddle, she called back, "Thank you, I see it."

He was right. It was clear and safe. “Should I have befriended that man? Would that have been part of my transformation from exploration?” she asked Mitch, who never answered.

Five

There was a happy dream Sonny wished for each night. Finding the rustic campground and depositing five dollars in the dropbox, she ate dinner after setting up camp. Swinging in the hammock and looking up to the galaxy, she hoped to dream that dream again.

Engulfed by a blend of hope and unease, Sonny found herself navigating a surreal landscape. The hope stemmed from the emotions evoked by this enigmatic dream, yet the fear that it might be her last loomed. As if from a distant, celestial realm, Sonny found herself returning home—a place both comforting and familiar.

Here, beloved aunts and uncles, childhood friends, and neighborhood acquaintances beckoned her, eager to share the transformations that had unfolded since her last sojourn. The discontinued Faygo Rock & Rye pop she adored in childhood filled the garage fridge, the scent of her mother's signature meatball dish wafted from the kitchen, and her father, pipe in hand, perused the newspaper in the living room, peeking over its edge to offer a warm smile and wink. A palpable sense of love and security permeated the air, promising a solace that felt real.

This sanctuary existed just around the corner, at the next bend, or behind a door, if only she could unlock it. Immersed in an intricate web of love, a potent spiritual energy enveloped her, guiding her onward. Upon awakening, the lingering after-glow from this ethereal visit suffused her life for weeks.

It had been ages since Sonny last experienced this dream, or even one similar. It had graced her slumber only three times in her life, a potent force that consumed her. She guarded it at arm's length. It echoed the descriptions found in near-death experiences. She couldn't help but ponder if death enticed the living toward a final light, flooding their senses with intoxication.

As more friends and family took up residence in this transcendent realm, their voices swelled into a chorus, calling to Sonny like the sirens of myth.

CLICK. Waking from the noise, Sonny told herself that it's the woods. Nothing had followed her this distance to eat her or attack. She was safe, cocooned in the warmth of her hammock. Billy had sold her the whole system, which included the extra padding, wind screen, mosquito net, rain flap, and cover. In one moment, she knew she was a hanging human Twinkie waiting for some bear to discover her and treat her like a piñata. In the next, she was off the ground and hard to reach for most critters to care.

Her eyes opened a few minutes before the sunrise, at her circadian rhythm. She started to do the math in her head to answer the question, "What day is it?" A day of travel, half a day to start, camping on the river's peninsula, and then yesterday. She had taken two days to get to where she wanted to be after the first. Her muscles sore, joints stiff, she was going to need momentum to get out of the hammock. She needed the first movement to get going. "Oil can," she quoted the Tin Man.

Unzipping the one layer, she could feel the cold creep in. It motivated her to get moving. Her legs were fine; it was her arms and shoulder that were the problem. Once the dry suit was on, things started to warm up again. On the floor of the woods, soft pine needles cushioned her knees on the earth. She began to stretch and warm up. A salute to the sun, downward dog, hip flexor, and butterfly, and Sonny was ready for the rest of the day.

The water pot she had put on the fire before her stretch was now boiling. Breakfast included the cinnamon oatmeal packet with her banana. The simple hot meal filled her with warmth and energy.

Her blue barrel packed fast. The dry bag closed with a click. The Prospector 14 rolled over with all the needles and overnight passengers evacuated. Snapping her life vest and checking her essentials, she looked downriver and thought, *This is going to be a good day.*

Minutes down the river, Sonny allowed her mind to time travel. They had decided to avoid any class reunions. People only got weirder with age. He didn't know anyone and played the supportive husband. She didn't know anyone in his class and played the dutiful wife. Decades later, those they did remember carried some unnecessary emotional baggage. He did this. She did that. One time they said that... It had always reminded her of a popular song by the Doobie Brothers when she was younger, "What a Fool Believes." That whole summer after it came out, she thought it was romantic and wonderful, being a fool for love. Reading the lyrics on the album changed that quickly. The "fool" was one of those boys she went to school with. Boys who always thought there was something more, when she hardly knew them, or remembered their names. At each reunion, they would come to her and explain something imagined between them. How they held a moment of silence the day she and Mitch married, knowing she was no longer available. Polite and patient, she would smile, nod, and give Mitch the signal. He always saved her from the awkward moments. She would miss that. Losing that one thing made her feel alone more than anything else in the world. It was something she might never be able to recover or recreate. Like a million little moments, there could never be anyone like Mitch.

All the drama helped Sonny appreciate what her girls were going through as they grew up. "Things were different back then" was a sentiment she often heard, but she didn't agree.

Under the age of twenty, everything seemed heightened. Feelings, passions, ideas, growth spurts, changes, but that's just growing up.

It was the intensity that seemed amplified for the young girls. As a child, Sonny had perceived it as the result of peer pressure and the need to fit in with the right clique. For the twins, the judgments were harsh and unyielding—if a girl didn't eat, she was anorexic. Overweight? Labeled morbidly obese. If she had slept with a boy, branded a whore. If she had never kissed, a prude. It required adherence to the perfect beauty routine. They must dedicate more time and attention to attire. Her girls got subjected to a myriad of social pressures. Similar to her experience, but more intense for the twins.

Sonny remembered the first time she quoted her mother, "I am not your friend, I am your mother. My job is to make sure you're better than me."

It surprised Sonny. She understood it completely in an instant. Once the words left her lips, she knew her mother was right. She called her mother an hour later and thanked her.

"You're welcome."

"It's tough being a good mom. How did you do it?"

"You weren't as difficult as you think. You were more of a molehill girl than a mountain."

It brought a smile to her face to think about her mom. What would she think of this adventure? Her paddle stroke pushed her forward around the bend to face another chance for portage.

The Two-Hearted held many turns. It made the distance

longer than the straighter rivers in the lower peninsula. It reminded her of one of those odd "fun facts" that Europe's coastline is 2-3 times longer than Africa's. Having fewer ports to support shipping kept Africa from being seafaring. Other parts of the world, with more natural ports, advanced to the waters, creating empires from navigable opportunities.

Having set down the blue barrel, she returned for the red dry-bag. That's when it happened—a hand-mine. Her ankle caught on a protruding root, sending her plummeting forward with no control. Instinctively, she stretched out her hands, hoping to save her teeth and avoid breaking her nose. Her hand reached out, and while falling, she heard the distant call of a loon echo, signaling the presence of a lake nearby.

Her eyes fluttered open, lashes sweeping dirt away. The metallic taste of iron from blood filled her mouth. Something had gotten cut or broken. Then, the familiar sensations of searing pain and electric jolts coursed through her nervous system to her brain. Her ankle, twisted and bruised, a consequence of her momentary lapse in attention. As for her wrist—was it sprained or broken? And what of her head—bruised or lacerated? She couldn't be certain. How long had she been out?

Six

It was surprise. No, shock. Wait, or was this confusion? Sonny cried out in frustration, furious at her own negligence that had led to this predicament. A momentary lapse in attention. Stupid. She began to squirm, maneuvering her body until she lay on her back, her face liberated from the dirt. The once comforting, earthy scent of pine and soil had lost its charm.

Pain radiated from various points on her body—her head, ankle, arm. She felt fortunate. She had escaped a serious injury like a bruised rib or broken neck. Despite the pain, she considered herself lucky.

Sonny lay on her back on the trail, halfway between the blue barrel and the red dry-bag. Which one held the medical kit? She shut her eyes, imagining and playing the day back, recalling the morning's packing. Not long ago, she had been optimistic about the day ahead, self-congratulatory, boasting about the benefits of her stretching routine. Now, the second wave of pain was setting in, the type that lingers long after the adrenaline has worn off.

A flash of past experiences—standing at a bus stop in biting winter cold, the wind slicing through her jacket at eight years old. Two years later, the first day at a new school, standing on the playground looking down at her legs, noticing they were hairy, embarrassed and ashamed. An unsettling tumble from her bike, the embarrassment of being different. She had always told her girls to pick themselves up; to push through the discomfort. "You are fine. Get back up."

She had to sit up. The movement was as simple as bending at the waist. She felt something warm trickle down her forehead. Bird droppings? Pine sap? Touching it, her fingers came away stained with blood.

The fleeting embarrassment subsided. She began to think. The blue barrel held the ropes and pulleys that could aid her mobility. It also contained food and water to sustain her. The red dry-bag held the emergency beacon and cell phone. If she could reach halfway, she could go all the way. The plan remained the same: red dry-bag first, then the blue barrel, then the Prospector.

She examined her wrist—was it broken or sprained? She pulled back the sleeve of her dry suit. Her fingers still moved—good. The bone was straight—good. The wrist was tender and turning purple. Her left foot throbbed with pain at the slightest movement.

"Here goes," she whispered to the wilderness. Sonny flipped over onto her stomach. With her elbows bent to protect her hands and wrist, she nudged herself forward. Right knee, push, move forward, shift hip, left knee, push, move forward. "A hundred more like that."

At this level, she noticed an early season mushroom. It was a detail she missed on the first trip and would have missed in each passing. To distract herself from the pain, she told herself a story. She thought about the Northwoods Giant Fungus from Michigan. A fungus the size of a blue whale, one single organism that was 2,500 years old and spanned 180 acres of Michigan forest. What was it called? The Armadillo? How was she going to remember it? Jerry Garcia? The Armillaria gallica. This story spilled over to another. The ant "supercolonies" that divided North America. Entire states of ants working together, unified in efforts, clashing with rival factions. And the poor fool in the story who built a house on the front line of the two fighting factions. He lost it all. She needed to be an ant.

Almost there. I can make it.

Seven

A bit further. One more nudge, two. "I have this within me," Sonny reassured herself. She hauled herself up the side of the Prospector 14. The red dry-bag, she remembered—hope. Using all her strength, she tipped the canoe on its side until it disgorged the red dry-bag onto her. She rolled aside, allowing the bag to rest on the ground. Within a few clicks, it opened and spread out. Her arm reached inside, feeling the useful items she craved to access. With a sigh, she faced the harsh truth. The medical kit was in the blue barrel.

The palm-sized orange satellite emergency beacon was in the red dry-bag. Hope. She had removed it from her dry suit's zipped pocket the day before to make room for more energy bars. *I am going to be okay.* She turned the beacon on by pressing the power for two seconds. She could see the simple black-and-white display come on. It buffered. A yellow light turned on. Its bars indicated full power. Each letter scrolled across the little low-definition screen. The message said "Welcome." *I am going to make it. Things will be fine. Stay calm.* "Please call our service number or visit our website to subscribe."

"What? WHAT? WHAT THE FUCK? You have to subscribe for service!" Her vulgarity echoed across the waters, sending two mallards to flight in fear.

Pain brought her priorities back in order. The yelp had strained something, creating a sharp headache. She ripped her pristine white cotton underwear, reserved for the journey home. One half—the elastic band and cotton prepped to fasten over her head. First, she plucked the foil hand sanitizer packets from a side pocket. Holding a small travel mirror, she put on a brave face before confronting her reflection. The face staring back was unfamiliar. She wished she had spared herself the sight. Using the "clean" water from her drinking bottle, she dampened a sports bra, also reserved for the trip home. She dabbed at the dried blood on her forehead. She cleaned her face as best she could. *How did I hit my head in the same place twice on one trip?* She opened a foil hand sanitizer packet and cleaned her hands. Another foil packet opened, and she braced for the inevitable sting. The pain forced her breath into short, sharp gasps, pained moans escaping her lips. But it still didn't measure up to childbirth. The clean underwear, fastened tight around her head, provided pressure. It would shield her from most dirt during her return trip.

"Ugh," she vocalized her frustration. "How am I going to

manage this, Mitch? I'm not sure I can make two trips, and I doubt I can haul it all in one."

The sun had retreated behind the clouds, bringing a chill to the air. The wind picked up. Sonny retrieved the map from inside the canoe.

The scooching technique proved least painful and most effective. Submerged in the chilly river, the flow of water around her legs provided a soothing massage. The temperature in her dry suit began to drop. The coolness offered relief to her injured ankle. She toyed with the idea of slicing off the dry suit leg to let the cold take over. Her emergency blade snapped back into place on her chest when she decided against it. She knew that indecision could be perilous. This only made her question each choice more.

Splashing about in the water like an overgrown child, Sonny began to assess her situation. She tried to muster clarity and focus. A paddle could serve as a crutch or a splint. A stick could also be a splint. Her folding saw, a green sapling the diameter of her thumb, could be cut for the splint. Stripping the bark in long cuts, she could weave fresh bark into a makeshift rope.

Returning to the Prospector 14, she extracted her reliable folding saw. Next, she scooted back into the woods where she found two saplings about the right size. After a few minutes of sawing, both trees fell, and she returned to the comforting muck of the river. Her injured leg went back in the water. The distraction of activity kept her mind off her wrist, though there was an occasional reminder that flashed, urging her to handle it with care.

With steady hands, she cut a quarter-inch wide line along each sapling. Once her pile of strips was complete, she took four slices and began a simple weave. This was like her friendship bracelets at camp. After about thirty minutes, she had created several feet of sturdy twine.

Next, Sonny's attention turned to the splints. Using the saw, she transformed the two stripped saplings into four equal lengths. She fixed them tight, not taut, to avoid cutting off circulation. She flexed again. Her stretching was not the usual morning routine. Instead, it was an effort in strapping the four matched pieces to her leg above and below the ankle under the icy water. Her final binding secured below the knee.

With the task accomplished, she felt a sudden decline in everything. Her energy, adrenaline, and motivation all plummeted. She shut her eyes for a moment. Just a moment. She reclined for a moment. Just a fleeting moment. Her legs, submerged in the water, felt quite alright. Her breathing slowed. Everything seemed fine, simply fine.

Sonny's eyes snapped open. Night had fallen. How long had she been unconscious? Or was it sleep?

Eight

Her leg, now numb, trailed behind as she attempted to inch toward the Prospector. Rolling over, she resumed her slow crawl. In the darkness, she reached the canoe. Her hand floundered inside for a snack bar but found nothing. In the uncertainty of the night, Sonny groped for the red dry-bag. "A strap!" She tugged it toward her, patting the sides until her fingers stumbled upon her secret stash. Tearing into the plastic wrapper, she crammed half the bar into her mouth. The rich, gooey chocolate, sweet and decadent, melted under the warmth of her tongue. The satisfying sensation of her molars grinding down the larger chunks was a delight she hadn't experienced in a while. That last bit of sustenance could carry her through the moment. The sensation of satiety tricked her mind into believing she had more reserves than she actually did.

She recalled an episode of RadioLab she and Mitch had once tuned into. It was about ultra-runners who deceived their bodies with a few drops of sugar water to endure the long nights. It was all a matter of the mind leading and the body following. That was an enjoyable long weekend with Mitch. Before the sadness, late nights, quarrels, and complications set in.

As she savored the final traces of chocolate sliding down her throat, she considered the second half of the protein bar. She ought to save it for the morning, ration her meals. But hadn't she earned this? If there was ever a moment in her life when she deserved a treat, it was now. A little nibble, a long lick of the outside—how she wanted to cheat. Logic intervened. There might be a more desperate moment between now and then when this meager sustenance would be vital. And so, she rewrapped the remaining half in its plastic shield. She tucked it into her pocket where the useless satellite beacon should have found a home but was now only dead weight.

Had the sun recently set? How long till morning? She reached into the red dry-bag again and pulled out her phone. She switched it on, watching the boot-up graphics. No bars. No signal. The clock read a quarter past nine. She had been out for a good six hours, lying half on the trail, half in the river. The next question was whether to relieve herself in the dry suit or attempt to remove it in time.

There was no modesty. Who would she be modest around? In one of the articles she read, it said she was more likely to meet a moose than a human on the river. The chainsaw man may have exceeded those chances.

She tugged at the hook and loop fastener to access the XX heavy-duty zipper. Billy had waxed the zipper for her in the store. It should move with ease. The dry suit was now loose. Billy's advice had proven invaluable. She'd been comfortable throughout the trip thanks to all this gear.

With her trusty paddle in her good hand, Sonny steadied herself. Her fingers traced the gunwale of the canoe until she found herself upright. Rising on her uninjured foot, she tested her weight. A good sign—not broken.

She fished out the little red flashlight from her pocket, the one with the magnetic end and hat clip. Sonny pulled the hat string tight. It had been dangling around her neck since she lost her ball cap at launch. She put it on, mindful of the makeshift bandage. The flashlight's clip slid onto the brim of the hat, providing a guiding light in the night that freed her hands. Now she could see where she was going.

The pressure began to mount. With careful deliberation, she moved toward the nearest tree sizable enough to bear her weight. The forest teemed with such trees. She faced away from the tree, letting her dry suit and hiking pants fall to the ground, followed by her underwear. Closing her eyes and taking a deep breath, Sonny leaned backward in a trust fall against the tree. The angle was steeper than anticipated and awkward. She adjusted her footing until it felt right. The ensuing release was the most satisfying sensation she could recall. The only sound was that of liquid hitting the ground, clear of her dry suit.

The relief, the sugar from the protein bar, and the accomplishment of those first steps filled her with renewed determination. "I can do this. I will make it," she assured herself. Reality intruded soon enough. The toilet paper was in the blue barrel. She was leaning against a tree without the strength, or the means, to stand back up. Any attempt might further injure her ankle. She couldn't risk dropping the paddle. She couldn't bend down to retrieve her pants or dry suit without it. Yet the flashlight still worked. She could see all the other trees she hadn't chosen. They stood silent and indifferent in the darkness. Looking down, she noticed the base of the tree sloped. Everything had run down, pooling at the bottom where the dry suit, pants, and panties rested. Gravity always wins. "Get back up," she murmured to the spirits of the woods. It was her mantra for her daughters, and a reminder for herself.

Positioning the edge of her paddle at the base of the tree, she pushed forward as if to take a powerful stroke, leaning ahead. The combined effort managed to lift her off the tree. As her instinct to stand upright took over, the pain returned. The splint held fast, aiding her to her feet. Bending at the knee, she stooped. Extracting her emergency knife, she cut the waistband of her $39 panties. She flung the sodden cotton into the wilderness. With her pants pulled up, she was going commando. Pulling the dry suit back on, her arms slid into the sleeves. Warmth crept back into her body. Paddle in hand, Sonny made her way back to the Prospector 14.

This was the reality she had signed up for. She was aware of the risks, the harrowing tales, yet she had thought this was a good idea. This was her fight now, alone in the wilderness. "I can do this, right?"

Nine

Billy had given it to her straight. Dragging the canoe was a big no-no. Yes, there were some good types of scratches on the hull that would testify to the adventure she would endure. Those were trophies of accomplishment. Rocks and branches in the water could do that. But there were also some nasty marks that could weaken the hull, rip the gel coat right off the thing. Those were the marks of the idiot—the idiot who dragged their canoe over land instead of taking the time to portage it; hoist it up on their shoulders like a real outdoors person. That was the right way. Billy had high expectations for Sonny, but now she was looking like a first-rate idiot.

All that mattered was the blue barrel. Sonny refused to get distracted by time or the darkness. She held the paddle in her good hand like a prized possession, while her bad hand clutched the bow deck handle. Lifting with her legs, she propelled the Prospector forward, one step at a time. The sound of friction on the dirt and pine needles filled the air, interrupted only by the occasional rough crunch of roots or the thud of the canoe dropping. She kept moving forward.

Sonny resisted the urge to look at her phone or check her watch. Time had no meaning in this universe. Only the blue barrel mattered. Her head turns and steps revealed a world that existed only in 50-yard slices, illuminated by the 1500 lumen light on her head. The reflective eyes of creatures watched her from the darkness, surprised by this crazy woman trying to prove herself. She imagined their thoughts before they galloped or crawled away. She entertained the idea of capturing a few of them, lashing them together, and training them to carry her forward. Such thoughts were distractions from the pain.

Many of these mammals were thirsty, longing for cool water from the river. But strange Sonny scared them off, and so she continued on alone, focused on reaching the blue barrel.

The world began to expand, unfolding between the dawning light and the enclosing darkness. Sonny's flashlight seemed less significant. The river resurged into her perception, its roar and murmurs trickling over the rocks. The water's motion was dominant, surging along its meandering course with tremendous force. Sonny had passed the halfway point where she had fallen, unnoticed. The smooth pine and earth path, the rough terrain with jutting branches where her canoe scraped and pushed forward, consumed her attention and focus. She hadn't imagined completing the journey in one go. But there it was.

"Where's the barrel?" she questioned the spirits, as though they would even bother to answer. The canoe now returned to the Two-Hearted, she surveyed the surroundings with her light to find evidence of a bear. The blue barrel had disappeared in the countless hours. *No point in calling for it like a lost pet,* she thought. Her phone had no signal; not even a tracker would do any good. She hobbled into the dark, ten yards from the trail, pursuing what she believed to be tracks.

The trail began with the bag holding the rope and pulleys. A few yards away, her tent and poles rested, followed by the hammock, stove, and medical kit. With the flashlight now in hand, she scanned the woods, but nothing else came into view. A few more steps, another scan at the edges of the light, nothing else.

She could feel her energy wane. Her enthusiasm was on a quick decline without finding more food. "Take only memories, leave only footprints," she muttered. Sonny bent down to pick up the litter the thief left behind. She traced her steps back, collecting each item, until she reached the rope and pulleys. From there, she gazed at the first light of morning reflecting on the water. Beyond it, in the distance, she imagined Lake Superior's pink and blue skies. Gulls and terns danced against the ceaseless winds.

She went first for the painkillers in the medical kit, the ones prescribed to Mitch in his final days. The ones that the pharmacist had reminded her not to flush or discard down the sink or toilet. The ones she had tossed in the kit "just in case." She swallowed two with water. After a while, she realized the pain persisted, but she didn't care. She didn't give a damn about her leg or wrist, the things she needed to do to survive, or how many days had passed. She recalled the half snack bar in her pocket as she fumbled with the zipper, then fumbled to unwrap it. It remained intact, warmed by the heat of her body during the night's journey. As she sat on a log, gazing across the river's expanse, she pondered when would be the ideal moment to consume it. Famished, was it enough to warrant devouring it? Or should she save it for later? As the drug-induced apathy continued to grow, gravity seized hold of the snack bar, causing it to plummet to the earth, mingling with the soil and pine. She looked down to where it fell. A lithe brown chipmunk bolted toward her. It snatched the remnants and dashed off five feet before turning to face her. The plucky creature nibbled away at the bar's edges for a spell. She couldn't catch it even if she desired to, and she had no intention of doing anything but sit there. Sonny reminisced about the chocolate from the night before. She thought on the caramel's gooeyness and the nuttiness's crunch. Her mouth began to water, and spittle sprayed out as she cried out, "Hey, that's mine!" But it was too little, too late. Her words reverberated to the world, sending the rodent scurrying into the dark woods.

The rough surface of the log proved to be far from hospitable. Exhausted, she yearned for slumber. So she gathered her belongings and stowed them inside the canoe. Instead of preparing for departure downstream, she fashioned a cozy sanctuary by arranging her possessions into a makeshift bed. She then nestled herself atop it and descended into sleep, asking, "Will I ever be the same as before?"

Ten

The world materialized before her, regaining its recognizable form. It appeared distant and hazy; was it "the dream?" Male voices murmured in the background, engaged in a conversation about fish. Sonny became aware of her surroundings. With effort, she pried open her crusty eyelids, revealing a timber beam ceiling. She found herself lying in a bed. Attempting to turn her head proved futile. Was she tied down? Captive?

"Looks like Snow White has finally awakened from her slumber," quipped the muffled voice of a man.

Leaning over her, a man's face came into view, peering down at her. "Hello, Ms. White. I'm Doc. That one's Bashful, and the other is Sleazy."

The other voice corrected, "Sneezy!"

"I... I can't turn my head to see them," Sonny managed to respond.

"We've immobilized your neck and bandaged your head. You had a substantial bump when we found you," explained the man.

"Where am I?" Sonny inquired, her voice filled with confusion.

"You are in the finest established hunting cabin in the Great Lakes. I am Pike, and the other voices you hear belong to Riker," the man replied.

"Hello, ma'am," Riker added.

"And the other one is Ranger," Pike continued.

A mumble escaped Ranger's mouth, resembling a greeting of sorts.

"What happened? How did I end up here?" Sonny asked, her curiosity piqued.

"We were about to ask you the same thing. How are you feeling?" Pike questioned, concern lacing his voice.

Pike placed a small flashlight in front of her, examining each of her eyes. "I must say, you have beautiful eyes to match that stunning hematoma," he remarked, before clicking off the light. "Riker, I'm going to remove the cervical collar."

"I concur, doc," Riker agreed.

Sonny breathed a sigh of relief. "Oh, thank God, a doctor," she uttered.

"Well, not technically a doctor, ma'am," he walked back the comment. "But the honorable members of the U.S. Marine

Corps ensured I received training for medical emergencies," Pike clarified.

A ripping sound resonated in the air as the hook and loop fasteners of the restraint were undone.

She felt Pike's weight shift as he settled on the edge of the bed beside her. "Just relax," he reassured her with a soothing and charming voice. "I'll check a few things while you lie there." His rough fingers touched her wrist, assessing her pulse. It had been quite some time since anyone had touched her.

"Please open your mouth."

Sonny complied.

"And close."

Another click, and the light returned, now focused on her injury instead of her eyes. "Nice stitching, Riker. Clean," Pike complimented as a beep signaled in the background. Within seconds, a series of beeps followed. He prompted her to open her mouth, allowing Pike to retrieve the thermometer. "Normal temp. Ms. White, your dwarfs are delighted to report that you're going to be fine," Pike informed her.

"Please, call me Sonny. Seems like I'm gonna run out of 'thank yous' with you three," she remarked.

“Sonny. Huh? I thought you’d smile more with a name like that.”

“Yeah, most people make that mistake.”

"Well, you're gonna be fine, Sonny," Pike reassured her. "You can sit up if you want, but take it slow and easy."

Assisting her, Pike helped Sonny sit up and swing her legs

over the edge of the bed. She found herself in a rustic hunting shack. A single room adorned with postcards, photographs, advertisements, pin-up girls, Skoal tin lids, and calendars covering most of the timber. It seemed like the place was built and decorated starting in the 1920s. "You boys look a little too young for the likes of Betty Grable, don't you think?"

"Betty Grable. Nice gams," remarked Ranger.

"Betty Boop, what a dish," replied Pike.

Sonny's curiosity piqued as she tried to recall how she ended up here. "How did I get here? Last I remember, a chipmunk was making off with my granola bar."

"That must have been one helluva chipper to give you a goose egg like that," Ranger quipped.

"No." Sonny's brow furrowed at the odd thought. "The chipmunk didn't—"

"I was about to say, that sounds rather unlikely," Pike interjected.

"I've been traveling the Two-Hearted River these past few days. You know, taking in the scenery and whatnot. Then, out of the blue, I stumble and take a nasty tumble, twisting my ankle and bashing my noggin. And, well, I suppose you stumbled upon me in that sorry state," Sonny explained.

"We couldn't help but notice your crafty ankle adornment. I took the liberty of replacing it with a shiny aluminum version. Our astute comrade Riker stumbled upon a mysterious blue barrel bobbing its way downstream, filled to the brim with all sorts of goodies. With his years of skills and training, he tracked its origin upstream, and lo and behold, there you were, out, lost in dreamland," Pike stated.

"We used your canoe as a stretcher to carry you here," finally spoke Riker.

"Well, Riker and I carried you. Ranger here isn't ready to shoulder that burden. He's still a growing boy," Pike said, glancing at Ranger.

"Hey, is that a short joke?" Ranger responded, standing up from the card table.

"Whoa." Sonny realized that he hadn't been standing that whole time. When he did straighten up, he had to stoop to avoid hitting his head on the rafters. "You're quite tall."

"Straight and to the point. I appreciate that in a woman," Pike quipped. "Ranger stands at a towering six feet, seven inches, Sonny. He's part of the 'less than one percent' in the world."

"You don't give him one of those ironic nicknames like Tiny? Shorty?" Sonny inquired.

"Nah, nah, they called me that in the Army. I don't go for that shit," Ranger replied.

"Riker and I call him Ranger. He served in the Army, where the boys go to play war. Marines have to live it," Pike taunted like an older brother.

"Well, military humor," Sonny replied. "Thank you for carrying me here. And thank you for finding me."

"Riker, why don't you rustle up some grub?" Pike suggested. "Our guest must be starved from fighting off wild chipmunks. You stay put for a while," he instructed Sonny. "Take it easy, okay?" Pike rose and made his way to the other end of the cabin, 15 feet away, near the door where a 1950s-era refrigerator and gas stove stood.

"I'm fine, I assure you," Sonny responded.

"Indulge me, please. When was the last time someone served you a meal in bed?" Pike implored with a playful smile.

Ranger, leisurely leaning against the crossbeam of the rafters like a child in a jungle gym, watched her and asked, "Sonny, what's a nice lady like you doing solo on the Two-Hearted? Couldn't wait for the summer tour?"

"It's quite obvious, she wanted to avoid those bloodsucking mosquitoes," Pike interjected.

"I despise mosquitoes. That's one thing we share," Ranger replied. "You wanna talk about bug bites, try Fort Jackson in June. Bug bites and sunburn. Whoa-boy. I tell ya."

"Right here, in the spring, we have mosquitoes and black flies the size of bats. Nothing worse. That's why we're here in May," Pike explained.

"That's the reason?" Ranger queried.

"That, and the fish," Pike added.

"Yeah, yeah, fish," Ranger responded.

"Did you boys manage to catch anything?" Sonny inquired.

"Riker landed five steelhead and three brook trout," Pike said, handing Sonny a cup of water and taking a seat on the lower bunk across from her. "Ranger got ten steelhead, and I hooked seven trout."

"Is that considered good?" Sonny asked.

Pike shrugged nonchalantly. "Depends. I was using a Hare's Ear, while Ranger had the Elk Hair. What were you casting, Riker?"

"They call it a Grannom," Riker replied.

"You threw your Grandma?" Pike quipped.

"Grannom, not Grandma," Riker clarified.

"Now, let me tell you something about Riker. That old soul is quite the expert when it comes to tossing grandmas." Pike spoke low, a knowing smile on his face, aware that Riker would catch his words. With a charismatic grin directed at Sonny, he posed a pointed question, “So, Sonny, are you truly interested in delving into the intricacies of fishing? Or, perchance, are you attempting to sidestep Ranger's inquiry?" Pike's expression carried a mischievous charm.

"What was the question?" Sonny feigned innocence.

Pike, undeterred, revealed the lingering inquiry with a playful tone, "Ah, the burning question on all our minds is, 'What's a nice girl like you doing in a place like this?'"

As if on cue, Ranger slid over to join Pike on the lower bunk, contorting to fit, offering a bottle of water to Sonny. "Bottle of water?" he suggested, his presence adding to the camaraderie of the moment.

"She's already got one water," Pike interjected, but Ranger persisted, insisting, "You can never have too much water."

Grateful for the gesture, Sonny responded, “Thank you” with a smile, as she cracked open the bottle and indulged in a long, refreshing sip. "I suppose I was more parched than I realized."

Pike's grin widened, displaying his gleaming set of teeth, as he responded with a touch of wit, "In the Marines, we have a technical term for that. It's called dehydration." His words carried a suave and charming tone, devoid of any sarcasm that might have been impolite coming from someone else.

However, the conversation took a heartfelt turn as Sonny opened up, sharing her personal truth. "I am a recent widow," she revealed, her voice carrying a delicate blend of vulnerability and resilience. "For the past two years, I stood faithfully by my husband's side, observing the gradual decline of his health, feeling utterly powerless. We shared countless conversations, always nurturing a glimmer of hope that we would embark on new adventures together, fulfilling the retirement dreams we never had the opportunity to pursue. Mitch, my late husband, possessed a deep admiration for Ernest Hemingway. We actually met at a book club where we bonded over our shared love for literature. He was particularly into Hemingway's works. Mitch would often revisit Hemingway's writings. Over the years, we saved and meticulously planned our journey to retrace the author's footsteps on a safari, envisioning a rainy springtime in Paris, and even daring to run with the bulls in Pamplona, Spain."

Pondering the question posed by Ranger, Sonny paused for a moment before responding, "You see, I came to the secluded woods of Michigan for my own Hemingway-inspired adventure. In 1925, Hemingway published a collection of short stories titled 'In Our Time.' One of the stories, 'Big Two-

Hearted River,' portrays his character traveling to Seney, Michigan to fish after the war."

Ranger interjected, "But we're nowhere near Seney."

Sonny nodded. "You're right. The story actually takes place on the Fox River, where Hemingway's character fishes for trout. I read in an article from the time that the good people of Newberry wanted to write Hemingway a letter clearly explaining. But Two-Hearted sounds better; it's poetry, has meaning. The entire area around Seney was ravaged by fire in the 1890s. It reminded Hemingway of Italy, bombed out. In the first part of the story, he alludes to the war, discussing it indirectly. And in the second part, he engages in grasshopper hunting as a means to fish, again addressing the war indirectly."

"The theory of omission," Riker chimed in.

Sonny smiled, acknowledging his input. "Exactly. Hemingway masterfully describes themes of home, friendship, and family, as well as the profound impact of war, all without explicitly stating, 'Hey, I'm dealing with the aftermath of war,' all before it was even referred to as PTSD."

Ranger, captivated by the conversation, exclaimed, "Whoa, I definitely need to read this story. Which war was this? Vietnam?"

“The Great War, World War I.”

“War is never great,” Riker said just loud enough to be heard. "Do you have any allergies? I probably should have asked that ten minutes ago."

Sonny replied, "No, no allergies."

Pike chimed in, his tone half-joking, "Was hitting your head and twisting your ankle in the middle of nowhere on your to-do list? Or perhaps only canoeing down a frigid river with rapids in the spring? Both sound pretty darn dangerous to me."

Sonny responded, her voice filled with a mix of nostalgia and resignation, "It was all talk, just talk. Then, after my husband's passing... well..."

Pike suggested, "Most people would consider taking a cruise."

“Ha,” Sonny explained. "Well, I bought a canoe and a paddle and drove eight hours north. That's how I ended up here."

Ranger remarked, "That's a bitchin' canoe you’ve got. Salesman must have made his nut on that one."

Pike interjected with a reprimand, "Dude! Using 'nut' in front of a lady? Haven't they taught you anything in the Army?" He then turned to Sonny, offering an apology, "Please accept my apologies, Sonny. He was raised by skink lizards."

Sonny smiled appreciatively. "It's been a faithful canoe, more like a companion, really. Its name is Prospector 14, and we've been through a lot this week."

Pike added with a hint of pride, "Sally—my rifle—and I share that kind of relationship."

Riker agreed, "Same here. Mine is called Daphne Blake."

Pike explained, "He has a thing for redheads."

Sonny, slightly taken aback, said, "Right..." unsure of how to respond to the banter. "That salesman, Billy, knew his stuff when it came to the equipment."

The clattering sound of a spoon hitting a plate emerged

from the kitchen, and Riker announced, "Okay," as he walked over with a plate and handed it to Sonny. He then squeezed onto the lower bunk beside Ranger, pushing him into Pike. From his shirt pocket, Riker produced a fork and knife wrapped in a napkin, then handed them to Sonny.

"Thank you," Sonny expressed her gratitude. Glancing at the three boys piled on top of each other in the lower bunk a foot away, she realized they were watching her intently as she was about to eat. "Eggs?" she inquired.

"Yeah, I figured, easy, fast, protein, mix in some vegetables. Those mushrooms, hand-picked and fresh. Did you know that the world's largest mushroom is right here in Michigan?" Riker shared.

"I think I've heard something about that," Sonny responded with a smile, enjoying the first bite of her meal. Holding back from shoveling the food in her mouth from the feeling of being famished, she sounded her satisfaction, "Mmm, it's delicious." Curiosity sparked within her, leading her to inquire, "Are you boys married? Do you leave any hunting widows behind each season?"

The three exchanged glances before Pike answered, "Not married. Ranger went on a date last year."

Ranger, with a touch of vulnerability in his voice, explained, "Ya know how things are. You get together, desperate to find if they meet, like, eighty percent of what you're looking for, and ya always feel like you're never quite good enough. She's got standards, see. And they end up finding someone else. Women today have high standards. No offense, ma'am."

Sonny responded with understanding, "None taken. Men don't have it easy. I've watched my daughters go through a string of boys. Each one supposedly better than the last, but never quite measuring up to some unrealistic expectation. Until one day, they found the 'right guy.' It took a long time. I used to say, 'He's a nice boy, treats you right, seems like a keeper.' But they would say, 'Mom, I'm not settling for just anyone. Did you settle for Dad?' Mitch told them, 'I was lucky to get your mom.' And I said, 'I was lucky to find your dad.' I can still vividly recall that conversation, sitting around the dining room table. The girls had graduated from university, very popular and sought after. But Sundays were reserved for family, and they always made sure to show up so I could feed them. They waited, both of them, for a long time. Boy after boy until my sons-in-law showed up at the table one Sunday. To be honest, my sons-in-law are both not the greatest. They may have impressive jobs, good backgrounds, and a certain social status, but they don't treat my daughters, well, right. As a parent, I can't help but wonder where I went wrong. But then I remember, it's their life," Sonny reflected, her voice carrying a mix of parental concern and acceptance.

Riker interjected, "You gave them the training and tools, but ultimately, it's up to them to carry out the mission."

"Yes, yes, exactly," Sonny agreed. "Are you from the area? I read an article where some downstate 'trolls' came to the Two-Hearted to fish and got into trouble. They were supposed to have known what to do, but when some local boys from Newberry found them, they were desperate. Nearly clinging to the Newberry boys, the locals had to give up their fishing trip, insisting they get them out of the woods and back to civilization."

"I'm from Berkley," Pike started. "These two are from Royal Oak."

Riker asked, "What other aid or comfort can we provide?"

"Too far, too far. Sounds like a porno," Ranger chided.

Eleven

Riker carefully added two more quarters of split log to the sturdy cast iron stove. Sonny, ensconced within the cozy confines of the room, drew a deep breath, relishing the warmth and dryness in the air. It was a rare moment of comfort for her, reminiscent of the days spent in that Newberry hotel room. Her attention drifted to Pike and Ranger, engaged in a spirited game of cards, their playful banter echoing the camaraderie of mischievous boys. They jested and challenged each other, staking their claims of dominance in the pack.

"In this vast expanse of nature, Sonny, what drove you here?" Riker inquired, his voice carrying a thoughtful timbre.

"Some *Eat, Pray, Love* shit?" Ranger interjected.

"Language," Pike gently admonished.

"What?" Ranger retorted.

“The title is nefarious,” Pike said.

"I wasn't particularly fond of the book, so no, no *Eat, Pray, Love* shit," Sonny replied. "In Gilbert's book, she abandons her partner for a younger man. The story promises self-reflection and rising above her circumstances, but ultimately, she finds herself entangled with another man."

Ranger's eyes widened at Sonny's words. "So, not a fan of men?"

"On the contrary, I have great affection for men," Sonny clarified, her voice carrying the weight of experience. "I've been fortunate to have many exceptional men in my life. But Gilbert's story speaks to the human condition. She traverses the lives of these men—committed, casual, and everything in between—only to end up in the same place. What troubles me is that she overlooks two crucial aspects. First, the man she left behind was superior in many ways to the one she ends up with."

“Stand by your man,” Pike said.

“Tammy Wynette, 1968,” Riker replied.

Sonny continued, “And second, she brushes aside the fact that real people cannot simply abandon everything and embark on a worldwide search for 'the answer.' Gilbert indulges in extensive introspection about the world's impoverished yet content inhabitants, all while failing to acknowledge the privilege of evading the burdens of everyday life."

"Kind of like buying an expensive canoe?" Pike interjected, a touch of dry wit in his voice.

"Valid point," Sonny conceded. "Not everyone can afford to splurge five thousand dollars on a boat."

"Five grand? Fuck me!" Ranger exclaimed, his eyes widening in disbelief. "Don't let me touch that thing, I'd break it."

"I have no plans for an *Eat, Pray, Love* escapade. No Oprah endorsements in the works," Sonny affirmed, her conviction ringing clear. "I'm just trying to get away from things—something."

Riker settled into a plush armchair near the stove, eyeing the metal wood bin. In a swift motion, he lifted the entire bin effortlessly and opened the stove door. With a flick of his wrist, he revealed a glimmering blade. Riker exuded an air of quiet competence—a man who could tackle any situation. With a discerning eye, he selected a split piece of wood and began to whittle it with graceful strokes, sending slivers and chips cascading onto the stove's door.

"That book somehow foreshadowed a disconcerting aspect of our culture," Sonny ventured, her voice filled with contemplation. "When I was young, Sundays meant attending church. I don't know if that was your experience as well, but it was mine. And to this day, that spiritual connection remains important to me. Yet I've noticed that the pews grow emptier, and the path to the choicest seats becomes easier."

"Times change, Sonny. It's the way of the world," Pike offered, his voice tinged with acceptance, laying down a card.

"Maybe. I see people still yearning for that connection, but instead of finding solace in churches, they seek tribes in spin classes, workplaces, gaming communities, or various social groups. It seems to me that while a gym trainer may excel at cardio, they may not possess the aptitude to offer spiritual guidance for grief counseling or infidelity."

"You've sought solace in group therapy?" Pike asked.

"A circle of folding chairs in a chilly basement, baring my soul to strangers—I've lived through that cliché of support groups recently," Sonny replied, her tone tinged with a mixture of weariness and resilience.

There was a moment of understanding and shared experience between them, as the weight of vulnerability hung in the air. The trials and tribulations of seeking healing and connection echoed true.

"How did we get on this topic?" Ranger asked.

"*Eat, Pray, Love.* Let her speak," Riker interjected, his tone encouraging.

"There's an abundance of groups one can join, tribes to be a part of, packs to run with," Sonny continued.

"God. Family. Country. Corps!" Pike barked.

"OO-RAH. Semper Fidelis," Riker responded instinctively.

"Yes, those crucial circles. God, family first, with a select few worthy friends. It's an exclusive circle. And the North Star of it all isn't found at work or in an adventure-seeking expedition club. Nowadays, people seem drawn to the allure of through-hiking—the Pacific Crest Trail or the Appalachian Trail. They traverse thousands of miles, yearning for extraordinary experiences and hoping to find a connection. This kind of spiritual quest used to find its home in churches, temples, or devasthanas..."

"Fifty-cent word, Sonny," Pike playfully commented.

"It means a Hindu place of worship," Sonny clarified.

"Roger that."

"But now, that community support is scattered. Even the coffee shop down the street seems to serve as a quasi-sanctuary for a group of regulars, treating it as a sacred space for grounded beans."

"A good cup of coffee is hard to come by," Pike added with a chuckle.

"It's the circle, and we should count ourselves blessed to have it. Because when it's gone, well, it's gone," Sonny concluded, her voice laced with a sense of finality.

Pike, Riker, and Ranger grasped the essence of Sonny's words—loss and the arduous journey of recovery.

Breaking the silence, Riker posed a question. "Have you ever heard of the Camino de Santiago?"

The three companions shook their heads in unison.

"It's an ancient trail," Riker began, his voice carrying a hint of wonder. "It starts in France, winds its way through Spain, and culminates at the majestic Atlantic Ocean. The Romans used to follow the path of the Milky Way, considering it a route to the world's end. What started as a mere trade route eventually became intertwined with the legend of Saint James and his sacred pilgrimage to Santiago de Compostela—a stunning church near the ocean." Riker paused in his whittling, lifting his gaze to the heavens as if seeking inspiration. "In Hebrews 11:13, there's a passage that says, 'These all died in faith, not having received the promises, but having seen them afar off, and were persuaded of them, and embraced them, and confessed that they were strangers and pilgrims on the Earth.'" Riker returned his focus to the wood in his hands, carving away with careful precision. "Those who embarked on this journey were known as pilgrims—sinners in search of penance. Today, nearly half a million people walk this path they call The Way. Each one carries a unique purpose, a different reason that compels them to tread its hallowed ground. They seek answers, hoping to find them along The Way or at its end."

"Do they find what they're looking for?" Sonny inquired, her voice filled with hope.

"Few find it on The Way itself," Riker replied, his words carrying a note of melancholy.

"Oh," Sonny responded, a hint of disappointment tinging her tone.

"Instead, they discover it upon returning home or attempting to reintegrate into their ordinary lives. I've met some pilgrims. Their eyes hold a distant gaze, forever scanning the horizon, longing to be back on that trail. The journey changes them, down to their very core, transforming every cell of their being along The Way. No matter how hard they try, the only way to truly return is to walk the path once more. They strive to live honorable lives, to become better versions of themselves, but it's only on the trail, during their quest, that they experience a sense of completeness. There's no grand revelation at the trail's end or a magical transformation brought about by their deeds. It's the journey itself that holds the key."

"Have you walked The Way?" Sonny asked, curiosity dancing in her voice.

"Not yet. Perhaps one day," Pike responded, his words tinged with wistful longing.

"It sounds utterly fascinating," Sonny remarked, her voice filled with awe.

"'The sharp edge of a razor is difficult to pass over; thus the wise say the path to Salvation is hard,'" Riker quoted, his voice resonating with wisdom.

"Where is that from?" Pike inquired.

"It's a passage from the Upanishads, an ancient religious text. The conundrum you're describing, Sonny, is not a new one. It's the query that haunts any awakened soul." Riker lifted the carving to reveal two links of chain perfectly crafted from the split log. "Sonny, do you recall the word 'timshel' from *East of Eden*? 'Thou mayest.' Everything is your choice."

Twelve

She woke last, stepped out first. They were readying for her return to the Two-Hearted. Riker cleaned the stove of its remnants of breakfast. Ranger packed, methodical and silent. Pike swept, a futile stand against the encroaching mice in the old camp.

At the break of dawn, each bead of dew clung precariously to the emerald pine needles, trembling under the kiss of the rising sun. Each droplet, a tiny prism, reflected the morning light, setting the forest ablaze in a cascade of crystalline brilliance. The woodland expanse shimmered in an ethereal ballet of dancing diamonds, receding into the velvety distance where the eye dared not tread.

A chilly zephyr whispered through the expanse of pine, carrying with it the promise of a new day. Every exhalation painted the frost-kissed air with the gossamer ghost of breath, a fleeting testament to life amidst the sacred silence. It was a spectacle of beauty so profound it snatched the breath from Sonny's lungs, an orchestra of light and shadow conducted by the whims of the sun.

This wonderland exacted a toll, paid not in coin but in the currency of the road less traveled: each scrap, scrape, and scar a voucher of the journey. Yet, as she let the words, "It's worth it" slip from her lips, they hung in the air for a brief moment before dissolving into the ether, a whispered testament to the beauty they bore witness to. A grand tapestry, woven from the threads of dawn's light and nature's quiet resilience, beckoned to the heart, inviting it to fall in love with the raw, unspoken poetry of the moment.

Pike's voice filled the air with a touch of reverence. "This sanctuary, nestled in the heart of North America's most fertile hunting and fishing grounds, was built by the hands of my grandfather and his brothers back in 1911. They carved out this piece of paradise, a refuge against the world's harsh realities."

His eyes took on a faraway look. "After returning from the trenches of Europe in 1918, the elder brothers would navigate a Duesenberg through the forest's maze. The younger ones, they came back from the Second World War in the late '40s, steering a Ford Mercury Woody through this very wilderness. Their spirits are etched into the woodwork, their stories whispered by the wind through the trees."

A warm smile spread across Pike's face. "I continue to tend to this place, keeping it alive, preserving the legacy. And the dream—well, the dream is to share this slice of heaven with my own kids one day. To have them understand the rich mosaic of their history, the resilience and dreams of their forefathers, and their deep, unbroken connection with this magical place. That's the ultimate dream, isn't it?"

“That’s a nice dream,” Sonny replied.

The sharp slam of the screen door jolted the quiet morning as Ranger swaggered out onto the front porch. His weight elicited a chorus of groans from the wooden boards beneath him. Unleashing a hearty belch, he grinned. "What? It's a compliment in some cultures."

Pike retorted dryly, "Maybe, but not in ours."

As the last vestiges of Riker's bustle in the kitchen echoed into silence, he emerged to join them outside.

"Are you sure about this, Sonny?" Pike asked, his voice laced with concern.

"I have to finish. I need to make it to the end. I can handle it," Sonny responded, her eyes blazing with determination.

Riker flashed her an encouraging grin. "I have no doubt you can, Sonny."

Meanwhile, Ranger strode over to the plastic tarp and whipped it off with a swift yank, scattering morning dew droplets in a shimmering spray. The droplets sprinkled down on the rest of the group, shimmering like stardust in the early morning light.

With a soft punch to Ranger's shoulder, Riker grinned. "You know, slower can sometimes be faster."

"It's just water," Ranger shrugged.

"It is just water," Riker conceded.

The sight of Riker next to Ranger brought the enormity of their task into sharp relief. Riker, at a meager five-foot-six, was dwarfed by Ranger's towering frame. With a gentle pat of Ranger's shoulder, Riker directed, "We've got this one. Why don't you take the rear and keep an eye out for bears?"

Sonny checked the blue barrel, snapping the lid shut. It contained only a quarter of what she'd started with. She hoisted it over her first shoulder, then wiggled it onto the second. Meanwhile, Ranger effortlessly hoisted the red dry-bag, making it seem as light as a balloon.

Pike and Riker fell into synchronization, carefully lifting and turning the green vessel overhead. Sonny followed behind, stepping gingerly on her tender foot. Ranger brought up the rear, rifle slung over one shoulder, red bag dangling from his hand.

The trail was a mix of dark gray sand and black dirt, a historical reminder, as Pike explained, of the forest fire in 1871, the same year as the Great Chicago Fire. Trees from this region were harvested to rebuild the city that burned. These tall trees, only one hundred and fifty years old, were mere children in the grand timescale of nature. "Any fan of Tolkien would know the importance of trees," he remarked.

Sonny noticed the lack of tree roots on this path compared to the one that had tripped her. Pike shared his thoughts, "I bet that's because this path was made and walked frequently as the forest grew alongside it. The river trail is a lot wilder, with fewer people until recent years."

The realization that she had never been more than half a

mile from people this entire trip was comforting. The wilderness was dotted with good people, like Pike, Riker, and Ranger, who shared a deep connection with the forest and its rich history.

Upon reaching the river, Pike handed Sonny a piece of paper. "These are our email addresses and phone numbers. Don't hesitate to use them if you need anything," he said.

Touched by their generosity, Sonny hugged each of them in turn. Every "Thank you" was echoed by their "Yes ma'am." Recognizing the pattern, she teased, "Well, I better stop this infinite loop, or we'll be here all day."

Sonny slipped into the fresh dry suit. It took a little longer than the first day, but she got there. With a final tug at her vest straps, she stepped cautiously back into the canoe, balanced herself with her paddle, and sat down. She strained with the paddle, and with a mighty push from Ranger behind her, the canoe sprang into the cold river, swiftly carried downstream toward Lake Superior.

Under the gentle propulsion of her practiced strokes, the Prospector surrendered to the playful whims of the current, making her journey downstream an unhurried waltz with nature. The familiar, soothing cadence of cool water lapping against her vessel felt like a serenade from an old friend, its lyrics an ode to solitude and tranquility.

Without warning, a swift shadow sliced through the air

above her, momentarily veiling the glow of the morning sun. Barely a stone's throw ahead, a spectacle unfolded that made time lose all meaning. An American Bald Eagle, a creature steeped in majestic elegance and raw power, dramatically unfurled its broad wings, breaking its speed with an air of graceful defiance. It hung suspended for an eternal second before descending like an avenging angel.

Its sharp, gleaming yellow talons, like the fingers of a seasoned pianist striking a decisive chord, extended and decisively latched onto its unsuspecting prey. A robust steelhead, a magnificent specimen that easily weighed twenty pounds, if not more, was the chosen breakfast. The eagle's talons pressed into the distinctive pink stripe running along the steelhead's length, between the green-speckled belly and scaled, finned top, as if imprinting its claim for the world to see.

The bald eagle's great wings, patterned in hues of brown, beat the still morning air, a symphony of strength, dominance. Each flap, each wave, lifted it and its heavy bounty higher into the sky's limitless canvas.

The spectacle was so close that Sonny felt herself synchronized with the rhythm of each powerful flap, each beat a palpable force that echoed in her heart. She thought about Ranger, with his rugged strength, effortlessly wrestling such a fish from the river, while the others might falter. The sheer idea of wrestling such a gargantuan catch from the icy river depths seemed like a Herculean task. Yet, the eagle, in its primal elegance, made the feat look as simple as drawing breath. It ascended steadily, gaining momentum until it was a mere speck above the tree line, then disappeared from view.

A wave of wistfulness washed over Sonny. This ethereal moment... she yearned to share it with her best friend, Mitch. Her mind wandered to her phone; a quick snapshot would have immortalized the moment. Was it stowed away in the red dry-bag or the blue barrel? But the thought came and passed too late. She mused about capturing the serene river or the emerald tree line, then narrating the thrilling eagle encounter. There was no shortage of fish tales in the world, but this encounter, this story... would others believe her story?

Mitch would have if he were here. Mitch.

The icy tendrils of fear crept upon Sonny, as swift and merciless as the eagle's dive. A sudden apprehension seized her —a dread that she might never have another soul to share her stories with. The stark prospect of a life shrouded in loneliness, of an existence devoid of shared laughter and silent companionship, terrified her more than she could express. It echoed the empty weeks since Mitch had passed, his absence a void she was yet to fathom.

When Mitch had been ambushed by the first stroke, he was left a shadow of his once active self, confined to a walker. The second, more vicious stroke ravaged his ability to communicate, consigning him to the unforgiving confines of a hospital bed in their back living room. Sonny watched, helpless and tormented, as the man she loved disintegrated day by day, slipping away from her like grains of sand through clenched fingers. Each sunrise brought with it a heartbreaking subtraction, each sunset a painful reminder of the man she was losing. It was like witnessing a slow-burning fire consuming her most cherished possession, bit by agonizing bit, until nothing but ashes remained.

At times, the enormity of their suffering made her wish for a merciful end. This guilt-laden thought haunted her, lacing her prayers with desperation. Yet, the spark in Mitch's eyes on the better days, the familiar touch, the whispered endearments all kept her tethered to the hope that the man she loved was still there, buried beneath the layers of his affliction. Oh, he made her feel so good. And there were moments of confusion when he would ask to be taken to his truck. He needed to get to the truck. Only now did she realize that in his truck, sitting under the passenger seat, was the path to freedom taken by Hemingway.

This was the fear. The stark loneliness that yawned before her, an unending chasm devoid of the love and companionship she had spent a lifetime cultivating. The family she had built with Mitch was a reflection of what once was, now their daughters enveloped in their own lives and loves. The past 24 hours spent in the warm company of three men had been a welcome distraction from her solitary existence. The fear whispered again, insidious and daunting, questioning her ability to find love and companionship again, warning of the potential pitfall of settling for less than what she deserved.

The fear of loneliness was intertwined with the dread of compromising, of settling for a life that was bereft of the joy and love she had known. Of sharing her existence with someone who was merely tolerable, or worse, cruel. The fear of being stuck, of being trapped in a loveless situation like so many women she had heard of, was as palpable as the fear of loneliness.

The house she had once shared with Mitch was now a spectral mansion, every corner echoing with his laughter, every room haunted by his memory. The fear of stepping into the garage to discover an emotional hand grenade, triggering a fresh explosion of loss and longing—this was fear. Fear of facing another day, of confronting her own human frailty.

As Sonny drifted down the Two-Hearted, the sight of an eagle's nest, nestled in the sturdy embrace of a treetop, brought her a moment's peace. Her male eagle brought the hefty steelhead to the nest, and Sonny watched as the female eagle fed, assuring herself of the eggs nestled within. It represented continuity, the unbroken cycle of life and love. It was a future. It was their future, a testament to survival and hope.

"Mitch," she called out to the spirit world. "I don't know if you can hear me, but I need to get over this fear. Can you send help?"

Thirteen

As Sonny navigated the major tributary, the low, ominous rumble of truck tires on the loose rock was an auditory cue to her precise location. She was nearest to the Coast Guard Line Road, just at the river bend where rental outfitters often dropped families for a long day of paddling in summer. Her study of the area maps reassured her that no more portages were in store. "Long and easy" was what the canoe livery promised.

The river had become familiar, a dance partner whose moves she had finally learned. Its turns, the way the sun pestered her eyes, the moments of respite when the river bent another way—she had grown attuned to its rhythm. The morning light, with its fiery persistence, ceased to bother her by eleven each day, when the brim of her hat, perfectly angled, shielded her from its searing rays. She would sometimes catch herself straining her ears for the distant crash of waves, for the faintest echo of Gichigami, the Ojibwe name for the great expanse of Lake Superior that contained ten percent of the world's fresh water.

The change was abrupt, like crossing an invisible barrier. The river's surroundings shifted dramatically from the shadowy deep woods and rugged banks to a barren landscape reminiscent of lunar plains, marked by steep dunes and sparse vegetation.

The Duck Lake Fire of 2012 had descended upon the Upper Peninsula of Michigan with a ravaging fury reminiscent of the fiery emblem of devastation in Hemingway's prose. In his story "Big Two-Hearted River," his description of the devastation of war he witnessed in Europe was similar to the devastation to the area of Seney, along the Fox River. Nature, in its elemental form, had wrought destruction on a scale that dwarfed all life in its path, casting an eerie gloom that blanketed the landscape, transforming it into a nightmarish tableau of ashes and charred relics of what once was a vibrant ecosystem.

The verdant canvas of the Peninsula, once teeming with life, was replaced by an expanse of blackened tree skeletons that punctured the ash-gray sky. The scent of singed foliage and the mournful silence hung heavy in the air, the birds that once animated the forest with their calls were silenced, and the once frolicking animals were absent. The water of the Two-Hearted, which had always mirrored the emerald forest and the azure sky, now reflected a somber reality, dark and devoid of color, starkly reminiscent of Hemingway's post-war world.

However, amidst this desolate spectacle, the resilience of life began to assert itself, stubbornly clinging to hope. The lush greens and the vibrant colors were indeed gone, replaced by a stark palette of blacks, grays, and browns, but within this monochromatic landscape were faint but certain signs of life's enduring spirit.

Since that year of the Duck Lake Fire, tiny, green saplings pushed through the scorched earth, dotting the blackened terrain with spots of defiant life. Birds began to return, their warbles tentative yet hopeful, breathing a certain cadence back into the silent world. Within this devastation, the tiny saplings, the returning birds, and the determined humans painted a picture of life's resilience and the enduring hope that even in the face of desolation, life found a way.

The aftermath of the Duck Lake Fire—the sights of the charred landscape—had filled Sonny with an unspeakable sadness. But as the chill of the winter day receded and the first signs of spring came in view, Sonny decided to beach her canoe on a particularly inviting sandy slope, the hull of the canoe whispering against the fine grains in sharp contrast to the abrasive sounds of branches scraping against the canoe's sides on previous stops.

She caught sight of a young white-tailed deer cautiously emerging from the edge of the recovering forest, its curious eyes scanning the surroundings before bending to taste the tender new shoots of grass. She held her breath, a tear brimming in her eye. It was a moment of pure, unadulterated joy—a sign of hope and renewal.

Taking a cue from Armstrong's legendary words, she said,

"That's one small step for Sonny, and one giant leap for Sonny kind," her voice resonating with the spirit world. She had to be careful on that ankle. After retrieving a full mountain meal from her blue barrel, she set up her pot and burner for a lazy, comforting lunch. The dune was an oasis, the sun beating down at the perfect angle to keep her warm without being overwhelming. The sand, forming a naturally ergonomic lounge chair, was more comfortable than Mitch's now neglected leather recliner back home.

Behind her shuttered eyelids, the sun's warm glow danced, weaving itself into the fabric of her dreams. Cradled in a cocoon of serene tranquility, Sonny slipped into a world painted by her subconscious—a pastel-colored canvas of her childhood home.

In the kitchen, she could almost taste the buttery richness of her mother's signature dish. It was real butter, spread generously over potatoes cooked to perfection, simmered in whole milk, and, rather than whipped violently, were mashed by hand. The tantalizing sizzle of hand-rolled Swedish meatballs seasoned meticulously, their aroma commingling with the simmering gravy, wafted through the air.

Her father was there, too, quietly positioned in the front room with his pipe and paper. She could sense his presence, a comforting certainty rooted in her childhood memories. Outside the side door, in the garage, stood the big white refrigerator, a treasure trove of her favorite drinks. They were always chilled to perfection, a blissful respite on sweltering summer days. With a satisfying pop and hiss, she opened a bottle of

Faygo Orange, its metal cap joining its compatriots in the bucket below, awaiting their party.

The first gulp was a delight, an explosion of sweetness that refreshed and invigorated her, its coldness tingling down her throat. She then emerged into the backyard where beloved faces of aunts, uncles, and grandparents lounged by the pool, their smiles radiant under the sun. "You're home," they said, their voices layered with love and welcome. Each smile, each word, wrapped her in warmth and love. In this ethereal landscape, she was never alone.

Mitch was there, too. In the pool, clad in those horrendous swim trunks he was so fond of sporting every 4th of July. A drink in one hand, he bobbed gently on an inflatable, his other arm beckoning her to join. His broad smile held an invitation. "Come on in," he coaxed. "The water's great."

A foreign sound crept into her idyllic world, faint at first but rapidly growing in intensity. Was it the neighbor mowing the lawn? Perhaps a malfunctioning weed whacker or a failing car muffler? An unsettling interruption in her otherwise perfect dream.

Sonny blinked open her eyes, feeling reality seep in, its daylight puncturing the lingering haze of her dream world. A sense of tranquility cloaked her. The weight of reality gradually returned, but it wasn't unwelcome. Her heart felt full. She felt a distinct smile that had been absent in her life for so long. It had been "The Dream" again, her favorite journey back home. The vibrant memories of the place she longed for, the people she adored, warmed her from within. Mitch was there, his happiness shining through. She was home, in a place she yearned to be part of, in a perfect world she cherished in her dreams.

The noise—it was real, not a figment of her dreams. The hum wasn't a motor's drone, rather a purr—or was it a growl? The low rumble had a feral quality.

Lifting her head tentatively, her gaze caught sight of its source: an enormous cat, its head bent low at the river's edge. As if sensing her scrutiny, it lifted its head, its eyes meeting hers. A primal, guttural growl resonated from its chest, a chilling sound that was foreign to her ears.

Sonny had known fear. The thrill of haunted houses, the terror instigated by horror movies, the vertiginous dread of roller coasters, but this fear was of an entirely different, more horrifying caliber. It was the kind of fear that held her motionless, choking her voice into silence. She was alone, help nowhere near.

The bear horn strapped to her chest was her only defense. Would it work against this beast? This creature was no mere pet. Its sinewy form, blanketed in golden fur, emanated raw power. Despite the paralyzing fear, a strange urge to reach out, to touch its fur crossed her mind. It was, after all, a cat—yet its eyes spoke of an untamed wilderness, a predatory hunger. Its paws, deceptively soft, concealed lethal daggers that seemed to grow sharper by the second.

A contemplation: *Should I go for the horn?* Her hand commenced a painstakingly slow journey, inching toward her chest where the horn was fastened. She visualized it—the horn's fireplug red figure, its nozzle that needed to point away from her, the button atop it that demanded a forceful push.

The cat's growl increased in volume with each infinitesimal movement of her hand. Its muscles twitched, contracted, primed like a powerful spring about to be released. The moment was a crescendo of tension.

Her hand shot toward the horn, fumbled, missed. Desperately, she patted the area, finally grasping the metallic canister on her third attempt. Her thumb traced the groove of the button as the cat's growl reached a peak.

A yelp split the silence, sending jolts of terror ricocheting through her body. Her sweat-soaked body emitted a palpable fear that seemed to enhance the cat's awareness of her. Its nostrils flared, taking in the scent of its prey. As she freed the horn, her thumb pressed hard against the button, her other hand tremblingly pointing the nozzle at the monstrous feline. The coiled spring was released.

The horn blared, its sound piercing the stillness. It reached the cat mid-pounce. The creature's reflexes worked in Sonny's favor, twisting its trajectory in mid-air. Its full weight missed her body. Its menacing gaze held her captive, but instead of teeth ripping through flesh and claws shredding her, it landed awkwardly on her right arm, knocking the horn away, then darted over the dune, disappearing into the underbrush.

Sonny was left gasping, her heart pounding a frenzied rhythm against her chest. The sand clung to her sweat-soaked skin, a testament to her visceral fear.

Her arm was an alien, sluggish and unresponsive. The pain

was a slow burn, then a sharp detonation, announcing its presence. Upon inspection, her dry suit bore the unmistakable signature of the wild cat's claws. Warmth flooded her arm, a familiar dread.

Her left hand, acting with swift efficiency, unsheathed the emergency blade from her chest and performed a hasty dissection of the sleeve below the elbow. The material parted reluctantly, revealing a spectacle of violence—punctures from the big cat's claws and a grotesque twist that her bones should not assume.

Her belongings, mockingly close, were a challenge to reach. She performed a clumsy ballet to rise without the aid of her right arm, a delicate balance of pain and determination. The dune's slope lent her aid, bringing her to her knees. "Good enough," she mumbled, a broken promise of effort. Descending toward her canoe, she prayed to the gods of gravity and grace.

The blue barrel's lid was a stubborn adversary against her single-handed assault. Her left hand pulled and tugged, fingertips turning an alarming array of hues until, with a triumphant *POP*, the lid surrendered. She rummaged blindly until her fingers brushed against the familiar fabric of her emergency bag. The contents of the barrel cascaded into the Prospector like a waterfall of neglect.

Zippers, it seemed, were no friends to the one-handed. Through a slow dance of frustration, she managed to tease it open. She laid the half-open bag delicately on the thwart.

Sonny fumbled with the foil packets, her teeth aiding where her fingers could not. A pristine wipe emerged from its silver tomb, only to be snatched by the river. The second packet yielded under the careful guidance of teeth and left hand. The wipe was a soft whisper against her ravaged skin. She swabbed the wounds, registering the deep furrows of cut flesh. The creature had left its mark.

The cap on the vial of liquid skin offered little resistance to the efficient teamwork of teeth and left hand. She gingerly placed the vial and cap on the thwart. Her fingers, now acting as an arcade mechanical claw, clamped down on the vial's brush. As she stared at the gory tableau of her arm, she realized she was short a hand. The needle and thread option was a challenge. It was then that her gaze caught a glint of chrome—a paper binder. Salvation in the form of office supplies. Billy had indeed recommended the best equipment.

Her fingers worked with purpose, prying out the chrome handles. The binder's maw opened, capturing the straight lines of her wound. The pain was a familiar enemy, an old foe in a new battlefield. She slathered the liquid skin over the injury with a thick application like Van Gogh might layer on canvas, standing between her and certain infection. As she waited for the solution to dry, time stretched before her, elongating each second. She watched the transformation with morbid fascination, the weeping wounds quieting under the healing salve.

Unclamping the binder sent a fresh wave of pain crashing against her resolve. Yet, with determined grit, she repeated the ordeal with each claw mark, sealing her body against the hostile world.

Her medical kit offered a wealth of options—large

bandages, squares of gauze, a testament to modern medical miracles. After a pause to collect her thoughts, she opted for the patches, their sterilized paper sheaths falling away under her teeth's insistence. Their use was a delicate choreography, the patches laid on the arm directly with an orbit of gauze wrapping unspooled, maintaining gentle but firm pressure on her wounds.

The flat, metal splint was in the kit as well—a prize she had crawled half a mile for days earlier for her ankle before taking the blue barrel bear wilderness adventure where Riker had discovered it. "Blue Barrel Bear Wilderness Adventure," she repeated, a mantra to distract herself from the grim reality of her situation. "I would go on that ride if Disney opened it. Blue Barrel Bear Wilderness Adventure." The splint was going to be bad. U-shaped, it promised correction at the cost of pain. For the ankle, the splint went under the heel of the foot, providing support up the leg. For the arm, it went under the elbow, righting the arm's length to the wrist.

Searching for a stick within hands' reach yielded no results. Her gaze roved the canoe for something similar, her desperation mounting. With a burst of inspiration, she reached for the orange emergency whistle now required on every life vest. It was a flimsy ally, but it was all she had in a last resort.

Bracing herself, she bit down on the whistle and forced her arm into submission. Bone grated against bone, a symphony of agony with friction. She fought through tears for clear sight into the operation. Her splint in place, it forced her arm to follow. Sonny wrapped another layer with gauze, each revolution a promise of stability. Hiker's tape served as the final seal between the two poles, ensuring the splint would remain straight and true.

Strangely, Mitch's "forget-the-world" pills were absent from the blue barrel. Instead, Sonny took extra-strength aspirin. They went down smoothly with a swig of water.

Her heart throbbed with a bitter agony, and a pang of hurt coursed through her arm. Tender tears welled in Sonny's eyes and began their sorrowful descent. It wasn't self-pity that provoked her suffering; no, it was genuine strife. This physical torment was simply the manifestation of a deeper, more intimate affliction—a crisis of the heart.

"Thirty years, Mitch!" Her voice echoed, reaching out toward the spectral realm. "For three long decades, I stood by your side as your wife. I provided support, remembered our special dates, guided you on the right path, nurtured our daughters, acted as your confidante and counsel. Thirty years, Mitch!"

Her voice cracked, the pain seeping into her words. "I was your unwavering ally, your constant. I stood by you until the very last breath. I gave you everything you asked for until the very last breath. But now, what is left for me? Who am I to become? I believed in us, Mitch. I thought I could do this, carry on in your absence. But I... I may not be able to. I don't know anymore, Mitch, I simply don't know."

With a sigh, she sank into the sand, exhausted from the events, the whisper of the river lulling her toward sleep. *What else will I need to survive?* she wondered, her mind teetering on the edge of consciousness.

FOURTEEN

In the misty landscape of her dream, Sonny looked down at herself, standing at the heart of an enormous stone labyrinth. She was draped in a threadbare robe, one arm hanging limp by her side. The stone walls around her towered menacingly, whispering of mysteries and dangers lurking in their cold shadows. With a start, she realized that the labyrinth was a manifestation of her current predicament; she was isolated, wounded, and lost.

Soon, she was not alone. A translucent, ethereal form materialized in front of her. It was Mitch, his familiar handsome face looking back at her with concern.

"Mitch," she called out, "I need you to send help."

His spectral image flickered as if caught in a gentle breeze, then steadied. "I already sent in the Marines, what more do you want?" His voice echoed, bouncing off the stone walls of the labyrinth.

"More," she called out to Mitch. "I need more!"

With a determined nod, Mitch's spectral form shimmered before fading away, leaving Sonny alone again. She felt a rush of wind and looked up just as an enormous raven descended from the sky, landing on a nearby stone. Jet black, the shaggy feathers around its throat moved with the turn of its head. The bird's long bill held something that glistened in the sun. Was it a ruby? With its head bowed, it dropped the item that fell for what seemed like an eternity until it splashed into the water below. *PLOP.* The ruby slipped beneath the surface. The world around her shook and trembled. She watched as the water below the raven's perch rose higher, spilling over the edges until the land began to flood. The water, lapping at her toes, rose quickly until she was ankle-deep. She knew that the ruby had caused this.

Sonny opened her eyes. She was still on the riverbank next to the canoe. She had fallen asleep only to wake with her arm and leg still bandaged.

Under the lingering sun, time stretched languorously, allowing for the day to unspool further. Painstakingly, and with a humility that solitude permits, she crawled to retrieve her stove, pot, and water bottle before managing to hoist herself into the waiting embrace of the canoe. She allowed herself a pause, a sweet surrender to the moment, an intimate rendezvous with her thoughts. Experimenting with the kayak paddle, she found it unwieldy, and her arm—swathed in protective skin—protested against its use. The wooden paddle gifted by Billy, however, caressed the water at an angle that promised both reach and control.

Gritting her teeth in determination, Sonny's body moved in a primal dance, pushing and pulling with her hips, until the canoe disentangled from the sandy river edge. In the river's heart, the current flirted with the canoe, twirling it around as she wrestled to control its course. Each dip of the paddle was a sweet whisper exchanged between her and the Two-Hearted, a quiet conversation of resistance and submission.

The river meandered, its path a lover's sigh between kisses, leading toward Lake Superior. The surrounding dunes, once barren, now donned a mantle of new life, the verdant aftermath of the Duck Lake Fire a decade earlier. Life's unyielding insistence on survival was on full display, sprouting seeds sprung in the wake of destruction, heralding a new beginning. The skeletal remains of the fire-kissed trees marked the passing landscape, rising and falling like the rhythm of a slumbering heart.

Fatigue tugged at Sonny, pleading with her to rest, to satiate her hunger. Ideal spots for her tent were absent, and the task of setting it up single-handedly loomed large. A hammock was an option, but the living trees were playing hard to get, too distant from one another. Resigned, Sonny decided to stay loyal to the canoe. An hour of journeying had bred familiarity; she knew she could endure, could cling to this vessel of survival.

As the sun began to flirt with the horizon, she fumbled for her flashlight and reserve, tools potent enough to pierce the impending darkness. As night's blanket began to unroll, the stars started winking down at her, celestial bodies that had once guided brave souls like Jason and his Argonauts, and explorers like Magellan, Columbus, and Vasco da Gama.

"Vasco da Gama," she murmured, finding solace in the gentle lilt of the name, whispering it into the gathering darkness.

The time seemed ripe for a touch of melody, a distraction, so she hummed "Moon River," her voice but a murmur in the wilderness. The words "Huckleberry friend" stirred memories of Johnny Mercer and a trip to Savannah, Georgia with her family. She pondered over Mercer's boyhood days picking huckleberries, his affection for Mark Twain which inspired the lyric. An owl, aroused by her song, returned a hoot that was hauntingly beautiful.

In the silence that had followed the change in landscape, Sonny became aware of the quiet symphony of the wilderness she had been a part of. The burnt terrain felt distant, while the rhythmic lullaby of Lake Superior's waves drew closer. She knew from her prior plunge that the waters of the Two-Hearted were chilly, and she expected the greatest of the Great Lakes to be more so, with icy specters of icebergs still adorning its surface this late in the season.

Her strength was ebbing, fatigue creeping in. Her thoughts meandered as she did, lazily steering the canoe to avoid the shoreline and the occasional eddy caused by a fallen cedar. Local tales whispered that the river was carved by a romantic Paul Bunyan, while others claimed it owed its name to the spirit of the place and people. Pike, Riker, and Ranger certainly proved this kindness. Looking at the map, many discerned a heart turned upside down in the split tributary. For Sonny, it would always symbolize the two hearts she shared with Mitch.

Distant voices floated toward her, surprising her. A campfire, though unseen, must be holding court to a few people, their voices reaching her at "three-beer volume" as Mitch might have termed it. As she approached a bend in the river, she noticed something reflected in the water. It was the hanging bridge near where her bike was chained, the voices from the neighboring campground.

She could halt here, declare her mission accomplished. But Sonny knew the journey wasn't over, not until the river's turbid water kissed the crystal-clear Lake Superior. Instead of turning, she watched the suspension bridge sail over her head, her flashlights catching glimpses of it. The voices from the camp grew louder as she approached, competing with the growing orchestra of waves crashing on her left.

As the towering dunes gave way to a flat beach, a celestial glow painted the horizon, the curve of the Earth dancing with the lake's lights. At the river's end, where the big Two-Hearted sped up to merge with the lake, she steered right, the canoe coming to a halt on the beach.

With labored effort, Sonny stepped out of the canoe, her legs crying out against the cold waters and cramped hours in the Prospector. Using her one good hand and foot, she dragged the canoe onto the shore. Exhausted, she lay on top of the Prospector 14, trying to shield herself from the beach winds and potential bug bites from sand mites.

Gazing up at the starlit canvas above, her eyelids felt heavy. Just as they threatened to close with a bang, a luminescent curtain unfurled across the sky. The Northern Lights, in hues of green, purple, and red, danced to celebrate her accomplishment.

FIFTEEN

"What year did that incident occur?" Sonny muttered to herself, hauling the Prospector by its handle over the pebbled wash of the river. "The Blue Pontiac LeMans... must've been '70 or '71. Around the same time, they stopped making the Tempest. I was wearing that favorite cream dress of mine, didn't want it sullied. Yet, in the span of a few moments, three cars pulled over. Each man eager to lend a hand. I knew the mechanics of it all, had the jack and the spare ready, but the prospect of ruining that cream dress... So I let them. They each took turns ordering the other around, asserting their authority, while one tried to charm me. The gentleman in the blue suit, he was the one lamenting the end of the Pontiac Tempest. Ten minutes, that's all it took, and I was back on the road, each with my number stashed away to call on me later. That was way before you, Mitch."

Her progress up the shoreline to the tree line was slow and measured, each step a delicate dance, punctuated by intermittent halts.

"I wonder what's become of those three. I wouldn't mind playing the damsel now. I wonder if that's still acceptable these days. Seems like chivalry is considered an affront now. Men can't even hold the door open for a lady anymore. That's not quite true, though. Pike, Ranger, Riker—they were gentlemen, through and through."

Packing provisions into the red dry-bag, she discarded anything cumbersome and redundant. Leaving the canoe tucked away under a Jack pine off the road, her joints were protesting from the night spent curled up in the canoe. The walk up the beach stimulated circulation. She had managed a solid four-hour sleep last night, she calculated.

The slow-paced walk toward her mountain bike was surprisingly therapeutic. She observed spring rabbits gamboling in the field, their noses twitching as they nibbled. Deer, still donning their winter coats, camouflaged against the landscape, visible only when they stirred. From her position on the road, she could see remnants of winter, patches of snow in the shadowy nooks of the woods.

"Well, I really botched this one up, Mitch," she announced to the spirit world. "Should've left the truck here and taken the bike on day one. It's all backwards."

As she unlocked the bike from the tree, she noticed the "three-beer choir" had already vacated the camp. If any souls had been lingering, she might've asked for a ride back to the truck. But this was a weekday, the off-season for most, and she found herself in one of the most isolated corners of America. Wilderness preserves were designed to protect the wilderness, which meant an abundance of wildlife and a marked scarcity of humans, let alone those in vehicles.

She laid the bike flat on the ground the way she'd been taught as a child and gingerly straddled the frame, careful to protect her right foot. As she bent down, her left hand taking the brunt of the weight, the tips of her right fingers barely made contact, guiding the bike upright. When the bike started to topple, her instincts kicked in and she tried to reach out, but her right arm didn't obey. The bike took a minor bounce, but she was back up within moments.

Everything had to be done in reverse, requiring careful consideration. The additional weight from the red dry-bag on her back didn't help, shifting uneasily at the slightest motion. Placing her left foot on the raised left pedal, she pushed off slightly and bore down on the left pedal. She sent deliberate commands to her right foot, guiding it to the right pedal, then pressed down gingerly.

Riding was only marginally quicker than walking, but it was the better choice nonetheless.

She delved into her memory palace, a mental storage for mid-length memories, such as the location of her parked car, upcoming birthdays and anniversaries, and due dates for bills. She pulled forth the image of a map that hung in the Edison

Room. She had taken her girls to the Henry Ford Greenfield Village every summer and adopted Edison's relocated workshop from Menlo Park, New Jersey as her personal workspace in memory. Among the maps on the wall was the one she needed for this journey: a 15-mile bike ride along routes 423, 414, and 407 back to the truck. Normally, it would be a 70-minute bike ride, but Sonny knew that today it would consume the better part of her daylight hours.

She engaged the bike's lowest gears to negotiate the uneven dirt road, skirting the sandy patches and adhering to the compacted tracks.

The first mental marker she'd stored in her Edison Room was a massive tree, bristling with directional signs at its crossroads. All 26 signs were secured to the trunk, and on this trip, she had time to count and decipher each one. The topmost sign, evidently among the oldest and weathered by the sun over many years, featured Larscoop and pointed south. Considering its height, it must have been affixed when the tree was young and crept upwards with the trunk's growth. From top to bottom, the other signs read: Camp 24, Jones, Peanut Camp, Grand Haven, Johnsons, Owl Club, Camp Buckeye, Alson, Beach Camp, East Firetower, Geoff Camp, Muskrat Inn, Elyson Club, Valhalla, East Branch Club, Camp Five, and DeFoe Camp. The last sign she read, Popp's Camp, faded from view as she continued her slow trek.

Further down the path, she passed a hand-painted saw blade from a lumber mill. Its depiction of a sunset over water, rendered in vibrant blues, reds, and yellows, seemed to be crafted with a broad, hefty brush typically reserved for furniture or house detailing. Each tooth of the blade appeared menacingly sharp, yet was rusted enough to impart a case of tetanus. *When did I last get a tetanus shot?* she thought, pressing on at a slow, steady pace.

Exhaustion was taking its toll, but her spirits were buoyed when she spotted the Princess Bride Rock. The sight signified that the paved road was not far off, providing her a ray of hope. The continuous crunch of dirt beneath her tires served as an auditory reminder of the journey she was undertaking.

Pausing to take water at the side of 407, just off the asphalt, a silver GMC decelerated and came to a stop a few yards ahead of her. The driver disembarked and sauntered back toward Sonny.

"You need a ride," she declared, without a hint of inquiry.

"I do."

"Where to?"

"High Bridge."

"That your truck parked there?"

"It is. You know this place well?"

"I make a point of it. Name's Grace. Let's get that bike of yours." Grace's statements held an air of finality.

Grace stood a good head and a half above Sonny, her facial features strongly hinting at Scandinavian roots. Her hair was silver, and her skin bore the wear of years, revealing her age. Together, they maneuvered the bike toward the truck and hoisted it into the truck bed.

Grace, still spirited, quipped, "You been out here wrestling bears? Or that come from your man?"

"No, no, nothing like that. Just canoeing the Two-Hearted."

"Where's your canoe?"

"Other end of the river, on Superior."

Grace emitted a grunt of acknowledgment. She seemed to know her way around, driving straight to Mitch's truck at High Bridge, cutting the engine, and hopping out. When Sonny caught up, the bike had already been removed from Grace's truck bed and was waiting to be loaded onto Mitch's.

Sonny reached into her pocket and pressed the ignition button on the key fob twice, hoping to pre-warm the truck.

Together, they heaved the bike into the truck bed, Sonny guiding the front while Grace pushed the heavier part in. The bike lay flat in the truck bed and was swiftly secured with straps.

"What happened to your arm?" Grace asked.

"I'm not sure you'll believe me."

"Give it a shot."

"I think it was a cougar, or maybe a panther..."

"We got those around here. Cougars have been caught on trail cams. They roam the entire peninsula, back and forth. Seen 'em in Dollarville, by the dam, getting a drink."

"One found me. Leapt onto my arm."

"It must have been startled. They usually avoid humans."

"I woke up, and there it was."

"Sounds about right. Tell you what, I'm going to follow you to your canoe and help you get it loaded."

"That's really kind of you, thank you. I truly appreciate it."

"Us folks need to stick together up here."

"Is it that obvious?"

"Nobody around here would be bold enough to take on the Two-Hearted this early in the year. I hope you found what you were looking for."

"I hope so too."

"Let's get going. The cab should be warmed up by now." Grace patted the truck twice before returning to her vehicle.

Their twin trucks trundled past a sign announcing "Authorized Vehicles Only." Grace reassured her, "Don't worry, sister. You're authorized" when Sonny had hesitated initially. The road she'd trodden that morning suddenly felt insignificant in the truck. What had been a near thirty-minute walk was under a minute's drive, highlighting the extent of her injury.

Sonny shared this with Grace, to which she replied, "Isn't that what we always tell ourselves? It will be different for us."

"Yeah. Yeah, that's right."

"Tell me about something you did recently."

They ambled side by side toward the canoe.

"Well, I canoed the Two-Hearted."

"And everyone warned you that it's dangerous, reckless even. And what did you tell yourself? That I'm different. That I wouldn't get hurt."

"It was just a canoe trip, like the ones from scouts."

"Exactly. Grab that end." Grace took the weightier end laden with gear by the handle, murmuring low enough for Sonny to hear, "Nice canoe."

One on each end, they hauled the Prospector 14 back to Mitch's truck bed.

"That's the tricky thing in life," Grace said. "Coming to terms with being human. Sure, you're unique in some ways, but not really. You're just like everyone else."

"I thought the lesson was to get back up, to keep going."

"Nah, that's kids' stuff. The real lesson? You do the best you can, improve a little every day. You'll stumble. Just like everyone else. Because you *are* everyone else."

As they set the canoe down at the edge of the truck, Sonny began loading everything into the blue barrel that would fit. Then, every item—the blue barrel, red dry-bag, wooden paddle, kayak paddle, medical kit—found a place in the back of the cab.

Hoisting the canoe's bow into the bed of Mitch's truck, Sonny retorted, "I canoed the big Two-Hearted in early spring. That makes me different, not like everyone else."

Assisting with pushing the canoe further into the bed, Grace replied, "You survived. That's what makes you different." Grace heaved the stern as Sonny closed the truck bed gate with a resounding slam.

"I survived."

"Yep." Grace flashed a crooked smile. "I'll tail you into Newberry, get you to the health center for that arm."

"You've already done so much."

"I'm following you into town. You're going to the clinic." It was a statement, not a question.

"Sounds good."

As they merged onto 500 South from 414, the satellite radio

sprung back to life. Sonny assumed her phone was also back in service. She followed her earlier route in reverse: 500 turned from dirt road to pavement as it merged into 123, leading her into Newberry, the heart of the Tahquamenon River Valley. *What will I tell the girls?* she asked herself.

Sixteen

Sonny followed the blue sign with the silver “H” that marked the entrance to Helen Newberry Joy Hospital & Healthcare Center. The substantial building appeared to serve all of Luce County.

The attending receptionist's face said it all as Sonny limped in. She reeked—a potent blend of Lake Superior, river water, the aftermath of relieving herself against a tree, body odor, and fear, along with other, more indefinable scents from the journey. "I need you to fill this paperwork out. Make sure to include your full name, date of birth, and your reason for visiting us today," the attendant instructed.

Living in a world turned upside down, Sonny attempted to pen her information with her left hand. Her scrawl was nearly legible—perhaps she was suited to be a doctor from this evidence.

A few minutes later, Grace entered with a man dressed in a brown uniform. They took seats on either side of Sonny. "This is my friend Rick," Grace began. "He's in charge of the DNR here in Luce County. I told him about your cougar."

"Ma'am."

"Hold on, your name is Rick? And you're a DNR ranger?"

"That's correct, ma'am. I get the joke."

"Ranger Rick, how can I assist?" Sonny couldn't help but smile at the absurdity of it all. In the scheme of the week's events, this was certainly a lighter moment. "I'm sorry, your name's not funny. It's just... this week has been... I—"

Rick pulled a map from his jacket and unfolded it. "Could you point out where you were attacked?"

"I wish I'd had this map with me earlier. Look at the details. It shows the terrain and everything."

"We provide these at the station. All you need to do is drop by and check-in before heading out into the woods."

"I was around here," she said, pointing. "The fire line had passed, and I was on a large dune. I fell asleep in the sun. When I woke, it was there, drinking from the river."

"I see. In the burn area, interesting."

"I used the bear horn, scared it off, but it pounced—it was just like an oversized, furious house cat."

"This one could rip your arm off."

"Well, besides that."

"What color was it?"

"Orange brown-ish."

"Goldie Hawn."

"I'm sorry, it has a name?"

"Goldie Hawn is the golden one; her black companion is Kurt Russell." Grace elaborated, "They've been around for a few years now. Hard not to name them."

"Goldie's spotted more often, due to her color. Kurt Russell is stealthier, harder to spot in the forest," Rick explained.

"Do you think they'll have kittens this year?" Grace inquired.

"She should be old enough to have cubs soon," Rick answered before turning to Sonny. "Did you see a red tag on her ear?"

Sonny closed her eyes, attempting to recall. "I don't know, I —I can't—maybe?"

"Sonny?" the attendant called. "The doctor will see you now."

As the attendant beckoned her, a nurse appeared from a hallway with a wheelchair, assisting her into it. He pushed her down a hall, clicked the wheel locks into place, and told her, "I'll be right back." True to his word, he returned a minute later, leading her into a room with eight beds, separated by white fabric partitions on a track in the ceiling. He helped her stand and remove her hiking pants. In the stark, real-world lighting, Sonny was taken aback by the sight of her legs. The colorful array of bruises resembled the topographical markings on Ranger Rick's map.

"Welp, you don't see that kind of coloring on a leg every day," he declared. He made quick work of the bandages she'd fashioned in the wilderness, revealing an ankle grotesquely swollen. "The doctor will be here soon. There's no cause for concern."

His manners were agreeable, his touch light as he began to work on her arm. As he endeavored to cut through the hiking tape, unraveling the layers of makeshift bandage that held her arm rigid, the scissors became lodged. When the layers of the handmade cocoon finally peeled away, it revealed what looked like Goya's Saturn with all the dark colors of bruised skin, the bend where the break happened, and three distinct gashes from the cat claw.

"What's this, here? Some sort of adhesive? Super glue?" he queried.

"Liquid skin," she replied.

He grunted, moving to a computer, fingers dancing across the keys.

"Sonny, I am Doctor Drake," the woman walking in introduced herself. "I understand you've had a rather eventful week. Care to share?"

Sonny paused, knowing full well her tale would sound ludicrous. "Would it be alright to take a few photos before we start?"

"Photos?"

"No one is going to believe my tale, not without some proof."

The nurse took three photos of her arm, three of her leg. While he was busy, Sonny told Doctor Drake about dropping in at High Bridge, tripping on the trail, and waking up to Goldie Hawn.

"You've met Rick, then?"

"I have."

"He does take pride in his names."

Following the cleanup, Drake called for X-rays. The medical center was small, nothing like the bustling places where Sonny had spent years with Mitch, a revolving door of strangers witnessing intimate moments of struggle and vulnerability. Here, it was just Doctor Drake and the nurse. They took the X-ray images, pored over them in a separate room, and then wheeled Sonny to a private room. They cleaned her arm once more and washed down her leg.

Drake decided against a hard cast. The lacerations on her arm necessitated a soft cast, one that could be easily removed for regular inspections. There was bad news, too.

The rebreaking and resetting of her arm was a kind of pain she'd never known, like a vicious explosion of agony. Nearest so far to giving birth to the twins. Of all the suffering that week, this was the whopper. Though the liquid skin had worked as intended, it was replaced by stitches. Painful, but nothing compared to the brute force of Goldie Hawn or the hand-mine that reached out and ensnared her ankle on the trail.

Once the procedures were done, Drake allowed her a few minutes to recover. "You're lucky to be alive, Sonny," she said. "What you did was remarkable. But don't do it again."

Grace peeked in. "Yeah, the admin wants the paperwork filled out again, I figure you might be right-handed. Why don’t we do this together?"

Seventeen

The seat warmer hummed into life, soothing Sonny's tired body. She flicked a glance at the dashboard clock. 8:15. *Now or never*, she thought, thumbing the cell phone to dial Glinda's number.

"Hello?"

"Glinda, it's Mom. I'm looping in your sister, sit tight."

With practiced ease, she activated the three-way call feature, dialing Evanora.

"Mom?"

"Hold on." One click later, she resumed, "Don't freak out."

Evanora scoffed, "Too late."

Sonny sighed. "Alright, fine. I'm okay."

"Now I really don't believe you," Evanora snarked.

"I knew this would backfire," Sonny muttered.

"Spit it out, Mom." Glinda intervened.

"To cut to the chase, my arm's broken and my ankle's twisted."

"We'll come to get you," Glinda immediately offered.

"No need, I'm in the hospital lot, got my arm set, ankle braced. And I can drive."

Evanora cut in, "Hold on. That's a load of bull. Your driving's compromised."

"I can handle it," Sonny assured.

Glinda's voice softened. "Mom, don't push it tonight. Get a room, sleep it off. We'll talk in the morning."

"Alright."

Evanora chimed in, "Yes, listen to Glinda. Do not, I repeat, *do not* drive."

"Mom." Glinda paused. "Evanora and I, we're worried. We care about you. There's this thing called the widow effect. People tend to—"

"Jesus, Glinda!" Evanora interjected, "Way to break it to her gently! Are you reading off a script?"

"It's also known as 'broken heart syndrome' or 'takotsubo cardiomyopathy.."

"Christ, she's got notes!" Evanora groaned. "Mom, don't mind Glinda. But we are worried. Call us if you need anything..."

"Yes, Mom, grief heals with time."

"Glinda, for crying out loud, shut up!"

"Girls—"

"Unbelievable! You had to go there."

"Girls."

They fell silent.

"Girls." Sonny sighed. "I won't be home as planned, but I'm okay. That's it."

"Check in later, Mom," Glinda requested.

"Yeah, call us."

"Goodnight, girls." Sonny cut the call, reclining in her seat, alone in the dimly lit parking lot.

Decisions didn't always need to be tough. The choice between truck slumber and a cozy hotel room? Simple. Unfortunately, the painkillers Doctor Drake had given her were hardly more potent than aspirin. It was a pain that gnawed, promising to keep sleep at bay until sheer exhaustion forced surrender.

Sonny spent the next hour and a half driving southeast, the Mackinac Bridge emerging in her path. Crossing it, she spotted a welcoming beacon of a hotel sign, "Vacancy" glowing brightly against the night. Sixty-five dollars awarded her a comfortable room and a splendid view of the illuminated bridge, a spectacle of red, white, and blue lights dancing on the water below. The faint rumble of truck engines employing their brakes to negotiate the bridge's descent was distant, more a lullaby than a disturbance.

Her ankle, it seemed, had taken the drive in stride, its protests subtle. There had been a moment, a flash of tawny fur, wide eyes reflecting headlight beams when she'd doubted her reflexes. The deer, however, had more sense, retreating just as swiftly as it had appeared.

One part of Sonny longed for "The Dream," the delicious warmth that came from being enveloped in the presence of her loved ones. Yet another part dreaded sleep, fearing a return to that desolate labyrinth of loneliness. Why would Mitch send her a raven in that dream?

She was supposed to live out the next few decades of her life alongside Mitch, her eternal love. But instead, she was grappling with the dawn of each day on her own. As she drove, her mind wandered back to the qualities that had drawn her to Mitch in the first place. Among many things, it was his thoughtful planning that had captivated her. He saw her as someone deserving of a meticulously crafted world, a world built on thoughtfulness and care for them to navigate together. Her prior boyfriends, on the other hand, had been nothing more than fleeting allies. They seemed intriguing at the outset, but their self-centeredness surfaced sooner than later.

It might seem old-school to see Mitch as a provider, but that's what he was and more. He valued Sonny not as a passing amusement, but as someone not to be taken lightly. Her past suitors reveled in the pursuit, but once they had her, they didn't know what to do. What would her dating life look like now? It was unrealistic to expect the high standard of Mitch, but was it too much to hope for someone who could at least come halfway?

They wouldn't have the same idiosyncrasies or shared memories. Did she have the patience or the inclination to train a new man? No, that wasn't quite right. Did she possess the patience and curiosity to spend that much time understanding a new individual? Many people she met seemed fickle and artificial. All she wanted was a reasonably attractive man who she could connect with and spend at least four hours a day with. Was that ask unachievable?

Eighteen

Dorothy's first inquiry about Oz was straightforward: "Is he a good man?" The response, arriving directly from Oz himself two-thirds of the way through the novel, was confessional: "I am a good man, but a bad wizard." Dorothy offered her own self-definition, "I'm just an ordinary girl from a strange land." As the miles passed on her homeward journey, with Mitch's truck dutifully sharing the labor of driving, Sonny's mind strayed to the pages of L. Frank Baum's tale for children. A tale she had cherished since her own girlhood, and which she had read to the twins as they grew, until memorized, the words becoming part of their shared childhood vernacular.

Her initial encounter with Mitch was wrapped in that memory, her asking of him that same question, "Is he a good man?" Mitch, in his way, mirrored Oz, a good man without a claim to wizardry, yet he wove an enchantment into her life just the same. Now Mitch had journeyed to that "undiscovered country," leaving her to wander, a stranger in this now unfamiliar world.

In the quiet of her arrival home, she sat in the truck, its lights extinguished, for a lengthy twenty minutes before marshaling the bravery to descend. Her left leg, stronger, facilitated her exit more easily than her entry. She had to twist her body awkwardly, relying on her left hand for balance as she carefully stepped down. There was no urgency. No expectant faces waiting inside for her. She anticipated a house as she left it, littered with untouched possessions she didn't really need. The encroaching darkness was soon to arrive. With methodical movements, the red dry-bag found its home in the garage, followed by the blue barrel, and the mountain bike resumed its usual place. A solution for the Prospector remained elusive, and it was left for the night in the bed of the truck. With her left arm aching from overuse and her right arm flinching with pain from moving the bike, she deemed the job done. Her gaze lifted to the sky before she entered the house. It was the same expanse, albeit with fewer twinkling stars. The trees in her yard stood as familiar sentinels, yet she was acutely aware of the neighbors, unseen but present, just beyond the fence. Alone, she faced this world, sobered by the depth of her loneliness.

The sting of Grace's words bore into her, an unwelcome tenant occupying her thoughts without paying rent. Sonny had long known she wasn't extraordinary, but for years, she had been the star in someone's universe. Not a superhero, not

Wonder Woman for the masses, but a marvel in his world. That realization served only to deepen her melancholy. Sonny was ordinary. When it came to societal statistics, she fell squarely in the majority. A suburban house, marriage, two kids, two cars, middle-class with some savings tucked away—Sonny was the very epitome of average.

Inside the sanctuary of her home, she sank into the chair at her computer desk, intent on substantiating the insinuations Grace had tossed so casually into their conversation. Life expectancy had indeed risen, now pegged at 78 years. A growing number of those over 65 lived in solitude—another tick on the list. Heart disease and cancer continued to reign as the leading agents of mortality. The data she unearthed only echoed her own somber sentiments, etching them deeper into the fabric of her reality.

Such a happy way to end her day, she went to bed.

The morning brought with it the scent of coffee and a modest breakfast, but more importantly, it brought clarity and sunlight to aid in her unpacking. Mitch's old workbench served as her platform, on which she meticulously sorted and cleaned each item from the red dry-bag and blue barrel. The hammock was hung out to air dry, and each vessel was vacuumed and wiped down, an effort to stave off mold and decay. She found an empty plastic tub, which would serve as their long-term storage.

Every item she laid hands on triggered a recollection, a fragment of the adventure they had shared. The overnight halt on the peninsula, the way it had been discarded by the bear after its brief fascination had waned, the way it had borne her down the river, over fallen trees, and across land during portage. Each memory was a testament to her resourcefulness, to the fitness of her body that made these adventures possible.

The gloom of the previous night was eradicated with the final grains of sand that she shook from the Prospector 14. She resolved to cling to these memories, to the adventure that made her feel like Wonder Woman, where she had accomplished feats of amazement. Surely, if any average person could achieve these things, the task would be simple and the Two-Hearted River would be teeming with tourists. But it wasn't, and that was a testament to her strength and endurance.

Sonny found a fiery determination to make the most of this day. The whiteboard on the kitchen refrigerator, once the home of shared grocery lists, was wiped clean of past requests—now irrelevant as her only need was to buy what she desired.

Her new list was straightforward:

1) Clean house, discard, donate. The subsequent steps were pragmatic: Hire a removal service. Schedule a pickup with Goodwill. Notify the girls to pick what they want.

2) Sell the house. This included: Identify a trustworthy real estate agent. Prepare the house for viewing.

3) Find a new home. Beneath this, she added a few options with corresponding question marks: Apartment? Townhouse? City?

A new beginning was clearly on her horizon.

Initiating a conference call with her twins, Sonny steeled herself for what she knew was going to be a challenging conversation. "I'm okay, girls. Made it back yesterday."

"That's wonderful, Mom," Glinda responded with relief.

"That's a relief, Mom. Can we come by to see you?" Evanora asked with concern.

"Of course. But there's a new house rule," Sonny declared.

"Oh dear, what's this about?" Evanora was curious.

"Each time you visit, you're required to leave with at least five items."

"What?" Evanora exclaimed, baffled.

"I'm planning to sell the house. So, if there's anything you want, you need to start taking it. If there are disputes, you'll have to settle them between yourselves—"

"I want Grandma's gold clock," Glinda cut her off.

"I want the China set," Evanora countered.

"The Afghan! I get the Afghan," Glinda shot back.

"The pendant. I want the pendant," Evanora insisted.

"Girls, it sounds like—" Sonny attempted to intervene.

"Dad's desk," Evanora said, staking her claim.

"Shit. Dad's first-edition, signed copy of *The Old Man and The Sea*, then," Glinda retaliated.

"No. Enough. Stop," Sonny commanded. "No one gets the Hemingway; that's mine. You take five items minimum each visit. If you've already made a list, which you apparently have, you can sort it out. I don't need to referee."

"Can I call dibs on the house?" Evanora asked.

“Pretty sneaky, sis.”

"You can make a reasonable offer. I am selling the house and the minivan. Also, I'm starting to clean today. A week from now, Goodwill will pick up the rest, and I've hired someone to remove what's left."

"Mom, that's really fast. What's your next move? What's the plan?" Evanora queried.

"I'm not sure yet. But it's happening soon. You better brace yourselves."

"Can we do this next week? This week is kinda full," Glinda requested.

"If you want anything, you'll make the time," Sonny concluded firmly.

Nineteen

"Just one meeting, Mom, that's all I ask. Will that really be the end of the world?" Glinda implored.

"I just don't see the point. They'll spend the whole time talking about themselves, and I won't connect with any of it," Sonny argued, pausing momentarily. "It will just be a waste of time."

"And what else are you doing?" Glinda challenged.

"Packing, cleaning, planning," Sonny retorted.

"Just one hour, Mom. That's all I ask," Glinda pleaded.

"All right, all right. I'll do it," Sonny finally capitulated. "But wait, before you go."

"Yes, Mom?" Glinda's voice changed pitch as if anticipating a heartfelt "thank you" or "I love you" as a token of her mother's appreciation for her efforts.

"You've only taken four items. The rule is five. You need to take one more thing before you leave," Sonny reminded.

"Oh, right, okay, Mom," Glinda responded, glancing at the small items on the entryway table. "I'll take this bowl."

"Drive safe. And next time, bring an empty car to load up," Sonny instructed. "Evanora, are you almost done? Have you gathered your five items for this visit?" she questioned.

"Mom," Evanora called, joining her mother and sister in the entryway. "Who is this in the photo?"

"Where did you find that?" Sonny's voice tightened.

"It was behind Dad's photo in the frame from his study." Evanora held up the folded photo that revealed an unfamiliar woman when unfurled. "Who is she?"

For a moment, Sonny looked cornered, but then her voice came out swift, like she was pulling off a bandage. "That's your father's first wife."

Evanora's jaw hit the floor.

"I'm sorry, I must have heard wrong. Did you say, 'your father's first wife'?" Glinda sounded incredulous.

"That's exactly what I said. Your father was married when we first met," Sonny stated plainly.

"But what about the literary club you met at? The story about your heart melting and knowing he was 'the one'?" Evanora questioned.

"All true," Sonny confirmed, her eyes distant. "I just didn't tell you about Lillith Worner." The name came out of her mouth like a bitter taste. "She was from Indiana. They met in college, I think."

"Mom, the date on this photo can't be right. You said you were 28 when you met Dad," Evanora interjected, her eyebrows furrowing.

"That's correct. Now, do you girls have all your things? At least five items?" Sonny tried to divert their attention.

"If that's the case, Mom, Dad was twelve years older than you," Evanora calculated, her eyes narrowing.

Sonny exhaled deeply. "Took you this long to do the math?"

"Mom," Evanora defended herself. "This just casts a new light on our lives."

"I knew you were younger, Mom, but twelve years? You made it seem like two," Glinda chimed in.

"Two, ten, what does it matter? We were in love," Sonny insisted.

"But you were the other woman," Evanora pointed out painfully. "You would never have approved that for us."

"I was another woman, not the other woman," Sonny corrected.

"I need to think about this," Glinda stammered, making a hasty exit. Her four items teetered precariously in her arms, the bowl looking ready to tumble off the top.

"Well..." Sonny began.

"Don't. My sister and I are in agreement on this," Evanora cut her off, heading for the door. "I don't know what to say."

Sonny stood in the entrance, listening to the sounds of car doors opening and closing; engines starting then fading into the distance. Alone again, surrounded by boxes she'd spent days packing, her mind wandered back to the day she met Mitch at the book club. It was the most charming of meet-cutes; he had accidentally spilled coffee on her blouse. He was so apologetic and insistent on helping her clean it up. She hadn't known he was married then. She only saw his kind eyes, his strong chin, and his gentle demeanor. His interactions with Lillith made them seem more like siblings or cousins, not a wedded couple. Sure, they shared some interests, but it was with Mitch that Sonny had discovered shared values. Lillith had always struck her as more of a free spirit with radical ideas for the era, which Mitch didn't seem to fully endorse. Sonny had never expressed it explicitly, but she had always gotten the impression that Mitch felt trapped in that relationship.

But how to explain that to the twins?

"Mom?" Evanora switched on the garage light. "Is that you? What are you doing in my garage at two in the morning?"

Emerging sheepishly from behind the crossover, Sonny replied, "Yes, it's me."

"Couldn't this have waited until morning?"

"I had a box of your things from your old room. I thought I'd save you a trip," Sonny explained.

"You thought you'd stow it away on my garage shelf in the middle of the night? It looks like there are two boxes, not one."

"Two," Sonny corrected herself. "I meant two."

"Mom, you're leaving emotional landmines everywhere. You're being an emotional terrorist."

"It's been days since either you or Glinda have been by, and I need to prep the house for the real estate agent and her photographer."

Evanora shook her head in disbelief. "You're so different, and it isn't just about Dad. Why are you rushing this? Why won't you attend a group session with the grief counselor?"

"Pastor John? No, thank you. He'll want to pray, and the others will get too chatty. I'm not interested. It didn't work for me when your father was alive. Drinking bad coffee in the hospital's function room with strangers... hearing all the stories... it's merely a distraction, not genuine help."

"Where are you rushing to, Mom?" Evanora asked.

"Rushing?"

"You ran off to the north woods thinking you could escape your problems, and you nearly killed yourself. Weeks later, you're still limping, dragging that cane everywhere, and your arm is encased in that inflatable swim toy. You need to recover."

"It's a prescribed air cast," Sonny clarified.

"Fine."

"I nearly lost my arm."

"I've seen the pictures," Evanora acknowledged.

Sonny glanced at her injured arm. "It's healing. The doctor said Goldie Hawn missed the tendon. My muscles are getting stronger."

"Didn't he also instruct you to take it easy?" Evanora queried.

"Her exact words were 'exercise caution.'" A note of optimism crept into Sonny's voice. "On a brighter note, next week I get a hard cast and the stitches come out."

"Great, Mom." Evanora sounded drained. "What's next? Why are you in such a rush?"

"I... I can't say, honey."

Tired and exasperated, Evanora flicked off the light. "Goodnight, Mom. No more boxes. Please, just donate the rest. We're all full up on crazy here, thank you."

Left standing in the dark garage, Sonny was uncertain of her next move. She considered placing the second box on the shelf next to the first but decided against it, leaving it on the garage floor.

Sonny made her way back to the truck, where two more boxes destined for Glinda's garage awaited delivery.

Twenty

"Mother!" Evanora's voice echoed. "Mother?" She moved cautiously, threading her way through the maze of boxes cluttering the hallways. "The door was open, so I..." Evanora halted in the kitchen doorway. "Apologies, am I intruding?"

Perched atop the kitchen island, Sonny sat cross-legged, beer in hand, resembling a nightclub chanteuse serenading her audience from atop a grand piano. Her audience, however, was a trio of young men—one alarmingly tall, another highly proficient, but all muscular and undeniably attractive.

"Not at all, dear," Sonny responded. "We're merely pausing from loading the truck. Evanora, meet Ranger, Riker, and Pike. Gentlemen, this is Evanora, one of my daughters."

"Sonny, you neglected to mention your daughter's striking

beauty," Pike interjected, offering his right hand to Evanora. His devilish grin widened. "A pleasure."

Matching his smile, Evanora responded, "A pleasure to meet you as well. How did you become acquainted with my mother?"

"They're my rescuers from the Two-Hearted," Sonny elaborated. "These are the Marines who saved my life."

The tallest of the three cleared his throat.

"My apologies, Ranger." Sonny swiftly corrected herself, "The soldiers who saved my life."

Evanora beamed. "It's an honor to meet you all. Thank you for saving my mother."

"Well, we didn't exactly do much," Riker admitted. "By the time we found her, she had already patched herself up. We merely ensured her safety for a while."

"Thank you," Evanora repeated.

Sonny grinned. "You'll find yourself expressing that sentiment often around these three. 'Thank you' seems to be their favorite refrain. I say it to them all the time." She extended her hand to Ranger, who gallantly helped her down from the counter. “Thank you.”

"Boys," Pike initiated, "let's finish with the hallway boxes and we should be all set."

They offered Evanora warm smiles as they moved past her into the hallway. The slight ruckus of their movement was quickly replaced with the first drawn-out notes of a familiar tune—"Heigh-ho... Heigh-ho..."—before the door clicked shut behind them. The melody continued, growing fainter as they headed toward the front yard.

Evanora turned to Sonny, confusion evident in her eyes.

"In short, they affectionately refer to me as Snow White and see themselves as my loyal dwarfs," Sonny elucidated.

"They're certainly young and handsome. You must enjoy the attention."

"It's rather agreeable, Evanora. Not unpleasant at all."

Evanora moved to a cupboard to retrieve a glass, finding it disappointingly empty. She glanced at her mother, questioning.

"Sold them all at the garage sales," Sonny informed. "Would you like a beer?"

"No, thank you. I'm driving," Evanora declined, disappointed. "Your friends were very kind to help with the move."

"They're good souls. I'm fortunate to have crossed paths with them."

"It's a little melancholy, seeing you nearly done moving out. I missed all the commotion."

"There wasn't much excitement, to be honest," Sonny explained. "Everything that wasn't sold in the garage sales, donated, or given away is heading to storage."

"What remains?" Evanora inquired, leaning on the kitchen island.

"The books, some clothing, a few mementos of your father."

"I miss him."

"I've missed the man he was for the past two years," Sonny confessed. "He changed."

"It's a shame you're selling the house."

"The thing is, Evee, it's just a house," Sonny attempted to comfort her. "It was a home when your father and sister were here. You have a home. It's just not here anymore; it's with your husband and children. This is a house. And it's far too large for me, alone."

"And what's next for you? Do you have a place to stay?"

"Well..." Sonny hesitated. "The boys and I are going on a trip."

"Really?"

"Yes, we're departing for France next week."

"France?"

"We're embarking on the Camino de Santiago, the pilgrimage of St. James. It begins in France, continues through Spain, and ends in the city of Santiago de Compostela."

"And where is that?"

"On the Atlantic coast of the Iberian Peninsula."

"That's quite the journey. Is this another one of your Hemingway-inspired adventures you and Dad planned?"

"Not exactly, although Hemingway did travel parts of the route. This is a personal venture, one I discovered through my three new friends."

"I don't understand, mother." Evanora's frustration began to show. "You're evading something. I can see it. Something's happened, or is happening, that you're not sharing. Something, I don't know, significant, perhaps trivial, but definitely something."

"Evanora, I think you're still reeling from your father's—"

"No, it's something else. You're not denying it."

"What if there *was* something, Evanora? A secret between Mitch and me that we chose not to share with you? Would you let it be if that were the case? If you knew that?"

"Well, I don't know."

"You keep secrets too. You don't share everything. Can't your dear, old mother do the same?"

"I suppose. It's just... it feels different. More substantial. You would tell me if it were something like that."

"When have I ever kept secrets from you, my dear?" Sonny approached her daughter for an embrace.

Evanora relished the warmth, the comforting knowledge of a mother's love and enduring presence. For a fleeting moment, she pondered how anyone without a mother managed to navigate life. Then, pulling away, she objected, "Wait. My entire life. That business about Dad's first wife. Your age, his age... you both lied."

"We were protecting you, Evanora," Sonny defended. "That's all. Parents desire nothing more than to safeguard their children."

Evanora's face reflected her lingering doubts. The sound of boxes being hefted and the echoing chorus of "It's off to work we go" resonated from the hall. Evanora studied her mother from head to toe. "I don't know you. You're not who I believed you to be."

"Evanora," Sonny pleaded. "Don't leave like this. Please, Evanora."

Twenty-One

The day was radiant with the signature Spanish sun as it cast a benevolent gaze upon Sonny. They'd made a decision to indulge, choosing to luxuriate within the comforts of a hotel room in Pamplona after journeying an additional three days to the city. Their wandering spirits guided them through the sacred halls of the Church of San Saturnino, along the infamous route of the bull run leading to Plaza de Toros, and finally to the heart of Pamplona: Plaza del Castillo, where they paused for a refreshing cerveza.

"I adore these chilled Mahou," Sonny professed, an expression of her love she'd repeated to the point of charming monotony.

"We're well aware," responded her towering friend with a fond grin.

A gentle zephyr swept across the plaza, tenderly cooling the band of travelers beneath the cerulean canvas adorned with fluffy white clouds. Sonny was submerged in a dream come true, basking in a sense of belonging, autonomy, deep-rooted friendships, and the satisfaction of daily accomplishments. An unparalleled sense of wholeness suffused her.

"That mountain ascent from France to cross the border, I was unsure if we'd make it," Sonny confessed to her trio. "But we made it. The challenges are mere memories. Spain has been a divine delight."

Riker, raising his glass in anticipation of a toast, suggested, “Cin-Cin.”

Sonny savored the ice-cold Mahou as it danced on her tongue and glided down her throat. From the corner of her eye, she watched Riker relish his beloved brew. She couldn’t help but imagine his strong arms around her. She studied the muscles in his forearms as they moved, curiosity swirling within her at the thought of such raw power pulling her close, pressing against her. With a mere hint or suggestion, she could envision herself surrendering to his will.

“After this one, I plan to indulge in a siesta,” Sonny confessed.

As the sun began its descent, the heat, intensified by light, was shielded by her sunglasses.

“I could do with a nap,” Pike proposed. “Does that make me lazy?”

“It’s not the desire; it's evidence of your laziness," Ranger rejoined.

The quartet ambled their way toward the Hotel Tres Reyes,

their steps steady and sure on stones that bore the weight of centuries and countless visitors. Their jovial camaraderie made the journey to their rooms a celebration, a respite from the sun's persistent heat.

Three hours into slumber, Sonny's phone buzzed against the bedside table. Its vibration rattled the tranquility, forcing her into wakefulness. Her mind lingered in the realm of dreams, where she felt nothing but warmth and love, trust and happiness.

"Hello?" she answered, her voice still laced with sleep and the effects of many Mahou.

"Hello, Mom," Glinda's voice came, its familiar, pleasant tone acting like a charm.

"Glinda, how are you? I am so happy to hear your voice."

"I'm well, Mom, but I'm worried about Evanora. She's distressed, feeling ostracized. She said it's as if a house has been dropped on her. Could you perhaps give her a call?"

Sonny sighed. "She won't take my calls, Glinda. I try every week, but it goes straight to voicemail. What do you call that?"

"Ghosting?"

"Yes, ghosting. That's exactly what she's doing."

"Mom, have you been drinking?"

"A little, there's this splendid beer here, Mahou. I've been having tastes most of the day."

"I'm glad you're enjoying yourself. But I'm still concerned about Evanora. She believes you're concealing something."

"I wouldn't know where to begin, Glinda. I've been feeling guilty."

“You always said it’s always best to start at the beginning.”

“Glinda... I just... it’s... you two might stop speaking to me if I tell you.”

Her daughter's voice was gentle, yet insistent. “It will take you home in just two seconds. You can tell me.”

Sonny confessed, her voice barely a whisper, "I was weak. After nearly two years, I couldn’t bear it anymore. I had a moment of weakness."

"Did you cheat on Dad? He would understand."

"No, no, nothing of the sort. I loved your father deeply. We fit together so perfectly. But it was never-ending. He kept asking for things. I couldn't sleep. The only person I saw was the grocery delivery man. I had no one to confide in."

"What happened, Mom?"

“He kept wanting me to carry him to his truck, but he was too heavy. He talked about Hemingway in that last year, after the plane crash.” Sonny turned in her bed, her hair disheveled, head spinning. “I was weak. I gave in. I did what he asked. I took his pillow, placed it over him, and pressed. Fuck, it took an eternity. He couldn’t struggle. Once I started, there was no end but to end it.”

Her voice cracked, tears spilling forth. “I was weak. I didn’t stop, Glinda. Don’t tell Evanora. Please, don’t say anything. She wouldn’t understand. Glinda? Glinda?"

Sonny stirred, her mind heavy with sleep, disoriented as she tried to grasp where she was. The deep slumber had taken its toll, clouding her memory. Then it all came back to her. She was a pilgrim, an ordinary girl in an extraordinary land, journeying with her closest companions in search of the answers to life. Was this a dream? Where did reality end and dreams begin?

As she bathed under the soothing spray of hot water, she let the day's stress drain away. "Breathe," she whispered to herself. "Just breathe and take the next day as it comes."

She took time to primp for the evening. The more she looked into the mirror, the better she felt about herself. She saw herself reflected back as a good person. She could look herself in the eyes and believe that she was a good person.

Descending the hotel's central staircase, she found Riker comfortably ensconced in the lobby, engrossed in a copy of *East of Eden* she lent.

“What do you think?” Sonny asked.

He turned to a dog-eared page he'd marked. “I believe a strong woman may be stronger than a man, particularly if she happens to have love in her heart. I guess a loving woman is indestructible.” He closed the book, a knowing smile on his face. “I see why you like this one. You ready to meet up with the boys? They’re saving us a spot.”

“I’m famished. Let's get lost.”

About the Author

Paul Michael Peters is a storyteller with an original voice who thrives at the edge of the human condition, blending humor and darkness with keen insight. His tales navigate the intricate dance between the mundane and the profound, capturing the ephemeral moments that define our lives with passion. His work invites readers into a world where the ordinary becomes extraordinary, exploring life's shadowy corners with narratives that resonate with authenticity and imaginative daring.

Dive into the work of Paul Michael Peters and discover stories that echo the complexities of life: "Broken Objects," "Combustible Punch," "The Symmetry of Snowflakes," "Insensible Loss," and several beloved short stories like "Mr. Memory and Other Stories of Wonder." Find free chapter previews at paulmichaelpeters.com.

Follow him at:
Website: https://www.paulmichaelpeters.com/

If you enjoyed this book, please consider leaving a positive review on one of these websites:

Bookbub: https://www.bookbub.com/authors/paul-michael-peters
Goodreads: https://www.goodreads.com/author/show/7077098.Paul_Michael_Peters

Also by Paul Michael Peters

RIGHT HAND OF THE RESISTANCE

In a world eerily parallel to our own, life is bisected by the Barrier—a monolithic edifice that symbolizes division and control. It segregates nations and dictates the very fate of those bold enough to cross. "Right Hand of the Resistance" by Paul Michael Peters melds the heart-pounding suspense of Tom Clancy, the speculative genius of Dan Simmons, and the prescient vision of George Orwell to capture the essence of a divided society. It challenges the Golden Rule by asking, "How well should we treat one another?" The narrative follows perilous treks to the north, fraught with danger yet illuminated by the hope of a better existence beyond the oppressive divide.

Paul Michael Peters maps a world where passage across the Barrier involves high costs and profound sacrifices, all under the watchful eyes of authorities dictating fates. Amidst this, a covert resistance emerges, daring to defy and dismantle the status quo, embodying the novel's core themes of rebellion and resilience.

Through a blend of suspense, intrigue, and fiction, Paul Michael Peters dissects themes of love, faith, family, power, and control. This narrative compels readers to question their realities. "Right Hand of the Resistance" is an exploration of human extremes, delivering a narrative that resonates deeply with our contemporary challenges while hinting at ominous futures.

COMBUSTIBLE PUNCH

Rick Philips isn't a fighter—but he is a survivor.

Haunted by memories of a high school shooting, not even the bottle can wash away the gnawing guilt and creeping feelings of inadequacy that batter Rick's conscience daily.

His life has been a mess of broken marriages, writer's block, terrible choices, and the morbid pity of others. When he meets Harriet at a writer's conference, the record doesn't scratch as he falls back—only this time, he may not get up.

Harriet Bristol Wheeler is a dark temptress—and self-confessed serial killer.

INSENSIBLE LOSS

If you had the chance to live forever, would you take it?

2053: An old man, Viktor Erikson, lies on his deathbed. Alone and with no known relatives, he is tended to by Olivia, a nurse. He has only one request: that she reads to him.

The request is not unusual, but the battered, leather-bound tome she must read is no ordinary book. Written in 1839, it chronicles the discovery of the fountain of youth by Morgana de la Motte—and Viktor Erikson.

What starts off as a swashbuckling adventure on the high seas in search of riches and eternal life soon transforms into something quite different: a clash between two personalities bound by love and deceit, locked together by a terrible burden of necessity.

THE SYMMETRY OF SNOWFLAKES

Hank Hanson's family is not only blended; it's pulverized by the weight of its own perfect symmetry.

To the casual outsider, Hank Hanson's life might seem idyllic. As a successful businessman on the verge of a major business deal and an all-around good guy, few get close enough to see the troubled soul underneath his open face.

The product of a family fractured many times over by his parents' multiple remarriages, Hank spends his Thanksgivings running a miserable, thankless gauntlet of visiting multiple family members.

One Thanksgiving, he takes an unscheduled detour and meets Erin Contee, a woman who might just be too good for him—but at the same time, perfect. As the two grow closer together, Hank believes he has finally found the missing piece in his fragmented life.

MR. MEMORY AND OTHER STORIES OF WONDER

Uttering the name Mr. Memory evokes the live performances and talk show appearances when he would impress the world with his abilities of recollection. His clarity of remembrance has kept listeners captivated for days while sharing the adventures of his life. In this collection of short stories, we learn the truth about Mr. Memory, the fantastic gone unseen, and a world of wonder which can inspire us to believe.

Made in the USA
Middletown, DE
29 July 2024

58046310R00239